The Shoppe of Spells

To Hadassah!
Welcome to Rutherford,
where science and magic
merge and nothing is
ever just as it seems.

Shanon Grey

THE SHOPPE OF SPELLS
by Shanon Grey

THE GATEKEEPERS – Book One

www.CrossroadsPublishingHouse.com

The Shoppe of Spells
Copyright © 2011, Shanon Grey
2nd Edition, November 2011
Print ISBN: 978-0615571621
Digital ISBN: 978-1452481968

Cover Art Design by Dawn Charles of Book Graphics

Trade Paperback release, November 2011
Digital Release, November 2011

Crossroads Publishing House, LLC
PO Box 723
Emporia, VA 23847

Crossroads Publishing House
http://www.crossroadspublishinghouse.com/

Acknowledgements

I want to thank my publisher, Crossroads Publishing House, for being as enthusiastic about this as I am.

To Becky, for being my beta reader, I can't thank you enough. You waded through the rough draft with gentle words and constant optimism.

To Josh and Andy: for reading this more times than I can count and still liking it.

To Pookie: for waiting for her walks until I got finished with a thought.

To my Mississippi girlfriends, Linda and Judy, thanks for putting up with me, for listening endlessly to my ideas and my hopes and dreams. I love you guys.

To my cousin and writer extraordinaire, Nancy Naigle, for all the reads, rereads, and last minute reads, for finding things I completely missed, for all the chats and phone calls at all hours, despite your schedule, I give you thanks and hugs.

To my family: I wouldn't be here without you.
You inspire me every day.
You believe in me.
Thank you.

Dedication

I would like to dedicate this novel to Mary Maloney. Friend, sister, and more mother than I'd ever had in my life, this incredible woman taught me to believe in myself, the universe and things unknown. She believed that the paranormal was just science that hadn't been proven—yet. She lost her battle with breast cancer last year, as I sat down to write this story. So, Mary, this one's for you!

Prologue

Morgan lay motionless, listening, struggling to define what woke her. A faint hum, almost imperceptible, thrummed through her body, battling the very rhythm of her being. There was something familiar about it. Was that hum from a smoke alarm going off in the distance?

The air crackled around her.

She released the breath she'd been holding and opened her eyes. Damp curls clung to her neck as she shifted up on her elbow and scanned the room. Streaks of light spiked beneath the closed bedroom door — the only light penetrating the room's inky blackness.

Panic seeped into her sleep-fogged brain. *Fire!* She threw back the covers, felt a slight tingle as something brushed against her leg, and watched a faint violet outline disappear into the darkness. Thank God, her cat was in the room with her. Morgan swung her legs over the edge of the bed, felt the soft carpet under her toes and tried to remember all the rules about fire as she rushed closer to the spikes of light snaking toward her feet.

She reached out and patted at the door with her fingertips. The wood was cool to the touch. Her heart hammered as she watched the sparking light sizzle across her feet. Not hot, exactly…more…electric. Her mouth went dry. She forced her hand around the doorknob and, not getting a shock, turned it and pulled the door toward her.

Blinding white light, like that from a welder's torch, filled the doorway, forcing her to shield her eyes.

"It's okay," a deep voice cajoled, "I've got you. Close your eyes and let me guide you."

Squinting, she looked down and saw a strong hand reach through the light toward her. She eased her hand forward to meet his. As their fingers touched, a sudden flash of violet, followed by a bolt of energy exploded between them, thrusting her backward—into nothingness.

Her arms flailed, her hands grasped, seizing empty space.

Morgan screamed—a soundless howl, as her breath was sucked into the void.

She tumbled backward, plummeting into a black abyss.

With a jolt, she sat up in bed, drenched in sweat.

Chapter One

Trembling fingers snipped grey-green branches of rosemary. Its delicate fragrance rose from the cuts as she laid them next to the basil. Morgan raised her face to the rays of the hot sun, letting it burn away the remnants of the dream. Her knee crushed a fallen leaf of chocolate peppermint, diffusing its scent into the air. She inhaled memories of hot tea and late night conversations with her mom, replacing the suffocating terror that still simmered beneath the surface.

The hot, humid weather was perfect for the plants and the myriad of butterflies that danced around them. Not so much for her heavy red curls. She pushed a loose lock away from her face with the back of her wrist, gathered her basket, stood, and contemplated the large Terra-cotta pots around her balcony. Someday she would have a real garden—after she left the ranks of the unemployed.

The doorbell chimed, breaking into her reverie.

"Coming," she called and tugged on the obstinate patio door.

Dropping the basket and garden shears on the counter, she hurried to the front door.

"Yes?" She peered through the peephole. She shut one eye and blinked; she squinted and tried again. A man with knobby knees came into view, impatiently shifting an overflowing mailbag on his shoulder.

"I have a registered letter for Morgana Briscoe," he called and she watched his face twist into a scowl. "I need a signature."

She flipped the deadbolt, glanced over her shoulder in case Mrs. T decided to make a break for it and, not seeing the long-haired Russian Blue lurking nearby, slipped into the hallway.

"I'm Morgana Briscoe," she said, careful not to make eye contact.

He shoved the letter toward her, along with a clipboard and pen. Placing the letter under her arm, she juggled the clipboard and noticed the dirt on her fingers. "Sorry," she flushed, "I was working in my garden."

"Yeah…sure," he smirked.

"I mean the pots on my balcony," she defended.

He reached out, all but yanked the clipboard out of her hand, and turned. "Have a nice day." He called the afterthought over his shoulder.

She stepped inside, closed the door with her hip, and twisted the deadbolt back in place. Keeping the letter safely tucked under her arm, she washed the dirt off her hands, slipped a knife out of the kitchen block, and moved to the table.

Knives weren't meant for ripping paper, her mother's admonition played through her mind. Morgan smiled to herself, sat, and slit open the envelope. Bask & Morrisette, Attorneys-at-Law. She shrugged at the unfamiliar name and unfolded the crisp linen paper.

Dear Miss Briscoe:

We are truly sorry for your loss. Please contact us at your earliest convenience regarding a matter of extreme urgency.

Again, we extend our condolences.

Sincerely,

Kristoff Bask, Esq.

The letterhead was longer than the message, displaying the embossed address and phone number prominently in an elegant script. Atlanta, Georgia. She didn't know anyone in Georgia. She placed the letter on the table and stared at it. Morgan reached for the phone and hit speed-dial.

"Mom?" She was cut-off by the answering machine.

She hung up and hit their cell number. Once again, a voice message. Her stomach knotted. She hung up, scanned the letter, and dialed.

"Bask & Morrisette," a female voice intoned.

"My name is Morgan Briscoe. I just got a letter from a Kristoff Bask—"

"One moment, please," the voice interrupted.

"Miss Briscoe?" a man's deep voice asked.

"Yes. I just got your letter. I don't understand?"

"We have an important matter to discuss with you. Would Monday be all right?"

"I'm in Virginia. A trip to Georgia is out of the question. Can't you just tell me what this is about?"

"When *can* you come?" He ignored her question.

"I don't have the finances..." she let the words trail off. Her finances were none of his business.

"Your travel expenses are covered." His voice was clip. "Your transportation and accommodations are all included," he explained, exasperated, as if pacifying a five-year-old.

"What's this about?" she demanded, growing more irritated.

"We need to speak in person, Miss Briscoe. If you will hold a moment, I will put you through to my secretary so you can make arrangements."

"But—"

Elevator music droned through the phone.

"Jerk," she muttered to herself and shook her hair back from her shoulders.

A few quick questions from the secretary and she was set to leave from the Newport News/Williamsburg International Airport on Monday morning. A car would meet her at the Atlanta airport and transport her to their offices downtown. Her return trip would be arranged from there. She jotted down the information and hung up, aggravated with herself for being so easily manipulated.

A deep-throated chirp drew her attention. Her cat sat on the balcony, tail aquiver, entranced by a butterfly precariously perched on some feathery dill in the corner. She let the scene on the balcony distract her until she calmed. First the nightmare—now this. That "oogie" feeling—the one she got when she sensed something wasn't quite right, but didn't know what—welled.

She hit speed-dial. Again, it went to her parents' voicemail. "Call me." Her voice hitched.

Just as the cat crouched, Morgan reached down and scooped her up. "Not today, old girl. With my luck you'll finally leap and it's a long drop." She nuzzled the soft fur with her chin. The cat emitted a low, deep growl. Morgan looked up.

"It's a butterfly!" She reproached Mrs. T with a smile. As she stepped back through the door, a faint outline caught her eye. She turned quickly. It was gone. She scanned the patio as she pushed the door closed and latched it.

A small current ran up her spine.

She shivered and rechecked the lock.

Mrs. T, having lost interest, squirmed to get down. She released the cat and called another number. Her best friend, Jenn, answered on the second ring, "Hey, kiddo."

Morgan tried to sound nonchalant as she described her conversation with the lawyer.

"Have you called your parents?"

"I can't get them," she explained, then anticipated Jenn's next question. "It's not their attorney. I know him. This guy's a royal pain."

"You're not going, are you?"

"I really don't have a choice."

"The hell you don't."

"It's not like I'm doing anything."

Morgan heard Jenn's muffled voice issue instructions to her assistant through the covered handset. Then she was back. "I'm coming over after work."

Morgan smiled. That was Jenn, rushing to the rescue. "I'm making rosemary chicken with tomato-basil salad," she tempted.

"—and your garlic bread? I'll bring wine."

"Thanks, Jenn. I don't know what I'd do without you."

"Somehow, I think you'd muddle through." Jenn laughed. "See you later."

Mrs. T's soft fur brushed up against Morgan's legs. Feeling guilty about spoiling her fun, she rattled a box of treats. Enough guilt and her cat could easily become a twenty-pounder.

****

Morgan opened the door to, "You look like hell."

"Gee thanks." Morgan hugged her. "Just a little tired."

"Have you lost weight?" Jenn squeezed Morgan's arms in assessment.

"No," Morgan wriggled out of her reach. "I just don't have the curves you do. I never will." Okay, maybe she had dropped a few pounds, not that she'd admit it to Jenn.

"Are you still having nightmares?" Jenn asked.

"Not so much lately," Morgan lied and followed Jenn toward the kitchen.

Jenn uncorked the wine to let it breathe and scrutinized Morgan.

"I promise," Morgan crossed her heart. She'd had nightmares since she could remember. As a child, she'd been diagnosed with night terrors—screaming hysterically, her little body drenched in sweat. Her parents had spent many a sleepless night by her bed. She claimed never to remember. Only she did remember—vaguely—because they were all, basically, the same. Thankfully, in the last few years, they seemed to have lessened. Now, once again, Morgan had awakened drenched in sweat. Only this time it went beyond Mrs. T crouching next to her, staring past the foot of the bed, puffed to the size of an overstuffed porcupine and hissing at nothing.

Morgan reached up and scratched the cat's chin as she passed the hutch. The cat nipped her fingers in a feline show of affection.

Jenn sniffed the air. "Wow. This place smells fabulous."

"It's the chicken." Morgan pulled out the broiler pan. "Come on. Let's eat."

Over plates of savory chicken, they rehashed the cryptic conversation with the attorney.

Grabbing a final piece of bread, Jenn barbarically sopped up chicken drippings, popped it into her mouth and pushed away her plate. "Damn, that was good."

"Just herbs."

"Yeah. Well, what you do with herbs amazes me."

Jenn refilled their glasses as her expression turned serious. "You understand that I'm not entirely comfortable with you taking off at the insistence of some strange attorney from some strange law firm you've never heard of. What'd your parents say?"

"They haven't called back." Of course, if she hadn't been so introspective of late, she wouldn't be wondering where they were. Normally, she talked to them every day.

"You don't think it could be the Stevens, do you?" Jenn speculated.

"Grace and Bill? Why would their lawyer be contacting me?" They'd been more than employers to her; they'd been like family.

"You didn't embezzle from them or something did you?"

"Of course not. Stop that." She laughed and buttered a slice of herb bread.

"I hope not; I like them." Jenn feigned a pout.

"That's because they gave you an employee discount."

"True." Jenn pondered the wine she swirled. "I'm going to miss that."

"Thanks for the sympathy. I'll try to find a job that'll give you a worthy discount."

"Regardless," Jenn ignored the bait, "I bet it has something to do with your job—compensation or something."

Morgan doubted it. Grace and Bill had demanded she receive a substantial severance package, although it'd been at her insistence that the shop close its doors. As their bookkeeper and friend, she couldn't recommend anything else. To go on would've ruined the old couple. At least they got out before eating up their modest retirement. She should be fine until she got another job, if it didn't take too long.

She smiled and said nothing, watching Jenn launch into speculation.

"You don't think they are going to appeal your unemployment." Jenn's face twisted. "No, you'd have heard from the Labor Department, not some fancy lawyer. Besides, Grace and Bill love you."

Morgan only half listened. Another oogie feeling made her shiver. She shook it off and tried to tune into Jenn's monologue.

"Am I even needed for this conversation?" Morgan quipped.

Jenn ignored her. "Speaking of jobs," she said, took a sip and set the glass down, "have you told your parents about the lay-off yet?"

Morgan shifted uncomfortably. "I was hoping I'd have a job by the time I had to tell them. I haven't had a single bite—not even a nibble. I can't avoid telling them for much longer."

"You know you have a job with us anytime you want it."

Morgan knew Jenn meant it. She also knew that the women's shelters Jenn operated were struggling just like everything else in the sluggish economy. Besides, Morgan needed more money than Jenn could afford. Still, she appreciated the offer.

"I don't think Claudia would appreciate me waltzing into her domain. I'll be fine." She tried to reassure her friend. "Besides, I've always wanted to go to Atlanta. I'm looking at it as an all-expense-paid vacation—before I go back to work."

"I'd feel better if your parents knew you were doing this."

"I know. That's your over-developed sense of responsibility speaking. You worry about those women and children in your care and let me worry about me. I'll be fine." Morgan started stacking the plates, hoping Jenn didn't sense Morgan's nervousness about the impending trip. Something was setting off small alarms in her brain. She pushed back her chair.

"Maybe I should go with you." Jenn seemed to read her mind.

"Don't be silly. And just who would look after Mrs. T with my parents gone?" She tried to remember if they'd said where they were going.

"I guess. I just hate this. I'll feel better if we do a little research of our own." Jenn walked over and flipped open Morgan's laptop.

Morgan watched Jenn's fingers fly over the keys. Her friend brushed back an errant strand of blond hair and took a sip of wine, all the while leapfrogging through sites. "Wow, it's an old firm," Jenn commented.

"So, I gather it's real?" Morgan scooted her chair in for a closer look. "Impressive. And large." The website was the epitome of quiet elegance. Not some shyster taunting, *Let me sue your employer!*

"Who's the lawyer you talked to?" Jenn asked.

"Wait." Morgan got the letter and opened it again. "Kristoff Bask."

Jenn typed, stopped and turned to Morgan. "He's head of the whole damn place. What *have* you done, girl?" she goaded, her eyes twinkling.

"Damned if I know." Morgan tried not to look worried. "At least we know they're legit."

"And then some. This firm has been around since 1759, originally begun right here in Virginia. It is one of the oldest in the country."

Jenn noticed the time. "I'm sorry, but I've got to run. Want me to leave this on?" When Morgan shook her head, Jenn shut down the computer.

"Thanks for coming over. I feel better," Morgan lied.

"Try not to stay gone too long; you know I'm not good with plants."

"Just don't over water them. Wait 'til the dirt feels dry," Morgan followed Jenn to the door, "not cracked, like last time."

"I'll do my best."

Morgan laughed. "It's all herbs this time. They're pretty forgiving. Besides, I won't be gone long. And Mrs. T will let you know when you've neglected her." A soft mewl sounded from atop the hutch.

"She and I do fine." Jenn glanced up at the cat. "At least until she decides to sneak out."

"Actually, she's never left this floor or the balcony. I think she just likes to prove to us she can, if she wants to."

Jenn threw the cat a glance. Mrs. T flopped over and stretched out a delicate paw. Jenn stroked the pad.

"How's Rob?" Jenn asked.

"We broke up." Morgan walked over to a cabinet, pulled out a package. "Before I forget. Here's your Patchouli soap."

Jenn took the package, inhaled, and let a languid smile form. "I wish you had money to open your own shop. You are so good with scents and all things herbal. By the way, this isn't distracting me from your Rob comment. What happened?"

"Nothing much." Morgan shrugged. "I just realized we weren't that compatible."

"And I thought you guys were so cute together. He was very handsome, in a geeky, professorish sort of way."

Morgan shrugged, not offering any details.

"Okay, I won't push. I know you'll tell me when you're ready."

The phone rang.

"Go get that. I'll let myself out." Jenn waved and pulled the door closed behind her.

Picking up the phone, Morgan saw her mom's cell number. "Where've you been?" she asked without preamble.

The phone crackled and her mother's broken voice squeaked back, "…went…tree Falls…"

"What?" she shouted into the phone. "You're breaking up."

"Crabtree Falls for anniversary…" It went dead.

Morgan stared at the phone. She'd forgotten their anniversary. How could she? Her parents usually started teasing one another three weeks in advance. It came from a long tradition of forgetting the actual date. Once she had slipped in and placed large sticky notes all over the house with nothing but the number "27" on them. Her mom still had one stuck to the photo of her grandmother, sitting on the dresser. Good for them. They loved Crabtree Falls.

She smiled. What they loved was each other. Oh sure, they squabbled. Hell, they couldn't paint a door together without arguing about how to do it and who was right. Nevertheless, no matter how much they teased, they still hugged and their eyes twinkled when they looked at one another—and at her. They considered her their late-life miracle. They said she was the best of both of them. With her mom's red hair and her dad's green eyes, she was a true compilation of the two.

Her parents were unsurpassed. Even her friends thought so. They gave her breathing room, yet let her know they were there for her. She could tell them anything. The only thing she hadn't shared with them was the disaster that was Rob. She felt a little guilty about that. Her mom and dad hadn't particularly liked him from the start—not that they'd said anything. It was more what they didn't say; they were too nice, too formal.

As for the joblessness—okay, she hadn't gone running to them when that happened. Working at the little book store/gift shop had been the closest thing to what she dreamed of owning one day. She hadn't wanted to worry her parents. Besides, with a degree in Business and a minor in Accounting, Morgan had had her pick of opportunities straight out of college. Who would've thought getting a new job would prove to be so difficult. She'd tell her parents about the lay-off and the lawyer when they got back. No need to ruin their getaway.

She picked up the phone, dialed the house number, and waited for it to go to voicemail. "Mom. Dad. Happy Anniversary. Something's come up. I have to go to Atlanta. I should be back about the same time you are. I'll fill you in then. We'll do an anniversary dinner celebration when you get back. Love you both. Have fun, you lovebirds. Bye."

Morgan fixed herself chocolate peppermint tea and settled down on the sofa. Soon, Mrs. T snuggled into Morgan's lap and they sat companionably while Morgan contemplated dreams of a simple shop, fragrant with her own special concoctions, and Mrs. T counted her names, as cats are wont to do—according to the musical.

****

Promptly at seven Monday morning, Morgan got a phone call confirming transportation to the airport. By seven-thirty, she found herself tucked into the back of a black town car, traveling the four miles to the airport. This wasn't necessary, she mused. The lawyers were certainly thorough with their door-to-door service.

She found very little congestion and got through the security maze in record time. Settled in first class—a "first" for her, she glanced out the window. The engine revved, the plane vibrated, and the sound built. This was the only part she hated. This—and landing. However, once up in the air, she loved the sensation that she was flying, wingless, above the earth, above the clouds. Morgan looked out the window and watched houses grow smaller until they blurred and disappeared.

The flight attendant served her orange juice and a warm croissant. She twisted around in her seat and peered over the top, trying to see if economy was offered anything. A man sitting next to the aisle behind her looked up and smiled. She swung back around and glanced down, letting her long bangs hide her eyes. What the hell. She wriggled in her seat. Definitely roomier. She smiled and settled back to sip her juice.

The crush of people exiting the plane forced her into motion. Like a lemming, she trailed behind them as they wound around a bit until they left the restricted area. She stepped away from the crowd and stopped.

"Miss Briscoe?" A man in a black uniform stepped up to her. Without waiting for acknowledgment, the stuffy, unsmiling man continued, "Will there be any luggage, miss?"

"No."

"Very good, miss. If you will follow me." He turned and led the way. She was so busy watching his back, she had no sense of the airport, except that it was crowded. The driver stepped through the doors where a black sedan waited. He helped her into the rear of the car with all the aplomb befitting a dignitary.

She leaned forward. "Where are we headed?"

He glanced into the rearview mirror. "Downtown, miss."

The vehicle moved further into the city. She craned her neck to look at the tall buildings. He pushed a button and the sunroof slid back. She looked up at the skyline and smiled at him in the rearview mirror. He turned onto a wide street shaded by heavily laden tree limbs overhanging each side. The concrete congestion disappeared. "Are we going to Bask & Morrisette?"

"Yes, miss."

The sedan passed palatial homes on magnificently landscaped lawns. Small neighborhood shopping strips, as

beautifully landscaped as their surroundings, sat nestled near
the estates. The car slowed and turned into a gated drive. As
they approached, tall iron gates slid back behind ivy-covered
brick walls. She turned around and watched the gates slide
firmly back into place. Even within the cool confines of the
elegant automobile, she felt her palms dampen. She turned
back and leaned forward to get a better view.

A long, stone drive curved in front of a Tudor-style
mansion. Dark green ivy worked its way up deep red brick.
She looked across the lawn. Perfectly orchestrated
landscaping obscured the mansion and its ancillary buildings
from the road. The chauffeur pulled in front of stone steps
and stopped, tugged at his hat as he walked around the front
of the car, opened her door, and extended his hand to help
her out. He turned and preceded her up the steps to a tall set
of ornately carved wooden doors. The chauffeur opened one
of the doors and stepped back. She stepped into a foyer that
smelled of wood and polish—the distinct smell of old
money—and was glad she had opted to wear the dressier
linen pantsuit.

A large reception desk, dwarfed by the mammoth foyer,
sat in the middle. The receptionist looked up from what she
was doing. "Miss Briscoe?"

"Yes."

"Follow me, please." The woman rose, took a step toward
the stone staircase, and waited for Morgan to join her. She led
her up the stairs. "Mr. Bask is expecting you."

The tapping of their footfalls echoed on the steps. The 15-
foot wide stairway rose a full story to a landing overlooking
formal gardens before splitting and proceeding to the upper
floor. Morgan paused at the window. Before her stretched
grounds that had taken years, if not decades, to perfect. A
maze, its age revealed by the grandeur of the hedgerow,
adorned the farthest portion of the terraced grounds. In an

instant, she was strolling along the paths of the maze, inhaling gardenia and lavender. She blinked. The receptionist waited patiently where the stairs split. Baffled, Morgan glanced back out the window before following her up the steps. They stopped outside of a mahogany door. The woman tapped lightly.

"Come in," a muffled voice barely carried through the heavy wood. The receptionist quietly opened the door and moved back. A distinguished man, about sixty years of age, rose, the epitome of an accomplished barrister. A stern expression marked his otherwise smooth features.

Morgan stepped into the room. Light filtered through lead-glass panes, casting prisms of color onto the thick Aubusson rug and anointing the room with a sense of reverence.

"Miss Briscoe," he acknowledged and waved her to the chair in front of the desk. He waited until she took a seat before sitting down in his ornate wood and leather chair. He rifled through the papers on his desk, its untidiness a contradiction to his austerity.

She stared at the front of the desk. When he looked at her, she ducked her head and glanced at him from under her bangs. "This is the most magnificent desk I've ever seen."

A glimmer of a smile broke his countenance. "Yes, isn't it? Early eighteenth century."

She reached over and gently touched one of the carved heads abutting the front and top. It was smooth as satin. Warm. Almost alive. "And," she added, "I think that's the friendliest gargoyle I've ever seen."

"D'Artagnan," he said, shuffling papers again. Not looking up, he added, "Athos, Porthos, Aramis—"

"The Musketeers."

"Yes." Having found what he was looking for, he sat back and looked at her. His quick intake of breath was all that hinted at his distress before he recovered. She immediately looked down, avoiding his eyes.

"I'm Kristoff Bask. Thank you for coming."

He pulled a thick sheaf of papers from the envelope he held. "This is the last will and testament of Melissa and Thomas Kilraven."

"Who?" she asked.

"Your parents, Melissa and Thomas Kilraven," he repeated.

"My parents are Rebecca and Talbot—"

"Your birth parents," he interrupted.

Chapter Two

"What?" Her throat constricted and a coughing spasm gripped her.

He reached over and pressed a button. "Ms. Gwynn, would you please bring Miss Briscoe some tea." He looked up at her. "I didn't think. You must be parched after your trip."

"Yes," she barely whispered, her voice failing her.

There was a tap on the door.

Morgan jumped. The woman must have been standing outside the door, teapot in hand.

"Come in."

She ignored the hot tea that was set in front of her. When she found her voice again, she asked, "My birth parents? The Briscoes are my birth parents. There's been some mistake."

"Your biological parents, Melissa and Thomas Kilraven, died when their plane went down three weeks ago."

"My biological parents?" God, she sounded redundant.

"Yes." He studied her. "The Briscoes didn't tell you?"

Unable to utter a word, Morgan shook her head.. She reached out and picked up the delicate china cup and saucer from the desk in front of her. The cup rattled as she tried to steady it and her nerves at the same time. She concentrated on sipping the tea, hoping he would give her a moment to get her pounding heart under control.

Her mind raced. But, she looked like them. Mom's red hair, Dad's eyes—well almost—at least the color. She was, after all, their late-life miracle.

His voice droned on, "...of course they were given the choice as to when they would tell you. However, it was their responsibility to do so—before now." His voice rose on the last.

Melissa and Thomas Kilraven. A dull ache formed inside her chest. She had no faces to attach to the names he bandied about. Why was she even here? It wasn't as if she cared. She didn't. They weren't her parents. They gave her away.

"Miss Briscoe?"

Morgan felt his eyes on her as she sat, mesmerized by the points of light playing through the leaded panes behind him. She knew she should look away. She felt numb. She didn't care if he stared. Finally, she forced herself to look directly at him.

He looked down and shoved the papers back into an envelope.

"I regret that I am the person to give you this information." He hesitated, then spoke quietly, "You look very much like her."

"You knew them?"

He nodded. She saw genuine sadness in his expression.

This was too much. She had to think. Suddenly, Morgan stood. "I need to go home."

"But there's..." his voice trailed off. He reached over and punched the button. "Ms. Gwynn, please arrange for our private plane to take Miss Briscoe home as soon as possible."

"Yes, Mr. Bask."

His voice was softer when he spoke. "Please sit down, Miss Briscoe. Drink your tea. It will take a few moments to make preparations. I'll arrange for you to return on Thursday.

There's still much to discuss and I'm afraid we're under a time constraint."

Morgan frowned at him but did as he asked.

He put some documents into a leather folder and stood. He handed the folder to Morgan.

"You go home. Talk to the Briscoes. I'll see you on Thursday." He walked around the desk and took her hand. "Ms. Gwynn will see you out."

****

Morgan—disgusted, disgruntled, and angry—shoved the key into the lock. She shifted the folder she'd read and reread under her arm and pushed open her apartment door. Her father leapt up from the dining room chair and her mother stepped in from the kitchen, a dishtowel in her hands. No one spoke.

Morgan walked over, threw the folder down on the bar counter, turned and stormed toward her room.

"That went well," Talbot muttered.

"Oh, shut up." Becky Briscoe tossed the dishtowel down and rushed after Morgan.

Morgan slammed the bedroom door in her face.

"Morgan," Becky called softly.

"Go away!" For a second she wished she'd never given them a key.

"We aren't going anywhere. You need to come out and talk to us."

Morgan could hear the plea in her mother's voice and wanted to open the door and rush into her arms. She took one step. No. Not now. She dropped down on the bed and reached for the box of tissues. She'd thought her tears were long dried. As soon as she saw them—her parents—a new onslaught threatened.

She listened to the low murmur of their voices in the other room as she walked into her bathroom. Bask must have called them. Naturally, they dropped everything and came running. She knew it was a two or three-hour trip from the falls. Good. She hoped they were as exhausted as she was. Taking her time, Morgan washed her face and contemplated taking a shower, even though she'd had one this morning. God, had it been just this morning when she'd stood in this very bathroom? Her whole world had tilted on its axis since then.

Feeling a little better and not finding anything to delay the confrontation, she opened the door and stepped out. Her parents sat at the table, across from one another. When had they aged so much? She hadn't noticed. They actually looked middle aged. And tired. Weary. The folder was open between them, the papers spread.

Walking over to the table, Morgan stopped. She glanced down. The beautiful face of the stranger she so resembled looked back at her. The eyes of her biological father stared out from under the edge of the woman's picture. She looked at the Briscoes.

"Who are you?" she asked. Then, pointing down, she added, "And more important, who are they?"

Talbot rubbed his rough fingers against his brows, pinching the bridge of his nose. Becky let a single tear fall before wiping it away. "We're your parents. You're our daughter. I don't care what the damn papers say. You're ours." She forced back a sob.

"Dad?" She turned to the man who had been her rock growing up. The man who had always had time to answer her questions. The man who always knew the answers.

Suddenly his shoulders shook. "I'm so sorry, Morgan," his voice cracked. "We never meant to hurt you. We just love you so much." He broke.

"Dad," she whispered. No matter how upset she was, these were the people that loved her. Morgan went to her father and put her arms around him, as he had done for her so many times. She looked at her mom, tears streaming. Becky rose and came to them, enfolding both her husband and her daughter in her embrace.

They stood silent—crying, loving. No one spoke.

And, for the first time in Morgan's memory, an awkward silence built.

****

Becky brought a fresh pitcher of iced tea over to the table. She sat down across from Morgan. The tears had dried—for the moment.

"We married young." Her mother raised red-rimmed eyes to meet hers. She took a steadying breath. "We met and that was it for both of us. He was my first." A blush crept up her neck. "We were naive. I got pregnant. We were thrilled. Our parents—not so much—we got married anyway." Her father reached over and took her mother's hand, gave it a squeeze. "Anyway, our blood didn't match. Our little boy was stillborn and I almost died."

Morgan reached over and took her mother's other hand.

"I don't remember very much." Becky shrugged. "When all was said and done, I couldn't have any more children." Her focus shifted as memories came rushing back. "For a while, we were all right. We went back to school with the help of our families. We had teaching and each other. However, it wasn't enough. We wanted a family. So, we put our name on an adoption list. For the longest time, nothing happened. Then we got a call from a law firm about a private adoption." Becky smiled and squeezed her daughter's hand.

Her father spoke, "We didn't know much, except that it would be a newborn and we would have medical affidavits, just in case. Anyway, the only stipulation was that we tell you that you were adopted by the time you were twenty-five."

"Oops." It came out a little more sarcastically than Morgan intended.

"I know," her father said. "We were planning on telling you. I can honestly say we talked about it. We should have when you were younger. Besides, we didn't hear from anyone and we figured—"

Becky broke in, "The money, Talbot. I bet this is about the money."

"What money?" Morgan asked and got up. She went to the kitchen, opening and closing cabinets—anything to expend some of the nervous energy building inside of her. She grabbed a box of scones from the counter and went back to the table. No one touched them.

"Well," her father explained, "when we went to the lawyer's office for the adoption—a big ol' house in Atlanta—Mr. Morrisette said that money would be put aside each month for you. We didn't want it. You were ours. We didn't want anyone having a hold over our family. However, he said it would be put into an account and, if we decided we had need of it—or anything else—we should contact him. That was twenty-six years ago." Her father smiled with pride. "We have taken care of our family ourselves, including your college."

Her mother took a sip of tea, set it down and folded her hands in the delicate fashion that was so familiar. "It has to be the money. It should be quite a tidy sum by now. It's yours." She glanced down to the papers strewn across the middle of the table. She lifted the picture of the woman, studying it.

"She's lovely," she said quietly. She looked at Morgan. "You have her eyes." She laid the picture gently back on the pile. "It's such a tragedy that they died. But, for whatever reason, she gave you up for adoption. We never heard from anyone…" She didn't finish her thought.

Morgan leaned back. She took a deep breath and let it out slowly.

"Mom. Dad," she addressed each of her parents, looking deep into their eyes. "I am your daughter. Don't ever doubt that. You raised me well and I love you." She hesitated. "I just wish I'd known."

Her parents looked at one another.

"No, don't feel guilty. That's not what I'm saying." Morgan stood, paced to the window and stared into the dark. "Hell, I don't know what I'm saying." She spun around to face them. "Inside." She touched her stomach, not her heart. "I'm curious—about so many things." She walked back to the table and plopped down. "I'm hurt that someone gave me up." Morgan grabbed her mother's sudden outstretched hand. "Not because of a lack of what I have. It's…oh… I don't know."

Becky spoke, "We understand. Or…we're trying to understand. We should have told you. I don't know why you were supposed to know by twenty-five. I know they couldn't have known they were going to die. It has to be the money."

"What did the lawyer say?" her father asked.

"I didn't wait around to find out. I was so angry. Shocked. I couldn't breathe. I had to get out of there."

"It's got to go back to the money."

"I guess." She thought for a moment. "But why make it so urgent?"

"Don't know." Her father shrugged. "Want us to go with you?"

She did. Oh, God, she did. Instead, she said, "No. I need to do this myself. I'll let you know as soon as I find out what's going on."

By the time her parents left, it was late. She tried to get them to go back to the mountains, but they refused. Instead, they offered to look after Mrs. T. Acquiescing, Morgan hugged them both. She knew this journey was just starting and God only knew where it would lead. She wanted to make sure they knew that, to her, they were her "real" parents.

With all that they had talked about, Morgan realized she had forgotten to tell them about the lay-off. And her break-up with Rob. Both seemed insignificant now.

Morgan turned out the lights and walked into her bedroom. Mrs. T opened her eyes from the little nest she'd created on Morgan's pillow, acknowledged Morgan with an outstretched paw, and went back to sleep. If only life could be so simple. Morgan stripped and stepped into the shower. She let the water cascade over her head and down her body, letting it dull the ache she felt. Her mind whirled with questions. The only way she was going to get answers was to take that flight back to Atlanta.

Finally, as the water started to run cold, Morgan turned off the shower and reached for her towel. She let the towel slide down her side, absorbing beads of moisture and glanced down to study the crescent shaped birthmark on her right hip. The report Bask had given her described an identical birthmark on her mother's—her biological mother's—right hip.

Morgan wiped the remaining steam from the mirror with the towel. Fingers trembling, she reached over, flipped off the lights, and forced herself to look at her reflection in the dark, something she seldom did. Her eyes shimmered an iridescent green, two glowing orbs. With a shudder, she switched back on the lights. Her eyes no longer glowed, but held a crystalline appearance, like faceted emeralds. The doctors said it was a birth defect. Maybe not.

Chapter Three

Thursday found Morgan standing in the same elegant foyer where she'd stood three days earlier. Had it only been three days? Now, she was no longer nervous; she was curious. Her parents, her adoptive parents—no, they would never be that—had, once again, offered to go with her. However, Mr. Bask made it clear to her that she was to come alone. So, she had. However, not unarmed. Knowledge was power and she felt very powerful. She knew who she was. Better yet, she knew whom she chose to be.

As before, the receptionist led her to Mr. Bask's ornately appointed office. He smiled, if one could call pulling his lips taut over his teeth smiling. There weren't nearly as many papers cluttering his desk today. In fact, a single folder rested neatly in the middle of it, closed.

They shook hands and she sat across from him.

"I gather you got things straightened out," he spoke as if to clarify an annoyance.

"Excuse me?" Morgan asked tightly.

Suddenly, his demeanor changed. "I apologize." His voice softened. His eyes warmed.

Her defenses heightened.

"Things are rather urgent just now, Miss Briscoe," he stated.

"Morgan."

He nodded and opened the folder. "This is the will of your parents. Do you want me to read it completely or go over the important points?"

"Biological parents."

"What?" he looked up at her. "Oh. Yes, your biological parents."

She glanced around, even though she knew she was the only one there, besides the lawyer. "Am I the only one in the will?"

"No. But the son has already—"

"Son? I have a brother?" Her heart tumbled. She never dreamed.

"Um, no. Not really." He ran his hand over sparse grey-white hair. "He's a ward."

"They gave me away and adopted another child?" Her voice sounded shrill, even to herself.

"No, no." It was obvious she was getting perplexed. "Dorian is their ward. And heir."

"I don't think I understand."

"That isn't important at this point and it has nothing to do with you." He was almost sharp.

Morgan was getting more frustrated as well. He was right. As far as she was concerned, none of this had anything to do with her. The sooner he finished, the sooner she could leave, get home, and go about the job of finding a job.

"Let's just get on with it, please."

"I'll just go over the part that pertains to you, alright?" She nodded.

"A sum of money, starting at $10,000.00, with monthly additions of $1000.00 was deposited each month in your name, with the Briscoes in guardianship, beginning on the day of your adoption. They did not access the funds at any time. Given interest, accrual, and compounding, and with some depreciation at times, the sum at this time is

$577,366.05. The account is already in your name, the guardianship withdrawn." He looked up.

"Miss Briscoe...Morgan..." He reached over and hit the intercom.

"Ms. Gwynn, would you please bring Miss Briscoe some water? And hurry."

Morgan stared at him. Her vision clouded as the blood drained out of her head. Someone placed a glass of cold water in her hand. Sipping, she offered the receptionist a weak smile. "Thank you," she whispered and set the glass on the desk. Every time she was in this office, she almost passed out.

He waited until Ms. Gwynn slipped quietly out of the room. "Are you all right?"

"Would you repeat the amount, please?"

The lawyer looked back at the document, running his finger down, "Five hundred seventy-seven thousand three hundred sixty-six dollars and five cents."

"That's what I thought you said."

"May we continue?"

"There's more?" She reached for the glass again, just in case.

"There is the matter of the shop and property." He looked up, obviously anticipating another reaction. When she didn't, he continued. "The shop and its contents, the property on which it sits in Ruthorford, Georgia, the cottage and all outbuildings and their contents are transferred to you and Dorian Drake as coheirs. As Dorian was raised by Melissa and Thomas Kilraven and taught the business," he shot a quick glance at her, "he was apprised of the situation immediately upon their death and is running the shop." He closed the document. "He is awaiting your arrival."

"I thought you said—"

"I said that the information regarding his lineage has nothing to do with you."

Well, that was just fine with her.

"Just where am I supposed to meet Mr.—" she faltered.

"Drake. Dorian Drake." The corner of his lip curled. "Ruthorford, of course." She couldn't tell if it was an attempt at a smile or a smirk.

"Where is Ruthorford?"

"About an hour from here. Our driver will take you."

Damn. There was no way she could go all the way out to some God-forsaken town and get back in time to catch a flight out tonight.

"Would you like some lunch before you go?" Mr. Bask rose. "If you wish to freshen up..." he didn't finish, just pressed that infernal button again. "Ms. Gwynn, would you please show Ms. Briscoe the facilities?"

She would hate to be Ms. Gwynn, she couldn't help thinking. Instead, she smiled at him and stood. "I'm not very hungry. I think I would like to get going, if you don't mind."

"I'll arrange a meeting with you and Dorian later on to finalize the estate, after you have had a chance to meet." He took her hand. Its warmth startled her.

Once settled in the car, Morgan looked at the leather case Bask had handed her as she left. Bask & Morrisette was embossed on the front. Her name was also embossed in the same style and lettering below the firm's name. She ran her fingers lightly over the lettering and the soft leather. She set it aside. There'd be plenty of time to read over the documents on her way to Ruthorford, wherever that was.

The driver wasn't particularly forthcoming with any information about the firm and he didn't know too much about Ruthorford. He went out there about once a month to take something to Miss Melissa or Mr. Kilraven or bring something back. Morgan found it interesting that he called Melissa by the southern familiar of adding "Miss" before the first name. Normally, that was reserved for venerated elders. They seemed well thought of, at least by the driver.

Morgan slipped off her pumps, sunk her feet in the soft carpet of the luxury vehicle and settled back for some boring reading. It was straightforward, given the legalese. It stated what Bask had said, except for some part about the firm of Bask & Morrisette being available to her "in perpetuity" as was the facility in which it was housed. That didn't make any sense, but maybe this Dorian Drake could enlighten her.

Every now and then, she glanced out at the passing scenery. She had no idea which direction they were headed, but the landscape was breathtaking. The summer had been good here. Everything was green and lush. What she wouldn't give to get her hands in the dirt. While the terrain wasn't mountainous, it was definitely more up and down than she was used to.

She happened to look up as they crossed a wooden bridge. A morning glory framed sign displayed *"Welcome to Ruthorford."* The road snaked around. Houses appeared on either side. Cottages—some Tudor, some Victorian—gave way to larger homes on more expansive lawns. One in particular caught her eye—a large Victorian, white with blue-gray trim. A beautiful "painted lady." The sign read *Abbott's Bed & Breakfast.* "Strange," she muttered half to herself, half to the driver, "Abbott House is the name on the mansion in Atlanta. Abbott must be a significant family in Ruthorford."

Morgan stole another glance at the bed and breakfast. She loved bed and breakfasts. Having grown up near Williamsburg, Virginia, there was an abundance of private lodgings. She tried to make it a point of choosing that over the sterile accommodations of a motel whenever she got the chance. Maybe she could stay there for the night. She smiled to herself. Perhaps this wouldn't be so bad, after all.

A large, grassy median split the lanes. Landscaped paths and wrought iron benches encircled tall fountains. Picturesque shops appeared on either side of the divided street. The car slowed and stopped in front of a dark brick, two-story Victorian building. Brick fencing with black iron gates set it apart from its neighbors. Bay windows flanked tall doors.

A sign in Old English read, *The Shoppe of Spells*.

****

"Thank you, Miss Alice. Remember to use this sparingly." Dorian Drake handed the older woman her package. "And give my love to Miss Grace."

"I will," the diminutive woman twittered. "You must come by for some of Grace's peach pie. She's in a baking mood this week—"

The tinkling sound of the bell above the door drew their attention.

"Oh...my," Alice whispered and glanced at Dorian.

"I'll come by this week." He spoke softly to the old woman, yet his gaze never left the woman now standing just inside the entrance. He would've known her anywhere. She *was* Melissa, some twenty or so years ago. The same curling, brilliant red tresses. The peaches and cream complexion. The cupid's bow full lips. This woman was taller and more slender than Melissa. There was something else—a wariness, as she peered at him through red bangs. She was self-conscious. Something Melissa never was.

The grief came suddenly, without warning. He'd thought he'd gotten a handle on it, until *she* walked through the door. How dare she look so much like Melissa? How dare she force his loss to the forefront? He swallowed, took a breath, and forced it back down.

Miss Alice edged around her, staring. "Oh...my," she said again.

The bell tinkled, announcing Miss Alice's departure.

The young woman's lips curved in a hesitant smile. She stepped forward. "I'm—"

"I know who you are," Dorian announced flatly and came around the counter. "Bask called me."

"Oh." She pulled back the hand she'd extended.

His eyes warred with hers.

She straightened to her full height, which was still a good six inches below him, and thrust out her hand again. "I'm Morgana Briscoe—Morgan." She flashed him a brilliant smile.

He glanced down at the hand, considering. Then, with a slight lift to the corner of his mouth, not quite a smile, he slowly let her hand slip within his grasp. "Dorian Drake." A current surged between them. She jumped, jerking back her hand. As if nothing had occurred, he slipped around her, flipped the closed sign on the door, and locked it.

He watched her as she looked around the shop, her eyes coming to rest on the sign above the counter, where he now stood, closing the old-fashioned register—*Merry Meet, Merry Part, Merry Meet Again.*

He saw her brow furrow. "It's an original sign," he said, "probably a hundred and fifty years or more." His voice sounded harsh to his own ears. Mel and Thom would never have treated anyone like that, especially not her. As he watched her move around the room, he offered up his own silent plea. *Hey guys, give me a break. I didn't expect her to look like this. I'm doing the best I can.* Seeing Melissa in his head, her hands on her hips, one brow raised, he added. *Okay, I'll try harder.*

"Excuse me?" Morgan stopped and faced him.

"Nothing." He shook his head. Had he said that out loud?

****

She wandered over to the counter with the oils and soaps. This was not what she'd expected, given the sign out front. She looked around. The inside was airy and inviting. Bottles of lotions, perfumes, and soaps rested neatly on glass shelves. Interspersed between the bottles were rocks and crystals. The effect was dazzling. On the other side were herbs and jars of—whatever—all neatly lined up. It looked like an organic gift shop. And, it smelled so good. Scents she knew. She sighed in relief.

He wasn't what she expected either. Hell, she didn't know what she'd expected, but it wasn't Mr. tall, dark and handsome with ice-blue eyes that seemed to cut right through her...and looked as though he was hoping to hit the jugular. Then, she saw the sadness in his eyes before he covered it with a glare. Up until now, all she'd felt were anger and confusion. It hit her. This man had just lost his parents—her parents. No. She still had her parents.

He followed her across the room and stepped behind the counter, pulling several bottles from the shelves. He put drops on a small white ceramic disk. "Basil, vanilla, and a light citrus." He closed his eyes and inhaled. "Yeah, that's about right." He held the flask under her nose. She sniffed.

"How did you...?" It was her scent. The one she made for herself.

He smiled at her for the first time. The smile didn't quite reach his stormy blue eyes. Still, Morgan had the strange urge to reach out and push back the wave of hair that fell over his brow. She felt her stomach tighten. She grabbed the counter. He didn't seem to notice.

"This has evolved into an herbal apothecary, with gifts," he said and waved his arm, encompassing the shop. "We don't specialize in spells much anymore. Oh, don't get me wrong," he chided, "there was a time."

He moved around the counter. "Tea?"

"Uh…sure." She followed him toward the back.

He led her down a small hallway, past a restroom and an office. A door to some sort of closet, she presumed, was tucked under the stairs. They entered a large kitchen.

"My workroom. Have a seat." He pointed to a table by a six-paned window. She looked around. Commercial appliances surrounded by lots of stainless steel. Nestled among beakers, flasks, and mortars and pestles were stones and crystals, softening the effect. She thought of the cramped galley kitchen she used to do her crafts. What she wouldn't give— She stopped the thought.

A sharp, single bark caught her attention. Dorian stepped to the screen door and opened it. "Meesha," he said to the dog, "this is Morgan. Go greet our guest." Tail wagging, the small Border Collie walked over and sat in front of Morgan. Ears raised and head tilted, she let out a soft woof.

"Nice to meet you, too," Morgan reached over and stroked the dog's soft fur. The dog inched forward slightly, positioning herself for a better stroke. Morgan laughed.

She watched as Dorian deftly poured hot water into a china pot, added a tea ball, and slipped it under a cozy to steep. He came and sat opposite her. She looked up and his eyes caught hers and held. She felt that tingle again. She looked out the window. Trellises lined the brick fencing. Roses and other flowers climbed and bloomed. Morgan leaned toward the window. Farther down, an espaliered peach tree ran along the brick wall in candelabra fashion.

"I will show you the back in a little while," he interrupted her musings, causing her to jump back, unsettling the teapot. Adroitly, he reached over and caught it with large, beautiful hands. Her gaze followed the sinewy arms to where they stretched out from rolled up sleeves and beyond, to well-formed biceps and broad shoulders. When she got to his face, she saw he was watching her.

The blood rushed to her face and she looked down. She hadn't been this awkward since junior high.

He poured the tea and sat back, studying her. Embarrassed, she concentrated on the tea. The aroma hugged her senses. It was heaven. She took a sip. It was strong, but very smooth and with a hint of spice.

"This is fabulous."

"Thank you. It's my own special blend." His voice was velvet.

Morgan set down her cup. "I know this is hard for you." Something flashed across his eyes and was gone. She rushed on. "I had no idea," she explained. "Until a few days ago, I thought I was the biological daughter of Rebecca and Talbot Briscoe. I'm not here to take your inheritance," she added.

"It's not really my inheritance," he muttered and stood, taking their cups to the sink.

"Let me show you around," he said, not giving her time to question. "I live upstairs," he nodded toward the stairs between them and the shop, but headed toward the back door. Meesha jumped up and followed, happy to join them. He held the door as both she and the dog moved past him. At her gasp, he smiled.

"Oh—God," she breathed. The late afternoon sun bathed the garden's colors in soft light. A large tree filtered more strokes of light into shadows that caressed a cottage and gazebo nestled in the back. A backdrop of ivy and flowering vines covered most of the high brick fence encircling the property. A warm breeze whirled floral scents, combined with those of herbs, making Morgan close her eyes and inhale.

He was watching her, as if he awaited her reaction. She didn't disappoint him. A smile played across her lips. "It's magnificent." She could tell he was proud of the gardens, cottage, and gazebo. The lushness told her it had been a particularly good year for the gardens. He led her down a path of bricks laid haphazardly in dirt.

"The gardens are arranged by type." He pointed to the left. "Culinary and beverage. On the right medicinal and fragrance. Floral interspersed. The sides of the shop harbor more shade loving plants while the fence walls have vines or espaliers, depending on the light and, mostly, on the determination of the plant."

She walked slowly. Thyme. Marjoram. Sage. Fennel. She smelled peppermint, rose, lavender, and bay. Somewhere there was patchouli. She thought of Jenn. Wisteria worked its way up the gazebo. It was her dream garden. All around her. She stopped, squinted into the setting sun. "Is that a Neem tree?" She turned her full attention to Dorian.

He nodded. A smile broke across his face. This time even his eyes smiled. "Yes. A beauty, isn't it."

"I didn't know they could grow here."

He shrugged. He took her elbow, "Let me show you the cottage."

The current ran lightly from him to her. She fought an urge to pull away—or move closer—not sure which she wanted more. "You are indeed self-sufficient here." Her voice sounded breathy. She stepped away from his touch.

"We're a true herbal apothecary. However, we also offer soaps, perfumes, and gifts, among other things. Meesha, let's show Morgan the cottage." Meesha barked and bounded to the side porch of the Tudor-style cottage. The sunlight touched the leaded glass panes, sparkling like gems.

He opened the door and held it as Morgan stepped inside. She thought she heard a hum, very faint, for just a second. She listened. She heard Meesha's nails tapping on hardwood. He closed the half door, unlatched the top and left it open.

"I've never seen one of those."

"A Dutch door? This will let some air in."

She walked over and let her fingers run over the leading between the panes of the front window, overlooking the garden. She could look across the gardens to the back of the shop, have tea in the morning and watch the birds. What was she thinking? She turned back to the interior of the room. A side window framed the gazebo. A stove, sink, and refrigerator snugged along the wall. On the opposite wall was a small fireplace. More stones and crystals adorned the windows and mantel. A comfortable sofa faced the fireplace. She took a step toward the open French doors in the back, saw the quilt-covered bed, turned and moved quickly back into the living area.

"There's a small bedroom and bath in the back," Dorian said.

"It's bigger than it looks."

"We use it as a guest house. I stayed here for a while—before I moved upstairs." She heard the sadness in his voice.

Meesha stood next to the sofa, whining. Morgan turned. The dog was staring at the space between the sofa and the bedroom. "What is it, girl?"

"Meesha," Dorian called. "She just wants to go out." He walked over to the door, pulled it open, and stepped outside.

She followed him. "It's lovely. Thank you for the tour."

He looked at her from beneath hooded eyes. His jaw was set, as if he wanted to say something, yet forced himself to remain silent. The discomfort between them escalated.

She looked at her watch. "It's been a long day. I think I better be heading out." She hurriedly took several steps toward the shop. "I think I'll stop at the bed and breakfast tonight. We can talk more before I go home tomorrow."

"No." His voice was sharp.

Morgan jumped.

"I mean," he carefully modulated his tone, "we have a lot to talk about. The cottage is freshly made. Stay here tonight. We can discuss things tomorrow morning and make some decisions."

"I don't know." She looked back at the cottage. The lights played through the windows and into the gardens. It was the most inviting little house. Plus, he would be inside the shop with a garden between them. Maybe one night.

"If you don't mind?" She was still unsure. He didn't look thrilled that she was staying, although he'd just insisted. "I didn't come prepared to stay. I don't have any clothes."

"Although you are more slender, I think Melissa has some things you can wear."

"Oh, I couldn't."

"Why not?"

She shrugged. What was one more thing to feel awkward about?

"Besides, you have to have dinner." Dorian opened the door to the shop and waited for her. Again, the perfumes from the shop assailed her senses.

"Let's go down to Abbott's," he said. His tone sounded lighter. "They serve a wonderful dinner. Then you can come back here and get a good night's sleep."

"I'll let your driver know you're staying," he added, finalizing the decision for her.

She watched as Dorian walked toward the front of the shop. The yawn she'd been fighting overtook her. When she opened her eyes again, he was surrounded by spikes of colored light. She squinted, shook her head, and rubbed her eyes. A *normal* Dorian opened the door, stepped through and pulled it closed behind him. She took a deep breath. She must really be tired.

In a few minutes, he was back. "I told him we'll call when you're ready to leave."

"Let me freshen up and we can go," she started toward the back door.

"Use the powder room here. I'll run over to the cottage and close up. I left the upper part of the door open. I'm always forgetting that."

****

Fifteen minutes later, they walked the few blocks to Abbott's in an awkward silence. He didn't say anything and she was too tired to carry the conversation. A young girl, who seemed to know Dorian, smiled adoringly up at him and seated them next to a window overlooking another garden. This garden was not nearly as opulent as the one behind the shop, but it made a beautiful dinnerscape. A fountain rose out of a small pond. Water bubbled up and over, falling back into the basin. Trails meandered around the pond and disappeared behind the building.

Dorian smiled at the young woman and proceeded to order for the both of them. The atmosphere had a calming effort on him. Once he lost the hostility, he became the perfect host. Morgan watched him as he talked about the shop and the group of people who frequented it. His eyes brightened and he leaned forward, smiling as he shared a story. His animation captivated her. It was obvious that he cared deeply for the people in this town. As he talked, she listened and tried to imagine him interacting with the people who raised him—the ones who gave her away. Suddenly, she wasn't smiling any longer.

Dorian stopped midsentence. "What's wrong?" He seemed genuinely concerned and reached out as if to touch her hand, stopped, and pulled his hand back, his fist clenched.

Feeling raw with unexplored emotions, Morgan looked down, shook her head and toyed with her napkin.

An older woman approached, a tray balanced on her shoulder. She set the tray on a stand, set plates in front of Morgan and Dorian, then stood and stared.

Morgan bent her head further down.

"Oh, I'm sorry," she apologized, "it's just that you're the spitting image of Mel. But, you know that."

Morgan smiled faintly.

"Morgan, this is Teresa Ruthorford."

Morgan extended her hand. Teresa took it in both of hers. Tears threatened to spill from the woman's eyes. "I am so glad to meet you. Mel was my best friend." Her voice broke. She turned and rushed away.

"Go," Morgan said, seeing Dorian's quandary.

"I'll be right back. Go ahead and start. Don't let your dinner get cold."

Morgan took a bite. The fish was grilled and served with a fragrant herb sauce that enhanced the flavor but didn't overpower it. It was incredible. The fresh asparagus was also grilled and served with just a hint of lemon. Her appetite rapidly returned.

Dorian returned and sat down. "How is it?"

"It's wonderful. Is she okay?"

He nodded, took a bite of his chicken, and looked at her. Suddenly nervous, she dabbed the napkin at her lips and looked out the window.

"Why do you do that?" he asked.

"Do what?"

"Look away. Or down. Or out from under your bangs."

Her cheeks flamed.

"It's your eyes, isn't it?" He reached over and gently lifted her chin with just the tip of his finger, barely touching her, until she was looking right at him, into those glacial blue eyes. She felt a slight tingle. "You have Melissa's eyes," he said. "Wonderful eyes."

"Eyes that bring stares and starts."

"Hmm," he nodded. "I forget." He went back to eating. "Here, we are all used to her eyes. Eyes that shined with kindness and love." He took a sip of coffee. "But, now that I think about it, she did have sunglasses she wore whenever we went anywhere else. Or, she'd wear a hat." His eyes crinkled at the memory. "I'd forgotten."

"You're sure Teresa's okay?" She changed the subject. Talking about Melissa felt weird, as it pertained to her.

"Yes. She'll be all right. They grew up together."

"Losing a friend and then having her likeness appear before you must be devastating," she acknowledged. *Finding out you've lost someone you never even knew isn't easy, either*, Morgan thought and realized she, too, was experiencing a sense of loss.

Dorian poured her a second cup of coffee and turned the conversation to herbs, soaps, and lotions. The things she knew and loved to craft. He seemed to have a real talent for concocting just the right blend. For a little while, he was warm and friendly, as though he'd forgotten to be mad at her. Morgan began to relax. They sipped coffee as candlelight flickered in the deepening dusk.

"You don't know how much you look like Mel. It took my breath away." He cocked his head and looked at her. "But you are softer, gentler."

"I wish I had met them."

"They would have loved you." He looked into the candle flame. A far away, sad expression passed over his eyes.

Wanting to comfort him, Morgan reached over and touched his hand. Zapped, she jerked back. "Ow! What is it with you? Every time we touch…" she let the words trail off as he looked at her, his brow furrowed. Obviously, he hadn't felt it.

"Shall we go?" He rose and came around to pull out her chair.

"Don't we need to wait for the check?"

"No. We… I have a running tab. Plus, I provide all the herbs for them."

The warm night and events of the day began to wear on her. By the time they entered the shop, she was exhausted. "I think I'll go on to bed. Thank you for a wonderful evening."

"Wait and thank me tomorrow," he said. He looked so serious. Then he smiled. "I'll walk you out. Make sure you don't need anything." He stopped, as if pondering something. "Wait here," he said and bounded up the stairs, taking them two at a time.

"Okay," she responded to his retreating back.

Turning, she saw the cottage through the back door. Like a painting, the small Tudor building cast fingers of light over the gardens. She watched flickers of color, entranced, and remembered the crystals decorating the windowsills and mantel. She moved toward the back door.

"This ought to do it." Dorian came up behind her.

She turned. He handed her an armload of clothing.

"I don't need all this."

"Well, I'm a guy. I wasn't sure what you'd need. If you want something else, just ask."

"Thank you," she said softly.

Dorian walked her over and said goodnight, leaving her alone in the cottage. She set the clothes on the bench at the foot of the bed and picked up the nightshirt. It smelled of

lavender. She put it to her face and inhaled, wondering about
the woman who'd worn it.

Her cell phone rang. Her mother's voice sounded
cautious. "Am I disturbing you?"

"Of course not, Mom," Morgan said and rushed on, "I'm
sorry I didn't call. It's been so busy." She sat on the side of the
bed and set the nightshirt at the foot, feeling guilty. For what?
Wondering about her biological mother? She pushed the
thought and guilt aside and launched into a detailed
description of her day, leaving out the hotness of her new
"brother."

She wasn't so lucky with Jenn, who called on the tail end
of her conversation with her mom. Her mother had insisted
Morgan take the call and promised to give hugs and kisses to
her father for her. Ever the romantic, Jenn jumped on the idea
of sparks flying between them, even when Morgan insisted he
didn't feel them, only she did. Jenn also reminded her that he
most definitely was not her brother. All in all, the
conversations with her mom and Jenn lightened her mood
and she grabbed the nightshirt and headed into the bath.

An antique claw-footed tub sat at an angle in the dusky
beige bath. An oval mirror hung pristinely over a pedestal
sink. Diamond panes set in a small window showcased the
vine covered brick fence behind the cottage. She lifted the lid
on a glass jar. An herbal infusion of lavender perfumed the
small space. It was becoming apparent that Melissa was a fan
of lavender. She looked at the tub and sighed. She was too
tired. It was all she could do to climb beneath the cool sheets
and turn off the light. Her last thought was how the pillow
smelled of lavender.

Somewhere in the distance, a dog barked. Again. And
again. Morgan pushed back the covers and padded into the
front room. Meesha? She moved toward the front window.

Moonlight streamed across the garden. Something scurried through the plants, rustling leaves. A cat? She couldn't quite make it out. Meesha barked again—from inside the darkened shop. The hair on the back of her arms stood on end. It moved again, whatever it was. She leaned into the window and squinted into the darkness, trying to make out the outline of the small animal silhouetted by moonlight. It looked hairless. Her breath caught. It stopped, rose up on hind legs and faced her. Violet slits glared at her. She screamed.

The hairless creature moved on all fours toward her, its body outlined in bluish violet. Morgan screamed again and stumbled further back into room. She saw the door of the shop fly open and Meesha and Dorian bound down the steps. Before she could turn, he burst through the door, pulled her away from the window, stopping just short of the bedroom, and pulled her into his arms. His initial contact with her sent a jolt, but before she could pull away, he gathered her close, resting his chin atop her head. The energy changed. It seemed to pulse—to catch and match a rhythm from him.

"Close your eyes," he commanded, his voice husky from sleep. Points around the room began to glow, including the edge of the rug on which they stood. She quickly obeyed, closing her eyes. He whispered soothing words to her, his voice taking on a crooning tone. She began to relax, become lethargic. The pulse changed to a hum.

She could smell the heat of his bed warmed body. She could feel the beat of his heart. For a moment, she felt like she could hear both hearts, then one, as if they'd become attuned. She breathed him in and snuggled closer. His arms tightened around her, then loosened. Slowly, he released her. She blinked, stepped back and looked around. Nothing glowed. Not the stones. Not the rug. She didn't hear a pulse or a hum.

He stood before her, watching her. Except for the fact that he was shirtless, in pajama bottoms, with mussed hair, he looked fine. Actually, he looked more than fine. She had an incredible urge to step back into his arms. Instead, she turned away.

She walked to the window and looked out. Nothing stirred. Warm scents wafted in through the still open door.

"What the hell was that?" She point toward the garden. "And what did you just do?"

"You were frightened," Dorian said simply.

"I wasn't born yesterday," she snapped at him.

His brow furrowed.

"Something happened here." She waved her arm inclusively. "I'm not stupid."

She faced the dog. Meesha sat three feet from the rug, ears forward, staring in rapt attention at the rug beneath Morgan's feet, as she had the day before. Morgan hopped off the rug. "What's that?" she pointed at the dog.

"Meesha?"

"No. Yes. But, what's she staring at?"

Dorian stepped off the rug, lifted it to reveal the wood floor. Meesha looked up at him and moved over to the sofa where she hopped up and settled down, resting her head on her paws.

He walked over to the door. "You must've had a bad dream. I'll go and let you get some sleep. Meesha," he called. Meesha looked up at him but didn't move.

"No!" Morgan's voice came out in a yelp. "I'm not staying here alone."

He smiled at her.

"You can have the couch." She walked into the bedroom, retrieved the blanket from the bench, and grabbed a pillow. "Here," she shoved them at him, marched into the bedroom, and closed the French doors firmly behind her.

"Oh…yeah…thanks for staying," she called from behind the safety of the closed doors.

"Meesha, down." She heard his command. A few grumbles followed and then silence.

Maybe he was right. It was so similar to her nightmares. They seem to be returning. She was so tired, she couldn't think straight. She pulled the covers up and was asleep before her head hit the pillow.

Outside, a pair of violet eyes stared at the cottage.

****

Morgan woke sprawled across the bed, the quilt piled in a heap on the floor. A heavy fog clouded her mind. She rolled over and stared at the ceiling. There was something flitting just beyond her consciousness. She turned her head. She stared at the closed French doors…and bolted upright, remembering that Dorian was on the other side.

She crawled off the bed, grabbed clothes off the bench and crept into the bathroom. Trying not to make too much noise, she bathed and got dressed, pulling her still damp red hair up off her neck and fastening a large silver clip to hold it. The jeans were a little loose, but when she tucked the chambray shirt in, they were just fine. She started out and turned back, pulled her make-up kit out of her purse. A little lip-gloss wouldn't be going too far.

She pushed on the doors. With a thunk, they finally pushed open. There lay Dorian, asleep, one long leg hanging over the end of the sofa, while the other was bent and resting on the floor. He couldn't be comfortable. His bare bronze chest rose and fell in an even pattern. She should cover him. She stepped over and looked down at Meesha, sprawled on her side in a nice little nest of blanket.

Her attention lifted to the window. She eased around the couch and tiptoed over to the large window. The happy faces of flowers turned upward toward the bright sun. The garden looked welcoming and safe. No animals of any sort. Maybe it had been a dream. It seemed so real. In all her dreams before, the threat was vague, the creatures undistinguished. She could still picture it, the malevolent eyes glowing. She shuddered.

"Hey."

She jumped.

"Sorry." Dorian sat facing her, his arm thrown across the back of the couch. His hair looked tousled and, with a night's growth of beard, he appeared quite the rake. "I didn't mean to startle you."

She couldn't help but stare at the muscles rippling across his torso. A shimmer of heat coiled in her belly.

He looked into her eyes. The shimmer of heat turned into a flame.

She looked down, letting her bangs curtain his view, then remembered his comments at dinner, looked up and brushed her bangs back.

He glanced at the mantel and was off the couch in one swift movement. "Crap. It's almost 7:30. I need to open the shop. Meesha, come." He was at the door with a panther's grace before he turned back. "Give me a few moments. Then come on over." He opened the door and turned back. "Coffee?"

"I can make some."

"No, I meant do you want some? I always get a pot going in the morning. Not the most herbal smell for the shop, but I've found I have no desire to go without my coffee."

She nodded. "Thank you. I will be over in a little while."

Without another word, he walked out the door with Meesha on his heels. Through the window, she watched him cross the garden to the shop—watched his magnificent muscles flex as he walked. "Down, girl," she admonished her thudding pulse. Instead, she concentrated on Meesha, who had raced off to the side and now bounded up the steps behind him and yipped as he opened the door to let her precede him.

Morgan turned and retrieved the blanket from the floor. She shook it and folded it, laying it over the back of the couch. She grabbed a throw pillow, used her fist to fluff it, and caught the scent of him. She stopped and inhaled. He definitely had an effect on her. A few bars from "Music of the Night" played. *Jenn!* Morgan raced into the bedroom and grabbed her cell phone.

Jenn, lovable geek that she was, had installed show tunes on Morgan's phone for several people who called her regularly. Her father got, "If I were a Rich Man," and her mother, "I Will Follow Him." Morgan chose, "With a Little Help from My Friends." Rob had not been impressed with "The Nutty Professor" and insisted it be deleted. She should have known then.

"Hey, girlfriend," Jenn piped.

"Hi. What's up?"

"I hope it's not too early. I wanted to catch you before you talked to your mom and dad today."

"What's wrong?" Her apprehension escalated.

"Nothing. I just wanted to let you know they were at your place when I went by to check on Mrs. T. We had a nice little chat."

"And?"

"Morgan, they're worried about you. I mean, about how you feel about them."

"Mom didn't say anything last night. I thought we'd cleared all that up before I left." She sat on the bed and thought of the fine lines around her mother's eyes. "I told them not to worry."

"Well, I did too. But, they are who they are." Jenn paused. "I just wanted to tell you that I sense that they feel like all this is somehow their fault."

Morgan closed her eyes. She felt like she was doing a juggling act and she didn't even know for sure what she was juggling. She wasn't sure if Dorian wanted her here. He was being kind—now. There was something under the surface she couldn't quite figure. Now, her parents.

"I'll call them later," she said.

"How's Dorian?"

She smiled. If there was a male within ten miles, Jenn was ready to hear all the details.

"Not much to tell," she said, waited a beat, then added, "except that he spent the night here last night."

"What?" Jenn voice became shrill.

Morgan laughed. "Sorry. I couldn't resist. Yes, he did. And no, we didn't. I will explain later. I promise. I have to get over there now." She stood and started smoothing the quilt back on the bed as she spoke. "Gotta run. Bye." Smiling, she hung up on a flurry of questions.

She took her time putting the cottage to rights. She lifted the top of the glass jar in the bathroom and let the lavender perfume the space. By the time she opened the door to leave, the cottage sparkled and smelled inviting.

****

The temperature was already climbing into the eighties. A warm breeze ruffled the morning glory along the back fence. She studied the gazebo. The swing stirred in the air blowing through the bright white structure. Tea roses trailed upward, climbing the latticework, their delicate fragrance wafting around her. She took a step toward the gazebo when she caught a movement out of the corner of her eye. A quick glance in the direction of the shop showed her there was nothing where she'd seen the creature last night. The hair on her arm prickled. She swallowed and willed herself not to run as she hastened to the back door of the shop. When she tapped on the screen door, Meesha gave a welcoming bark.

"I'm in front. Come on in," Dorian called.

She looked back at the garden. The picturesque cottage was nestled in a cornucopia of summer color. Her unease momentarily squelched, she followed the voices. Dorian stood behind the counter, wrapping dried herbs in brown paper. Deftly, he formed a small packet and secured it with twine. Five women clustered on the other side, tittering. All eyes turned to her. She smiled, but kept her eyes slighted averted.

"Ladies," he said, amusement in his tone, "this is Morgan Briscoe, co-owner of The Shoppe of Spells."

They rushed forward, surrounded her, touching her arm, shaking her hand. A bunch of chattering squirrels would have been less disturbing. She nodded, smiled, and was assailed by a flurry of comments and questions.

"You look so much like her, dear."

"We are so glad you are finally here."

"Will you be staying?"

"Where have you been living?"

"They never said anything about you, did they, Dorian?"

The bell above the door tinkled. All chattering stopped. Morgan looked up. A tall, svelte woman with short raven hair seemed to flow in, her eyes never leaving Morgan. She proprietarily moved around the counter, stepped up to Dorian, slid one bronze fingernail under his chin to turn him toward her and planted a kiss on his lips, which he rigidly returned.

Morgan noticed the muscle in his jaw tighten. The vixen took no notice. She flowed back around the counter and invaded the small circle of women surrounding Morgan, extending a hand full of long bronze fingernails.

"I'm Jasmine. But, I'm sure Dorian has already mentioned me."

Morgan felt the tips of the nails dig, ever so slightly, into her hand. Determined not to acknowledge the discomfort, she tried to ignore the pressure. "No. Can't say that he has," she said, looking the other woman directly in the eyes. The battle lasted mere seconds before Jasmine let go. Morgan saw fire flash in her eyes before they turned, petulantly, toward Dorian.

"Jas, she just got here last evening." There was no pretense in his tone.

Jasmine moved back around the counter and sidled up next to him, letting her fingers make a long, smooth stroke down his arm.

Morgan watched them. Every time she came in contact with him, an electric current sparked between them. To her vexation, Jasmine didn't have the same problem. Now, why would that bother her?

The little group of woman moved as one toward the door, quietly, trying not to draw Jasmine's attention to them.

Too late. "Leaving, ladies?" The vixen's voice dripped venom.

Not turning, the smallest of the five whispered, "We just stopped by for some herbs." "Sure you did," the viper hissed. The little group scuttled out the door.

Morgan raised her head and looked directly at her.

Jasmine turned her full attention to Morgan. "Why look Dorian, she has the same weird eyes Melissa did."

"That's enough, Jas." Dorian took her arm and led her toward the door.

"But, darling," she purred.

"Morgan and I have business to discuss. I'll call you later."

Jasmine reached up and kissed him, narrowed her eyes, and glared at Morgan.

Morgan flashed her best smile.

Dorian reached around Jasmine, eased himself out of her clasp, and held the door.

"Until tonight." She smiled a seductive promise.

Dorian didn't answer, just closed the door behind her.

He thrust his hand through his hair. "Well...that went well," he muttered to himself.

That one statement—one made often by her father—totally disarmed her.

"Coffee?"

"Sure." She followed him into the kitchen.

Chapter Four

Morgan slipped into the same chair she'd occupied the night before and watched him pour the piping hot brew into two mugs. "Scone?" he asked, not turning around.

"Okay." She shrugged. The little scene in the front of the store had robbed her of her appetite.

He set a white china plate in front of her. "I think they're still warm."

"You made scones?" she asked just before letting the warm cinnamon play on her tongue.

Her eyes widened. "Wow."

"Teresa brought them down. She seems to think I'll starve if she doesn't bring something in the morning."

She saw the pain, still fresh, cloud his eyes as he sat across from her.

"I'm so sorry for your loss," she said softly.

He acknowledged her with a nod. Meesha gave a whimper. Dorian broke off a small piece of scone and offered it to the dog. "Your breakfast is over there," he said. As if in understanding, she gave his hand a quick lick and moved over to her food bowl.

"I'm sorry about in there…earlier," he said.

"It's okay. They didn't mean anything." She made careful reference to the group of women.

"Them?" he choked back a snort. "I don't apologize for them. They are what they are." He shook him head. "And, they'll drive you crazy with their good intentions." He rose and took her plate, talking back over his shoulder. "I was referring to Jasmine."

"Your girlfriend?"

"Actually, no." Dorian turned back around and leaned against the counter. "She would like it, if—"

The bell tinkled. He looked relieved. "Back to work." He pushed away from the counter. "Come on, I will try to give you some shop initiation as we go."

Morgan wondered what he would have said had they not been interrupted.

The next few hours passed quickly. For what it was, the little shop seemed to do a brisk business. Or, everyone in town was curious and wanted to see her. Items were purchased, introductions made. For Morgan, it was nice to be active in a shop again. Before long, she was able to find what someone needed and ring it up without asking Dorian for help. She loved the smells of the products and wanted to ask for the recipes so she could incorporate some into her own scents when she got home.

As the hours passed, Morgan began handling more and more up front, allowing Dorian to do more apothecary work. He would disappear through the door under the stairs, take ingredients into the kitchen and come out with the compounded item. She had so many questions. Occasionally, she caught him watching her. At first, she thought he was evaluating her work, but it was more than that. It was as though he was studying her, not just her work. Before she could ask, someone would come in and interrupt them. Each person was very pleasant and tended to linger, visiting with her until another customer took her attention.

Dorian had just suggested they break for lunch when a woman came in with an older man. Morgan could have sworn a cat had slipped in with them, the way that Mrs. T would do, given half a chance. When Meesha whined from the back room, she was sure of it. She walked around the counter just as two women opened the door to leave. The cat, or whatever it was, slinked past them and out the door. Morgan blinked. She would have sworn the outline shimmered.

She heard a commotion behind her. As she turned, the woman who'd arrived with the older man was hugging him.

"Papa?" She heard the catch in the woman's voice. The woman's eyes swam with tears.

"Cathy?" The old man looked at his daughter, then around, confusion etched on his face.

"Yes, Papa," she said and hugged him again. She turned to Morgan. "He hasn't said my name in three weeks."

"Dorian?" the older man said. Dorian stepped forward.

"Melissa?" He looked at Morgan.

"No, Mr. Parker," Dorian corrected gently, "this is Melissa's daughter, Morgan."

"It's nice to meet you, Mr. Parker." She turned to his daughter.

"I'm Cathy," the woman smiled at Morgan.

"Does he need to sit down?" Morgan asked, watching the man's gaze dart around the room.

"No...I think we'll go home now." She turned back to her father and guided him to the door. "Oh, Papa, it's so nice to have you back."

"I've had such a bad headache," the old man commented.

Cathy quietly closed the door behind them, watching her father carefully.

"Do we need to call a doctor?" Morgan asked. "He said he's been suffering from headaches. It could be a stroke."

"It's not," Dorian said flatly, as he turned the sign over and locked the door. "We need to talk."

She followed him into the kitchen. He didn't stop. Meesha danced out the door as he held it open. Without another word, he walked over to the cottage and held that door, once again adjusting the top to stay open. It seemed a little warm to keep the door open, but Morgan said nothing, just followed him inside.

"You need to do as I say. It's extremely important."

She stopped, nerves tingling. "What?" she looked at him.

Dorian walked over to the carpet where he had dragged her last night and held his hand out to her. "Come," he beckoned. She resisted.

"Hurry. Trust me, Morgan. You won't get hurt. But we have to hurry."

She stepped toward him. When he started to pull her into his arms, she stepped back. The shock was quick, stinging. "Okay, we'll try it another way." He held out both hands. "Five points of our bodies have to touch. We'll try hands, feet, and forehead." When she hesitated, he urged, "Hurry." Then, softening his voice, added, "Please."

Morgan stepped in front of him. He took both hands simultaneously. The jolt wasn't as strong but she could still feel the current flow from him to her. He positioned his feet just outside of hers and bent his head, touching his forehead to hers. They were close, intimate. She could feel his breath as he spoke. "Close your eyes. Or open them. Just don't move, whatever you do."

"You're frightening me." She pulled back. He held fast.

"Don't break contact," he ordered. Frightened, but compelled by his urgency, she stepped back toward him.

Out of her peripheral vision, she saw the stones begin to glow. The fibers in the rug beneath her shimmered. She heard rustling. He held her hands tighter. She swallowed. She could feel sweat on her palm. Morgan wanted to pull back—she definitely didn't want to sweat into his hands. Then she realized that was the least of her problems. Sitting over by the window, Meesha started to whine.

"Quiet, girl," Dorian soothed.

The dog quieted but continued to stare at the rug.

"You're still frightening me," Morgan whispered.

"I'll explain. Just don't break contact until I do. Understand?" His voice was deep, firm.

"Yes." She swallowed and held fast.

"The creature you saw last night was real. It's what was making Mr. Parker sick. Together we can send it away. Several of them have been roaming free since Melissa and Thom died. With your help, I think we can control them."

"What?" She impulsively yanked her hands. He held tight. She felt something brush against her leg. She glanced down. The rug glowed silver and she saw a faint violet outline of movement. She moved in closer to Dorian. Now, they stood, body to body. Far more points than five were touching. She heard the hum.

Morgan closed her eyes. *Oh, God.* She couldn't be awake. This had to be a dream. One long continuation of her childhood nightmares. She would wake up any moment. She squeezed her eyes shut. Her body trembled. Sweat beaded on her upper lip. She stood stiff as a statue, afraid to budge. She could feel Dorian's thumbs begin gently massaging the back of her hands, the back and forth motion her only reassurance.

Dorian stepped back. She held on, too frightened to let go.

"It's okay," he said softly and broke contact with her. The edges of the rug beneath her still shone a silvery hue. She leapt off the rug and looked around. Everything looked normal. Meesha stretched out and put her head down, but watched them, waiting for some command, some piece of attention. Like, Meesha, Dorian watched her.

"What happened?"

"It's gone back through the portal."

"Portal?" She edged the rug with her toe, lifting it. The shiny wood floor lay underneath, it's pattern unmarred.

"Morgan, it's a dimensional portal."

"Yeah, sure." She moved away from him, stopped and turned. "Like I know what that is."

She studied him, waiting for some sarcastic punch line.

He didn't say anything, just watched her.

She narrowed her eyes at him. "What kind of joke is this?" She headed into the bedroom and grabbed her purse and the folder. He stopped her as she headed into the bathroom for the small make-up kit she'd left on the sink. She jerked her arm away from the shock of his hand on her arm.

"And you—what is it with you? Every time you touch me, I get shocked. Yet, you don't seem to feel it." *To hell with the kit.* She could buy more make-up. She swung around toward the French doors.

"Oh, I feel it," he said, the timber of his voice slightly lower. His eyes now dark like a stormy sea. He took one step toward her before he stopped. "Believe me, I feel it," he all but whispered and turned away.

As she scrutinized him, heat curled in her stomach. A small throb punched deep inside. *Damn.* Needing to do something, she went back and grabbed her make-up kit.

She came out of the bathroom to find him standing in her path. She carefully stepped around him. She wasn't going near him. "That...that thing..."

"...is gone," he said. "Please. Let me explain. Give me a day. Then, if you wish, you can leave."

She stopped, turned toward him, her eyes full of questions.

Dorian pushed his hair back from his forehead, closed his eyes and took a deep breath. *Who am I kidding? I'm not sure I understand.* It would take more than a day with her. She knew nothing. He had practiced this speech for three weeks, since he'd first gotten word of Melissa and Thomas's death and of her arrival. He knew it was coming—it had to come. He'd been fighting against the inevitable most of his life. He'd wasted a lot of time being angry that his destiny wasn't his to make. Angry with a woman he hadn't met. What he hadn't anticipated was her naiveté. She'd had no idea of her future—of him. He looked at her. Her face was flushed. Perspiration dampened her upper lip. She watched him warily, like a frightened wild animal ready to bolt. He wasn't sure what he would do if she left. That had never been considered. So many things hadn't been considered. Suddenly, he was pissed at them for dying.

"Let's get out of here." His voice was edgy. "We'll go get something to eat. You're probably hungry."

As if by suggestion, Morgan's stomach rumbled. Her hand went to her stomach. "I'm not hungry," she started to say. Her stomach gave another loud protest.

"It's natural to be hungry afterward…" He was just relaying what Thom had told him…he didn't know for sure. It was his first time as well. He'd been taught. And practiced with Mel. But never the real thing. As long as they were alive, nothing happened.

He walked to the door and reattached the top and bottom and stood waiting for her. She walked past him and stepped into the bright sunlight, stopping just out of reach. She waited for him to precede her. He led her around the side of the building, along a plant-lined path to a high front gate. She stopped several feet behind him.

"Are you going to walk behind me all the way to Abbott's?" he asked.

"Just don't touch me," she said.

"Okay. I'm sorry about that. We aren't quite in sync yet."

Before she could question him, he opened the gate and waited for her to go through.

"Stay here, Meesha," he called over his shoulder. The dog sat.

"She's not going to sit there the whole time, is she?"

He smiled for the first time. "Trust me; she's just putting on the good girl act for you. I wouldn't be surprised to find a plant or two uprooted when we return."

Morgan smiled back and seemed to relax a little. Yet, the way she hugged her purse to her side, she looked as though she was ready to bolt. After all, what did she owe him, or this town? They needed her; he needed her. He would have to make her understand.

Morgan studied the way his brows drew together when he thought. He looked as though the weight of the world rested on his shoulders. She would give him the courtesy of listening. If she didn't like what he had to say, she was out of here. No one had cared about her before; why should she care about them now. This whole thing unsettled her. Yet, she had a feeling he held the answers to her night terrors, as well as other things. Things she wasn't even aware of—yet. However, she wasn't making any promises, other than listening.

She was busy silently reaffirming her convictions when they stepped out onto the sidewalk. This was the first time she had walked around during the daylight. It was bright and airy. The well-tended median erupted in a profusion of color. The fountain shot water high into the air, letting it splash down into the basin. A toddler, closely watched by his young, very pregnant mother, raised back his arm and threw a coin with all his might. The coin fell short of the fountain. The young mother gingerly placed a hand under her burgeoning belly as she bent to retrieve the coin. Handing it to her child, she gently urged him a little closer and clapped heartily when the coin plopped into the water. In a motion belying her ungainliness, she quickly grabbed his arm as he tried to follow the coin into the fountain. He pointed at the fountain, tears streaming down his face. Drying his tears, she spoke softly to him. Morgan watched him take another coin, scrunch up his little face in concentration, close his eyes, make a wish, and toss the coin. This time it clinked as it hit the upper lip before splashing into the water. Beaming, he took his mother's hand and they crossed the street.

Happy chatter preceded two teenage girls exiting a boutique near the woman and child. They stopped, made much over the little boy, and then bounded down the block to catch up with their friends. All perfectly normal activities for a hot summer day in a small town. She relaxed a little more as they crossed the street and began walking under the shade of the overhanging trees.

"Ruthorford is a very old town," Dorian told her. "Originally considered very sacred ground by the Cherokee and Creek tribes, they began allowing a few white men to settle here. Which is ironic, since the tribes wouldn't settle here themselves. A joint tribal council gave the final okay on the people. Surprisingly, no matter what uprising or war ensued, the people who were allowed to settle in Ruthorford remained untouched. Disturbances just seemed to flow around them. The few "unauthorized" people who made attempts to settle here without permission were—how should I say this—forcibly discouraged. More than a few of the families here today can trace their lineage back to the original settlement."

"You?" She looked over at his handsome profile. The sun glinted off deep red highlights in his black hair.

"Oh, no. I was born in Washington, D.C." He thought for a moment. "I say that, but I guess anything is possible." He reached down and snapped a daisy, holding it out to her.

Careful not to come in contact with him, she accepted the flower. Its pretty face beamed at her. She smiled back.

They had stopped walking. He turned and watched the pleasure play across her face. She lifted her emerald eyes to his. His breath hitched. Quickly, she looked away. "I'm sorry," she said quietly.

"Stop that."

"Sorry." She looked down and studied the pavement.

He started to reach out, but stopped. Instead, he let his words sooth her. "You have beautiful eyes."

"According to your friend—"

"Ignore her. That was all an act." Risking it, he dampened his energy and touched her chin, lifting her face upward until he was looking into her sparkling emerald eyes.

Morgan felt a tiny tingle tickle her chin as he touched her. She ignored it, although she had trouble ignoring the heat she felt moving through her veins.

"Melissa had beautiful, expressive eyes. You got them from her. They shimmer, like faerie dust. They're very special." His breath feathered against her lips and she realized how close they were standing.

She swallowed and watched his focus move to her mouth, not her eyes. She stepped away. Without a word, they both turned and began walking again.

Dorian picked up the story. "Ruthorford remained isolated from the rest of the country. Whether by intent or accident, the people remained close to their Native American sponsors."

"I haven't seen any Native American descendants that I know of," she mused.

"You won't. The Native Americans wouldn't and won't inhabit the area around here. They still say it is very special, sacred."

"Then why allow outside settlers?"

They had arrived at Abbott's Bed & Breakfast. Without answering her question and instead of going inside, he led her to the side of the building and through a black iron fence. They walked through the gardens she had seen the night before from inside the restaurant. As they passed the fountain, its spray cooled the air around them. In the back, century-old trees provided deep shade. Iron tables with glass tops were scattered around the lawn, the spacing giving good separation and privacy to each table. Dorian didn't stop but moved down a slope toward the water. He parted the hanging branches of a huge willow, allowing her to pass. Another small table and chairs sat cozily sheltered under feathery limbs. He walked over and held the chair. Morgan slipped into it and looked around. She peered through the veil of branches, hidden but seeing. A light breeze whispered around her.

"This is exquisite." She smiled at him.

"It's my favorite place to hide—besides our gazebo during a light rain."

She noted his use of the word "our." Was he referring to the Kilravens or her? That was something else they needed to deal with, and, given the circumstances, the sooner the better. She wanted to get out of here. Yet, the thought of never seeing him again tugged at her. She felt a slight ache.

His chiseled features softened and she followed his gaze. Teresa was making her way over to them, waving and smiling. Morgan, too, smiled.

"That is also an interesting story," he said, then added, "for later."

Teresa swept through the branches, leaned over, and gave Dorian a loud smack on the cheek. "Heard you pissed off Jas," she chortled.

"Now, how'd you hear that?" He lifted a brow.

"Well," she drawled out, "if I hadn't gotten an earful from Julia Emerson and that group—"

"The little old ladies from this morning," he interjected for Morgan's benefit.

Morgan smiled and nodded. She'd liked them, as invasive as they were.

"Jasmine, her royal self, decided to grace us with her presence for lunch." She turned an eye on Morgan. "Haven't been in town twenty-four hours and already you have her hackles up."

"I didn't mean—"

"Shoosh." Teresa waved her quiet. "Everything gets that girl's hackles up, especially if it pertains to Dorian here."

"Teresa," he implored.

"Well, honey bunny, she sure is upset with you. Both of you. Good thing that girl doesn't have any might in her magic or you'd be croaking—as in ribbit." She turned on Morgan, her smile full beam. "I don't even want to think what she'd like to do to you," she laughed long and loud. "Does my heart good. She gets away with way too much as it is. Now, whatcha gonna have?" she asked without taking a breath.

Morgan realized there were no menus. "Whatever is good?"

"You?" she glanced at Dorian.

"Oh, I'll have the same," he said, his eyes twinkling.

"Be right out. You two enjoy." With a wave, Teresa was off toward the house, waving at other seated guests as she passed.

"I like her," Morgan said.

"And she likes you. Especially since you let her do the ordering."

"There weren't any menus."

"You noticed." He laughed and added, "You did just right, and you'll have the best lunch you've ever eaten. Plus, you pleased her."

Morgan found herself focusing on his smile. When he smiled, really smiled, his blue eyes sparkled and the fine lines in the corners of his eyes crinkled, showing her he knew how to laugh and did so often—just not with her.

"How's that?" she asked, forcing herself back to their conversation.

"Jasmine's her cousin."

She sucked in her breath. "Oh, Dorian, I'm so sorry."

He laughed. "Don't be. She had it coming. She and Teresa are as different as night and day." He sobered somewhat. "They are both from founding families, as are you."

"Melissa?"

"And Thomas," he nodded and waited until the approaching young girl set down two drinks, very nearly dropping them, her eyes so attached to Dorian. He thanked her, ignoring her blush.

"A fan?" Morgan teased when she left.

"I used to babysit her, believe it or not. Somewhere in there, she began to grow up but she never quite outgrew the crush. She's a sweet gal, so I try not to hurt her feelings."

"She's cute."

He gave a husky laugh. "Well, I'm afraid I won't have a chance much longer. She's going to Emory University in the fall."

Morgan watched the pretty young girl clean one of the tables, eyes still lifting repeatedly to look their way. "I don't know," she teased. "Looks like true love to me." She laughed and took a sip of her tea. Peppermint with a hint of lime. Perfect. She let the cold drink run down her parched throat and let her gaze wander around her surroundings.

Across the water, a wall of what looked like stacked granite rose upward, forming the backdrop for a small waterfall. A pair of swans glided effortlessly across the lake. It was lovely here. When she looked back, Dorian was watching her, a thoughtful expression on his face. "A penny," she said and smiled at him.

"Not a million," he looked away, flustered.

"Dorian, you started telling me about yourself," she encouraged, ignoring his comment.

"There's not a lot to tell," he evaded.

"You were born in D.C. and yet came to be raised by *my* biological parents. But, you were never adopted by them." She paused, hoped he wouldn't pick up on her emphasis.

"It's complicated."

Morgan shook her head and placed the napkin in her lap. "That seems to be a pat answer for you, doesn't it? Well, I am in over my head here," she chided softly, "and you're all I've got for answers."

"In this case, answers only beget more questions."

Morgan actually growled in frustration.

A different waitress approached with a large tray. She expertly swung a stand she had looped over her arm, flipped it open and set it next to the table, all the while balancing the large tray on her shoulder. Her movements were quick and efficient. Morgan winced, knowing that, had she tried that trick, all the food would have landed on the ground.

The aroma rose from the plate as the girl placed it in front of her. A steaming slice of quiche with a side of spinach-strawberry salad adorned the plates. The waitress set a basket of fragrant herb bread in front of them. Nestled next to the bread was a crock of honey butter. Dorian broke off a piece of bread, slathered it with butter, and handed it to Morgan.

She looked down at the fare in front of her and mentally declared a truce until she had time to savor what was in front of her. All the questions in the world—and she had some doozies—couldn't compete with the enticing smells making her mouth water. Waiting for the waitress to finish loading their table, she glanced around her tree shelter once more. It was terribly quaint. Even romantic. Just what was he up to? Cold one moment, hot the next. He was obviously trying to impress her. And, there was no doubt, Ruthorford was gorgeous. An ideal place to live. Well, minus the small hallucination or delusion she'd had earlier. Once she was fortified with a full stomach, she intended to pin Dorian down on a lot of things, complicated or not. She slipped a bite of the quiche into her mouth and moaned.

"That's a common reaction to their food."

"God, this is heaven. And I thought last night was good." She took another bite. "Do you eat like this all the time?"

"No. The shop keeps me pretty busy. However, if I don't make it by a couple times a week, Teresa will show up, food in hand."

"Do they have some famous chef?"

"Actually, her husband, Bill Ruthorford, is the chef."

"As in Ruthorford? This Ruthorford?"

"The one and same." He handed her another piece of bread generously adorned with the sweet spread. When their fingers touched, he didn't pull back. Neither did she. The current, less shocking and more throbbing, ran up her arm and settled deep in her core.

He kept talking but watched her with darkening blue eyes. "He actually left, made a name for himself in Charleston. He came back on a visit, but because he was a little on the outs with his folks, he stayed at the Abbott Bed & Breakfast, run by none other than Teresa Abbott. And the rest, as they say, is history." He slowly pulled back his hand.

"So, Teresa is related to the Abbott House in Atlanta?" Her voice sounded husky when she spoke. She took a quick bite of bread and nearly choked as the velvety sweetness spread across her tongue.

"Uh-huh." He popped a final bite and sat back. "If I let her keep feeding me like this, I am going to be too big to get through the door," he said, deliberately lightening the moment.

"It's fabulous. Thank you."

His expression changed. "Now," he said pouring her more sweet tea from the pitcher that had been left on their table, "time to get down to the nitty-gritty. About the Gulatega."

She tensed. "The what?"

"The creature you saw earlier."

"Oh, that." She waved a nervous hand to dismiss the aberration. "That's from my nightmares. It isn't real. Probably too much heat."

"No, Morgan." He leaned forward, demanding her attention. "It's real and has been for a very long time."

"What are you saying?"

"I tried to explain in the cottage," he said with an edge of frustration. "There is still a lot we don't know. The Abbott House has been researching it for forever, it seems."

"A bunch of lawyers are doing research?"

He ran his hand through his hair, pushing back the curl that tended to brush his brow. "Abbott House is much more than just lawyers."

He saw her confusion and he didn't feel like taking on more than one complicated topic at a time. For now, he'd prefer the Gulatega.

Dorian tried another tact. "Do you know anything about String Theory?" Her expression said she didn't. "It's a theory in physics that basically leads one to explore the idea of multiple universes, multiple dimensions. The Gulatega is from another dimension."

"Yeah—" she stopped at his expression. "Gulatega," she sounded out the word. "You've called it that several times."

"The name came from the tribes. It's more or less a bastardization from several languages. Basically, it means naked raccoon."

Remembering the creature she saw in the garden, she sniffed, "I can see that. But what about those glowing eyes and the violet outline?"

"I don't know. I can't see them."

"You can too," she countered. "You knew exactly where it was."

"I took my cue from you and from what I learned being around Melissa. Only some woman can see it that I know of. Apparently, women with tribal heritage can see it."

Three questions popped into her mind all at once. She opted to stay on track. "Them? There's more than one?"

"Yes. But, I don't think that there are that many. When you and I connect, we set up some sort of harmonics. With the rocks—the universe. Hell, I don't know, except—supposedly—we open a portal and back it goes."

"If you can't see it, how do you know it's gone back?" Her voice sounded shaky.

"Meesha can sense them, even if she can't see them. I understand cats can see them."

Morgan immediately thought of Mrs. T and her nightmares. Maybe the cat hadn't been hissing at nothing. Maybe—oh God—maybe her nightmares weren't nightmares at all.

Dorian watched the color drain from Morgan's face. He was up and around the table in one motion, pulled her around and shoved her head down between her knees. She winced at his touch.

"Breathe slowly," he ordered but removed his hand.

"What's wrong?" Teresa rushed through the branches. She knelt beside Morgan. "Honey?"

Completely embarrassed, Morgan sat up. The world tilted slightly, then righted itself. "I'm fine. Heat, I guess," she defended.

Teresa rounded on Dorian. "What did you do?"

"Nothing. I was just trying to explain—" He stopped when she punched him in the arm.

"Men," she hissed, exasperated. "Why don't you take Morgan back to the shop for a while? Let her relax." She turned to face him. "You hear me, Dorian? She's had quite a few shocks in a short period of time."

She turned to Morgan. "Unless you would rather stay here? We would love to have you."

As much as Morgan would have loved staying at the bed and breakfast—almost as much as she didn't want to stay in that cottage—she realized there was too much information Dorian possessed, and that she needed, to avoid the inevitable. "I'm fine now. Honestly. I do think I will go back to the shop though."

She stood up, reached over, and hugged Teresa. "Please give the chef my compliments. And you, too. Thank you." She thought for a moment, then added, "I hope we can be friends. I would like to know more about Melissa."

"I would like that too, honey. I'm here, any time."

She looked away, at the people at other tables—people that probably knew her parents. The parents she hadn't been allowed to know. She looked at Dorian. "Can we go?"

"Are you all right?" He started to reach out to her and stopped, knowing his touch wouldn't be comforting.

She nodded. Without waiting for him, Morgan started walking toward the side of the building.

Dorian turned back to Teresa. She patted his arm and nodded her head toward Morgan. "Go on. She's gonna need you. I can feel it."

He kissed her on the cheek and raced to catch up. As he rounded the side of the bed and breakfast, he saw Morgan, looking back at the house, a wistful expression on her face.

"There's quite a history here, too," he nodded back over his shoulder.

"I bet there is. I was just thinking about how I had planned to stay here and luxuriate."

"We could probably arrange something," he offered.

"No." She sighed. "That seems like a million years ago." She turned and headed back toward the shop.

They walked a few moments in silence. Morgan looked at him. "Tell me more about yourself, Dorian. I feel like I am missing something and I don't want to feel this...this animosity," she said, still searching for the right word. Animosity was too strong a word for what she felt. It was frustration, or confusion. Right now, it was directed at him. He wasn't being particularly helpful either, with his continued evasiveness.

"Well, I was born in Washington, D.C. to a drug addict," he stated and moved around her so he was walking on the roadside edge of the pavement.

Given what he was saying, Morgan knew that little point of etiquette had to have come from Melissa and Thom.

Morgan stopped, realizing the tale wasn't going to be pretty. "Look, I don't mean to pry."

He shrugged. "That's okay, it's ancient history. The story is that someone from Abbott House, the one in Atlanta—that's another story we need to explore—heard about my mom and came looking for her. Unfortunately, by the time they got there, she was gone."

"She left you?"

"No, she OD'd."

"Oh," Morgan whispered.

Chapter Five

Morgan didn't know what to say. He'd made the statement so cavalierly, as though it had happened to a stranger. A sense of remorse replaced the resentment she'd allowed to build. Where would he be if they hadn't rescued him? These thoughts slowed her steps until they stopped in front of the Boutique across from the shop. She looked across the street at the building that had been his home. It no longer had the macabre feel that it'd had when she first saw it. It looked welcoming.

A loud scream pierced the air from the direction of the Boutique. Dorian and Morgan swung around.

"Damn wasps!" Jasmine shrieked, as she came flying out of the building, a spray can shooting streams of liquid chaotically at the windows, ceiling, and out toward them. Dorian threw out his arm as he saw the stream heading toward Morgan. He blocked most of the spray, but not enough. Morgan screamed and covered her eyes. In one swoop, he yanked the can out of Jasmine's outstretched hand, swung Morgan into his arms, and ran across the median to his shop.

"Open," he commanded and the door creaked and began to open. He backed in with Morgan squirming in his arms. "Don't rub your eyes," he told her. "Try to cry."

Not a problem. Tears ran down her cheeks. Her eyes burned as though fiery embers had landed in them.

He rushed to the sink, reached out with one hand to twist the nozzle of the faucet upward and turned on the water. He set her down and, none too gently, shoved her face into the stream.

"Open them, Morgan," he demanded. When she pushed back against his hand, he held her in place, "Don't fight me."

She did as he commanded.

"Keep rinsing them. Both of them. Don't rub." He turned his attention to the can. It was organic, so it was the oils, including some mint, that were the problem. He reached around her and turned down the pressure. "I want you to keep rinsing. Gently. I am going to prepare some drops that should help."

"Don't leave me," she begged in panic.

"I'll be right over here. You'll be fine," he soothed. "Don't step back. Meesha's right behind you."

Dorian worked quickly, compounding several items and mixing until he'd made a salve. Then he a grabbed a bottle of distilled water and pulled down small flasks marked tinctures of dilute boric acid and green tea. He glanced over his shoulder as he mixed. Morgan was gently switching one eye for the other over the fountain of water. He could see her hands shaking as she held on to the side of the sink. Water dripped down the front of her shirt. He looked back at the bottle and the dish. Slowly, he raised his hand over each and let a current jump from his hand to each container.

"What was that?" There was panic in her voice.

"Nothing." He turned toward her.

"I thought you touched my hair."

"No, but I'm about to." He moved to the sink and lifted her hair back from her shoulders. She didn't flinch. He was surprised at how soft and heavy her hair was. Like heavy silk. He reached onto the windowsill and pulled twine from a spool, yanked it against the cutter and then wrapped it around her hair, pulling it into a loose ponytail.

"Thanks," she whispered.

"I think that's enough." He shut off the faucet.

Morgan heard a drawer open as she lifted her head. Something soft touched her face.

Dorian dabbed at her skin and around her reddened eyes with the soft towel. The skin around her eyes was beginning to swell slightly. Dorian prayed that she didn't have an allergy as well.

"I'm going to pour soap in your hands. Wash them." He flipped the faucet back around and guided her soapy hands under the water. His hands massaged hers as he helped her clean them. He washed her wrist and forearms as well, and then pulled them under the warm water. The current from his touch sent a slight tingle up her arms. This time it didn't hurt, or even bother her. Maybe she was getting used to it.

She blinked. Everything was fuzzy. She started to reach up. He grabbed her hand. "Come over here," he urged softly and guided her to a chair. "I have a solution that I'm going to put in your eyes. It should help dilute the oil base of the spray. It won't hurt. Then, I'll put a salve on your eyes and cover them with patches. You should be fine by tomorrow."

He knelt down in front of her. "Let me see your eyes."

Morgan opened her eye and gazed toward the sound of his voice. She heard his intake of breath and immediately glanced downward. His hand raised her head back up. Then she felt the warmth of his breath across her face as he leaned in to examine her eyes. She blinked.

Her eyes were pools of shimmering emeralds surrounded by red. Her pupils expanded and contracted rapidly. He could see diamond shapes in the iris enlarging and shrinking as the pupil changed. He had never seen anything like it. He assumed Melissa's were the same but he had never been this close or noticed them change this abruptly. He hoped what he was about to do wouldn't do any harm.

"Your sclera," he saw the furrow in her brow and amended, "the whites of your eyes are very bloodshot. Lean your head back so I can put drops in them."

She tensed.

"I won't hurt you. I promise."

"I know," she said, visibly trying to relax. "I just don't like people messing with my eyes."

Dorian put several drops in each eye. He waited. She blinked. He gently wiped away the excess as it ran down her cheeks. Already the redness was going away. He tilted her head back again and once more applied the drops. Again, they waited. He dabbed at her closed lids and her cheeks with a clean cloth.

"How's that?"

"They don't burn as much." She looked at him, squinted, blinked again. "I can't see very well." Her voice hitched.

"It's okay. I'm going to put some salve on them. By tomorrow they should be good as knew." Mentally, he crossed his fingers.

He had just finished putting tape over the gauze when he heard Jasmine call from the front room. "Dorian?"

"We're in the kitchen." His voice was cold.

"Oh, Morgan, I'm so sorry." Jasmine rushed into the room. She gasped and dropped to her knees in front of Morgan. "Oh my God. She grabbed her hand. "I am so sorry."

Morgan flinched and pulled back her hand.

Dorian reached out and grasped Jasmine's arm, pulling her to her feet. "She'll be fine. I just didn't want to take any chances." He glared at her.

"I didn't do it on purpose," she whined.

"It was an accident," Morgan said. "I'll be fine. But I think I would like to lie down, Dorian, if you don't mind."

"I could stay—" Jasmine started to offer.

"No." His voice was harsh. "Turn over the sign when you leave, Jasmine."

"But Dorian," she pleaded.

"Not now, Jasmine," his tone softened. "Let me get her to bed. We'll see you tomorrow."

Jasmine nodded. "I really am sorry."

Morgan heard the bell as the door closed. Dorian walked over and locked it.

"Come on," he took her arm.

"Dorian," she hesitated, "I don't think I want to stay in the cottage alone. Not like this."

"It's okay. I'm putting you upstairs in the other room. That way I can hear you, if you need me. Meesha will watch you, too, I'm sure." He bent down and ruffled the fur of the eager Collie. She let out a soft yap.

"Thanks, Meesha," Morgan said. She did feel better. "Can I stop at the powder room down here first? I remember its layout."

"Sure," he said and led her to the little room off the hall. "I'll get you something to put on. Just wait here."

"I'm not going anywhere," she called through the closed door.

****

Morgan stretched and felt her muscles come awake. She opened her eyes to blackness. Her hands automatically grabbed at the bandages. Then she remembered yesterday. Yesterday had been a nightmare, even compared to her recurring ones. Luckily, last night had been nightmare and incident free. Given all that had occurred the day before, a quiet night seemed like a miracle.

The patches were loose enough to allow her to blink. She felt her lashes rub the soft gauze. At least there was no more pain. She groped around for the pillows and pushed herself up.

"Good. You're awake," Dorian spoke from the doorway. "Do you need some help?"

"If you don't mind." Tilting her head, she heard him approach the bed. "Can't we just take these off?"

"Not yet." He reached for her arm and eased her out of the bed. She anticipated the tingle of his touch and didn't jerk back.

"Here. Let me guide you," he said and led her across the room. "You can use the master bath. I'll show you where the basics are." He guided her in and placed her hand on the sink. "Now follow the edge of the sink to your left. Next to it is the toilet. You okay?" He watched her nod, saw the tension in her shoulders. He retreated toward the door. "I'll be right outside."

"Toothbrush?"

"It's on the edge of the sink." He placed her hand on the toothbrush. "Toothpaste's next to it. Cup next to that. You can yell if you need help."

She nodded and waited until he closed the door.

Morgan managed everything until it was time to leave the room, then she had no idea where the door was—how far or in what direction. In fact, she had no clue how big the room was. Did it have a shower? Realizing she could walk into a wall or a closet, she surrendered and called Dorian.

Before the last syllable left her lips, the door opened. He was beside her in an instant, guiding her back to bed.

For the first time, Morgan realized that his touch hadn't caused pain. She still felt the current move from his body to hers, but it wasn't as sharp.

"Dr. Yancy's here." Dorian said as he helped prop her up in bed. "He was Melissa's doctor. I called him last night," he added when he felt her tense. He pulled the quilt up for her.

"After I told him what I did, he said you should be all right until he got here this morning."

"Morgan. I'm Dr. Yancy." A warm hand took hers and squeezed. "Let me help you back onto the pillows. I want to take a look."

Her hand automatically went to her eyes. The bed gave a little creak as his weight settled on the edge. He pulled her hand away and spoke softly. "It's okay, Morgan. I was Melissa's doctor," he said in a deep warm voice. "I understand you have her eyes."

Morgan yielded to his touch. As he pulled each patch off, she blinked. A face etched with wrinkles came into view. She blinked again. Silver grey eyes smiled at her. She smiled back.

He held her lid up and shined a light into the pupil. It contracted. As expected, he saw a second contraction. "Good," he said and repeated the process with the other eye. "Very good."

He applied several drops of a solution into each eye and had her blink repeatedly. His face came into sharp focus. She saw movement and shifted her focus. Dorian stood at the end of the bed, wearing the same clothes he'd had on the day before. She frowned.

"I told you I wouldn't let anything happen to you," he defended.

The smile she offered stunned him. Her luxurious red hair spilled about her shoulders. The quilt nestled beneath her breasts, affording him a glimpse of rose tipped nipples pushing against the thin nightshirt. He felt an undeniable tug in his gut. As her now clear gaze followed the focus of his eyes, her face tinged with pink and she pulled the quilt higher. He shifted uncomfortably.

"Dorian...would you mind getting me some tea?" she asked softly.

She waited until she heard him in the kitchen, then looked at the doctor.

"You said Melissa had eyes like mine?"

"Yes, dear, she did. Yours seem to be more…" he looked for the right word, "intense."

"Intense?"

"Have you ever been to an ophthalmologist?"

She looked down. "Yes," she whispered, "he said I have a birth defect."

He tilted her chin until she looked him in the eye. He stared at her. "You have an anomaly, not a deformity." He was emphatic. "Your mother, as well as many of the women in your lineage, had the same anomaly. Hell, it may be evolutionary advancement. It serves a purpose. It enables you to see the Gulatega."

She started. "You know about the creature?"

He smiled and patted her hand. "I've been employed by Abbott House since before I became a doctor." He laughed. "So, yes, I know about the Gulatega."

"Then, I haven't been dreaming?"

"No." He rose and walked over to the window. Turning, he studied her. "Morgan, your eyes have a double lens. I have studied it all my life and still don't completely understand it. However, it seems to allow you to see in the ultraviolet range. That somehow enables you to see the Gulatega. The only other animal, I think, that seems to have the ability to see it is the cat. Dogs can sense it." He took a breath and slowly shook his head, "I am only speculating, because, thus far I haven't gotten either a cat or a Gulatega to cooperate with any experiments."

It took her a moment to realize he was teasing. Mrs. T came to mind. The idea of her highness cooperating with anyone for anything that didn't involve dinner… She laughed. "I have a cat. You're right. There would be no cooperation."

He smiled and walked over. "Just know I am here for you, just as I was for your mother."

Simple words and reality slapped at her. He knew her mother. Dorian knew her mother. In this place, everyone knew the woman who'd given her away. Maybe this man knew why she gave her away.

He seemed to read her mind. "No. I didn't know of your existence until after her death. However, I did know her. Trust me when I say this, Morgan, she wouldn't have given you up if she hadn't had a damned good reason."

Dorian appeared at the door with an inlaid teak tray holding several cups, a pot of steaming tea, and a plate of croissants.

"Ah, refreshments," Dr. Yancy exclaimed and shifted a tray table toward the bed. Dorian set the tray down, pulled chairs forward and poured the tea. From beside her bed, he pulled an elegant smaller tray, which he placed on her lap and set a cup of tea and a croissant on it.

"Teresa?" The taste of butter floated across her tongue.

"Actually, yes. She's the baker." Dorian stated.

The doctor sipped his tea. "How are Teresa and Bill?" he asked but didn't look up.

"They are doing well," Dorian said. "You ought to stop by the B & B while you're here. I know Teresa would love to see you."

"Can't this time." He set down his cup. "In fact," he said, looking at his watch, "I'm late as it is." He wrapped the croissant in a napkin and slipped it into his pocket. "I'll finish this on the way back to Atlanta."

Dorian rose. "Thanks for coming. She's okay?" He followed the doctor to the door.

Dr. Yancy turned. "She'll be fine." He looked back at Morgan, "Take it easy today." He held out his hand to Dorian, "Stay. Finish your tea. I know my way out." He shook Dorian's hand. "You're a good pharmacist, an even better compounder. Apply more salve if she has pain. Several more drops won't hurt either."

Dr. Yancy looked back at Morgan, sitting regally among the pillows, the spitting image of her mother. "It's been a privilege. Remember—if you need me." He smiled at her and headed out the door. "Amazing," he muttered as he trod down the steps.

They both listened for the faint tinkle of the bell. When Dorian turned back to her, she asked, "Pharmacist? Compounder? And here I thought you were a shopkeeper."

"I am. I apprenticed under Thomas after I finished my education. I figured, with the kinds of things people were asking for, it would behoove me to avoid legal ramifications." He walked back, sat, and reached for his tea.

How a man could drink tea out of a dainty cup and still appear so devastatingly masculine—Morgan felt the warmth spread through her limbs. Her voice squeaked when she spoke, "Where did you go to college?" She felt her face flame.

If he noticed, he gave no indication. "Emory in Atlanta. Biochemistry and Pharmacology."

"Wow."

"But I'm a lousy bookkeeper," he added.

She laughed and wondered if he knew about her accounting minor.

The bell sounded downstairs. "Damn," he hissed, "I thought I left the closed sign up."

"Yoo-hoo, Dorian?" a familiar voice called.

"Coming, Miss Alice," he called. "Sorry," he whispered to Morgan and left.

She leaned back in the pillows, listening to his warm voice flow over the chatter below. She looked around. She lay in a queen size four-poster in the middle of a truly Victorian bedroom suite. She could have been time-warped to the 1800's except for the cool air blowing out of the air conditioning vents. An ornately carved armoire stood in the corner with a matching dresser and tilted cheval mirror across from it. A fainting couch covered in a delicate stripe sat beneath the window.

Morgan's breathing stopped. She was in the master bedroom. Her parents' bedroom. She pushed back the covers and rose, setting the tray on the bed and walked straight to the dresser. She recognized the man and woman in the picture from the photos in the folder. They were standing in the garden; he had a hoe in his hand. A child played at their feet. Dorian. The picture went blurry. She blinked and wiped her eyes. Why was she crying? She didn't know them.

As she turned, she caught sight of herself in the long mirror oval mirror. Her hair tumbled down her back. The thin cotton nightshirt danced just below her thighs. Bikini panties hugged her hips. Her rose nipples hardened when she looked up and saw Dorian looking over her shoulder into the mirror, his eyes riveted on her breasts.

"Are you up to getting dressed?" he asked tersely. Not waiting for an answer, he left the room.

She followed behind him and closed the door. Her hand trembled. Never had she reacted so immediately or so strongly to a man. Even an angry man. At times he was so nice to her and at others—he seemed hostile. Morgan glanced around once more. Had she met him somewhere else, some other time, she could see letting her attraction to him take a different course. This was just too awkward.

Morgan allowed herself time to take a quick shower, having found fresh towels laid out for her on the sink. She reached for the shampoo sitting on the tile ledge in the shower. As the floral scent encased her body, she inhaled the scent of the woman who gave birth to her. Somehow comforted, she finished the shower. When she walked back into the bedroom still wrapped in the towel, she found a fresh pair of jeans and a yellow oxford shirt on the bed. A drawer in the dresser was ajar. Morgan walked over and shook her head, barely suppressing the laughter at Dorian's sense of decorum. She found the garments she needed and closed the drawer. Her fingers reached for the picture. They looked so happy, so complete. With renewed resolve, she tucked the shirt into the jeans, pulled her damp hair back, twisted it up, and clipped it.

As much as she regretted not being able to keep her half of the shop and those, oh so magnificent gardens, Morgan knew it was only right to offer it to Dorian. He grew up here. He trained to take over. It was obvious that he loved it. This quaint little town. Remembering the conversation the night before, she knew he loved the people and the people adored him. Everyone had been extremely kind to her. Even Jasmine, after she nearly blinded her. She looked like Melissa and people reacted to that. Nonetheless, she wasn't Melissa. She just didn't fit. Letting determination bolster her, she started down the stairs, a spring in her step.

"Dorian," she called. Better to get this straightened out so they could get out of each other's way and on with their own lives. She was sure Jasmine wouldn't miss her and would be thrilled to have Dorian all to herself once more.

Midway, she saw Dorian and another man turn toward her. Her step faltered and she grabbed the rail to keep from falling.

"Rob!" she exclaimed. She didn't miss Dorian's scowl.

Dorian's brooding, dark handsome features stood in direct contrast to Rob's blonde Adonis charm.

"Morgan," Rob flashed a smile and pushed up his glasses. Taking the steps two at a time, he stopped on the step below her. Now eye to eye, he leaned over and kissed her lightly on the lips.

"What are you doing here?" She stood on the steps, not moving.

"I talked to your parents. They told me where you were."

She glanced at Dorian, who watched them, his chiseled features unmoving.

"They send their love." Rob smiled at her.

She studied him, wondering what he was up to. Surely, her parents hadn't told him what had transpired. Then she remembered they didn't know she had stopped seeing him. God, too damn much had happened in the last few weeks. She let a huff of breath escape.

"Why are you here?" she asked, her voice flat.

He stepped back one step. "Oh," his smile disappeared and he threw a look at Dorian, "I see how it is."

"No." Morgan and Dorian spoke simultaneously.

Rob raised an eyebrow. Morgan steadied herself and stepped around him, preceding him down the steps. "Dorian and I have business to conduct." She didn't elaborate. "This was not a pleasure trip."

"Well, it should be," Rob's smile was suddenly back in place. "I am staying at the most charming bed and breakfast a few blocks down the street. Where are you staying, Morgan? We could—"

"I'm staying here." She walked to the counter and leaned against it. Her knees felt weak.

Her eyes hurt and her head throbbed. Suddenly pissed that Rob got to stay at the bed and breakfast before she'd had a chance, she scowled at him.

Rob frowned.

Dorian interjected, "I have the paperwork. I'm ready any time you are." He hoped she appreciated his saving her ass. "I'll be in the cottage when you're ready."

"Oh, I can see I've interrupted." Rob took her hand. "I'm sorry."

Morgan grew more exasperated by the moment. Rob was giving every indication that they were a couple. She jerked her hand away.

Unaffected, he continued. "Say, why don't we meet at the bed and breakfast later." He turned to Dorian, who had stopped in the kitchen. "You're welcome to join us," he added reluctantly.

"Sounds good to me," Dorian called over his shoulder.

"Hang on, Dorian. I'm coming with you," Morgan called. She didn't want a confrontation with Rob just now. She didn't feel like playing games with either one, but especially not Rob.

Dorian whirled mid-step and walked back to the front door. "We'll see you later, then." He held the door open for Rob.

"Sure," Rob said, taking the none-too-subtle hint. Morgan stepped away, barely avoiding a second kiss.

As soon as Rob was out the door, Dorian shut it, locked it and turned the closed sign over. He walked over to Morgan and grasped her arm, leading her out the back door. "Now we really have to talk."

Chapter Six

Morgan paced back and forth in front of the cottage fireplace. She stopped, looked at Dorian sitting calmly at the table by the front window, and started pacing again. "Let me see if I have it right." She pushed back her bangs. "This creature…this Gulatega…is some sort of parasite. It attaches to people," she shuddered, "and sucks out their brains!" Her voice rose to a shriek.

Dorian watched her. She'd heard him. She'd understood him. She was being dramatic. "No, it's not like that," he emphasized. "Here's what we know. It's attracted to some people. It gets around them and they start having headaches, confusion, difficulty remembering. It doesn't suck out their brains." He rolled his eyes. "The longer they are attached—" he shook his head when she whirled on him, and corrected, "around—the person, the worse the symptoms become."

"And just what do I have to do with this again?" She'd resumed pacing.

"You can see them. I can't. Together our energy does something to the portal and they go back through. Unharmed. We don't want them harmed because we don't know what effect that would have on their dimension…or ours."

She studied him. He still wasn't telling her everything. She damn well knew it. "What about us?" She placed her hands on her hips. "Can it suck out our brains?"

He ignored her sarcasm. "For some reason, people like us are immune."

"People like us?" Morgan felt like she was repeating herself.

Now Dorian was brushing back his hair. "Yeah. You know that crescent moon birthmark high on your right hip."

Remembering the sleep shirt, her lips tightened, "I thought I dressed myself last night."

"Don't worry. You did." He stood and unfastened his jeans.

She stepped back.

His blue eyes flashed. "Don't get excited. I'm only going to show you my hip." He pulled the one side of his jeans down, exposing his left hip. A crescent moon like hers rested lower on his hip, except it faced the opposite direction of hers. He hefted his pants back up and tucked in his shirt.

That flash of his golden skin tempted her to reach out, run her fingers across his hip, his abdomen. She didn't realize that she had actually extended her hand toward him until his eyes drew hers. For an instant, she stood mesmerized. He took a step forward. She leapt back.

"The...the shocking thing?" she stuttered.

His lips curved into a smile, washing her in warmth. "Yeah, that. It hasn't been so bad lately, has it?"

He was right. Since the accident, they had touched several times and a mild tingle was all she felt. Well, not all she felt, but he didn't need to know that.

"We carry a current that, when combined, changes the harmonics of the stones, which in turn can open the portal. But, unless we're aligned, we zap one another."

"Then we can't—" Her heightened color finished the thought.

"Yes, we can," his voice was changing as he spoke. "In fact, the more we touch, the more in sync we are."

He watched the flush move up her neck. There was innocence about her he couldn't ignore. She drew him like a magnet, and he didn't think it was the harmonics. The rebel in him still fought beneath the surface, not wanting her—or anyone—to be his mate by design or destiny. However, he wasn't sure any more that he wanted her to leave.

Then there was Rob. He knew he didn't like that guy. He wasn't sure she liked Rob all that much, either. Something he saw. A flatness in her eyes. Not like when she looked at him. Dorian let his eyes draw hers. Her eyes met his. Sparkled. Yeah, she wasn't doing that around Rob.

When he started talking again, Dorian's voice was lower, huskier. He cleared his throat. Morgan did that to him—made hormones flood his system, made his brain turn to mush. He fought for control. This was too important to let attraction muddy the waters.

"I don't know all the history. Abbott House in Atlanta has volumes of journals and information on the Gulatega, your lineage—"

"Does everyone here know about the creature? Why aren't they frightened?"

He shifted in the chair, obviously uncomfortable, got up, walked over to the sink and filled a glass with water. He took a long drink before turning around to face her, letting the liquid cool the heat building inside of him. "Actually, very few know about it. And since most people can't see it," he shrugged his shoulders, "why cause panic?"

He took a step toward her, held the glass out. She looked at it, then at him. He took another step and stood right in front of her—lifted the glass to her lips.

Mesmerized, she sipped. The water was ice cold. Delicious. She licked a drop from her bottom lip, still drowning in the ocean of his blue eyes. He was staring at her lips, his own mouth slightly open. His breath fanned her face, warm and inviting. If she leaned forward just a little....

Abruptly he turned away, inhaled sharply, and set the glass down with a thud.

"Aw, hell," he cursed and spun around.

In one swift movement, before she could think or react, he stepped forward and swept her into his arms, enfolding her body fully against his. His mouth covered hers, seeking, asking. His tongue touched the seam of her lips.

Morgan's hands moved to his sides. There was no zap, just heat. Her eyes closed as her lips parted, welcoming him into the warmth of her mouth, like a long lost lover. She grasped his shirt in both hands, pulling him even closer and felt his hands spread across her back, heat spreading a trail of fire across through her shirt. She heard herself moan and felt the staccato beat of his heart against her own.

She was drowning in the desire that was coursing through her body. She could feel her legs getting heavy and her head became a little fuzzy. A strange pulsing seemed to drag her forward, until she felt she was becoming one with the response demanded by the hard muscular body against her.

She couldn't breathe. The room was spinning. She gasped. A soft blackness crept around the edges of her mind and she fell into darkness.

****

Morgan eyes fluttered open to the soothing coolness of a damp cloth over her forehead and eyes. Her arms felt as though they had lead weights attached. She took a deep breath, reached up, eased the cloth away from her eyes, and blinked at the brightness in the room. She was lying on the bed in the cottage. Light streamed in through the windows in the bedroom and the front rooms, suffusing the bed in sunlight. She blinked again and felt the weight of the bed shift. She glanced over. Dorian was sitting on the edge of the bed, a frown creasing his handsome brow.

"What happened?" Her voice sounded forced, husky.

"You fainted. Are you all right?" He reached up, took the cloth and set it on a plate on the bedside table.

Memories came flooding back. Morgan shook her head slightly to clear the cobwebs and raised up on her elbows. She looked at him incredulously. "You made me swoon?"

His face took on a boyish charm as a flush crept up. He raised his eyebrows and grinned. "Can't say that's ever happened before."

"Oh, good grief," she huffed and shooed him off the bed. As soon as he rose, she swung her legs around and sat up.

"You might want to take it easy." He automatically reached out to steady her.

She flinched.

"Don't worry. I don't think I'll zap you again."

Morgan looked up into his concerned eyes and hesitantly reached out a finger, touched his arm and jerked back. Nothing. He didn't move. She slowly reached out her hand and laid it tentatively on this bare arm. Nothing. Except the feel of his well-formed muscle moving slightly at her touch.

She looked up and found herself staring into darkening pools of blue. A streak of lust rushed through her. Good God, she had to get a grip.

Sensing her unease, he stepped back, but stayed closed enough to catch her if she fell. He watched her. Her hair had come loose and cascaded over her shoulders. She reached up in an automatic motion, undid the clasp, pulled her heavy tresses up, twisted it and refastened the clasp. Dorian found himself spellbound by such a simple task. The upward movement of her arms gently lifted her breasts beneath her shirt, the nipples hardening as they brushed the fabric.

His eyes moved downward to her small waist and the gentle flair of her hips and thighs as she sat on the side of the bed. He swallowed, knowing he wanted nothing more than to push her back on the bed and cover her body with his. The flicker of movement brought his eyes up to her mouth and he watched as her tongue peeked out to moisten her lips. His groin tightened. He swallowed.

So much for his angst about her resemblance to Melissa. From this vantage, she bore little resemblance to Melissa and, probably, never would again. Yes, there were similarities, but they were so different. And this woman—Melissa's daughter—was driving him to distraction.

Morgan watched him and watched his eyes change as his thoughts drifted away from her. Given a moment of reprieve, she stood and stepped around him, walking into the front room. Now where were they—before he'd knocked her socks off with that kiss? Oh yeah, the Gulatega. Playing back that part of the conversation, she rounded on him.

"This Gulatega thing. Just how dangerous is it?" she found herself looking around, searching for it. She went into the front room and settled at the table by the window.

He followed and sat across from her. "Depends. To us—not at all. We seem to be immune. And, before you ask, I don't have any idea why." He heard Meesha whine, walked over to the door and let her out. Looking out he saw Meesha chase a butterfly, not catch it, and wander off to the side of the gazebo. He turned back to Morgan.

"For those who are susceptible, it can progress until, like Alzheimer's, the individual's personality disappears and the body degrades."

"Is it Alzheimer's?" she asked, thinking ahead.

"No. We wish it were. We could run around, put those creatures through the portals and be done with it." He shook his head. "Melissa and Thomas tried. They had a dear friend who developed Alzheimer's at an early age. They didn't see a Gulatega but they tried to "flush" the portal anyway—that's what they call it when a creature can't be seen but seems to be playing havoc in an area." His eyes went distant, remembering. "They tried repeatedly, over the years. Nothing helped. Mrs. Lawson is now in a nursing home. She doesn't have much longer."

She could see his pain. She reached out and placed her hand on his arm. He looked down at her and smiled. "She used to babysit me. I adored her."

"I'm sorry."

He nodded. "Anyway, with Melissa and Thomas here, there weren't any creatures to speak of. If they came through they would be drawn to Melissa, and she and Thomas would send them packing."

"Drawn to Melissa?" Morgan couldn't help the unease that statement brought. She shivered.

That sheepish grin appeared. "Must be the irresistible charm," he teased. "But women such as yourself and Melissa draw them like bees to flowers."

She squirmed. "Gee, thanks."

He shrugged. "No problem. Morgan, I mean it. They won't harm you. And we can send them back."

Morgan had so many questions. Creatures. Harmonics. Dimensions. She sat, staring out the window into the gorgeous play of colors in the garden, trying to grasp everything. Then she remembered. He'd said portals. Multiple. She turned her head, her eyes wide.

"You said portals, as in more than one. How many are there?"

"I don't know. The Abbott House could probably tell you. I only know of two others on the east coast."

"And these are watched by…?" She wasn't sure she wanted the answer.

"People like Melissa and Thomas."

Then it struck her. "Or you and I." It was a statement, not a question. She got up from the chair and walked over to the sink, picked up the glass he'd set down, and took a drink of water.

She stood, staring out the window at the gazebo. Her fingers tightened on the glass. She set it down before she broke it and whirled around to confront him. "We're their replacements, aren't we?"

She watched him close his eyes. He opened them and she saw sadness. He nodded. "I've known for a long time that I was. I didn't know about you." He shook his head. "Not until recently," he amended. "I found a picture of you. You were in your teens, I think."

"They had a picture of me? In my teens?" She walked back to the table and slumped down. "I don't understand. They knew where I was but they never tried to contact me. Why?"

Tears welled. "I don't understand."

Pain tugged at her. She tried to console herself with thoughts of her parents—her adoptive parents. A door opened in her heart and the pain rushed in. She would never know the people in that picture upstairs. She got up and went to the bedroom, pushing the doors closed behind her. She crawled onto the bed and let the tears fall. She cried for herself. For not ever knowing them. She cried for Dorian. For the situation their deaths had thrust them into. The tears turned to sobs.

She heard the doors open and felt Dorian's weight settle on the bed before he gathered her into his arms. She tried to turn away, but he pulled her back against her chest. His breath caressed her hair and he whispered soothing words to her and let her cry. She held on and let the sadness and doubts wash out of her.

Finally, the tears stemmed; she closed her eyes and slept.

Dorian eased her back onto the bed and pulled a blanket over her. As he walked out of the room, he turned back and looked at her. He could only imagine the hell she was going through. He'd been rescued from his life and raised by two loving people as though he was their son. When they died, the people of Ruthorford wrapped their arms around him and gave him comfort. Ruthorford was more than his town, it was his family. He wished he could impart that love and warmth to her. He wished he could erase all the pain and fear the last few days had wrought. He shook his head and gently closed the doors.

He walked over and looked out the window at the gardens in all their magnificence. He remembered the look on Morgan's face when she realized her part in all of this. A beautiful prison was still a prison.

Chapter Seven

Morgan awoke to the sun casting late afternoon shadows across the bed. The French doors were pulled closed but not shut. Her eyes stung. She reached up to rub them and caught herself. Remembering the bottle of ibuprofen on the bathroom shelf, she eased off the bed and trod into the bathroom. She filled the glass with water and glanced at her image in the mirror. Slightly swollen orbs, the green accentuated more than normal by a tinge of pink stared back at her. *Great.* She smirked at her reflection. *I look as bad as I feel.* She tidied herself as best she could. The shirt was hopelessly wrinkled, the jeans not too bad. She tucked the shirt firmly into the waistband, hoping to pull out a few of the wrinkles, and headed to the front room.

Dorian sat at the table by the front window, hunched over a laptop, papers strewn on either side. Hearing her, his typing stopped and he looked up. "You okay?"

"My eyes are bothering me a little, but I'm okay." She crossed over and sat opposite him.

"I thought they might be." He rose and picked up a small bottle. "Lean back. Let me put some drops in them."

She did as he asked and tried to relax as he gently pulled her lid back and dropped a couple of drops in her eye. Relief was instantaneous. She tilted her head slightly for the other eye. When he was done, he smiled at her and handed her a tissue. "Blot gently," he reminded her. She nodded and obeyed.

He went back to where he had been sitting.

"What're you working on?" she asked as she dabbed a remaining drop on her cheek.

"A short paper for Dr. Yancy. He was very pleased with the effectiveness of the compounded salve I used and the drops. He asked me to write it up and send it to him for 'The Herbal Apothecary'."

"I've never heard of that."

He raised a brow and looked at her.

"Snob," she countered his look. "For your information, I'm a bit of a geek when it comes to herbal magazines and journals," she defended. "I thought I knew most of them."

"Well, I will have to put you on the list. This is actually an in-house magazine that the Abbott House publishes for distribution among its various sites."

"We are back again to the size of this…consortium…or whatever."

"Hungry?" he changed the subject.

"Famished. What time is it?"

"Almost six." He raised his hand at her gasp. "Don't. You've been through a lot. You needed to rest. Oh, by the way," he began, reached in his pocket, and pulled out her phone, "I brought this over when I went over to check on the shop. It was ringing when I went in. I didn't answer it."

The shop. Things had been so convoluted that she had completely forgotten that he was running a shop. "I am so sorry. I completely forgot about the shop," she said as she flipped open the phone. She had three messages, two from her mother and one from Jenn.

"Not a problem. The Shoppe of Spells is kind of an institution around here. We seldom close." He laughed as he shut down the computer. "And when we do, people actually tape notes to the door."

Morgan remembered the bevy of little old ladies that had surrounded her in the shop. She could imagine them peering through the windows and taping notes on the door. She laughed and watched him lower the computer lid. She was taken by the elegance of his long tapered fingers and wondered how a man with such large, albeit beautiful, hands could type on such a small keyboard.

He held up a yellow sticky note. "One of the notes was from Miss Grace. She has a pie waiting for us. She left it at the B & B. Guess we should face the music." He rose and tucked the computer under his arm.

Morgan looked down at her shirt. Pinching the front she pulled it outstretch and looked at him pleadingly. "I don't want to go anywhere looking like I slept in my clothes."

"But you did," he teased.

Her cell phone rang. She flipped it open and saw her mom's pretty face in the caller ID. "I'd like to take this, if you don't mind."

"Not at all. Come on over when you're ready. I'm sure we can find you another shirt in the closet upstairs." With that, he walked out the door, closing it behind him, leaving her alone in the cottage.

With a small shiver, Morgan answered the phone. "Hi, Momma," she said, eyes still darting about the room, anticipating something creeping across the floor.

"Hi honey. I tried earlier but couldn't get you. Everything okay?" Morgan could hear the concern in her mother's voice.

"I'm fine, Mom. Just busy." No need to alarm her mother at this point.

"Morgana," her mother's voice took on that *mom* tone. "I know *busy*. I'm not hearing *busy*. Is everything all right?"

Morgan took a deep breath. "Actually, I don't know. I think so. Everyone here is so very nice and kind. It's just a strange place. This has been a lot to face."

Her mother was saying something in the background, her hand over the phone, probably to her father. Then she was back, "I can be there in a heartbeat, Sweetpea. I don't mind."

Morgan smiled. "I know, Mom." She was tempted. Then she remembered the creature. "No!" she said too emphatically and tried to make her voice sound calmer. She wanted to keep them away from here until she knew just what she was dealing with. Yet, if her parents sensed she might be in danger, they would risk everything to be at her side. "I need to do this myself. I promise I will call you if I need you to come. Mom, you guys know I will always need you."

She heard her mother's voice crack. "I know, baby."

Becky hushed her husband in the background, then asked, "By the way, did Rob call you?"

"He's here." Morgan sighed. "Mom, I meant to tell you—we broke up."

"That…that," her mother hissed. "I knew something was wrong. It was the way he acted. Sneaky. That's what it was. He showed up at your apartment. Before I knew what I was doing I told him where you were."

"Did you tell him anything else?" Morgan prayed she hadn't.

"No. Actually, your father stopped me. He couldn't understand why Rob didn't know where you were, if you two were as close as Rob was letting on. He was right, too."

"Mom," Morgan hesitated, then decided to throw the whole ball of wax on the fire, "I need to tell you about my job."

Her mother interrupted her. "I already know, Sweetpea. I went by to tell them you had to leave town unexpectedly.

When I saw that the shop was closed, I called them. They told me everything. They send their love and said to tell you they're sorry the shop had to close."

"Me, too, Mom. Me, too," she sighed.

"They also told me that it was you who convinced them to do it."

Morgan didn't say anything.

"That was kind of you, Morgan. You saved their retirement. We're proud of you."

Tears welled. "Thanks, Mom. I needed that."

"You sure you don't want us to come?"

"I'm sure. I can take it from here."

"Dad said to tell you to kick Rob in the butt for him. He's more than a little ticked off."

"Thanks. Tell Dad I intend to. Love you guys."

"Love you back."

She disconnected and looked around the room. So far, nothing had scurried. She sank down onto the sofa facing the fireplace and took a deep breath. She knew the sacrifices she'd be willing to make to protect her parents. Moreover, she knew damn well how far they would go to protect her. Maybe she did understand a little why Melissa and Thomas Kilraven gave her up. She tried to imagine herself with a child. Would she be willing to give up her daughter? She wondered what circumstances would make her consider that as an option. She didn't know. However, she felt she was on the right track. Maybe she wasn't unloved, but loved well.

Without the creepy gargoyle creatures running around, Morgan could imagine enjoying the little cottage. Everything about it was homey and light. She could envision a fire in the fireplace, the scent of a pie baking in the oven, strong arms wrapped around her, warm breath against her neck. She leapt up from the couch.

She scoffed, knowing full well that Dorian's kiss was still planted firmly in her mind. Without him near, she could think about him a little more clearly. When he was near, it was all she could do to think, period. There was something about him—other than the fact that he was devastatingly handsome. As soon as he got near her, her whole body became attuned to his. He drew her, like a magnet. And, when she was in his arms—she tried but couldn't come up with an explanation. It was like nothing she had ever experienced. She wondered if he felt anything near what she felt.

Had it been that way for Melissa and Thomas? Was it some sort of destiny compulsion for two "marked" people to be drawn to one another? Was it magic? He had used the word sync when describing the shock that had happened in the beginning. She didn't experience the shocks anymore. Were they now synced? She definitely vibrated when he got close. There was almost a need to get even closer. When she was near him, thinking was damn near impossible. That had never happened around any man before. Maybe she was just a late bloomer. This was one hell of a time for her hormones to finally kick in. She would definitely have to get control over them.

Morgan stepped up to the fireplace and picked up one of the crystals, noting its exact location. She didn't want to throw anything off by setting it in the wrong place. She turned it over in her hand. It was a rough crystal. It looked like it had been chiseled out of a mine, wiped off, and placed here. She hadn't handled many crystals before, but she assumed they would be cool to the touch. This one wasn't. In fact, the longer she held it, the warmer it became. Holding her rising anxiety at bay, she gently returned the crystal to its precise location and picked up another one. This one looked more like a stone of some sort. Again, it became warm in her hand. She set it back. She added another question to her mental list of things to ask Dorian.

She picked up the coverlet from where it had slipped off the back of the couch, refolded it and placed it over the back. Reaching down, she grabbed a pillow, fluffed it, set it down, and smiled. It was a quaint little cottage. She pulled the door behind her and crossed through the gardens to the shop. Without knocking, she eased the back door open and stepped inside.

Dorian's voice carried from the front room. He didn't sound happy. "Good God, man, don't you think she's been through enough?"

She moved forward quietly. His back was to her. "No, I haven't told her. Shit. All this happened so fast. Then she got injured. Yes...yes, I'll—" he turned and saw her. "I have to go." He pocketed the cell phone.

"Tell me what?" She moved into the room and faced him, daring him to evade her question.

He looked tired. "Morgan...," he began and shook his head. "Look, you don't have to do this. This is all new to you." He ran his hand through his hair and turned away.

She reached out and stopped him, gently turned him back to her. "Tell me."

Even now, she could feel the energy begin its rhythm, pulsing between them, flowing one to the other. Dorian sighed, put his hands on her shoulders and leaned forward, letting his head rest on hers. Such an intimate gesture, yet it felt so right. She put her arms around him and drew him in closer. They hugged. She felt the steady beat of his heart, a slow strong rhythm.

"Tell me," she whispered.

He pulled back gently and let his hands slide down her arms until he took her hands in his. "You have another

talent," he said. "Besides seeing the Gulatega, you can see
people's auras. In particular, sick people's auras."

She frowned into his eyes. "No, I can't." She searched his
face. He gave her a half smile.

"I would have known," she stated. He remembered the
spikes around him earlier but said nothing.

"It happens when you are attuned to your..." he searched
for a word, "...mate," he said softly.

"My mate? I don't have a—"

He squeezed her hand.

"Oh."

"Listen, Morgan," he began and let his hand cup the soft
skin of her cheek, "I wouldn't do this to you if it wasn't
important. Something's happened."

"What?"

"You don't know them." He let go of one of her hands
and while still holding the other, led her to the kitchen,
motioning for her to sit down. "Right around the time Melissa
and Thomas died, a young girl was attacked. She's thirteen."

"God," she whispered.

"She's Native American. She's like you."

"Like me?"

"In fact, there is a strong possibility you could be
related."

"I don't understand."

He sat across from her. "The people who came here to
settle mostly came from Scotland. Many married people of
the local tribes. Women of the lineage—Melissa and
you—inherited traits specific to descendants. The eyes and
the birthmark. The males with the birthmark are supposedly
direct descendants from the Scots. When the male and female
come together—"

"I know the birds and the bees, thank you," she
interjected.

"That wasn't where I was going, actually. We, the males, have the ability to control electrical current flow—ours, the earths."

"Ah." She nodded, grasping some meaning, "The zapping."

"When you and I are close, our currents align, shifting harmonics." He held up a hand when she started to speak. "It also enables you to see electrical fields around animals, people, plants—"

"That Gulatega creature?"

"That one you do on your own. You don't need..." his voice trailed off.

"My mate?" She watched his discomfort and felt a little better. "So, what does this have to do with the girl?"

"She was found wandering, unable to talk. She can't tell us what happened. Testing has come back inconclusive. However, we know something is wrong. She's growing weaker and weaker."

Morgan didn't know how she could help. None of it made sense, but she was willing to try. She'd been around Jenn long enough to see firsthand what attackers could do to a child. She had to give it her best. "Where is she? What do I need to do?"

Before Dorian could answer, there was a sharp rap against the front door. He rose, stepped around her and went to open it. Morgan followed behind him.

One of the most beautiful men she had ever seen stepped into the room. He was Dorian's height, but about thirty pounds heavier with straight black hair tied in the back. His skin was the color of bronzed honey. His chiseled features were strong. His lips firm yet sensual. Black eyes met hers head on.

He smiled. "You must be Morgan," he said and took her hand in his. "I'm John Davis." His voice poured over her like warm whiskey.

He turned, took Dorian's hand and thumped him on the back. "Thank you."

"Wait, I was just explaining to Morgan—"

"Let's go," she broke in and grabbed her purse.

Dorian shrugged. John smiled at Dorian. Dorian smiled back. Meaning passed between them.

Morgan hopped in the back of John's BMW. "I hope I can help. I don't know what to do but I'll do whatever I can."

John glanced over his shoulder at her. "Just follow Dorian's lead. He'll guide you."

Chapter Eight

They rode for about twenty minutes, most of it in silence. Morgan watched John's cheek muscle twitch. It was obvious this girl meant a lot to John.

The car moved into a densely forested area and climbed higher, leveled out, and started downhill once more. Shortly after they began the decline, John swerved to the right and drove down a narrow road. It had to be hard to see, even if you knew where it was. Small buildings, set back in the woods, dotted the road on either side. The road wound around further into the trees and circled back on itself. John pulled to a stop in front of a concrete block building. Dorian opened the door for her.

As she stepped out of the car, Morgan's nerves failed her. What was she doing here? How could she help a child who had been brutally attacked? Her hands trembled. Dorian quietly reached over and took her hand. They entered the plain, squat building.

The room was oppressive. Heavy drapes covered the windows. The only air seeped in through the screen front door and was immediately drawn out the back. Beads of sweat popped out across Morgan's brow.

In the corner, on an iron cot, a small, frail figure lay curled up. Morgan halted. She looked down at the woman-child. Straight brown hair spread loosely across the pillow.

Her forehead shined with dampness. A light sheet covered
the tiny body. Morgan gripped Dorian's hand tighter.

A woman moved forward from the shadows. Of obvious
Indian heritage, she had John's beauty, except in a completely
feminine way. She was much shorter than Morgan but
projected such a regal bearing, Morgan dipped her head in
acknowledgment. John spoke. "This is my cousin, Kayla.
Meadow is her daughter."

"Thank you for coming," Kayla said quietly. Tears filled
her eyes.

"I don't know what—"

The little girl moaned. Morgan stepped over to her and
knelt down. "Hello, Meadow. That's such a beautiful name."
Meadow tried to smile. She raised her innocent face. Vibrant
green, facetted eyes stared back into her own. Morgan felt a
lump in her throat. She looked around at Dorian.

"I am going to stand behind you, Morgan, with my hands
on your shoulders. Take Meadow's hand. Close your eyes.
When I tell you to open them, look at Meadow and tell us
what you see."

Any vibration she felt she was sure was from fear. The
small hand reached out and took hers. Morgan smiled at the
trusting child. With her free hand, Morgan gently brushed
back the damp bangs from the small face. Dorian's legs
brushed against her back and he rested his hands on her
shoulders. The heat from his body encased her. The familiar
pulsing began between them. She closed her eyes.

She waited and concentrated on the flow between them.
The current synchronized until the individual rhythms of
their energies became one. She inhaled and could smell his
scent above all else.

"Morgan, open your eyes," his voice resonated behind
her.

She could do little else but obey his command. The form in front of her shimmered in a multitude of colors, vibrant and muted, some light, some dark. She wasn't sure what she was looking at, but concentrated on what she was seeing, looking for inconsistencies—anomalies. The little girl squeezed her hand, as if encouraging her. Morgan smiled at her. The colors heightened and became more distinct.

A rainbow of spiking colors emanated from Meadow's body, similar to what she had seen around Dorian. Morgan was drawn to her eyes. Green, like hers; faceted, like hers—they glowed the same iridescent green as her own. Except the glow was weaker and it pulsed. She watched as it took on a rhythm similar to the one flowing between her and Dorian. Maybe she was drawing energy from the two of them. She prayed it helped. Morgan let her gaze travel down Meadow's body. Part of her abdomen was bluish-green with a dark center. *Maybe an infection*. However, what drew her was the child's head. Above her left ear was a greyish-brown area, devoid of light. *That's it*. That was what was making her sick. She couldn't explain how she knew, but she did. She scanned the body one more time, squeezed the child's hand, and broke contact. She closed her eyes and took a deep breath. Air rushed into her lungs like she'd held it the entire time. When she opened them, Meadow, once again, appeared as she had when she first saw her.

Dorian helped her to her feet, not questioning her silence. They walked outside, Dorian's arm steadying her. The eighty-some degree breeze felt cool after the inside. She turned to the mother.

"I am not sure of what I am saying because I have never done this before. Her body is surrounded with a vibrant rainbow of colors."

Kayla grabbed John's hand and smiled. Obviously, this was a good thing.

"In her abdomen there is a bluish-green color with a dark center. I believe she may have an infection." She faltered, then decided to give the information as she saw it. "It doesn't feel like a pregnancy. I can't tell if she was raped."

Kayla leaned against John.

Morgan hated the fact that she had to go on. She hesitated before speaking. Kayla looked her in the eyes and nodded, waiting. "I saw a greyish-brown area above her left ear. It emitted no light." She took Kayla's trembling hand in hers. "You need to get her to a doctor, preferably a neurosurgeon. I think she may have a tumor." She knew instinctively that what she was saying was correct. "I'm so sorry."

Kayla nodded and let tears fall. "Thank you," was all she said before she turned back toward the building. John walked with her, his arm around her shoulder, holding her up.

Morgan turned to Dorian. "Oh, Dorian..." she whispered and moved into his arms.

He pulled her close and pressed both hands against her back, letting a low current flow from him to her. He hoped it would ease some of her torment.

"How did Melissa do this?"

"I know this was hard." He didn't say anything about Melissa. "You probably saved her life."

Sadness swept through her. She was too drained to think.

Dorian helped her into the back seat and told her to try to sleep on the way back, if she could. Something kept nagging at her. The house was too desolate for the bearing of the woman who occupied it. It didn't match. She sat up.

John walked back to the car, his steps heavy.

Morgan waited until they were on the road to speak. "John, I know it's none of my business," she said and put her hand on his shoulder, felt it tighten, "but I have to ask. Why are they there? I didn't see any other families. And that house is too...too hot..." she didn't quite know how to go on.

"They're in hiding. The man Kayla married is very powerful. He would like nothing more than to take Meadow away from her." Morgan sensed the anger roiling beneath the surface. He continued, "I believe the attack was his fault. She went missing for a couple of days. I think her father sent someone to take her. She got away. But not before the bastard hurt her. Police found her outside of LaGrange, a city near the Alabama border. She hasn't spoken since."

Morgan's heart stopped.

John's hands gripped the wheel. His knuckles had turned white. "We searched for days. The police combed every square inch of three counties, thinking she had wandered off—possibly with friends. That devil denies knowing anything and is now using it as justification to get custody. As soon as Kayla got her, she came to me. They have been hiding there because it's a deserted area. Not many people know about it. It has no air conditioning and is minimal..." His voice cracked. "I know they can't stay there..." He couldn't finish.

Morgan squeezed his shoulder. "I have a friend who owns several women's shelters. The closest to here would be the one in North Carolina. However, the one in Virginia is near an excellent children's hospital. Would you let me call her?"

She could tell he was thinking. He was also hesitating. "Trust me; this woman knows what she's doing," Morgan said. "Nothing will happen to Kayla and Meadow once we get them to Safe Harbor. They will be protected and Meadow can get the treatment she needs."

John looked at Dorian. Dorian gave a barely perceptible nod. "Call her." John's voice was raspy.

Morgan pulled out her cell and dialed Jenn. No service. "I can't get a signal."

"We're too far in the country. Keep trying," Dorian said.

They were almost in Ruthorford when Morgan got Jenn. She explained the situation and spoke loud enough so John could hear her part of the conversation. She said she would call her later with more details. Jenn said to give her a couple of hours to make some calls and get things set it up. Morgan could almost feel Jenn's mind racing, figuring, planning. Morgan smiled. John didn't know it, but Kayla and Meadow were going to be in the best of hands.

John pulled in front of the bed and breakfast. He turned to Morgan. "I don't know how to thank you."

"Don't. I'll have Dorian call you when everything is set and we'll tell you what to do. This is Jenn's vocation, her passion—her life. Let her help them." She leaned over and brushed a kiss across his cheek.

He smiled. He looked at Dorian, his eyes twinkling, "If—" he started to make a comment to his friend, before he was interrupted.

"Not a chance." Dorian clasped John's arm. "I'll call you later."

"Too bad," John chuckled, then turned serious once more. "Thanks," John said and drove away.

Morgan looked at the gorgeous Victorian in front of her. She had no energy. Her legs felt cemented to the ground. She was tired beyond words. She was wrinkled. She wasn't sure she didn't smell. Then, the faint aroma of rosemary wafted out and her stomach growled. She grinned in spite of herself. It seemed her stomach talked incessantly in this town.

Dorian grabbed her hand and pulled her toward the porch. Teresa burst out of the door and planted herself in front of them. "Don't go in there!"

"Why?" Dorian asked.

"Jasmine's in there. And she's having dinner with Morgan's friend."

Morgan let out a groan. "How in the hell...," she gave up and shook her head. She'd forgotten about Rob. And Jasmine. There was no way she was ready to confront that combination.

"Go back to the shop. I'll have a basket sent over. I promise you, it'll be better than being here." She hugged Morgan. "You look beat, little one." She threw a scathing look at Dorian.

"What'd I do?" he asked.

Teresa ignored him. "I'll throw in a little something special for you," she winked at Morgan and ushered them back down the steps. She looked behind her, watching the door, and waved them on.

"I adore that woman," Morgan said as she walked beside Dorian. As tired as she was, Teresa had a way of putting a spring in her step. She wondered if that was Teresa's "gift." She wondered if everyone in Ruthorford had a "gift." She put that on her growing list of questions.

With the next breath, she stopped smiling. She had forgotten Rob was even in town. And now he was with Jasmine. That couldn't be good. Had Jasmine told Rob about her parents, about her? She looked over at Dorian and frowned. He and Jasmine were close. She wondered just how much he'd told Jasmine about her.

He stopped. They were outside the shop. He looked at the knob, reached down, turned it, and pushed it open.

"You didn't lock it?"

He just smiled at her.

"What was that look you gave me?" he asked.

"What look?"

"The one before the door. The worried look?"

"Nothing." She was too tired to worry about anything except helping Meadow.

The soft light shining from above the kitchen table drew
Morgan forward. She started to sink down in the kitchen
chair, only to rise when she heard Meesha's bark from the
back door. Dorian waved her back down. He opened the
door. Meesha gave Dorian no more than a glance, pranced
over to Morgan, and pushed her nose under Morgan's hand.

"Hey, Meesha," Morgan let her hand run over the soft
fur.

"What am I, chopped liver?"

"No," Morgan laughed, "cause if you were, she wouldn't
have come to me."

At the sound of the dry food hitting her bowl, Meesha
forgot Morgan.

A soft tap on the glass of the front door had Dorian
moving quietly through the shop. She heard him speaking
softly to someone at the door and then heard it close. He came
back carrying a large basket. "Here or in the cottage?"

"Where are we least likely to be found?" Morgan couldn't
handle Rob or Jasmine for a good eight hours—or more.

"Not a problem." Dorian turned back toward the shop
and pulled pocket doors out of the walls, shutting off the
shop completely. Morgan stared. She hadn't noticed them
before.

Dorian's sigh turned her attention back to the table. He
was wrestling a chilled bottle of Pinot Grigio out of the
basket. He deftly set it on the table, swung around, and
grabbed two wine glasses. "You *do* drink wine?"

She held up a glass and grinned.

She settled back as Dorian produced a light Caesar salad,
herb butter biscuits, and chicken penne from the basket. He
brought plates and quickly had the table set, so, had she not
seen the basket, she would never have guessed the
sumptuous meal before her hadn't been produced right here.

The aromas teased the taste buds. She sipped her wine slowly and savored its crisp cold flavor.

She watched the man across from her. In spite of the fact that they had spent part of the afternoon in conditions that would wilt the hardiest person, his white shirt still appeared crisp and his scent still clean. Jenn would love the faint hint of patchouli. He ate with determination and yet with elegance. Refined.

Dorian glanced up at her. Her fork stopped halfway to her lips. His gaze focused on her mouth.

She swallowed. Took a sip of wine to avoid choking. Feral. That was it. She wondered if there such a thing as elegant wildness. She felt like she was getting a buzz and she felt certain it wasn't the little bit of wine she'd consumed. The hair on her arm tickled. She looked down. Tiny blonde hairs stood on end.

"Stop that!"

Dorian smiled at her and sipped his wine. Her arm went smooth again. "When you're friend calls—tell her we can arrange for Abbott House to transport."

"I can tell you right now, she will be coming down to go with them."

"That's fine. Let me know when and I will set it up with Bask."

"I thought he was an attorney."

"He's a lot of things."

Which was true of everything around here. Morgan sensed she had only seen the tip of the iceberg where "different" was concerned. She needed time to collect her thoughts. Except things kept happening. She wondered if it had always been this hectic for her biological parents.

Her phone rang. She flipped it open. "Jenn. Thanks"

"No problem. I am coming down—"

"Wait." Morgan put her on speaker. "Dorian says he will set up transportation. Just let me know when."

"I think the sooner the better. Set it up for tomorrow. I've cleared my schedule. I'll fly down, meet up at your place, and go back with them. We will be going straight to the hospital. I can have one of our vans waiting."

Dorian spoke for the first time. "Let me arrange all transportation. That way we can control security—at least to the hospital. We can arrange for security personnel as well."

"That bad?"

"He's an angry, powerful man."

Jenn's voice was controlled. Tight. "Did he do this?"

"No. We think one of his henchmen got out of control. I doubt we will ever see that man again."

"Ahh," Jenn said in understanding.

"Talk with Morgan. I'll call Bask." Dorian got up.

Morgan held up her hand, grabbed the pen on the table, jotted down Jenn's number and handed the paper to Dorian. He smiled, pulled his phone out of his pocket, opened the pocket doors and eased through, sliding them closed behind him.

"Am I still on speaker?" Jenn asked.

"No." Morgan put the phone to her ear.

"Wow!"

Morgan knew what Jenn meant. Where John's voice was warm whiskey, Dorian's was a little deeper, thicker, like brandy. "Yeah," she breathed.

"You are so in trouble."

"You have no idea."

"Everything okay?" Jenn was quick to pick up cues.

"Rob's here."

"What the—"

Dorian walked back in. "Tell her to be ready at nine."

Morgan spoke, but didn't add any more about Rob. "I can't wait to see you. We'll have you all on a flight back to Virginia," she looked at Dorian for cues, "late afternoon." She read his hand movement. "Four-thirty, Dorian says. It'll be tight, but I know you can do it."

"See you tomorrow. I'll call your mom. Anything you need?" Jenn asked.

"My own clothes," Morgan almost whimpered.

"I can take care of that. See you tomorrow. Love you." Jenn disconnected.

The phone trilled again as soon as Morgan shut it. Morgan started to answer. Dorian grabbed the phone and held it in front of her face. Rob's cell number flickered across the screen.

"Thanks." She took the phone and set it on the table.

"Are you ready?" Dorian asked. Before she could answer, he swung around with a plate topped with two, large, scrumptious confections—some sort of pastry—like a tart, but flakey, dusted with sugar.

He waved them under her nose. "This is your treat..." he teased and moved away as she reached out.

"Wait. Let me warm them just a touch..." He smiled at her, popped them into the microwave, licked the sugar off of his fingers as the microwave counted down 13 seconds. He had done this before. When he opened the door, she salivated. The smell was heaven.

He lifted one and held it. She took a bite. The crust was light and broke off in her mouth. A very light hint of berry touched her tongue. She knew she had powdered sugar on her mouth. Just as her tongue slipped out lick it off, Dorian captured her mouth, his tongue sliding across her lips. She moaned.

He put the plate on the table and pulled her up into his arms. His mouth went from warm to hot. She sank into him.

He tasted of berries and wine. She knew she was losing control.

Dorian realized he was in trouble. He couldn't help himself. When her pink tongue had slipped out to lick that light dusting of sugar from her upper lip, his mind went blank. Her lips became a magnet to his. He felt as though he would die if he didn't get a taste of her. Right then. And it was worth every moment of purgatory ever invented—her warm lips parting for him, the feel of her unbound breasts against his chest, the curve of her waist tapering in and then flaring softly under his hands.

She moaned into his mouth. He moaned back. Then, using the few brain cells left in his head, he pulled back. Her eyes were shut. He hands caressed her shoulders and he watched her eyes flutter open. Those emerald facets shimmered, then darkened as her pupils dilated. Her desire pulsed.

Pulsed. The word shot through his brain like gunfire. Shit. He stepped back quickly, right into the closed doors leading to the shop. He edged around her until he was against the sink. He turned, pulled the handle of the faucet up and stuck his head in the cold water.

Morgan watched him leap away from her like she had shocked him. *Finally*, she thought. She continued to watch him as he moved his body around the corner of the refrigerator toward the sink, staying as far away from her as possible—as though she brandished a hot poker and was aiming it directly at his middle, or lower. She cocked her head, watching him jam his head under the faucet, amusement overtaking the flagrant longing coursing through her veins.

What the hell was going on? One minute he's pulling her against him with a force that could have melded their bodies. Then he's leaping away. This pull me/pull you behavior had been going on since she arrived. Dorian was one big contradiction. One minute angry, the next loving. One minute wanting, the next avoiding. She seemed to be the central theme or cause of his actions—or inactions. Well, this wasn't any bowl of jellybeans for her either. Suddenly, as if some floodgate opened, the stress of the last week washed over Morgan. Her hands shook; her eyes burned. Knowing she was losing control, she turned and fled up the stairs.

Dorian pulled the dishtowel from his wet face to see Morgan's back disappear up the stairs and into the master bedroom. He heard the door close softly and ascended two steps when he thought better of it. He trod back down and slumped into the chair he'd pulled her out of just moments before. What had he been thinking? She wasn't ready for this. Hell, he wasn't ready for this—whatever this was.

He rested his chin on the palm of his hand and stared out the dark window. Why hadn't he listened to Mel and Thom when they'd explained things to him? *Because I was a bloody teenager,* he countered in his own defense. *And—you were supposed to live forever,* he added sadly.

Memories flooded his mind. Melissa calling from the garden for them to take it outside when he and Thom started throwing small electrical balls at one another during one of his "compounding" lessons. Thom had such an impetuous sense of humor and everything was done in fun and with great love and laughter. When caught, Thom could look at Mel with that sheepish twinkle and she would just melt and shake her head. Now, he not only had to remember their teachings, but impart them to Morgan as well. He pushed himself away from the table and strode out the back door, calling for Meesha to follow. The door slammed behind them.

It was dark in the garden. No lights emanated from the cottage. He could barely make out the structure of the gazebo as he headed that way. Feeling the weight of loss, he fell into the swing in the gazebo and felt the uneven jostle as Meesha hopped up next to him. She laid her head in his lap, waiting for his caress. He obliged, softly stroking her fur—taking whatever comfort he could get.

"Poor girl," he spoke softly to the dog, "we forget you miss them too." She whined softly in response.

Meesha had sensed Mel and Thom were gone before he knew. She had come scratching at the back door, drawing him away from his work out front. He would let her in, she would wonder around, lie down for a while, and head back to the door, wanting out. After about the fourth time in as many hours, he'd lost patience with her and wouldn't let her inside. She stood at the door whining until he relented. She laid down at the foot of the stairs, watching him. It was shortly thereafter that he'd gotten the phone call from Bask. They'd spent the night huddled on the floor in the master bedroom, wanting it to be different, waiting for the sound of the couple's familiar laughter as they came up the steps.

Now Dorian had to face the fact that he was alone here. He was in charge of The Shoppe of Spells—and all that implied—and had to decide what to do about Morgan. Obviously, it was Mel and Thom's wish for her to be brought into the shop and trained. But why now—so late? He was sure Bask would have some answers. If not, he was sure Bask knew where to look or who to ask. One thing was for sure—Dorian didn't have any answers, only more questions. Well, at least he could be honest with Morgan.

He glanced up at the light coming from the bedroom window. She must have turned on the bedside lamp. The light filtering from the window was muted, barely casting its glow to the ground. The gardens were quiet, quieter than it had been since Mel and Thom had left. As soon as they died, it was as though the creatures had gotten a free pass to come out. He couldn't see them, but with Meesha aware of them, he knew more were about. That and Mr. Parker suddenly becoming forgetful. He knew he and Morgan had only sent a couple back—unless more had gone through at each opening. Dorian looked into the garden and squinted. He hated the fact that he couldn't see them—that he had to rely on someone else.

With a huff, he gave one last stroke across Meesha's back. "Come on, girl, let's go inside," he warned her before he moved. On cue, she lifted her cute face, looked up at him—just to make sure he wasn't joking—and hopped down. He rose and headed inside, drawn by the light in Morgan's room.

Morgan had closed the door to the master bedroom before she realized her quandary. Was it okay to escape up here? Should she have gone to the cottage? Well, he could tell her to leave, if he didn't like it. She needed to be away from him for a little while. She needed a shower.

She turned on the bedside lamp and went into the bathroom. The soft scent of lavender permeated the air. She turned on the shower and pulled off the clothes she had worn for what seemed like days. As she stepped under the steaming spray, she closed her eyes and let the hot water stream down her face and body. Every muscle relaxed, one at a time. She washed from head to toe, thoroughly—trying to wash away her confusion about Dorian and the memories of that little girl lying helpless on that cot. With brisk strokes, she dried her skin until it glowed, applied the lavender lotion, wrapped a towel around her head, put another one about her body, and stepped into the bedroom. Padding quietly across the floor she opened one dresser drawer after another, looking for a nightgown. As she pulled out a pretty, lightweight muslin, an envelope fell to the floor. She pulled off the towels, put the gown over her head and let it slide down her body. Melissa's signature scent wrapped around her like a hug. She bent over and grabbed the envelope. She flipped it over. In a beautiful script, her name was written across the front. Numb, leaving the towels on the floor where they had fallen, she crossed to the bed. Piling pillows against the headboard, she climbed upon the feathery mattress and turned up the lamp.

It was a woman's handwriting. It had to be from Melissa. To her. She smelled the envelope. The same scent—the same one that scented the nightgown donning her body—floated from the paper. Her fingers trembled as she tore open the envelope and pulled out the letter. A necklace fell onto the bed. Morgan lifted it. The head of a tiny owl with emerald eyes looked back at her. She laid it gently on the comforter and opened the letter.

Dear Morgana,

Since it is well past your 25th birthday, I am assuming that the Briscoes have told you of your adoption.

Writing this is the hardest thing I have ever had to do, besides giving up my child—my lifeblood. I am your mother. Before you get angry, please understand that I am, in no way, trying to usurp the Briscoes' place. However, it is time for you to fulfill your destiny.

Your heritage began in the 1700s, when Ian Galbreath took an Indian maiden to wife. He called her Mary after his Grandmother. Their daughter was the first (that we know of) born with our distinctive traits—eyes and birthmark—and our abilities. Abbott House has journals of our history. They can give you a much better accounting than I can.

I know you are wondering why we gave you up. It was a decision Thom and I fretted over my entire pregnancy. Ours is not an easy life. It is one of service and commitment to others and our legacy. We took one look at you and knew we wanted you to have more—at least a semblance of normalcy—before you took your place. We decided to give you a chance to know the outside world and to enjoy living in it. We couldn't have asked for better people to love you than Becky and Talbot. We have kept tabs, without their knowing, as we didn't want to interfere. Your life has been more than we could have wished for you and something we couldn't give you. We will always be grateful to them.

Now that you are an adult, it is time to show you our path and enlighten you as to your abilities. We understood the risk we took letting you live in the outside world and that you might choose to stay there. It was a risk we felt was worth taking. It was done with love. Always with love.

I have enclosed the Necklace of the Owl. It is our symbol. The owl leads souls and the emerald protects and enhances our abilities. You will understand later.

We look forward to meeting you, Morgana. No, that is wrong. We are beside ourselves with joy at the prospect of meeting you.

Know, always, we love you,
Melissa and Thomas Kilraven
(your birth parents)

The warm smell of lavender eased under the door and caught Dorian by surprise as he raised his hand to knock. For an instant, he pictured Melissa, fresh from a shower, in her favorite robe, opening the door and reaching up to ruffle his hair, a smile on her lips. He tapped lightly. When Morgan didn't answer, he eased open the door. She sat cross-legged on the comforter, wearing Melissa's nightgown. The light danced off her still damp, tangled curls. She looked and smelled freshly scrubbed. When she raised her face to him, he saw the tears sparkle. She held papers in one hand and Melissa's necklace in the other.

"Where did you get that?" he demanded and saw her flinch. The sight of the necklace tore through his heart. He could have sworn Mel had worn it the day they'd left.

Morgan blinked, frowned, looked down at the necklace, and held out the letter.

He crossed the room, took the papers and dropped on the edge of the bed. He read in silence. When he looked up at her, his eyes were moist. He blinked them away. His voice was softer, but raspy, when he spoke. "Where did you find this?"

"The envelope fell on the floor when I pulled out the nightgown." She held out the necklace. "I'm sorry."

"No," he said, his voice much kinder. "Don't be. I didn't mean to snap. She gave it to you. It just surprised me to see it. She never took it off. Here. Let me." He took the necklace from Morgan's other hand, stood, and undid the clasp.

Morgan pulled her hair up. Dorian eased the necklace around her neck and secured it in the back. She let her hair fall. When her fingers touched the owl, it felt warm, much like the crystals had earlier.

"Let me see."

She turned and lifted her head.

For a second it looked as though those tiny eyes winked at him. He blinked. "It looks great."

Morgan climbed off the bed and went to the mirror. She looked at the necklace resting smoothly against her skin. It looked as though she'd always worn it right there.

She looked up and saw the flicker of pain in Dorian's eyes, turned and padded back toward the bed. "I could use a robe," she suggested.

It took a moment for him to tear his eyes from the outline of her naked curves showing beneath the thin material. "Sure." He went to the armoire, pulled it open, produced a light seersucker robe.

"About earlier," he began. He didn't turn but looked at her in the mirror on the armoire door as he closed it. She looked ethereal. A faint glow emanated from her body. Heightened color spiked from her eyes and from the tiny eyes of the owl nestled just above the cleavage of her breasts. He felt his loins tighten. He clinched his jaw.

"Don't worry about it." She shook her head. "So much is going on, and now with this…" she let her voice trail off. Suddenly, she wanted to be alone. She wanted to reread the letter and think about them—her parents. She pulled back the comforter. She looked over at him. He was looking at her in the mirror, a haunted expression on his face. He still held the robe. "I'm exhausted. I think I'll call it a night, if that's okay. Climbing onto the high tester bed, she punched the pillows, and nestled down.

Dorian walked over, laid the robe across the foot of the bed, shoved his hands into his pockets, and looked at her for a moment. She was so damn beautiful. "John is bringing Kayla and Meadow over first thing. I'll wake you about seven." He walked to the door, reached over and turned off the light.

"Please leave the door cracked," she called to his retreating form.

He pulled the door slightly ajar and went downstairs.

Chapter Nine

Morgan woke to a still dark room and stretched. She'd had the best sleep she'd had in years. No dreams, no fears. Just pure, undisturbed sleep. She went to the armoire, pulled out a fresh pair of jeans and a shirt, dressed and clipped the mass of red curls atop her head.

She crept down the stairs, hoping not to wake Dorian. However, the smell of fresh coffee rebuked that thought and drew her to the kitchen. There was no sign of Dorian or Meesha. Her hands cupping a mug of the rich black brew, she moved into the shop. The closed sign was still flipped, the lights off. A sound at her back made her spin around, almost spilling the coffee.

Dorian emerged from the open door under the steps. His startled expression told her he wasn't expecting to see her downstairs just yet. He pulled the door closed behind him. "You're up. It's early yet." He walked over, poured a cup of coffee and took it to the table.

Morgan eyed the closed door. "What's in there?"

"It's just a workroom." He changed the subject. "John brought Kayla and Meadow at about four this morning. I put them in the cottage. I hope you don't mind."

Morgan sat down across from him. Dorian had shadows under his eyes. She could tell he hadn't slept well the night before, if at all.

"Why would I mind?"

"Well, it's where you were staying. Want something to eat?"

"Not really. Dorian, I don't feel any claim to the cottage. Or here, for that matter."

She studied him. He appeared to be uncomfortable with her this morning. She still hadn't confronted him about what happened last night in the kitchen. "We need to talk."

The air seemed to leave his body. His shoulders slumped ever so slightly. "I know.

Can we get Meadow settled first? Then, I promise, I will try to tell you everything you need to know."

She noticed the choice of words but decided to forego the questions. "For now, let me know what I can do to help in the shop. Oh, and I am fixing dinner for us tonight, barring any unforeseen circumstances."

"Like Rob?"

"Crap," she put down her cup and pushed out of the chair. "I completely forgot about Rob."

"And the fact that he had dinner with Jas last night, don't forget that." Dorian's eyes twinkled.

Well, she was glad she provided him with some amusement at least. She walked to the back door. "How much does Jasmine know about me?"

"You're Mel's daughter. She probably assumes, given the similarity, that you are like her."

"I thought you said not everyone knew."

"She's from a founding family." He shrugged. "I wouldn't worry too much about Jasmine. She has an effusive personality and a quick tongue, but she's good people. Our people."

Morgan decided now was probably not the time to discuss Jasmine.

"Where's Meesha?" she asked, changing the subject.

"Oh, she's staying in the cottage with Meadow. Believe it or not, Meesha has a comforting effect."

"She's one incredible dog."

"I know." He watched her as she moved about the kitchen, opening random cabinets and drawers. "Are you looking for something?"

She pushed in a drawer and let her hand drop. "I was just thinking about dinner and realized I didn't know where anything is and…" she faltered, not knowing what to do.

"It's okay, Morgan. I was teasing you." He got up and pointed out the layout of the kitchen. It was very neatly organized. He went to a sidewall that led to the door under the stairs. "This is for the pharmacy. I keep it separate. You can do anything you want with anything, except here. Okay?"

"Got it." She saluted.

Morgan looked through the huge double door refrigerator and freezer and found some salmon in the freezer. She moved it to the other side. She thought about the herb garden and knew they would have a scrumptious dinner.

Dorian had moved into the shop and was organizing one of the shelves. Morgan busied herself figuring out what was where and what she had to work with.

She heard a knock at the front door. Although they had been working for a while, she knew it was still early. Not moving to the front, she listened.

"Well, hello handsome," came a throaty feminine voice from the front.

"Jenn," she squealed and raced into the other room.

Jenn set the suitcase and large pet carrier she was wielding on the floor and rushed forward. "Hey, kiddo." She wrapped Morgan in a tight hug. "God, I've missed you."

She pushed back and held Morgan at arm's length. "You *have* looked better, but you'll do." She hugged her again, stepped back and turned to Dorian. "And who is this gorgeous hunk of man-flesh?"

Morgan watched the red creep up Dorian's neck.

"Dorian," Morgan laughed. "This is Jennifer Davis, my best friend in the whole world and woman extraordinaire. Jenn, this is Dorian Drake, my brother." The last was said with a twinkle in her eye.

"I am—"

"—not," Jenn finished for him. "I know. Morgan told me who you are but not how you are." She laughed, stood on tiptoe, and kissed him on the cheek.

Morgan saw him fluster and decided to save him. "It's okay, Dorian," she said and wrapped her arm around Jenn's waist, "she's all bark."

As if on cue, an indignant meow came from the crate.

Morgan stopped cold. "Mrs. T?" She walked over, leaned down, and was greeted with a soft mewl. "Mrs. T," Morgan cooed and knelt down, opened the door, and hefted out the large, gunmetal grey cat. Mrs. T turned her head, looked at Dorian with eyes the color of Morgan's and pushed her ears back. Then, seemingly comfortable that her disdain had been noted, she nuzzled Morgan's neck and managed to turn herself upside down in Morgan's arms. A loud purr erupted from her throat.

Dorian and Jenn watched as Morgan and Mrs. T shared their moment. When Morgan finally looked up, Jenn lifted her hands in supplication, "Hey, don't look at me. It was her idea."

Morgan didn't doubt it for a moment.

Jenn supplied the rest. "I got a call from Bask late last night. He had the plane coming by Norfolk at four this morning and, as they say, the rest is history. Look, I can take her back with me since we are going back on the plane. She travels very well—settled down in the seat next to mine and went to sleep, after conning food out of the flight attendant, mind you."

Morgan looked at Dorian. "We'll talk," was all he said. It wasn't a no, per se, just qualified.

"Meesha?" Morgan asked

"Who's Meesha?" Jenn looked from one to the other.

"My dog," Dorian stated. "She won't be a problem. She loves all animals. Now, whether...Mrs. T, is it?...will take to her...that's another question."

"She likes dogs. Just not some people," Morgan teased. She had rested her chin on top of the cat's head. It was disconcerting having two pairs of what appeared to be the same eyes staring back at him.

Jenn interrupted. "I brought clothes," she twirled and pointed to the large suitcase.

"Oh, thank you," Morgan sighed. "Not that I don't appreciate the loan," she added quickly to Dorian.

"It's okay." Dorian moved past Jenn toward the kitchen. "Coffee, anyone?"

"Sure," Jenn piped up. "I could use some high octane." She followed Dorian into the kitchen.

At that moment, the back door opened and John walked through. His long black hair was still damp from a shower and his bronze skin glowed. Morgan heard Jenn suck in her breath and waited for some quippy remark to follow. When none did, she looked over at her friend. Jenn stood rooted, staring. John was pretty much doing the same. Cheeks pink, Jenn looked down.

Well, that's a first, Morgan thought. "Jenn, this is John Davis. John, this is my friend, Jennifer Davis."

Jenn looked at Morgan, laughed and quipped, "Wow, if we got married, I wouldn't even have to change my na..." the words trailed off and she turned bright red.

Morgan smiled. At least Jenn's brain was still engaged, at least partially. Morgan decided to rescue Jenn. "Sit down guys, coffee's almost ready," she turned to Dorian who had been watching from near the sink and rolled her eyes. As she turned back, John was holding Jenn's chair for her. And Jenn was letting him.

"Here…sit, Morgan," John's liquid voice softly commanded. "You appear to have your arms full. I'll help Dorian."

"Thanks, John." Morgan slipped into the chair across from Jenn and widened her eyes at her best friend. Jenn was watching John's back with a dreamy expression on her face. Oh, good grief. Where was the Jenn that took nothing from nobody? Apparently, she'd slipped into John's pocket, not that that wasn't one handsome pocket to slip into.

"How's Meadow?" Morgan addressed his back.

He brought mugs of coffee over to the table, put one in front of her and placed one in front of Jenn; then, just as Morgan reached out, he moved the cream and sugar from next to her over to Jenn.

Morgan watched as Jenn added cream to her coffee, something she never did. Damn, it went both ways.

Jenn looked down and toyed with her napkin.

Morgan wanted to groan.

It took a few seconds, but John finally realized that Morgan had asked him a question. "She was sleeping when I left," he said, sat down and faced Jenn.

Then, as quickly as it had appeared, the self-consciousness Jenn displayed was replaced with the victim-rescuing acumen Jenn was known for. She drew a notepad from her purse and launched into questions, hammering John with one after another, writing fiercely as they spoke. Morgan and Dorian sat quietly, sipping coffee and listening. By the time the mugs were empty, Jenn was done.

"Now, I'd like very much to meet Meadow and Kayla, if they are up?" She flashed her power smile at John.

"Yes," he stammered and almost knocked over his chair rising.

As the four of them trekked over to the cottage, Morgan pointed out some of the features of the garden to Jenn. Jenn looked at her and smiled. She knew. They were standing in Morgan's dream garden. Jenn reached over and squeezed her arm. Morgan shook her head ever so slightly at Jenn. Jenn frowned. "Why?" she mouthed. Morgan shrugged.

At least Jenn was back to herself, or at least as close to herself as she would probably get while John was around. That tall, overly handsome Indian was having one hell of an effect on her outspoken, curvy blonde friend. Too bad Jenn didn't live closer. Or not. Morgan didn't know if John was married or committed to someone. He, too, seemed smitten.

She could hear Kayla in the cottage talking to Meadow as they approached. Dorian opened the door and Meesha shot past, heading for the far side of the property.

"Potty break," he affirmed.

Not so much as a snarl escaped Mrs. T. Either she hadn't noticed or didn't care. However, as soon as they entered the cottage, she squirmed out of Morgan's arms and took off toward the bedroom.

"Mrs. T," Morgan called, apologized to Kayla, and rushed into the room. Mrs. T was already curled up next to Meadow's stomach as Meadow lay on her side on the bed. "It's okay," she started to reassure Meadow, afraid the cat had frightened her. Meadow just smiled and put her arm over the cat. Mrs. T's purrs could be heard in the other room.

"Well, I'll be," Jenn shook her head.

Morgan had never seen Mrs. T act like this. Normally, the cat was the epitome of nonchalance. Yet, here she was curling and cooing as if she'd found someone she'd lost.

Dorian came up behind Morgan and took in the scene. "Can I talk to you?" Dorian took her arm. "Please excuse us," he called to the others and led her outside. They walked toward the gazebo.

"I've never seen her act like that. I hope Meadow isn't allergic."

"I doubt it." He said and sat down on the swing, patting the space next to him. Morgan sat. Dorian gently pushed, setting the swing in a smooth motion.

When he'd pulled her out of the bedroom, his tone had seemed urgent. However, now, as he looked over the garden, his thoughts appeared elsewhere.

Morgan followed his gaze across the floral beauty in front of them. She felt a real sense of peace. "It's beautiful here."

"Wait until I show you the rest of the property."

Morgan looked around at the enclosed area.

"It's through that gate in the back." He pointed behind the cottage. "It spreads out and covers about thirty acres. Most of it's wild, but Mel and Thom had been working on some of it. I want to show it to you."

She nodded and looked at his gorgeous profile as he studied the garden, lost in thought. A slight frown broke his countenance.

"Now," he interrupted her musings, "I need to talk to you about Mrs. T. You are welcome to have her here, of course. However, she is like you in that she can see the Gulatega. Cats don't generally react well being in such close proximity to them. They don't seem to be in any danger, but it makes them kinda weird."

"How?"

"Well, you figure, they can see them move about, but they can't smell them. It upsets them. Meesha will let me know when they are around, whine and watch an area even though she can't see them, but she doesn't become agitated."

"I see." Morgan sounded sad.

"We could try it for a while."

"But I'm not staying," she countered.

Dorian expression was one of surprise. "You're going back with them?"

Morgan fiddled with a piece of loose wicker on the seat of the swing. She had come to the decision last night, right before drifting off to sleep. She could think better away from Dorian. In fact, when she was anywhere near him, her brain didn't want to function, period. Unfortunately, her body was all too ready to take over. So much was happening—so fast. She needed time to think.

Although the shop and the gardens were compelling, she wasn't quite ready to take on all this hoodoo stuff that kept happening to her. Until a week or so ago, her life had been simple. Predictable. She even complained to Jenn that her life was *too* predictable. What was the old saying, *Be careful what you ask for; you might get it?* Now, she would give just about anything to go back to simple and predictable.

Morgan knew in her heart that she couldn't make things be the way they were before. Her life was forever altered. It would have happened anyway, sometime in the future. She understood that. She also knew that, before Melissa and Thomas Kilraven had died, she'd had more options. They knew it, too, and, from what the letter said, they wanted to allow her to make her choices.

She decided to be as honest with him as she could. "Dorian," she began and turned in the swing, rested her leg on the seat between them, keeping some distance, "things are happening so fast. With this," she looked down and added quietly, "and with you."

Dorian put his hand under her chin and lifted it, looking into her eyes. Those pools of green that drew him in like a beacon reminded him of the dark waters in an unexplored grotto. He wanted to fall into her eyes and never look back. He started to lean forward, to touch his lips to hers, and stopped himself. This was what she was talking about. He could feel the current between them. He dropped his hand.

Morgan also felt the electricity sizzle. It no longer hurt her, it was just there. More compelling. It was as though she was beginning to crave the feeling, whenever he touched her.

"It's this," she said. "This thing that happens between us. I don't understand it. I've never felt it before. Is it just you? Me? Us? I feel as though I can't get enough of you—I mean this." She felt her face heat up.

"I know," he tried to reassure her. "I've never felt this before either—with anyone. And, if you think you are drawn to it, trust me, you have no idea."

Morgan laughed. She couldn't help herself. It was the expression on his face. It helped lighten the tension.

He smiled at her. A megawatt smile. His eyes crinkled at the edges. "Look," he said, running his hand through his unruly hair, black waves being ruffled by the breeze, "I'll make a deal with you. I'll try." He shrugged, "Can't say I'll always succeed—you are one tempting woman. But I'll never go any further than you're willing to let me." He caught her sound, put a finger to her lips. "I'll also try to control this thing for both of us. Just stay. For a little while. Until we can talk things out and you can get a better feel for this place. It's not always like it's been this week. I promise. Actually, it can be downright boring."

Again, she laughed. "Yeah, right."

At that very moment, they heard Meesha scratch at the cottage door. Before they could yell, "No!" Kayla opened the door and Meesha bolted inside. Dorian and Morgan leapt from the swing and raced to the cottage, colliding with each other as they tried to pull open the door at the same time.

"After you," he yanked open the door.

Morgan ran inside and straight to the bedroom, expecting a flurry of fur from a cat and dog fray. She skidded to a stop, Dorian bumping into her. Mrs. T lay curled up as they had left her, guarding her young ward. Meesha lay on the foot of the bed, her head resting on her paws, quietly watching Morgan and Dorian stumble over one another. Meadow laughed. Except no sound emerged. Morgan forced herself to smile down at her.

"I see you have everything under control," Morgan said, choking back the emotion as she thought of what the poor child had been through, and the fact that, even though she didn't look it, this frail body, nestled between two loving animals, was thirteen. A budding woman.

Not speaking, Meadow gave a slight nod of her head.

"Then we'll just tiptoe back out of here and leave you to your menagerie." Morgan turned, avoided walking right back into Dorian, and walked through the cottage and out the door, hoping to make it before the tears fell.

She was outside, in the garden area, when Jenn caught up to her and placed a hand on her arm. "You okay?"

Morgan could only shake her head no, afraid her voice would crack.

Jenn saw Dorian coming out of the cottage and waved him away. He kept coming but skirted around them. Not looking back, he called over his shoulder, "I'm going to Teresa's to pick up some buns and sweet stuff for the sweet stuff." He disappeared around the side of the shop building.

"Let's go inside," Jenn urged Morgan forward.

"Oh, Jenn," Morgan said as she sank into the kitchen chair.

Jenn brought them both coffee and sat across from her, patting her hand. "She's going to be all right. I promise."

Morgan looked into Jenn's baby blues, "You've never lied to me before—"

"—and I'm not now," Jenn stated. "She's a sick little girl, but I have a feeling she's going to be fine. The physical will be taken care of...and we have incredible specialists working with us to deal with the other. She's going to be fine."

"Have you decided where they're going?"

"Yes. I was talking with Kayla and John."

Morgan raised her brows at the mention of John's name.

"I know. Don't go there. I completely lost it. Me! Goofy. There is just something about him. It's a good thing I'm going home."

"Jim?" Morgan asked, referring to the man Jenn had been seeing.

"No. Yes. I mean...well...we've been having some problems. Nothing huge," she added at Morgan's wide eyes. "It's just that we seem to be heading in different directions lately." She took a deep breath. "I would never consider anything...I mean, I want to give Jim and I a chance... It's complicated," she finally finished and took a gulp of cool coffee.

"Complicated's something I can relate to. About your talk with Kayla?"

"I want her placed in *my* house. It's got the tightest security." Jenn was referring to the largest of their facilities. It was located in Williamsburg and, although she traveled to all the homes, this was where she kept her offices. Because of the sensitivity of records, it had been built with the heaviest security features and the most personnel. It was also where she housed the "highest risk" families. It was a huge facility on a lot of acreage done in a Colonial Williamsburg style. Jenn loved the buildings and the grounds. It was her crowning achievement.

"Morgan," Jenn began and bit her lower lip.

"What?" The tension in Morgan skyrocketed.

"No. Nothing like that, sweetie. I was just wondering. Well, Meadow and Mrs. T seemed to really hit it off. Do you think I might borrow Mrs. T to travel back with us and stay with Meadow until she gets better? There are all these postulates about animal therapy..." Jenn left it hanging—even she knew she was reaching.

"They are generally referring to dogs, Jenn," Morgan said with a laugh. The idea of Mrs. T as a therapy anything... Nevertheless, she had seen how the cat had taken to Meadow—an instant bond of some sort. Morgan wasn't sure she wasn't a little jealous. Then remembering what Dorian had said, she knew this was the perfect solution.

"I think it's a great idea," Morgan said. "If anyone or anything can bring that girl to talk, it'll be Mrs. T."

Jenn rose to go tell Meadow the good news when they heard the front door unlock.

"That must be Dorian," Morgan commented. "With treats. Jenn, you haven't tasted anything, until you've tasted Teresa's baking."

Dorian walked through the shop laughing. He had someone with him. "Look who I ran into outside the shop?"

"I just wanted to see how your eyes were doing."

"Dr. Yancy. Hi." Morgan turned and grinned.

His warm eyes crinkled with humor.

Morgan loved it when people smiled with their eyes. "Oh, by the way," she began and turned to see an odd expression on Jenn's face, "this is—"

"Uncle Mike?" Jenn sounded dumbfounded.

"Jenn?" Dr. Yancy's face blanched. "What are you doing here?"

Jenn threw her arms around the thin man. "Morgan, this is the favorite uncle I'm always telling you about. What are you doing here? I thought you were someplace near Atlanta?"

"I am. Morgan just happens to be a patient."

"What?" Jenn looked from her uncle to Morgan.

Morgan shrugged. "When Jasmine got the bug spray in my eyes, this is the doctor they called to treat me." Remembering what he had said about her "mother," Morgan cocked her head to study him a little closer. She looked at Jenn, but Jenn seemed truly surprised to see him here.

"Talk about a small world," Dorian spoke up, setting packages on the counter. "And to celebrate this little family reunion, I have brought hot cross buns from the B & B." He lifted the bag and waved it around the room. The sweet smell of yeast, cinnamon, and sugar filled the air.

"Teresa sent Meadow a special plate, just for her." He set one package aside. Whipping out a tray from below the counter, he set up a plate, added a small flower in a little vase from the window, grabbed an extra bag of goodies and backed his way out the door. "Don't stand on ceremony. And don't let them get cold," he called through the screen door. "Oh, and save me one or two."

Morgan got up and set plates around the table, leaving Jenn and her uncle to talk. She filled a plate with buns, poured fresh coffee for everyone, including Dorian, and returned to the table.

"Can you believe it? He actually works for that place we were looking up?" Jenn shook her head.

"Bask & Morrisette?"

"No, actually the whole place is called Abbott House," Jenn corrected. She reached for a bun, placed it on her plate and licked her finger. "It must run in the family. I have a foundation, he works for a foundation." She filled her mouth and stopped talking.

Morgan watched her friend eat. Jenn approached food as she did life. Like it was a treat and not a morsel should be missed. She found it amazing that Jenn kept her athletic, yet curvy figure. As far as Morgan knew, Jenn never dieted and never gained an ounce—not in all the years she'd known her, anyway.

Dr. Yancy turned to Morgan, "Before I get Teresa's sugar all over my fingers, let me take a look at your eyes."

Morgan turned to him and opened them wide. It was fun to do that and not be afraid of some comeback.

"Doesn't she have the most gorgeous eyes, Uncle Mike?" Jenn asked.

"Yes, they are quite beautiful and have healed nicely." He offered no mention of Melissa's, put his light away and grabbed a bun, took a bite, closed his eyes and moaned. "Made by the hands of an angel."

From the look on his face, Morgan sensed there was more to that comment than baking skills. That, and the way he'd avoided the suggestion he go see Teresa the last time he was here, made Morgan wonder about the real history between those two.

Jenn was watching Morgan. "So, can I take her?" she asked between bites.

"Take who, where?" Dorian asked as he piled in beside Morgan.

Morgan spoke, not looking at him. "She wants to take Mrs. T back to be with Meadow for a while. I guess that'll be all right. She can be her feline nurse."

"Just make sure you ask Mrs. T," she commented to Jenn.

Not missing a beat, Jenn teased, "Already have. She said it was okay with her if it was okay with you."

Morgan sensed the tightness in Dorian's body and added, without casting him a glance, "I think I'll stay around here for a bit. Until we get things straight."

She felt him relax next to her. He smiled and popped half a bun in his mouth.

Morgan smiled as well, taking a sip of coffee. God, she hoped she was doing the right thing.

"Oh," Dorian piped up. "I have news...or gossip, as you ladies might prefer."

Jenn and Morgan put down their food and looked attentive. "Yes?" they encouraged simultaneously and smiled at one another.

"Well," he stretched out the moment, watching the anticipation grow. "Teresa says Rob has checked out. He said something about having to get back to the University earlier than expected. He told her to tell you," he looked at Morgan, "to call him when you get home."

"It'll be a rainy day in hell," she muttered under her breath. Her body relaxed, not having to deal with him as well as everything else.

"And to give you a hug," he threw his arm around her, squeezed and let go. "Mission accomplished." He reached for another bun.

John came through the door. "Sorry guys. Got a call from Abbott House. Driver's on his way. Plane's waiting at the airport. Looks like weather's heading this way. He wants to be up and gone before it gets here."

Everyone sprang into action.

Chapter Ten

For a group of people unfamiliar with one another's ways of doing things, they became synchronized fairly quickly. Jenn made phone calls to confirm the hospital was set up for an early arrival, while Dorian and John conferred on security set-ups. Kayla was getting their things together. Morgan, a little out of her element, decided it would be a good time to talk with Meadow about Mrs. T.

"You're sure you won't mind taking care of her while you get better?" Morgan watched the young girl beam, a smile spreading from ear to ear. She hugged the cat tightly to her. Mrs. T, for all the indignity, seemed not to mind. She looked up at Morgan from beneath Meadow's chin, as if to say, *Don't worry. I'll take care of her.*

Morgan reached over and took one paw, holding it gently in her hand. It was astonishing to look at the dual pair of eyes so alike—and like hers. The cat seemed truly content with Meadow. Morgan felt her chest tighten. It would be the first time in two years, since she'd found Mrs. T on her doorstep—meowing indignantly, as though she'd forgotten to let her in—that they had been separated for any length of time. Morgan knew this was goodbye. She could never take Mrs. T away from Meadow. They belonged together. Just as the image blurred from sudden tears, she felt Meadow's hand on her arm, squeezing. She blinked. Meadow was frowning and when she caught Morgan's attention, she looked from her to Mrs. T.

"Oh, no, sweetheart. It's okay. This is where Mrs. T wants to be. I'm going to miss her, that's all. You promise me you'll keep in touch and let me know how she's doing, okay?"

Meadow stroked Morgan's arm in reassurance. Morgan leaned over and kissed the young girl on the forehead.

Dr. Yancy stepped into the room. "Sorry to interrupt. I just wanted to take a look at our patient, if you don't mind?"

Morgan stood. "Here, let me take Mrs. T for a moment. I can say goodbye while you visit with the doctor." Meadow handed the cat to Morgan, who immediately turned and looked back at the bed. "We'll be right in the other room," she said, not quite certain if she was telling Meadow or the cat.

Dr. Yancy took her place on the bed and proceeded to explain to Meadow what he was doing. Kayla stood, ever vigilant, at the foot. From the slight droop in Kayla's shoulders, Morgan guessed that Kayla hadn't slept in a while. Once they got Meadow to the children's hospital and through surgery, Kayla could relax and get the sleep she obviously needed. Morgan opened her mouth to say as much and closed it again, knowing Kayla wouldn't take reassurances at this point. Instead, she walked into the outer room.

The room was bright and cheerful with the daylight flooding into it from the myriad of windows. The crystals and rocks sparkled in the sunshine. It seemed so different with Meadow here. She'd almost forgotten the darkness it hid. Mrs. T squirmed, wiggled out of her arms, and scooted through the door Dorian opened.

Morgan started to go after her when he grabbed her arm. "She has her own potty place and will return shortly. I've seen her do this several times."

"Really?" Morgan had been so vigilant about keeping her indoors, she now felt a little guilty.

Dorian nodded and realized he was still holding her arm, letting the current flow between them. She pulled away as he let go, each aware that they were prolonging the contact.

Dorian cleared his throat, yet his voice still came out a little husky, "Everything's about ready. The car's here. As soon as Dr. Yancy finishes, we can get her situated."

As if on cue, Dr. Yancy appeared. "She looks okay. I think I'm going to go up with them." Morgan saw concern in his face.

"Dorian," the doctor motioned for Dorian to follow him outside. Morgan followed.

"She's weak," the doctor stated. "Also, a bit dehydrated—"

"I keep Ringer's Lactate in the pharmacy. Also saline. Will either of them do?" Dorian said.

"Let's go with saline; she's pretty small. That'll keep her hydrated until we get her to the hospital."

"Be back in a minute." Dorian took off for the shop.

Morgan and the doctor stepped back inside. Mrs. T slipped back in before she closed the door, walked past everyone and went into the bedroom. Instead of lying next to Meadow, she carefully curled up at the foot of the bed. Kayla reached down, stroked her, and looked at Morgan. "Pretty remarkable cat."

"Pretty remarkable kid," Morgan replied and left for the main house.

She walked in on a discussion between Dorian and John. Jenn stood to the side, her expression tense.

"I think I need to go with them," John's warm voice rose.

"John, think about this. That son of a bitch is crazy. It would be a lot easier for him to track them if you're with them, than if they go by themselves. You know I'm right." Dorian tried to keep his voice calm, steady.

"You're asking me to just let them fly off to God knows where…" he sighed the last words.

Jenn stepped in, touched his arm. He jumped. She quickly removed her hand, but stayed standing next to him. "Listen." She spoke softly but firmly. "I know you don't know me, but this is my job; I'm damn good at my job." Her voice got stronger with each word. "I haven't lost a family yet. And I've helped one hell of a lot." She turned to Morgan.

"She's right, John. Her safe houses are in five states and opening on the west coast. She knows what she's doing. Trust her. She won't let any harm come to them."

He turned to Jenn and looked at her. "I didn't mean to offend you…they are my family…" he spoke quietly but she saw the fear in his eyes. "He's one scary son of a bitch."

"I understand. I've talked with the people from Abbott House. They are backing up my security teams. We've got them covered. No one, and I mean no one, is going to find them once they come into my care."

"What about me?" John asked.

Jenn laughed. "I think we can fix things for you to be in touch. However, it will have to be through me. That's the only way." She looked at Morgan. "Or through her or Dorian, which might be even better—the less direct access the better."

Dorian, having disappeared into his workroom, reappeared with IV in hand. "Sorry, I need to get this to Yancy," he stated and left.

Morgan fixed a cup of coffee and urged John to sit down while they got Meadow situated.

When she saw Jenn's fingers tremble, she went to her friend. "Hey, before everything gets hectic," she laughed, "why don't you let me show you my room? We can take this suitcase upstairs and make sure you brought enough of my favorite things. Come on," she grabbed the huge suitcase and trudged it up the steps.

John stood. "Want me to—"

"No!" both women answered a bit too quickly. Their laughter followed them up the stairs.

Jenn followed Morgan into the master bedroom and headed straight to the picture on the dresser. "Wow. I hadn't seen any pictures. You really do look like her." She set it back gently.

"We can talk about me some other time. What's going on?" Morgan flung the suitcase up on the bed, unzipped it and flipped back the top. "Oh, Jenn," she sighed and pulled out her underwear, "you are definitely my best friend."

"Nothing like wearing your own," Jenn sat up on the bed.

"Speak," Morgan commanded.

"It's John. I was terrified he was going to come with us."

"You're afraid of him?"

"No. I'm afraid of me," Jenn looked down at her hands. "There's something about him. I want to focus on Kayla and Meadow and I'm afraid if he were around, I wouldn't."

Thinking of Dorian, Morgan nodded. "I know exactly what you mean."

"Yeah," Jenn drawled out the word. "Dorian's some kind of gorgeous. And, it's not like you're involved with Rob anymore. Speaking of which, what was he doing here, anyway?"

"I don't know. He just showed up. Now, he's left. Rather strange, if you ask me." Morgan hadn't had time to think about it at all. However, she planned to, as soon as things calmed down. There was something not quite right about him "just showing up."

"Your parents felt badly about letting him know where you were." Jenn jumped off the bed, "God, I almost forgot." She dug into her cargo pants pocket. "They sent this for you." She handed Morgan an envelope. "Said it's not urgent."

Morgan took the envelope, saw her mother's neat scrawl across the front and held it to her breast before setting it on the bedside table. "Then I'll read it later, when I have more time. You'll let them know I'm okay, won't you. I know they're worried and I haven't had time to talk with them. I should call them."

"I think that's what that's about. They told me they wanted you to feel free to take all the time you need. Not to worry about them." Jenn saw the tears in Morgan's eyes. She put her arms around her. "Honey, they know you love them. I know that you know they love you. We've been friends too long for me not to feel like you guys are family. I'll look in on them. You just do what it is you have to do." She pushed Morgan to arm's length and stared into her green eyes. "Somehow I know it has to do with things I probably don't understand. Things that make you and Meadow alike." She handed Morgan a tissue.

Jenn turned and walked over to the armoire. "This place is to die for, by the way," then realized what she'd said. "Oh God, Morgan, I'm—"

"Not a problem, girlfriend. I miss those feet sticking out of your mouth." Morgan threw her arm around her shoulders. "We better get back. You're going to have a busy day."

"Don't forget me..." Jenn whispered as they headed down the steps.

"Never," Morgan promised.

****

It was after eleven and Morgan was snuggled under mounds of comforter, freshly bathed, and wearing her own pajamas. Finally—she didn't feel like she was staying on someone's borrowed dime. They had supped at the B & B, not wanting to tackle making a meal, despite Morgan's earlier offer.

The promised storm broke during dinner sending them back to the shop in torrential rain pushed by howling winds.

Jenn had called and said that Meadow was resting comfortably in the Children's Hospital and surgery was scheduled for the morning. Kayla was set up in Meadow's room, the hospital having private rooms for their patients with large window seats that converted to beds for a staying parent to sleep. Dr. Yancy was staying close by and had already conferred with several of the doctors.

Morgan was glad Dr. Yancy was there. He was the one physician that knew about patients like herself and Meadow. Since Meadow couldn't or wouldn't speak, he was more than her doctor; he was her advocate.

From what little Morgan had gleaned from Dorian, Mike Yancy had been around for quite some time. Long enough, in fact, to have been engaged to Teresa Abbott before she met Bill Ruthorford. Morgan bet that was one interesting story. It might also explain why he always asked after them but wouldn't go see them when he was in town. She wondered just how long it had been since they'd spoken to one another.

John was a nervous wreck. He was going to go down to the B & B but Dorian convinced him to stay in the cottage. Morgan had left them strategizing about Kayla's ex-husband when she got so tired she could barely keep her eyes open and excused herself to go on to bed.

She'd found it amusing that for about an hour after Jenn had left, John had done nothing but question her about Jenn and Safe Harbor. At first, she figured he was getting information to reassure himself about sending his family off with a virtual stranger. As the questions progressed, however, they became more personal. Finally, Morgan told John that some of those answers would have to come from the source herself. He'd reddened slightly and changed the subject.

John hung around until word came that Meadow's surgery had been successful and they expected a complete recovery. They'd found a benign tumor and removed it. They also expected her speech to return, believing the loss to be because of the tumor, not from the attack. John planned to take a trip to Virginia once she was settled in and healing. He wanted to know what had happened to her and Jenn assured him she had the right staff of psychologists to help gain that information, without overly traumatizing Meadow. Morgan caught certain expressions on John's face that told her retribution would be swift.

Mrs. T was safely ensconced back at Morgan's apartment for the time being, until Meadow was released from the hospital. Jenn said she'd lifted her head, crooked her tail and assumed her customary position atop the hutch as though she'd never left.

Morgan's conversation with her parents had been another matter. Their letter had been sweet and loving, trying to let her know they supported whatever she chose to do. She'd picked up the phone and spent the next half hour with the three of them talking, filling them in on everything she could think of. At one point, both of her parents were firing questions simultaneously, first at her, then at one another, until the conversation was completely between the two of them. Picturing them standing not five feet apart and talking to each other on the phone had her doubled over in laughter. She missed their easy banter and the camaraderie the three of them enjoyed.

Explaining about herself proved to be a more difficult task, not because of her parents, but because of her. She had been *different* all of her life, but it had always been thought of as a birth defect. Now Morgan knew it wasn't…she really was different—in ways her parents couldn't comprehend. Or, maybe they could, Morgan pondered, suddenly remembering her mother's study of parapsychology. As an expert on hypnosis, she'd attempted to use it on Morgan to squelch the nightmares, with little success. Maybe, Morgan thought, when things settled down, she would bring her parents down and discuss "things" in more depth, getting their take on the situation—after she made damn sure it was safe for them to be here.

Through Dorian, the powers that be—The Abbott House or Foundation or whatever it was—tried to tell her the need for discretion. Did they think she was going to go around shouting it from the rooftops? She didn't understand what she had, or even what she was, by a long shot. She intended to find out as much as possible. She'd never been one to hide from herself. She understood that open knowledge of the creatures and the portals could cause panic. She certainly didn't want to cause panic. So, she had sworn her parents to secrecy, which, in her mind, was pointless, knowing they had kept the secret of her adoption for twenty-six years.

****

The next several weeks flew by for Morgan. Very quickly, she and Dorian established a routine. By the time she got a shower, dressed and went downstairs, he was already up and had hot coffee waiting for her. She watched the shop the first part of the morning, which was generally quiet, except for the occasional pharmacy needs. This allowed Dorian more time in his laboratory. She'd finally been granted access to the room under the stairs. It looked like a well-stocked pharmacy, albeit surprisingly large. She would come out, stand in the kitchen and look back at the stairs, trying to figure out how that size room fit under the stairs. Catching her quizzically staring one day, he laughed, grabbed her hand, and led her outside and around to the side of the house. The side was flat. For the life of her, she couldn't figure it out. Then Dorian stepped through the bushes, put his hand next to some decorative brick and, voila, a door handle appeared. Clever. It was a false side, built out flush to the building and providing a storage area on one side and access to the root cellar—which was far larger than she imagined a root cellar to be—on the other. He took her back inside and showed her several more hidden doors—one on that side of the building at the top of the stairs and one behind the counter in the shop.

"It was built with possible raids in mind. This area was under a great deal of conflict between settlers and Indians in the beginning."

"I thought Ruthorford was immune to the problems."

"It was, for the most part. The raids were done by the white settlers, not the Indians. In fact, during one of the attacks, it was the Creek who protected the inhabitants from their own countrymen."

She was fascinated by the history of the area and hoped to get some books on the subject. Ruthorford had its own library, but it was Abbott House that held the true records about the area and its people. Morgan definitely wanted another trip into Atlanta. She remembered the will—full access into perpetuity. Plus, she didn't know how long she could avoid the confrontation with Bask. He was pushing her to make a commitment to stay in Ruthorford. That was one commitment she wasn't quite ready to make. Luckily, his urging had been filtered through Dorian, who was adroitly keeping the man at bay.

In the afternoons, Dorian took over the shop, giving her full access to the gardens in the back. She was in heaven. They were well-designed, well-planted, and well-tended. By the third day, she knew every plant occupying the copious beds, where it was, and what it needed. She stooped and pulled weeds as she went—not that there were many. Meesha normally joined her, lying along the walkways, not wandering among the plants. At night, her muscles ached from overuse, but the hot, lavender scented showers eased the discomfort.

True to her word, Morgan had gathered herbs and made Dorian several meals she knew he would like. The sounds of pleasure he made while eating told her she had done a good job. She refused, however, to take on total kitchen duties, no matter how much he begged.

Late afternoon was the most active in the shop. Morgan figured just about every inhabitant in Ruthorford had passed through the shop at one time or another. They were sweet people and seemed saddened by the loss of Melissa and Thomas, but welcomed her with open arms.

Miss Grace sent a pie by way of Miss Alice. It turned out to be every bit as good as she had heard. So good in fact, she and Dorian demolished half of the pie after dinner.

The twittering group of women came by several times and fussed over her. She never did get all of their names—the constant chattering seemed to interfere.

Teresa came by, always bearing a basket of one goody or another. Morgan, in turn, returned one of the baskets filled with her freshly made herb rolls. Teresa begged for the recipe, and, if she couldn't get that, asked if Morgan would consent to producing such delicacies for the B & B. Teresa repeatedly asked after Meadow. Her interest had definitely piqued when they informed her that Dr. Yancy had traveled north to help.

The only person who hadn't put in an appearance was Jasmine. Morgan just couldn't work up any sadness over that slight. She apparently had gone on vacation shortly after Rob left, leaving her boutique under the care of a couple of the younger crowd. Morgan didn't think Jasmine would be too thrilled when she returned to find some of her wares had gone rather punk.

As for the Gulatega, there had been no known incidents regarding them as yet. She still didn't know if they came singularly or in multiples. Just the same, she had opted to stay above the shop. Even though Dorian assured her they were no threat to her, she wasn't quite comfortable being alone in the cottage.

Besides, she like being close to Dorian. There was something about him—other than the handsome factor. When she was around him, she felt whole. All her life she had felt something was missing, like some part of her was just a little less. Around him, she didn't feel that way, and that drove her crazy. She didn't know him well enough to feel so strongly, but it wasn't just a feeling, it was more tangible.... It was a need.

****

It was late when Morgan pounded the pillow into shape for the umpteenth time. Having worked in the garden most of the afternoon, her shoulders ached. She'd let a hot shower ease the tension in her muscles, put on her softest jersey pajamas, and crawled under the cool covers. She began to drift off when she suddenly sprang up. She felt itchy. *Must be too much sun.* She got up, rubbed the lavender scented lotion up her arms and across the back of her neck and laid back down. She felt as though something was crawling on her skin. She looked down. The hairs were standing up on her arms.

Dorian. The thought slammed into her. She shot out of bed and ran for the door, yanking it open. The hallway was quiet. A dim light filtered up from the kitchen, the one they left on when they went up to bed. She listened. She heard Meesha's soft whine on the other side of Dorian's door. She crept over and reached for the handled. A tingle ran up her arm. She pulled back. Meesha moaned. She reached fast, grabbed the doorknob and turned it, pushing at the door. Meesha sat on the floor facing the bed. Dorian lay on his back, his arms flung across the sheets. The rumpled covers were pushed over the end of the bed. He was wearing pajama bottoms. Morgan caught her breath. Every exposed part of Dorian's skin glowed—a vibrant white-gold. It sparked. Her hair began to dance lightly off her shoulders. A static current filled the air. Perspiration dotted his forehead, sparkling like tiny diamonds in the glow. He moaned. She wasn't sure she could get close to him. At first, as she stepped toward the bed, the current beat at her, pushing her back. Suddenly, it stopped, grabbed her, and tugged her forward. She tried to step back. That wasn't happening. The energy had formed a wall behind her. The force grew, the aura rose higher. She was pulled to the bed. Then, it was as though someone shoved her. She slid across his body. His eyes flew open and he stared at her, unseeing, his eyes a deep sapphire. She pushed back but could only get so far as an arm's reach. He blinked, brought her into focus. He was looking at her mouth. His hands gripped her shoulders. A pulsing force pulled her head toward his. When she opened her mouth to protest, his lips captured hers.

His mouth was hot. The tingling sensation turned into a hot flame that laved her entire body. His tongue swept her mouth and the current flowed one to the other, a slow pulse connecting the two. Slowly, he slid her off him and rose on one elbow. She stared into lust filled eyes.

"This isn't fair," he breathed, his voice deep. "You don't understand."

Morgan let her hand ease up his chest and around his neck. "I don't know that I ever will," she breathed back. "I want you to…" she looked at his mouth and let her tongue slowly lick her bottom lip, "…complete me." She heard his moan as he let her pull his head down to hers. His hands stroked down her body. His mouth followed, spreading liquid fire where his lips touched.

Dorian knew he should stop. Knew he must. The feel of her softness next to him, beneath his hand, was too much. She drew him like a magnet. He grew harder with every beat of his heart. He'd done everything to avoid this, to give her time. He'd lived through hell. The longer she stayed in the house with him, the more impossible it was for him not to want her, to crave her.

He let his hand cup her warm breast, feeling its softness. The peak hardened beneath the teasing touch of his fingers. Her breath hitched. She was his. He could take her, make her his without thought, without guilt.

"Damn," he moaned and pulled away from her. "Morgan, I can't." He sat on the side of the bed. The energy in the room dissipated.

She blinked. It took her a moment to get her brain back in order. He looked as though he was in agony. She let her eyes peruse the length of him. All evidence indicated he wanted her. So, what was the problem? He had a warm, more than willing woman in his bed.

She raised up on her elbows. "Is it another woman? Jasmine?"

He turned back to her. Her hardened nipples thrust against the thin jersey tank she wore. His mouth went dry. He forced himself to look at her face; otherwise, he was lost. Code or no code.

"You don't want me? No, I don't believe that." Her breathing became a little more even. She sat up. "Oh, God, you're not...I mean it's okay if you are," she stammered. "I mean—"

"No, Morgan, I'm not gay." He smiled at her perceived blunder. "Oh, I want you. And there is definitely no one else." He ran his hand through his hair, stood, and walked away from her, looking out the window into the darkened night. He could see the garden almost clearly. A full moon—that explained it. Hell, what was he thinking? That didn't explain it at all. She was the reason. Her. A piece of his puzzle. A perfect fit. But she had no clue. He turned back to her. She sat on the side of the bed, her hands folded neatly in her lap. She looked down, dejected.

He walked back to her and knelt before her, looking up into her beautiful cat eyes. "We haven't covered this part of it, yet. There are things I want you—I need for you—to understand before we have a physical relationship."

She was looking at him with such trust. It was a good thing he was who he was or she would be on her back and him in her in a heartbeat. He wanted her—to complete her, as she put it—in the worst way. Fighting his desire, he took one of her hands, put it to his mouth and kissed the palm. "I don't think we are going back to sleep tonight. Why don't you put on something less revealing—like a suit of armor—and we'll go downstairs. I could use a cup of tea."

Morgan nodded. All she actually wanted was to turn around and crawl back into his bed. It smelled of him. Warm spice. She wanted to wallow in it, with him. Without a word, she stood and walked back into her room and closed the door. What had she been thinking? What had happened tonight? She threw a pair of jeans over her boy shorts and a sweatshirt over her tank, swiped on lip-gloss for good measure, and went to meet him downstairs.

He was letting Meesha out when she walked in. He looked mussed, evidence of their tussle in the bed. There was a darkness about his eyes. Worry lines creased his forehead. She went over and sat, waiting. As he had done so many times, he fixed a pot of tea, put a cozy on it, and brought it to the table to steep. Setting two mugs, with spoons in them, next to the pot, he sat.

For the longest time he looked at her, studied her face. "I don't know exactly where to begin," he said and chuckled. "I feel as though I'm about to tell you about the birds and bees for the first time."

"Trust me, I already know about the birds and the bees." She smiled a devilish smile that went straight to his gut.

"Oh, I'm sure you do," he moaned, feeling his insides tighten. Even her slightest smile went to his groin. "This is more like the wolves and the owls, I should say."

Morgan cocked her head thinking. "I don't understand."

"Animals that mate for life." He heard her quick intake of breath.

"For us, it seems to be a compulsion—to find the one that matches us. Those of the crescent moon. That's what the Abbott House deemed us. The children of the moon. Some such nonsense. They've got a million of them. Sayings for everything."

"I still don't understand. Melissa's letter indicated I had a choice."

"Did she?" he asked.

Morgan concentrated on just what the letter had said. Something to the effect that she was afraid Morgan would choose not to come to Ruthorford, but stay outside.

"Yes, she did."

"Well, I'm sure she was going to go into more detail when you got together. It seems that women of your descent are strongly attracted to men of mine—so much so, in fact, that we have an extremely difficult time staying away from one another when we come within range."

She watched Dorian make that statement matter-of-factly while pouring tea into their mugs. He set hers in front of her and she smelled the sweet scent of clove and orange peel. For fortification, she dumped a huge spoon of sugar in the mug and stirred.

"You make it sound like some kind of rutting season," she huffed. Maybe she was reacting to the realization that that was exactly what it felt like they had been doing since she arrived. In all the years since her puberty, she'd felt incomplete. She wasn't a virgin; she hadn't been for a long time. Yet, she felt like it. Never quite satisfied. She'd had lovers whose technique was superb and she'd responded, as she should. Yet, she was left strangely unsatisfied, wanting them to leave—permanently. That had been her problem with Rob. As handsome and competent as he was, he left her cold. She thought she had a problem with her libido. She looked up at Dorian. Maybe it was time to find out.

He noticed the look in her eye and choked on his tea. "Whoa, girl. I'm not done yet," he laughed.

"Oh." She couldn't help but pout. She looked at him from beneath her lashes and blinked a long slow blink. "Go on." She heard him swallow and had trouble restraining a smile of gratification. At least she wasn't the only one suffering.

"You don't know what you do to me."

It was her turn to swallow. His voice was pure sex.

"When we do come together, we will be bound," he emphasized the last word. "We will be one with the other. We will feed off one another. Need one another. We will be in sync."

"Kayla didn't stay with her mate," Morgan pointed out.

"Kayla isn't like you. She has the crescent but not all the genes. Together they produced Meadow, who does. She will find a match-mate, hopefully. I'm not saying you and I can't be with others. We can. I dated Jasmine for a while. She has the crescent but not the 'vision' genes. If Jasmine and I produced a child, she would be like Meadow or you.

Unfortunately, the pull just wasn't there for me. She wanted it to be but it wasn't. I couldn't help that."

"Rob…" Morgan said softly.

Dorian's eyes hardened. "Yeah. Rob. I don't like him on so many levels."

"Jealous, much?"

"Yes, but that wasn't all. I don't know what it is…" he didn't finish.

"No need to worry. We didn't…how did you put it… match."

"If we do become a pair, as they say at Abbott House, we become so attuned to one another, we develop a form of telepathy. I don't mean you can talk and I'll hear you. Nothing like that. It's more like I'll think something and you'll feel it. You'll know, as though it was you." He studied her a moment, then added, "I think. The truth is I am only repeating what Mel and Thom tried to explain. I've never experienced it. For the most part, I would have sworn Mel and Thom did read each other's mind."

He took a drink of tea. He didn't look up. "It also enhances our abilities."

"I'm not sure what abilities you're talking about." Morgan was still having trouble accepting the enhanced vision and the aura thing.

"The abilities you have and haven't used. Your vision becomes stronger. You can read auras without me touching you. You can push with your mind. Mel used it in healing. Oh yeah, you can heal, somewhat. There's more, I just don't know what they are."

"You are spinning my brain around." Morgan set the cup aside. This conversation was no longer sexy. It was weird. She wasn't ready for weird. She stood. "One more thing…before I call it quits…alone…for the night—what happened tonight. I felt itchy. Then, suddenly, you came to mind and I thought you were in trouble, so I came running. You were glowing. And…well…you know the rest."

He gave her the satisfaction of looking uncomfortable. "I was dreaming." Silence spread between them. "About you."

"Oh… Oh!" Her eyes popped open and she reddened. "Well, goodnight." She turned and fled up the stairs. She heard his low laughter behind her.

Chapter Eleven

"Come on, sleepy head—out of bed!"

Morgan felt the cool air tease her body as the covers slipped away. She squinched up her face and peeked out of one eye. Dorian, fully dressed, and as handsome as ever, was tugging away her covers. She grabbed the end of the comforter in a last ditch effort, only to feel it slowly ease from her grasp. There she lay, cold, curled in a ball, in boy shorts and tank. She felt the weight of the robe land on her.

"It's sunny and bright. We're going exploring. Get dressed. Meet you downstairs in twenty minutes," he called by the doorway. "Oh, might want to wear jeans and bring a light jacket or sweater. Plus," he added, "sneakers—boots, if you have them.

She heard him bound down the stairs, whistle for Meesha, and slam out the back door.

She opened the other eye and looked at the clock. It was a little after nine, which wouldn't have felt so early had she not been awake most of the night. She had lain awake, contemplating all that he'd said. At one point she seriously considered getting up, getting in bed with him, and saying "to hell with it" while letting the cards fall where they may. Fortunately, she had fallen asleep about that time.

So, what was he up to and why was he so damn chipper? She dragged herself off the bed and into the shower. She'd just finished tying her sneakers when he called up the stairs.

"Breakfast is on."

"Be right down," she called back and grabbed her favorite, albeit worn, sweater and tied it around her waist. *Bless Jenn for remembering my sweater.* The aromas drifting up the stairs made her stomach answer in a loud response.

"Sit down," Dorian laughed at her growling stomach, "food's on the table."

Morgan sat down before a feast. Crispy bacon, cooked to perfection, surrounded a sunny yellow omelet with bits of tomato and spinach peeking out and topped with melted cheese. The coffee steamed up from the cup. A variety of muffins sat in a basket between them.

"Wow." She held her plate as he served. "I know you didn't make the muffins."

"Nope, but I made everything else. Eat up; we have a hike ahead of us."

She took a bite. She could get used to this. She eyed him while taking another bite.

He looked up and smiled at her as he shoveled omelet into his mouth. "What?" he said through a mouth full of egg.

"Just what are you up to?"

"Nothing. Really. Well…almost."

She set down her fork, took a sip of coffee and sat back waiting.

He set down his napkin. "I realized you haven't seen all the property. It is half yours, you know. I thought we'd take the day off and explore. I want to show it to you and today is a perfect day for it. I even have our lunch packed in a backpack for us."

"What about the shop?"

Morgan had begun to enjoy the shop. As soon as Dorian had figured out her accounting skills, he had turned a lot of the paperwork over to her. She was surprised at how well the

shop did. The books were in perfect order. The books for the
gift shop were kept separate from the pharmacy.

There were several people who had standing accounts
with the business and not one of them was delinquent. She
did notice that Miss Alice and Miss Grace had asterisks by
their names, as did Mr. Parker and several others, most of
them elderly. She had asked Dorian when she'd had a
moment. He had been working more in his lab since she'd
been there and a whole day could pass before they'd get a
chance to talk. He explained that The Shoppe of Spells had a
tradition of offering discounts for senior citizens and those
less fortunate. Upon examination, she found some of those
discounts were quite steep. Another family, whose account
included baby formulas and such, paid almost nothing.
Dorian explained that the husband had recently passed away
and the mother was trying to keep three children, all under
the age of four, fed and clothed. It turned out she was one of
the young waitresses that had waited on them at the bed and
breakfast. She had thought the young woman looked tired.
Even with all the discounts, The Shoppe of Spells held its
own.

The largest account holders were the bed and breakfast
and John Davis. The Shoppe of Spells supplied a large
amount of herbs to both. She understood the bed and
breakfast, but couldn't quite figure John. There were also
many miscellaneous pharmacy items. It worried her. She
considered the possibility of drug dealing and approached
Dorian about the purchases. Dorian laughed and reassured
her that everything was on the up and up—but would go no
further.

"The Shoppe of Spells is closed for the day. We pretty
much do that around here. Teresa will answer the phones—I
have any calls forwarded. As you've seen, there's a pad of

sticky notes in the mailbox so people can leave messages on the door. If there's an emergency, I have my cell."

He took their empty plates, rinsed them and loaded the dishwasher, then grabbed the backpack and headed out back. Meesha waited on the back steps. Dorian locked the back door, a rarity, and headed toward the back of the cottage. Morgan remembered the gate behind it. She followed, curious now. He held open the gate and Meesha dashed through. Morgan stepped through and stopped, causing Dorian to slam into her.

"You gotta stop that." He pushed her ahead.

She couldn't move. Before her lay a panorama of hills, meadows, trees, flowers, and a stream ribboning its way across the back. A field of lavender perfumed the air. She turned and stared at Dorian, dumbfounded.

"Your mouth is hanging open," he teased. He pointed to the stream. "That's the same stream that runs behind the bed and breakfast, down by the willows," he commented. "I don't know if you remember, but when you came into town, you crossed a bridge."

"I remember. It had that welcome sign encircled by morning glory."

"That's the one. Well, the stream flows under it. It encircles three sides of Ruthorford. There's a bridge on the other end of town as well. It's a bit farther out. But it crosses our property here."

She looked excited. "Our property? All this is our property?" Her eyes widened.

"Yep. Over thirty acres. Come on." Dorian led her down a path that was well worn.

"I can see you've come this way before," she mused and followed him. His pleasure was contagious.

He just smiled and pointed. It took a moment for Morgan to see the doe and her two yearlings standing on the other side of the lavender meadow, just inside the trees. Having caught a hint of their scent, the doe turned and led her little ones deeper into the woods. Quickly, they disappeared from sight.

She swung her arm. "This is why lavender is so prevalent." She inhaled and let her senses absorb the beauty before her.

Dorian led her down the side of the field, then followed a path that meandered into the trees. The path steepened. More granite popped up between the trees. She looked around. Pines, maple, poplar, oak. Dogwoods were tucked under the taller trees. The trees thinned on one side as they stepped onto a slope of granite. He led her across it, then down the side. She heard the trickling of water. Twenty-five feet away from her, water streamed down a granite slope and fell into a rock pool, carved out by eons of cascading water.

Dorian led her around the pool, jumping over the tiny creek and moving around the side of an ivy covered slope. He stopped in front of an opening. If he hadn't stopped, she would have walked right past it.

He led her inside the cave. About twenty feet in, the passage narrowed and darkened. "I know you can see in here, but I need some light." He took out a pin-light.

He was right. Morgan's eyes adjusted quickly. She could see fine. Funny, that had never occurred to her. She thought everyone could see in the dark.

She followed him along the passageway. The walls here were damp but smelled fresh. Another twenty feet or so and it looked like they'd come to a dead end. Dorian disappeared to the left. It opened into a stone cavern. A pool with glistening blue-green water occupied the middle.

He had stopped and turned to watch her expression. Her face lit with surprise; her eyes glistening like the water behind him. He took her hand and led her around the pool to a raised area of stone. He put his hands on her waist and lifted her easily until she sat on the edge. He pulled himself up and sat beside her. "Welcome to my grotto."

She looked at the shimmering water in front of her. In places, the walls sparkled like diamonds. She had never seen anything like it. Morgan turned and flung her arms around him.

"Thank you. I never…it's so…there aren't words…"

He hugged her back. As she pulled away, he pushed her hair from her shoulder, leaving his hand cupping the back of her neck. The warmth of his hand and the energy he emitted moved down her spine. She closed her eyes in pleasure. She felt his mouth move on hers, asking. Her lips parted in answer. Their lips melted into one another; their tongues explored. The tingling quickly changed to a pulse. He slowly pulled back.

"Look," he whispered and gently turned her head with his hand.

The grotto had come alive. Stones and crystals embedded in the walls glowed as they hadn't before. The water seemed to vibrate, tiny sparks dancing across the surface. Little balls of mist floated above the surface, like faeries in flight.

"What? How? I don't understand." She looked at his now deep blue eyes, the desire molten in them.

"It's us. We did that." He let his hand run down her back.

They sat silently, watching the image change as they calmed down. When all was back to normal, she turned to him. "I've got to ask. Just how did you know? And with whom?"

He laughed loud and hard and fell back on his elbows, looking up at the ceiling. The black curl that so often escaped, caressing his forehead. "It's not like you're thinking. Not that a pubescent boy wouldn't have liked that," he said, memories carrying him back. "I was about thirteen at the time. Mel and

Thom had gone for a picnic lunch, leaving me in charge of the shop. I was so proud. I felt like such a man." He turned on his side looking at her, devouring her with his eyes. "Miss Alice fell off of a ladder, trimming back some wisteria. Miss Grace ran to the shop to get Thom and Mel. She was almost hysterical when she saw they weren't in the shop. I sent her to get Bill Ruthorford and I ran for Mel and Thom. I knew about the grotto. They'd brought me swimming as a kid. I ran as fast as I could. I ran right into a scene out of a fantasy. They were in the pool, entwined. They heard me. I was so entranced with the scene around me I couldn't speak. Thom brought me out of my stupor long enough to tell them about Miss Alice. He sent me back to stay with Miss Grace. I snuck back the next day. It didn't look anything like it had when they were together."

Morgan looked down. He had begun playing with the fingers of the hand that she was leaning on. He had such beautiful hands. Their eyes met.

"Needless to say, I got a lesson in the birds and the bees shortly thereafter. At least our version of it."

The tension between them was palpable. The stones began to glow.

Morgan felt lust and need move through her body. She felt her breasts swell and become sensitive. She began to throb and thought if he kept looking into her eyes, she would orgasm from the current of energy moving through her enflamed body.

His voice was deeper when he spoke. "I wanted to show you how different we are. Other people make love, we change the environment."

"Dorian," she murmured, her voice husky with need, "…shut-up."

"Morgan, be sure," he whispered inches from her mouth.

"I am," she said and took his mouth with hers.

It felt right. For the first time in her life, Morgan had no reservations about offering herself to a man.

Dorian slowly peeled her clothes away, one piece at a time. The air was charged with their desire, the mist dancing. As the last piece of clothing fell away, he stopped and looked at her. She was perfection. Her long, red hair curled across her shoulders and breasts—her dusky pink nipples hardening under his gaze. Her waist tapered and her hips flared, joining with the longest legs he had ever seen. Her skin was flawless, except for the small crescent moon on her hip. He ran his hand over it. It warmed under his touch. She arched.

Morgan felt wanton. She had always been so private, so shy. Yet, here she lay before this man, who was about to become her lover, and she felt completely free, completely open. She looked into his eyes.

Dorian's intake of breath was enough to tell her that her eyes had changed, yet he wasn't moving away from her, but coming closer. They watched one another as their lips met, clung, until her eyes closed with pleasure. She felt the heat of his tongue and the graze of his teeth down her body.

He suckled the hardened nipple until she groaned. His hands, barely touching her, sent tingles everywhere he moved. The current ran hotter and hotter.

She couldn't get enough of him. Her hands explored his body as though he were a sculpture yet to be formed under her care.

Her caress left him weak.

Morgan felt like she was on an altar, a sacrifice to a god of love. Slowly, he entered her, his deep blue eyes enslaving her gaze. He began to move. The air swirled around them caressing them with warm, damp tendrils. He took her hands in his, locking their fingers, raising them above her head. She could feel the current moving from him to her and back. The more excited they became, the faster the current flowed, wrapping them in a pulsating blanket. His look held hers and he breathed, "We are one." Simultaneous orgasms ripped through them.

As her breathing returned to normal, her eyes fluttered open. He was lying on his side, his head resting on his hand, watching her. She glanced over his shoulder and sat up. The whole cavern had taken on an amethyst hue. His fingers traced down her side.

Then, he sat up and jumped down from the formation. Holding out his hand, he laughed, "Come, my grotto nymph, unto the waters."

Morgan took his hand and followed him. Several rocks jutted out forming steps and they stepped down, walking until they were waist deep—his waist, her breast—in water. The water was warm and felt like it fizzled.

"I thought it would be cold, being fed by a spring." She let her hand float across the surface. "It's like swimming in a giant fizzy," she laughed, then lay back in the water and floated.

The color had returned to the brilliant blue green. The rocks sparkled.

"It's so beautiful here," she sighed and let the bubbles break against her skin.

"No, you're what's beautiful," he said, his eyes devouring her body.

Time slipped away. They played. They made love. They explored one another and the cave. They ate lunch, sitting naked on a blanket in their own private world. He showed her how he could throw electric balls of light, having them burst against the walls. He held his hands up, moving them slowly down, and she felt them glide down her body, stroking her, even though he stood five feet away.

When they had dressed and were ready to head back, Morgan took one last look. She wanted to memorized every feature, every nuance. Her body felt languid and had that pleasant ache of being well loved.

"We'll be back."

"I know. It's just that this was so special."

He leaned in and kissed her. They clasped hands and began the trek back.

Meesha came dashing across the meadow. Bounding, leaping through the lavender, she yapped and danced around them as though they'd been gone a year. Dorian knelt, ruffling her fur. "We haven't been gone that long. You didn't starve."

She circled around them, sat back and cocked her head. Then, she went first to Dorian, licked his hand, then to Morgan, giving her the same attention.

"I guess it's official," he laughed, "we're a couple."

Morgan laughed, "Well, as long as she approves."

As they approached the back gate, Meesha stopped, her fur hackled, and she growled a low, warning growl. Dorian threw open the gate and rushed inside. Everything looked normal. He flew up the steps to the shop, started to unlock the door when he noticed Meesha wasn't staring at the shop, but the cottage.

"Damn," he exclaimed and ran back to the cottage. Although the door was closed, it was obvious the lock had been jimmied. He pushed the door open with his foot. It creaked.

Morgan grabbed his arm. It was warm to the touch and she felt his energy heighten. "Be careful," she whispered.

"I think they're long gone."

She could see the frustration in his expression. He pushed the door open the rest of the way and Meesha dashed inside. "If someone was here, we'd know it."

They followed the dog into the cottage. It was in shambles. Cushions on the floor, the bed tossed. Morgan looked around. "What were they after?"

"They got what they came for..." he frowned and went to the mantel.

The beautiful stones were gone. Morgan looked at the window. It, too, had been cleared of stones and rocks. She walked into the bedroom and the bathroom. Every last one of the crystals was gone.

"We better call the police." Morgan looked more closely. The braided rug, which had lain in front of the French doors to the bedroom, the one they'd stood on the first day they opened the portal, was gone. Dorian moaned.

"Oh, Dorian, I am so sorry."

"It was made generations ago, by a woman who fled here after being accused of witchcraft. Hence, The Shoppe of Spells. This was the one place that understood that what she did was not evil. She actually wove tiny fragments of crystals and stones into the rug. There's no other like it."

After one more trip about the cottage, taking note of what was missing, Dorian held the door for her, then closed it behind him. The lock was broken, but he laid his hand above the latch, his hand shimmered, and she heard the door tighten.

"Nice trick," she murmured.

"Too bad I didn't think of it earlier. I don't understand. I've never needed it before."

"Let's call the police."

"No. We need to call Bask."

He unlocked the shop door and walked inside, half expecting it, too, to be torn apart. Luckily, nothing had been touched. He went to his lab, opened the door, flicked on the lights, and looked around. His equipment was intact; his mortar and pestles were just as he's left them. He closed the door, pulled out his phone, and hit speed-dial. The conversation was quick.

"Someone's coming," he said and put the backpack down. He ran his hand through his hair. It was a habit, Morgan realized, one he did when he was stressed. The black wave of hair slid across his brow.

Morgan didn't know what to do. She knew he had been through so much, and now, to lose personal items of such meaning... She went in the kitchen and started the water for some tea, fed Meesha, whom, she figured, would be a better guard dog with food in her tummy, and unpacked the backpack.

"Who would do this? Why?" Morgan asked.

"I don't know anyone stupid enough—" He stopped cold, reading the sticky notes he'd taken off the front door. He turned to her, fury in his expression.

"What?"

"We would have found them eventually," he stated, his voice cold, "all we needed was a place to start. And I have that." He slammed the papers into her hands.

Confused, Morgan read the sticky notes. One was from Ms. Alice. *Just wanted to let you know I ran into that handsome blond gentleman. He said he tried the back. I told him "this" was how we contacted you. Oh, we left you a pie at Teresa's, if there's any left. Miss A.*

"Handsome blond gentleman?" Morgan read aloud.

"Oh, come on, Morgan," he paced in front of her, "what blond gentlemen might one of those two old women meet either here or at Teresa's?"

"Rob." His name came out in a slow breath. "But, what would he be doing—"

"Stealing from the shop?" he asked, his anger palpable. "I don't know, Morgan. You tell me."

"Now wait a minute. I had no idea." Realization struck. He was as much as accusing her of conspiring with Rob. She wasn't going to take it. She spun and marched toward the kitchen, stopped and spun back around, hands on hips. "Just what do you think I did? I wasn't the one who pulled someone out of bed this morning to go on a hike. I wasn't the one who left it unprotected. I have no idea what Rob is up to. What would a professor want with a bunch of rocks and a rug?" She turned and went into the kitchen slamming mugs on the counter as she fixed tea—for both of them. This was stupid. He was upset. She would have to be the bigger person here. She carried the mugs over to the table. "Come," she ordered. "Sit down. We'll figure this out."

Dorian sat down, took her hand and held tight when she tried to pull away.

"This is me saying I'm sorry." He pulled her hand to his mouth and kissed her palm. She felt the heat to her core.

She wiggled in her chair, hoping he wouldn't notice, and gently took back her hand. "Let's think this through. Why would he rob you?"

"Us," he corrected.

"Us," she amended. "I still don't get it. What could Rob want with those stones?"

"What does he teach?"

"College physics."

He looked at her. "Morgan, we have our own team of physicists at Abbott House."

"Yes, but…" she hesitated, "I met him at the bookstore. He wanted to order…" she thought for a moment. A frown creased her forehead. She closed her eyes and said, "…some books on Indian Folklore." Her shoulders slumped. She'd been used. But how? *She* hadn't even known her connection to The Shoppe of Spells until recently. It couldn't be.

"It could have been coincidental," Dorian laid his hand over hers. "Some of the stories talk about an 'emerald-eyed maiden.' He may have just lucked out finding you and kept watch."

"Well, that would explain his anger when I didn't want to see him anymore."

"And his appearance here, which led him to the stones, the rug…" his voice trailed off.

"Oh God, Dorian, I led him right to them."

"You had no idea. We'll get them back."

"What does he want with them?"

Dorian got up. He seemed to be concentrating on something. He turned to her. "I would say, off hand, that he, being a physicist, has some inkling of the portals. Maybe he's figured out something and is trying to recreate it." He watched her frown. "Or, he's a lousy scumbag who wants some precious gems."

She looked up. "How precious?"

"Well, the rug itself has fragments of red beryl, amethyst, taaffeite, benitoite, and painite."

"I've never heard of most of them."

"That's because they are all very rare. We still don't know how the woman who wove them into the rug came by them, but not many know about the rug. Mostly, Abbott House."

"So, it's worth a fortune."

"I don't know. Never thought about it." He pushed away from the counter and returned to the table. "Most people wouldn't touch it. There's a spell on it."

"I thought you said—"

At the look on her face, he couldn't resist—he walked over and kissed her hard. When he finally pulled away, they were both breathing a lot faster. "I said that we don't do spells much anymore." He grinned. "Doesn't mean it wasn't done or can't be done."

"The stones are charged. They leave a marker. You and I, especially now," he raised an eyebrow, "can detect the markers."

"We can?" She realized she was leaning into him again and sat back.

"Unfortunately, we better be ready to grab the damn thing, cause it's gonna glow."

"Oh…" she trailed out the word, remembering the rug's twinkle when she stood on it.

Her next comment was cut off by a knock at the front door. Dorian got up and walked into the next room. Morgan listened but didn't recognize the voice. Dorian came in, followed by a woman. She wore a shirtwaist dress and flats, carried an oversized purse and could have been anyone's grandmother. When she smiled, her whole face lit. She took Morgan's hand, not waiting for introductions. "Hi. I'm Jane Barnes. I'm from Abbott House."

Morgan stood, took her hand and exchanged a firm handgrip. A woman of substance, Morgan thought to herself. "Tea?"

"Sure, don't mind if I do."

Morgan listened as they talked. Not letting appearance belie capability, Morgan soon learned that Jane was one of Abbott House's security administrators. In that oversized bag, she withdrew several folders, and out of one of the folders, several pictures of the rug. They'd been taken at various times over the years, the earliest being from the 1800's. There were also some copies of detailed drawings of the rug, probably dating back many years prior to the photographs. Dorian stepped into his lab and returned with a list of all of the rocks and crystals in the cottage. It soon became apparent that nothing about that cottage was haphazard, no matter how quaint it looked.

He also filled Jane in on their speculations regarding Rob, all the while watching Morgan.

Feeling uncomfortable under his scrutiny, Morgan gave the addresses and phone numbers she had on Rob—at least the one's she'd used the last time she'd had contact with him. She hoped this would dispel any lingering doubt Dorian might have about her. It bothered her that, especially after the time in the cavern, he was so quick to doubt her.

Jane stood. "Now, I'd like to see the cottage. You haven't moved anything, have you?"

"No. Locked and sealed."

"Good." Her voice was clipped as she dug around in her oversized purse, pulling out what appeared to be a very fancy camera. "Let's go have a look, shall we?"

"I'll think I'll stay here, if you don't mind. I have a slight headache. I think I'll go lie down."

Dorian looked torn.

"Go ahead. I'll be fine. Just give me a few minutes."

His side-glance at her cell phone answered the question running around in her mind. He still didn't trust her. Her heart ached. Leaving it on the table, she rose. "Here, you keep it." Her voice was flat. She forced herself move slowly up the stairs and not look back. Tears stung her eyes. She blinked them back. She'd be damned if she'd show any emotion. She heard him call her name but didn't answer or look back, hurt and fury blinding her.

Morgan slumped on the side of the bed. What made her think sex would make things better? Some sort of romantic notion she had. Did she expect him to feel the way she did? Everything had happened so fast. She pushed herself up and walk to the back window, watching them enter the cottage. He glanced back at the shop, right at her, but his expression was unreadable. She felt an ache deep inside. She needed time to think. Time away from this place, away from him.

The weight of the world on her shoulders, she picked up the bedroom phone and dialed.

"Mom?" she tried to keep the pain out of her voice when her mother's happy voice answered the phone.

"Morgan, I was just thinking about you. How are you, honey?

Morgan heard the slight hitch in her own voice. "I'm homesick, Mom. I miss you guys so much."

"We miss you, too." Morgan heard her mother's voice quiver in return. "Any idea when you might make it home?"

"I'm thinking of taking a break and coming now. I haven't made reservations yet—"

"Oh Morgan, that's great!" Her mother's excitement dampened any doubt.

She laughed. God, she missed them—their all-encompassing love. Her heart lightened. "I'll make arrangements and let you know when I get home. It'll probably be late, so don't wait up. I'll call you in the morning."

"Just come over for breakfast. Or, whenever you get up."

"Give Dad my love. I'll see you guys tomorrow."

As she hung up, Morgan realized her spirits had risen. She had enjoyed her time here, and, yes, she knew she would return, but going back to the happiness she felt in the arms of her family was the balm she needed.

Her family. Morgan looked around the room. The room of her birth parents. Strangers. She had no concept of their capacity for love. Dorian had obviously loved them and they, him. She wondered how they would have felt about her. She didn't know and didn't care. Morgan appreciated the fact that she had grown up the way she wanted to grow up. Sure, this was to become her life, but it wasn't who she was. Her essence. The Briscoes, with their love and kindness, trust and understanding, had imbued her with that.

She'd finished packing, had reservations for a flight and a cab on the way, when she heard Dorian on the stairs. The door to her room was cracked, so, when he knocked, the door slipped open. He stepped in and glanced from the suitcase to her.

Her fingers trembled. Trying not to show her raw emotions, she pulled a band off her wrist and pulled her hair back into a ponytail. Her eyes refused to meet his, but in a surprisingly calm voice she asked, "Did she get all the information she needed?"

"Yes." His voice was low as he stepped toward her. "Going somewhere?"

Then she looked at him. She let him see the doubt in her eyes. "Yes, Dorian. I'm going home to see my parents."

"But—"

With fingers to his lips, she silenced him. "I want to see them. No...I need to see them. I miss them more than you could know." She turned away at the pain she saw in his expression, as he looked around the room.

"I'm sorry, Dorian. I know you miss Mel and Thom desperately. We've had a tumultuous start, to say the least. I know I have to come back. I just need a break. So do you."

"I was angry," he whispered. "I didn't think."

"No, you didn't. And, you hurt me deeply. Now, I need time to think."

They both heard the knock on the front door and turned.

"That's my cab," she said and started to lift her suitcase. He took it out of her hands. They went down the stairs in silence. Meesha sat in the kitchen whining. At first, Morgan thought of the creature, then saw the thumb of the tail and stepped into the kitchen while Dorian took her bag to the cab. She picked up her phone, as she'd left it, on the table.

"That's a good girl." She smoothed the soft fur, her voice thick. "I'm going to miss you. I'll be back." Meesha gave a soft woof in response and licked her hand.

As she climbed into the cab, she looked up at Dorian. "Just to ease your mind, in case you're wondering, I won't be contacting Rob." She pulled the door closed and faced forward, not giving him a chance to respond. She was halfway to the airport before she let the tears fall.

Chapter Twelve

Dorian was still slamming around the shop, shocking himself from pent-up energy when Teresa knocked on the front door. He flung it open.

"Geesh, news travels fast," he hissed.

"Small towns, gotta love 'em." She marched past him and into the kitchen, setting a box on the counter. "Dinner. I figured you wouldn't do it yourself, so…" she poured herself some coffee, sniffed it, poured it in the sink and turned on the faucet.

"Look, Teresa. I appreciate what you're trying to do—"

She turned around to him and held up her hand. "Don't you even," she began and stopped, fire in her eyes. "I'll fix the coffee, we'll sit down, you'll eat, and we'll talk."

He shrugged and went to sit at the table. Hell, she'd been bossing him around since he could remember and was the closest thing to an aunt that he'd ever had. But, he didn't want to talk with anyone. Not right now. He was hurting and he was angry, and he didn't know which was the stronger. Nevertheless, Teresa wasn't going away, so he caved.

Coffee brewing, she fixed a plate and brought the pasta dish over and set in front of him. She went back, grabbed the crusty, small rolls, and returned to the table, briefly touching his shoulder before she sat across from him.

"You're as close to a son as I'm going to get, so deal." She smiled at him.

Pouting, he picked at his food. She watched the handsome, strong man and burst out laughing. He looked up and couldn't help but smile in return.

"That's better. Why did she leave?"

He glared at her.

"Hey, she left in broad daylight, on Main Street. Word travels. What can I say?"

"I pretty much accused her of being in cahoots with Rob on the robbery."

She frowned. Took a sip of her coffee and studied the cup before carefully setting it down. "I know about the robbery because Jane Barnes stopped by for something to eat before heading back. In fact, she was still in town when Morgan left. She thinks you're wrong about Morgan, by the way."

He flung down his napkin, stormed over to the counter and poured more coffee. "I don't think I ever really thought... I just started thinking of that pompous...and having been so bitter in the beginning, before she arrived..." Disjointed thoughts flowed from his mouth.

Teresa watched him and felt such sorrow. Bask had gotten her to come with him when he'd told Dorian that Melissa and Thomas had been killed. He was a basket case for two days; there was no other way to put it. She remembered walking into the shop, seeing him smile up from the register as she shut the door and turned the closed sign over. She'd watch his face drain of color and heard the low moan that escaped him as he sat on the stool behind the counter, torn with grief. She'd held him as his body shook with sobs of grief.

For two days, he'd sat in the master bedroom, on the floor by the bed, with Meesha refusing to leave him. It was a good thing she'd had a key. It took a lot of coaxing to get Meesha to leave his side and then she'd only run outside and come straight back in and up the stairs to lay her head on his lap. It had taken her goading him with guilt over his neglect of his faithful dog that'd finally brought him out of his state. His energy had been down, depleted. She could feel it. She gathered the lodestones kept in the lab and brought them to the bedroom, shoving them into his hands. He stared at them blindly, then at her. She nodded once, then left.

When Dorian reappeared, he seemed better. He kissed her on the cheek, ate what she put before him and took care of Meesha. When the cremated remains had arrived, he had taken charge of the urns. To this day, Teresa didn't know if he still had them or he'd interred them somewhere. She didn't ask. She knew, wherever they were, they were together.

She studied him now as he stood, drinking his coffee, looking past her, out the window, his mind a million miles away. Actually, more like five hundred. She would bet that his thoughts were on Morgan, heading to Virginia and away from him. She studied him closer.

"Dorian, you slept with her." She made it a statement. Watching him, there was no question in her mind.

His body shifted. He didn't speak.

"Son, do you know exactly where she's gone?"

His voice was soft, far away, "Doesn't matter. I can find her. I'll always be able to find her." It was no more than a whisper.

Her breath rushed out. "You're paired," came out as a gasp.

Finally, he moved his eyes from the scene beyond the window to meet hers but said nothing.

"Damn it, Dorian. Does she know?" She was on her feet coming toward him. For a moment, he saw Melissa in her. The way she moved. Her unbridled personality. He almost smiled. He set down the cup and waited until she was directly in front of him. He could feel the anger and concern vibrate off her. She almost shook with it. He took her by the arms and drew off some of the energy to calm her. She pulled away. "Don't do that," she hissed.

"I just don't want you having a stroke," he said low-key, a tinge of humor in his voice.

She smacked him in the arm. Not bad for a five-foot-three ball of fire. Not bad at all considering the energy he'd drawn off her. He rubbed his arm.

"Don't you doubt for one moment I won't take you in hand." She put her hands on her hips and stared up at him, fury in her amber eyes.

Part of him wanted to rise to his full height in a childish attempt at rebellion, but he knew that it was just that, childish. It wasn't her fault. She had every right to be angry. Instead, he let out a breath and walked to the back door to let Meesha in.

"Sit down, Teresa. I'll explain."

She marched back to the table and sat, ramrod straight, like an angry schoolmarm.

"I was going to tell her today. I mean..." A red flush crept up his neck.

"Go on," she urged.

"We went to the grotto for a picnic. I was trying to explain things then. Things got out of control."

"You think?" Sarcasm dripped from her mouth.

He sighed. "You know how strong attraction can be." It was her turn to blush. He knew about Bill. He went on. "I've been fighting it all along. But when she started..." again, he faltered. "I asked her if she was sure." He shook his head, knowing she was going to protest. "I know. I should have been stronger. The male in me figured she was here to stay anyway and eventually... I thought we'd have dinner. I'd explain the pairing." He slammed his fist on the table. "God damn, Rob!"

"Don't blame him. You acted like a lunkhead and she went home. About right?"

He nodded. "I know it's a long way, but I can probably ease the pull for her, without her knowing."

"Yeah," she sat back, "and who's gonna do the same for you?"

"I'm strong. I can handle it."

"Sure." She stretched out the word. "I remember Mel and Thom tried that—and they were prepared, mentally, emotionally and 'magically'—she made quote marks in the air—it lasted all of a week and they were miserable. Poor Morgan has no idea what's going to happen to her or what's causing it. You might want to think about going after her."

"Oh, I am." He looked up suddenly. "I'm not a complete ass."

"Jury's still out on that one, boyo."

He ignored her. "I just want to give her time to see her folks first. She really misses them."

Their phones rang simultaneously. As Teresa pulled her phone out of her pocket, she saw the expression of hope on Dorian's face fade to disappointment as he looked at his. She got up and walked into the other room. She listened for a few moments and hung up, turned around and waited for him to finish his call. When he did, she spoke.

"I'm sorry, Dorian, we have another problem. Jasmine's missing. She never came home. She was due in several days ago. The girls watching the boutique didn't want to cause problems for her so they kept it quiet, thinking she was on one of her 'larks', as they put it." She took a deep breath. "I don't like this."

"Well, here's more good news. That was Jane Barnes. She found out that Rob quit the university months ago. He's moved out of his place and left no forwarding address. Pretty much disappeared off the radar screen."

"Do you think they're together?"

"I want to say yes, but I don't have a clue. However, if Rob has the stones, you can bet I'll find them—and him. If Jasmine so much as—"

She cut him off. "Jasmine's headstrong, self-centered, and willful, but she wouldn't do anything that would endanger her community or her family. That includes you, Dorian."

"Even if she's jealous?" He'd lived around Jasmine all of her life and knew she could be vindictive, but Teresa was right—she wouldn't do something to harm Ruthorford. She loved it as much as anyone did.

"Besides, I saw her and Rob at dinner. She flirted. She was Jasmine. However, about ten, she left and went home. Rob went upstairs and he left the next day, without seeing her again. She didn't leave town until the next week. Plus, that vacation was planned. It had been for months."

Dorian didn't like the recent developments. Rob missing. Jasmine missing. Suddenly, he was up and moving toward the counter in the shop. He pulled out a file folder from underneath, scanned through a couple of pages, found what he was looking for and looked up at Teresa, who had followed him into the room. "I'm going to let you handle Jasmine for now. See what you can find out. Call John, he's a PI. Get him on it. Call Bask." He smiled and shook his head. "Poor Bask. He hasn't seen this much excitement…" The words trailed off, his smile gone.

Teresa patted his arm. "Since I ran off with Bill?" She urged him to happier thoughts.

"Yeah, that." He appreciated her caring. "I'm calling Morgan's parents, give them a head's up. I don't want Morgan getting any surprises."

"You got it, sweetie," she said as she walked to the door. "Call me later. That's an order." She blew him a kiss and was out the door, heading across the street to the boutique.

The phone call to Morgan's parents went better than he'd expected. For some reason, he'd figured she'd cried on their shoulder. She hadn't. At least not about him. They were friendly and open, had put him on speaker so they could both talk to him. Morgan's Dad was livid when Dorian suggested the possibility of Rob being connected to the thefts. Dorian said nothing of Jasmine, since they didn't know her. He emphasized that he wasn't trying to pry or take time away from them but wanted Morgan aware of what was happening. He ended asking them to have her call him, if they would.

After hanging up the phones, and separated by 500 miles, both men commented, "That went well."

Chapter Thirteen

Morgan pulled off the sunglasses and laid them on the kitchen counter. She'd hastily purchased them at the airport to avoid the stares. Being in Ruthorford had afforded her the luxury of familiarity. She'd forgotten what the flagrant stares and comments from strangers felt like. Suddenly, once again, she'd become an oddity. She'd felt herself withdraw, falling back on old patterns, pulling her bangs over her eyes and looking down. At the first kiosk she'd come to, she'd plunked down twenty dollars for the first pair of sunglasses she'd picked up, and had joined the anonymity of the masses.

She looked around. After the shop and the cottage, her apartment, which had been home for four years, felt barren. Of course, Mrs. T not being there to greet her opened a void in her heart as well. Maybe she'd go see how she was getting along. The place felt so empty. She stepped out onto the balcony. Her mom and dad had taken good care of her plants and they thrived. There were so few. She reached down and grabbed a tiny weed, just poking its head through the soil. The dill had gone to seed. She would have to replace it. A wave of sadness washed over her. She thought of all the plants in the garden at Ruthorford. Maybe she could take these back with her. A slight chill swirled around her. She shivered and glanced around for a violet outline. Seeing nothing, she realized that, up here, fall had arrived. She rubbed her hands up her arms and went inside, pulling the obstinate door in place.

Morgan wandered through the rest of the place, flicking on lights, resetting the thermostat. When she got to the kitchen, she pulled open the refrigerator door. A box sat on the shelf, a note taped to the top.

Sweetheart—I picked this up at the bakery today. Just a few seconds in the microwave should do it. Love, Mom

She grabbed the box. Her heart twisted. However, when she opened the lid, the sugar-dusted confections Dorian had teased her with weren't nestled in Teresa's special paper. A single bear-claw, a favorite since childhood, sat alone in the plain box. A tear trickled down her cheek. She gently put the box back in the refrigerator.

She went to her purse and pulled out the cell phone. After two delays at the airport, it was too late to call her parents, or anyone else for that matter. She hit the buttons. No new messages. Carrying the phone, she lugged the suitcase back to her bedroom and hefted it onto the bed. Setting the phone next to the bed, she started pulling clothes out of her suitcase. As she reached the bottom, the light seersucker robe appeared. She hung it neatly in the closet, grabbed a nightshirt, and stripped. Naked, she walked into the bathroom and started the shower. As she turned back to the sink, a tiny light winked in the mirror. Startled, she looked up to see the eyes of the owl catching the light. Her fingers brushed over it before she unclasped the fastener and laid it on the counter. It seemed to watch her. She reached out and touched it once more before stepping into the shower.

She inhaled. Basil and citrus rose in the steam. Not the lush lavender to which she had become accustomed. She felt a tug at her heart. Upset that she was becoming morose, she lathered and scrubbed until her skin tingled. Similar to what she felt when Dorian...*oh, good God.* She turned off the water and dried herself and her hair, put the necklace around her neck, and went back into the bedroom, only to stare at the small, plain, very empty bed. She had hoped that tonight they would share a bed. Morgan pulled the nightshirt over her head and snuggled into the bed, trying to grasp a vague scent of lavender, the shop, or Dorian, as an exhausted sleep overcame her.

Morgan followed the path to the grotto. She didn't remember it winding so, or it being so long. It was darker than she remembered. Why wasn't Dorian's light in front of her? She felt the slight tingle at her back. Somehow, he had gotten behind her. That was okay. She smiled to herself. She could see in the dark. She would lead him this time. When she came to where the wall abutted, she turned to the left—and ran into a stone face. She stepped back. Reaching out, she felt the cold stones, following them back around. The bend was to the right. She turned and moved forward. The path continued to wind and seemed to take her down an incline. Then, the path narrowed, barely letting one pass, never two. She stubbed her toe on loose stone and realized she was barefoot. She looked down. She was wearing a nightshirt. When she looked up the path was opening to a large cavern. She listened for the sound of water. Nothing. She looked for the mist faeries. It was still dark. The tingling ran up her spine. This time it felt different. Sharper. Almost painful. She stepped away, careful that she not fall into the pool. She eased her feet forward slowly until she was in the middle of the room. She should be in the middle of the pool, except there was no pool. Morgan felt the current of his fingers run up her arms. She stilled. The current began to pulse. The room lightened. The colors were grey green, the glow putrid. She shivered. The pulse beat at her. What was he doing? She turned and large violet eyes stared into hers.

Morgan bounded up, hauling deep gulps of air into her lungs. Perspiration ran down her face and between her breasts. She turned on the light and blinked to adjust. She scanned the room. Nothing. It was a dream. She was in her own bed, in her own apartment. But, that...that thing. It was huge. It had to be as big as she was. Was it a Gulatega? In her dreams, it had never appeared so large. Evil. It felt evil. In her dreams, she'd been frightened, but because it was unknown. The dream in itself had never felt evil—until now.

She pushed herself off the bed, trudged into the bathroom and turned on the lights. Her face was flushed. Her skin glowed pink, as though she'd been sunburned. She felt her forehead. Was she coming down with a fever? Definitely clammy, but no fever. Just to be on the safe side, she grabbed a couple of acetaminophen and washed them down with cold water from the tap. As she closed the medicine cabinet door, her eyes reflected back at her in the mirror. They had deepened to a dark green, almost black. She dropped the plastic cup. It rolled around inside the edge of the bowl before settling over the drain. She blinked. Slowly her eyes returned to their brilliant emerald shade. She returned to bed but lay staring into the lighted room until day broke. She got up grateful not to have fallen asleep again.

Knowing Jenn would be up and about, Morgan went in search of her phone. She was exhausted. How Jenn could go on so little sleep baffled her. Somehow, she did and it worked.

"Wow, I was just thinking about you." Jenn's jovial greeting never failed to make her smile.

"I'm in town," Morgan stated simply. It was met with silence.

"I got in last night."

"You want to tell me what's going on?" Jenn's voice was low, careful.

"Yeah, I do, but not over the phone. I needed to get away for a while."

"How far away?" Jenn's voice sounded more chipper. "Why?"

"Well, I was just looking at my schedule. With Meadow doing so well, I was thinking of coming down to see you. But, since you're here...how about..." she drew it out, "we get away for a girls vacation? Spend some time together. Really catch up."

"Really? You mean it?" It had been years since they'd done that. One or the other was always working. They had such fun together. It would give her a chance to fill Jenn in and maybe, just maybe, work out her thoughts and feelings about Dorian, and everything else, at the same time.

"Yep. I just *inked* you in. Not penciled, mind you, but with indelible ink."

"Well, I'll repack," Morgan found herself laughing. "I'm going over to my parent's for breakfast, and then I'll meet you at your place, say, around eleven. Will that do?"

"Don't you want to know where we're going?"

"Nope. Surprise me," she said and ended the call laughing.

****

As Morgan wound down the curving driveway to the home she'd grown up in, she felt a sense of relief, of welcome. This remained familiar. Nestled on two acres in the rolling hills just outside Williamsburg, the house was the classic Williamsburg cottage—a gabled, deep roofed, white clapboard, with twin brick fireplaces hugging either end. Built just after the Civil War, its bones were good. Her parents had covered the front steps with a small porch when she was in her teens. Her mother had complained about getting rain in the house for years. They'd studied many historical designs and finally found one in keeping with the classic architecture. They even had the classic picket fence and the customary garden in the back. Funny, Morgan thought, the garden had a similarity to the one behind the shop.

She climbed out of the car and looked over at the house. Her upstairs bedroom was on the end closest to the drive. One of the gables held the window seat where she'd sat on winter days, looking out at light dustings of snow and reading romance novels. Dorian's image played across her mind. He would make one hell of a hero.

Her gaze caught the narrow windows on either side of the fireplace. In her room, they fit perfectly on either side of her bed. On nights when her parents had that fireplace going, her bed was warm and toasty. She saw a flicker of movement. Her mom waved from the window. Morgan waved back and headed toward the house.

The door flew open before she could touch the handle. Becky pulled her inside and into strong, soft arms. Morgan closed her eyes and sank into her mother's embrace, hugging her tight. She inhaled the scent that was *mom*—warm vanilla with a hint of spice. She was never sure if her mother smelled so good from cooking and crafting or if she actually got it from a bottle. Over the years, Morgan had given her many scents. Okay, mostly experiments Morgan was dying to try out, but her mother always accepted them and immediately would touch pulse points. Funny, Morgan couldn't remember her smelling of anything other than vanilla and spice.

Becky slowly stepped back, letting her hands run down Morgan's arms until they were holding hands. Morgan blinked and her breath hitched as she looked at her mother's aura. Her mother glowed. Spikes of color pulsed around her mother, just as it had around Meadow. She could hear her mother commenting but Morgan concentrated on the aura. It was vibrant and sharp, except for a small whitish area around her abdomen. Morgan remembered the hysterectomy. She held on to her mother's hands a moment longer, taking one last scan before she released the grasp.

"You're looking great, Mom," she said, closed her eyes and stepped away. When she opened her eyes, her mother's image had returned to normal, but she had a look about her eyes. She started to say something.

"Hey, don't I get a turn?" Talbot grabbed Morgan in a bear hug. She slipped her arms around him and closed her eyes. He wore Old Spice. She would forever think of her father and Old Spice. She held on to his hand, stepped back and looked him up and down. His aura wasn't as vibrant as her mother's, but she'd never studied a man's before. Its pulse was a little off as well. That scared her. His heart? She didn't see anything murky or had any "feelings" like she'd had with Meadow. She rose on tiptoe and planted a kiss on the cheek. His skin felt warm and soft from his morning shave. She blinked and stepped back.

Her mother was watching her. She never missed a trick, Morgan realized.

"You feeling okay, Dad?" She asked, having smiled meekly at her mom.

"Funny, you should mention it. The doc changed my cholesterol medicine last week. I've been feeling a little off this week."

She relaxed. "Well, you'd better call him. You know some people react differently to some of those. I thought you were doing great on the one you were taking." It was more of a question than a comment.

Becky led them back into the kitchen. "You know how they are…" She pulled a pan of muffins out of the oven. "Still warm," she said more to herself and brought them to the table in the bay window. Then she looked at Morgan, "Those doctors now have it in their collective heads that cholesterol should be even lower." She waved Morgan into her seat, returned to the stove, gave the perfectly scrambled eggs a quick stir, dished them up and brought the steaming plate to the table. "Let's eat," she proclaimed and sat down. They took hands and closed their eyes in the blessing they'd said since before she could talk.

She inhaled. God, it smelled like home. She felt tears well up.

"Stop that." Becky patted her hand. "You're home now."

"Eat," her dad said, loading eggs onto his plate.

She glanced at her mother.

"I've put one yellow per two whites. I'm doing my part." Morgan smiled and picked up the crisp bacon.

"You seem different," Becky commented.

The bacon broke between her fingers and fell to the plate. She looked at her mother, who innocently took a bite of eggs and purposefully didn't look at her.

"A little, maybe," she said.

"You love him?" Talbot slathered butter on a muffin. Becky took it away and handed him another one, unbuttered. He glared at her, or what appeared to be a glare, then nodded and smiled.

Their dynamics never changed. Morgan loved that about them. Her throat felt tight.

"I asked you a question." Talbot said softly.

Morgan took a breath and let it out. "I don't know. Maybe." She didn't know. Desire him? Definitely. Respect? Absolutely. Trust? Love? Those questions were harder.

"Well, something's changed," Becky smiled at her.

Morgan wondered if she was blushing. "A lot has happened."

Her mother reached over and took her hand, squeezed and let go. "I know, honey. It's been, what, a month? A lot can happen in a month." She cocked her head and studied her daughter. "But it's something else. You seem more confident. Your eyes are sparkling."

Morgan looked down. Her mom reached over and lifted her chin. "Hey, it's us." She smiled at her daughter. "I meant they looked brighter, happy."

She smiled back and grabbed the last muffin. "Last muffin!" she announced and bit into it. A rule of the house since she could remember—stemming from her dad finishing off her mom's favorite snack, without leaving her a bite—demanded the pronouncement that the last item was taken, eaten, or whatever. She even did it alone. She wondered if she would pass that tradition to her own family.

"The airport was chaotic, both in Atlanta and here. I did buy sunglasses in Atlanta. You know, you'd think I'd have thought of that years ago."

"You tried once. You said they made things look funny."

"They do. But, that's not nearly as bad as having people stare at me. It's been so different being in Ruthorford. I guess because Melissa lived there and people were used to her...nobody pays any attention to my differences. It's rather nice."

"So you're going back?" Morgan could see that her mom was trying not to sound disappointed.

"Yeah, I think I have to." She took a last sip of coffee, dabbed her lips, and sat back. "Wow. That was fabulous."

Becky stood. "Talbot, you've got dish duty. Morgan, come with me. I've got something to show you."

"Sorry, Dad," Morgan brushed a kiss on his cheek and followed her mother upstairs.

She followed her mother into the guestroom opposite hers. It'd been converted into a workroom or studio. "Wow. This is fabulous."

"Your dad did this for me. It only took him three weeks, once he got started. He said he got tired of having my stuff all over the kitchen table."

"Yeah, but he's going to miss being able to harass you." Morgan walked around the room. A long worktable covered the center of the room. One wall had shelves and those shelves had drawers with clear fronts, so Becky could see her supplies. On the end, between the small windows, instead of a bed was a sewing table, forming an L along another wall to the dormer. It held a sewing machine on one end and an embroidery machine on the other. The large dormer had shelves on either side, with fabrics lying neatly stacked. The lighting had been upgraded as well.

As she watched, her mother pulled the door closed a bit. Behind it was a recliner, a side table and a light. She saw her father's glasses sitting on the table. She shook her head. "Next, you'll have him crafting."

"Well, he does help me cut out patterns, now and again." She laughed. "He just looked so damned uncomfortable sitting on a stool across from me."

"It's great, Mom. You should have done this years ago."

"Years ago, this was our only guest room."

Morgan swung around and looked toward her bedroom. She walked slowly toward the room where'd she'd grown-up. She let out a sigh of relief. Other than a new quilt in a beautiful fall motif, it still felt like her room. Of course, she'd never been one to junk up her space with the latest teen fads. Other than the princess canopy bed she'd had until she was thirteen, she'd always loved decorating, following in her mother's steps.

Becky followed her daughter into her bedroom. "Honey, this will always be your room. You never were a messy child. I could vacuum, dust and make the bed and, voila, a guest room." She put her arm around her daughter and squeezed. "Anytime, Pumpkin, you know that."

"Thanks, Mom." She turned and hugged her mother. "I love you."

"Me, too, Pumpkin. Me, too."

Morgan bounded back down the stairs. "Look, guys," she included her father, wiping his big hands on a dishtowel. "Jenn and I are going to go away for a few days. Put our heads back on straight."

"Jenn called. She apologized for taking you away. I told her to promise to join us for dinner when you get back and all's forgiven. She wanted to know if we still had the hiking sticks your Dad made for you two." Becky pointed to the corner by the stairs. Two five-foot limbs, carved, stained and polished, each with initials in it, stood in the corner."

"Oh wow!" She walked over and picked hers up. "I haven't thought about these in years."

"Where're you headed?" Talbot asked.

"She's going to surprise me. But wherever it is, I gather we'll do some hiking." The tradition had started in their sophomore year, when Jenn had come home with Morgan on fall break. At first, it was small walks around the wooded property. With each trip home, the hikes got longer and further afield. Her father had given them matching walking sticks for Christmas the next year.

Morgan looked at her watch. "Yikes, I'm supposed to be there in fifteen minutes."

"Wait," Becky walked to the kitchen. "I packed some sandwiches and stuff." She walked out with a real picnic basket.

Morgan shook her head. "I should have figured."

She threw her arms around her mom and dad. "It's great to be home. I've missed you."

"We've missed you."

"Dorian called, by the way," her Dad said, almost hesitantly.

"He did?" Morgan felt her pulse jump and tried to appear nonchalant.

"What'd he want?"

"He'd like you to call him, for one. But, he also called to mention the stuff about Rob."

Morgan heard the edge in her father's voice when he said the name. "Apparently, the old boy has left the university and dropped off the radar."

Morgan's interest peaked. "Wow. I would never have thought him capable of robbery."

Becky rubbed her hand down Morgan's arm. "I'm glad you're getting away. You girls be careful."

"We will. Love you guys."

****

Morgan pulled into the parking lot as Jenn loaded her bags into the large black Chevy Tahoe. Morgan whipped in beside her, opened the back door and brandished the hiking sticks.

Jenn grinned and held out her hand. "They found them."

"Of course." Morgan handed them over, hugged her friend, and pulled out her bag and the picnic basket.

"I do love your mother," Jenn said and took the basket, inching up the lid to peek inside.

"Need a pit stop or are you ready to go?"

"I'm good. Where're we headed?"

"Turns out, Uncle Mike has a cabin on Gwynn Island."

Morgan finished wrestling her suitcase next to Jenn's and turned to look at her friend.

"I don't think I've ever seen you in sunglasses," Jenn commented. "It's weird."

"Weirder then my eyes?"

"I don't think your eyes are weird. They're you."

"Thanks. Back to Gwynn Island." She and Jenn had found the small Virginia island, located in the Chesapeake Bay off Mathews County, when they had taken off exploring one weekend during college. They loved it and used to fantasize about owning one of the little cabins that dotted the island. She wondered which one of those belonged to Dr. Yancy.

"Oh, yeah. He and I have had a chance to talk. Boy, have I got a lot to tell you."

They climbed into the Tahoe and pulled out. Morgan yawned. Without looking Jenn spoke, "You look beat. Why don't you nap? If you haven't awakened by the time we arrive, I'll get you up. Or, maybe not. I could let you sleep and eat all the great stuff your mom packed."

"No you won't," she laughed. "Mom made enough to feed an army. I think I will take a nap. I didn't sleep well."

"Nightmare?"

Morgan nodded, leaned back and closed her eyes. Jenn watched as she began to snore softly. Quietly fishing the phone out of her pocket, she dialed, and then spoke softly into the phone, "I've got her." She clicked off.

Chapter Fourteen

Morgan and Jenn sat in Adirondack chairs they'd lugged down to the pier. Having finished off the cranberry chicken sandwich and her mom's incredible potato salad—the best Morgan had ever tasted—they now sat, Merlot in hand, watching a spectacular sunset. Come morning, if they pivoted the heavy chairs 180 degrees, they would be enjoying a spectacular sunrise. They figured this was why Uncle Mike, as Morgan was beginning to think of him, had chosen this site for his cabin.

It definitely wasn't one of the ones they'd spied years back. This cabin was rustic as done by an architect—wonderfully appointed kitchen and baths, beautiful furnishings. The only thing truly rustic in the whole place was the wide plank flooring. It appeared the Abbott House paid very well indeed.

"So," Jenn was saying, "little did I know that when they took me out of that flea ridden hole they called a school and plunked me down in Virginia to room with you, it was intentional."

Morgan afforded her little more than a glance, since Jenn had already explained that "Uncle Mike" had been instructed to keep an eye on her. As a doctor, he had access to her medical records. Having a niece her age, and in college, definitely was an advantage. Of course, he was taking a chance, not knowing if they would get along. He'd figured everyone got along with Jenn, why not Morgan? Jenn, being none the wiser, relayed information home, and Mike's sister was always more than willing to discuss her daughter and her daughter's best friend with her brother. The good doctor then relayed the information to Abbott House and they, in turn, passed it on to the Kilravens.

Morgan wasn't sure how she felt about the whole situation. She was feeling a bit down, but she wasn't sure she could attribute it to plans to keep tabs on her. Thinking logically, it made sense. If Melissa and Thomas cared as much about her as they indicated, she could see them going to great lengths to make sure she was well and happy. She shuddered—to be watched all of one's life and be unaware of it. She ran her hand over the back of her neck. It felt clammy. Maybe she was coming down with something. That, too, would be a first. She hadn't been sick a day in her life.

"So, tomorrow...hiking or boating? Uncle Mike mentioned that he's got a bass boat in a little boathouse around the bend."

"Let's play it by ear, okay."

"You okay?" Jenn turned and looked at Morgan. Then she squinted at her, reached over and put her hand on her forehead. "You don't look so good, girlfriend. Maybe we ought to head inside."

"I'm just tired. It's gotten a bit chilly out here as well." She stood with some difficulty. "What'd you say we put on jammies and watch a movie?"

"Let's make it something funny, okay. I don't particularly want to burst into tears tonight." Jenn took Morgan arm as they started up the path.

"Still nothing from Jim?" Morgan patted Jenn's hand.

"Nope. Not a word. I don't expect to, either. He said, and I quote, 'I'm tired of playing second fiddle. I know what you do is important, but I should be, too.' About that moment my phone rang and I had to dash off to an emergency."

"I'm sorry, Jenn. I know you love him."

"Loved, Morgan." Jenn's voice was almost a whisper. "If he can't understand that what I do can't be scheduled, then..." she let her voice drift into the night.

Morgan squeezed Jenn's arm. "Then funny it is," she assured her.

"I'd say it sounds like a plan. There's nothing we have to do, except relax." They trudged up the trail back to the cabin. Inside, as Morgan went into her bedroom—the cabin had three—Jenn called after her, "I'm going to take a moment to call and check on Meadow." She walked into her own room and closed the door.

Morgan walked into the bathroom and turned on the water. As she wet a cloth, she looked at her reflection. She did look pale, more than usual. Waves of sadness washed through her. She wrapped she arms across her stomach. *Dorian.* A tear escaped and rolled down her cheek. She grabbed the counter and turned off the water, hoping to stem the sadness overwhelming her. She ached. Was he all right? What was he doing? Did he miss her?

She made her way slowly into the bedroom and sat down on the bed. Maybe if she rested for just a moment. She fell sideways onto the pillow and, with her last bit of effort, kicked off her shoes and pulled her legs onto the bed....

"It's okay, sweet baby, I'll take care of you." Dorian whispered in her ear. Morgan shifted to make room for him. She felt his warmth as he lay next to her. "I know it's bad, love. Let me take away the ache." His breath brushed over her mouth and cheek. She felt the warm tingling sensation move through her body as his hand hovered just above her skin, letting the current flow, yet not quite touching her. She felt her blood heat and her pulse deepen, its beat

coursing through her veins. She felt the ache to her core, wanting him inside. She arched. The hot current eddied in her abdomen and spread outward—down. She shifted her legs. Her breathing became shallow. "Let it go, my angel." She heard his deep voice resonate against her hair. "Give me your desire."

Morgan stretched. The sun filtered through the blinds and across the bed. She sat up. She was still wearing the jeans and sweater she'd had on last night. A small blanket lay across her. Her door was closed.

"Dorian?" she called. Birds chirping outside the window were the only response.

She remembered the dream and bolted upright. She had never had such an erotic dream. She still lay on the side of the bed where she'd fallen asleep. The other side was undisturbed. It seemed so real. She knew her response had been real. A hallucination brought on by fever. Possibly. She felt better than she did yesterday. Maybe she'd had a fever after all. A twenty-four hour bug.

"Jenn?" she called out.

Morgan walked into the main room of the cabin. Jenn's door was closed. She eased open the door in case Jenn was still asleep. The quilt was pulled taut, the pillows positioned just so. Jenn's bag sat on the floor at the foot of the bed.

"Jenn?" Morgan looked in the bathroom and then walked into the kitchen. A crisp piece of paper, folded in half, rested in front of the coffee pot.

I didn't want to wake you. You dropped like a brick last night. I got an urgent call. Don't I always? It shouldn't take too long. Hope to be back by late afternoon. You've got my cell number. There's plenty of food. Relax. You need it. Love, Jenn

****

Jasmine blinked once, trying to focus out of her swollen eyes. She licked her lip and tasted her own blood. Her arm was numb, pulled taut over her head and chained to a timber. Her other arm lay at her side, useless, the excruciating pain intensifying when she attempted the slightest movement. The dirt and rocks beneath her dug into her flesh. The cold from the ground seeped into her bones. She shivered and listened. How long had she been out? Was she alone? Please, God, let her be alone. Using her bare feet to gain leverage, she tried to push herself up into a sitting position. She felt the dirt grate between the cheeks of her bare buttocks and winced. She shifted her legs and felt the drying stickiness pull on her thighs. Tears fell from her swollen eyes. Her breath, when she inhaled, was shaky—shallow. Her chest hurt. The torn sleeve of her blouse pulled on her injured arm. Her breast was tender. A shuffling sound came from somewhere nearby. She stopped moving and tried to remain very still, listening. She whimpered, forced her lips together to keep the sound from escaping. She didn't want to draw his attention. Then she remembered—he was gone—at least for a while. Blackness began to overtake her. She didn't care. She let it.

****

Morgan scooped fresh coffee grounds into the basket, pressed the button, and sat at the breakfast bar, anticipating the aroma. *Poor Jenn.* Jim had seemed so understanding, so encouraging. He wasn't the first that'd had trouble being second to Jenn's dedication. He probably wouldn't be the last. A sense of pride welled inside for her friend. Jenn had sworn she would help the helpless and she had. She hadn't lost a woman or family yet. She'd had to do some convincing at times, but she was the best at that.

She picked up her phone. It was off. She went to her suitcase, then her purse. No charger. *Damn.* In her hurry, she must have left it in Ruthorford. A chill went through her. No car. No phone. She looked around. No house phone. This was just great.

Gurgles from the coffee pot beckoned. She grabbed a mug, inhaled the rich aroma as it filled the mug, and carried it over to browse through haphazardly arranged books. She picked up one by Jane Austen.

Morgan pored through Jane Austen, took a long shower, lounged on the dock, and meandered around the lot. She didn't want to stray too far since she couldn't find a key. Not that she feared anyone breaking in. They were pretty isolated. She didn't have a clue how far the next cabin was. And, with the school year having started, she doubted many families were heading up this way.

Dorian kept drifting into her thoughts. When she was sitting on the dock, the skin on her arms tingled, like it did sometimes when he would walk near her. She looked around, half expecting him to come sauntering down the path—wanting him to come sauntering down the path. It took some real concentration for her to remember why she'd left—his lack of faith in her. As the day progressed, Morgan replayed the conversations over in her mind. She could see where he would be concerned, not knowing her. But, they had just made love, for God's sake. And it had been making love, not just sex. The word "love" played across her mind. She tested it, weighed it, then forced it from her mind.

When Jenn didn't appear by dinner, she finished off the chicken salad and put a movie in the DVD. Forced relaxation wasn't all it was cracked up to be. It didn't take long for her to drift off. She awoke to the sound of gravel crunching outside.

"Jenn must be back," she said softly and was startled at the sound her voice made in the quiet. She got up and looked outside. The Tahoe wasn't in the drive. She glanced around. Maybe she'd dreamed it. She locked the front door, closed all the blinds, and turned the movie back on. Her ears listened for every sound and her heart pounded at the slightest noise.

When the lights flickered, Morgan froze. She hadn't heard thunder. Grabbing the clicker, she switched from the DVD to the television. The room plunged into darkness. *Oh God*. She listened. She heard bugs chirping outside. Her eyes began adjusting to the blackness. She blinked. She began to take in the room. *Shit*. She remembered her eyes glowed. She eased off the couch and tried to remember where she'd put her purse. Those stupid sunglasses would shield her eyes. Finding it on the bar chair, she fumbled around inside until she felt the glasses.

She heard a creak.

Morgan squatted to the floor, shoving on the glasses. Everything went dark. Damn it, the glasses screwed up her night vision. She moved on her hands and knees around the bar.

Another creak. She stilled, listening.

A hand grabbed her hair and yanked her head back. Before she could scream, a cloth covered her mouth. She struggled and was jerked backwards, twisting her foot beneath her. Pain shot up her leg, yet she couldn't get her leg out from under her. Her limbs felt heavy. *Dorian,* she concentrated every fiber of her being on him. *...help me.* The world fell away.

****

John saw the drink drop from Dorian's hand, reached out and grabbed it before it hit the ground. Tea splashed across his shirt, yet Dorian remained still, staring off.

"Dorian?" John set the cup down. "Hey, man. You okay?"

Dorian blinked. He looked at John, his brow furrowed. He concentrated, then spoke, "She's gone."

"Yeah. That's why we came to Virginia."

"No." Dorian reached out and clasped the other man's forearm. "She's gone. Dropped from my radar." Agitated, he marched back and forth in front of the outside bar where they'd stopped to grab something to eat.

Having been friends with Dorian for most of his life, John knew to wait. Illumination would follow, eventually.

"We're paired." Dorian ran his hand through his hair. "I can feel her. I *can't* feel her." His wild eyes focused on John.

"Hey, congratulations." John got the paired part, first.

Dorian grabbed his arm again. "Pay attention, John. I *cannot* feel her."

The message sank in. "Her parents said she was with Jenn," he reminded Dorian. They went away to relax. Maybe they got drunk and she passed out."

Dorian shook his head. "No, this is different."

John pulled the small phone from his pocket and searched through numbers. "Jenn gave me a number to call if I needed to reach her." He dialed. When it went to voice-mail, he ran through some more numbers and dialed another one. "This is the security number for the home where Meadow's staying."

"Hey, this is John Davis. I'm Kayla's cousin—"

"John?" Jenn voice came through the phone. John looked at Dorian. Dorian couldn't stand still. He kept looking around the surrounding street.

"Jenn? I thought you were with Morgan?" John hit a button and Jenn's voice, albeit tinny, came through loud. Dorian stopped pacing, his attention riveted on the small phone.

"I was. I got called in. Someone tried to hack into our system. She's at the cabin, probably bored out of her skull by now." Jenn laughed. "What's up?"

John thought for a moment on how to present this to Jenn. "Dorian thinks something happened to Morgan. He can't reach her."

"I tried earlier. It keeps going to her voicemail. I bet she forgot to charge her phone. I was getting ready to head out myself—"

John's and Dorian's simultaneous "No!" stopped her.

John spoke. "Don't leave. Make sure everything's secure." It was a command. "Give me the address."

Jenn voice was quieter, very controlled. "What's going on?"

John hesitated for a moment. "Dorian and Morgan have a connection of some sort. Psychically, I think. It suddenly broke. He can't find her."

Dorian hissed through clinched teeth, "It's not like I misplaced my damn wallet."

Jenn voice sounded muffled. Then she was back. She spouted the cabin's address. "Someone's trying again..." she yelled at someone behind her, "gotta run. I'll wait to hear from you." She hung up.

John looked at Dorian. "I don't like this."

They were racing toward the truck. "Where's Jenn's from here?" Dorian asked.

"About ten minutes. Less, maybe."

"I'm dropping you off there. I'll be in touch."

John guided Dorian through the streets toward the safe house. To make sure they weren't being followed, they maneuvered through some side streets a couple of times. They still made it in under eight minutes. As they pulled in front of tall, iron gates, security lights flashed on. John stepped out of the truck and turned back.

"You sure you don't want me to go with you?"

"No. You stay with Jenn. Since I don't know what's going on, I want to make sure you're there for Jenn and Meadow."

"Call if you need me," John shouted. Dorian was already moving as the truck door slammed.

The GPS had him arriving in about an hour. "Let's see if we can cut that down a bit," he commented to the device attached to the windshield of the truck.

Every so often Dorian would try to concentrate on Morgan. It was ironic. Her presence in his mind had become so natural he barely noticed it. Not so in the beginning. The hint of recognition had hit him the moment she'd walked in the door of the shop that day, her red hair flaming around her. However, he'd been too angry, too determined *not* to be waylaid by those embedded traits—the recognition of his match, his mate—to pay attention. The only thing he'd think about was the fact that he didn't want his future dictated, yet he knew that it was.

When they'd come together to open the portal, the first tendrils, although invisible, had linked. Those invisible threads had strengthened again when they did it the second time. Their kiss, hot and demanding as it was, further cemented their connection and his fate. He'd been so damned determined to fight it.

In the grotto, he'd known. He'd seen her essence vibrate under his touch and he'd wanted her. He'd wanted *them.*

Warmth shot through him as he remembered her touch on his body, tentative though it had been. He smiled remembering her blush and how he'd watched desire push away her shyness.

He now used those feelings to focus on her, sending out a call, hoping for an answer. There was none. It was as though she'd disappeared off the face of the earth.

Dorian hit the brakes and turned hard to the left, skidding on the gravel. It was pitch black. There was no moon to help guide him. He inched the truck forward, trying to stay on the narrow gravel path and see in front of him. A pine limb brushed the top of the truck. He edged over to the right, barely staying on the path. Suddenly, the path fanned out and the high beams spotlighted the cabin. It looked deserted. He shut off the engine, left the lights on and grabbed a flashlight.

The truck door slamming shut resounded in the dark. He listened for the crickets. Gradually, their chirping started back up, as did the croaks of the toads. Not fond of the exposure he had in the light, he shifted off to the left until he was at the door and had no choice but to step into the glare of the high beams. The knob turned easily in his grasp and the planked door edged forward. It was unlocked. He moved his hand in, felt for the switches and hit every one he could reach simultaneously. Nothing happened.

He pulled back. Using the flashlight, he moved around the side of the cabin, looking for a breaker box. He'd almost completed a circle of the cabin when he found it—open. The main had been tripped. He reset the breaker and quietly moved back around the cabin. Light poured out of the windows.

A quick scan of the place told him it was highly unlikely that anyone was there. A bar stool was knocked over, a book on the floor. An end table lamp lay on the couch. She didn't go without a struggle. His blood ran cold. *Stop it. Don't do this. It won't help.* He took a deep breath, went through the cabin, then ran back to the truck and turned off the lights. He didn't need to get stranded as well.

Dorian dialed John as he re-entered the cabin. As he crossed the threshold, something pricked his brain. A tiny twinge. It didn't feel like Morgan, but it was something familiar.

"She's not here," he spat out as soon as John answered. "It's been tossed and it looks like she put up a fight." He walked through the room, slower this time. On the kitchen side of the bar, he saw her purse on the floor, emptied. Her phone lay next to it. He picked it up. It was dead. "Damn it, Morgan, where are you?" he muttered.

"What? Did you find her?"

"No. Sorry. I was talking to myself," which reminded him of the feeling he had when he crossed the threshold. He walked back over to the door and stepped through. The same feeling assailed him. "Let me call you back," he said and closed the phone. He backed up, kept stepping back until the feeling went away. He stepped forward again. Like a human Geiger counter, he eased this way and that, looking all around him. Something sparkled near the door. He knelt down. A small crystal.

"Now, I've got you," he said aloud, tossed the stone in the air and caught it.

It took three rings before Bask answered his phone, his voice hoarse. "This better be important." The man sounded more like a military commander than a lawyer.

"It is," Dorian shot back.

"I'm listening."

"Remember when those people wanted to buy the rug from Mel and Thom and got so belligerent that you threatened to put a tracking chip in it."

"Yes."

"Did you?" Dorian almost shouted.

"Yes. Took a pretty penny to have it inserted just right, but Mel finally agreed. It eased her mind. I've been following the damn thing all over the place."

Dorian let a small smile play at his lips. "Where is it now?"

"You told me to hold off on retrieving it until you were sure. Something about not pissing off Morgan."

"She's missing."

"Oh, God. You don't think she took it, do you?"

Dorian let frustration push him. "No," he snapped. "I think whoever took the rug might have her."

"I'll call you back."

"I want to go after the son of a bitch, got it?"

"I'll call you back."

Dorian walked back through the cabin. In her room, he saw the open closet and Mel's robe hanging there. Lavender still clung to the material. He let his fingers run over it. He couldn't lose both of them.

His phone went off.

"Yes."

"It stopped moving a while back. It seems to be in the old Hollis Mine in North Carolina. I'm texting you the coordinates. I can get someone there—"

"I'll call if I need backup. I don't think so."

"I don't, either," Bask mused. "Be careful, just the same."

"I will."

Dorian grabbed Morgan's phone and purse, opened the refrigerator, took out several sodas and headed for the truck.

John was harder to persuade than Bask had been. "I'd rather you take care of Jenn and Meadow. I'm already on the road."

"You're not Superman. Remember that."

"I know. Thanks."

Dorian stopped in Emporia, Virginia, filled the tank, and grabbed something to eat. As much as he hated the delay, he needed to eat since he and John had left without eating anything.

Around Oxford, Dorian thought he could feel Morgan for just a moment. Like she slipped in and out, faintly, briefly. He slammed his hand against the steering wheel. *Come on, girl. Think of me. Think of us.* Nothing. Try as he might, it escaped him. Pulling into a rest stop, Dorian turned off the engine, closed his eyes and let his mind flow to Morgan. Again, that faint tinge. *Morgan, I know you can't hear me. Just feel me, baby. That's all you have to do.* The current flowed. Warmth filled him. He smiled. It flickered and was gone. "Damn it!" he bit out.

He started the engine and headed back to the interstate. Something worried him. It didn't feel like she was in this direction. However, since this was the only direction he had, he drove forward.

His insides ached. Was this what she been feeling the other night when he'd come to her in her dreams? He'd been guided by lust, a need so great he couldn't fight it, but it hadn't hurt. This hurt. He opened one of the now warm drinks and let it burn down his throat. A shiver ran up his spine. Concentrating so strongly on Morgan, he nearly passed the turn-off. Daylight was just breaking.

The road, no longer used, was overgrown. Kudzu reached out its tendrils to entangle his tires. He could see where a vehicle had been through here before, enough to tamp down the foliage. He could feel his current pulsing. His anger fed it. The engine sputtered. Shit. He took one hand off the wheel and forced himself to calm down. The last thing he needed was to stall his truck.

Dorian crept forward. He could see the opening to the mine. It was clear, not a vehicle in sight. That didn't mean no one was here. They could've hidden a vehicle easily. He backed up, turned around, and parked down the road a bit, off to the side. He made sure that, if he had to, he could get the hell out, fast. Remembering the flashlight, he checked it. His nerves were hopping. He forced himself to keep from running.

Dorian eased into the entrance of the mine and listened. It was quiet. He walked as far as he dared without using the flashlight. Not wanting to fall down an open shaft, he switched on the flashlight and adjusted the beam. He had no clue what kind of mine this was. The gradual decline and the lack of tracks led him to think it was hand done. Timbers seemed well placed for support. About a hundred feet in, he heard a sound—a moan. It was all he could do not to run; it could be a trap.

He moved forward as quietly as possible. He let his senses open and felt nothing. If she was conscious, he should feel her. His hand tingled. He shook it, trying to keep his energy down. Now he knew why Thom had forced him to learn those stupid meditation exercises. He was damn near ready to shock himself.

Another moan, this one louder. Then, a scream.

He ran. Suddenly, he was in an area about the size of his grotto. He heard shuffling to his right and swung the light down the wall. He gasped.

Jasmine turned her head away from the light. Her lips, cracked and coated with dried blood, tried to move. She felt him kneel next to her.

"Jas," he whispered.

She tried to draw her arm across her naked body. It wouldn't move. She winced as pain shot through her.

"It's okay, sweet," he soothed and tore off his shirt, laying it across her.

"Do-r-r-y?"

"Yeah, it's me. Let me help you."

"He...he..." she couldn't get the words out.

"Is he here?"

She shook her head slightly. "He...hasn't...come..." She took a deep breath.

Dorian pulled out his phone and hit 9-1-1. Nothing. "Damn it," he cursed and turned back to her. "I can't get a signal." He stood.

She screamed. "No!" Then more softly, "Please."

"Okay, okay." He eased the light up her arm. "Jas, I can get this off you, but it's going to hurt."

He shone the flashlight across the floor, saw a piece of material, probably the rest of her blouse, grabbed it and gently forced it between her wrist and the chain and lock. He knelt down beside her and took hold of the lock. Concentrating, he pictured the lock and let his current flow.

Jasmine moaned. The lock opened. He pulled it away from the chain and eased her arm down. She groaned. Her hand was like ice. There was no telling how long she'd been hanging here.

"I'm going to carry you out."

She nodded slightly, tried to move the damaged arm and sucked in her breath.

Dorian felt her shoulder. "Jas, your arm's dislocated. I'm going to try to put it back in, okay."

She looked away. He put his knee under her armpit to give him leverage, let a small amount of current flow to warm up the joint and pulled. He felt it snap back. When she didn't say anything, he looked down. She'd passed out. It was just as well.

He shoved the flaring flashlight into his back pocket and lifted her as gently as he could. She felt so thin. He could barely see for the anger. That son of a bitch was dead.

Alert to the slightest movement, Dorian made his way back to the truck carrying his abused friend. He had no doubt he could end the man's life with a look right now, but he didn't want to chance hurting Jasmine any more than she already was. Her struggles warned Dorian that Jasmine was coming to in a panic.

"Jas...it's me...Dorian. I have to get you to the truck. Hang on, sweet."

She stopped struggling.

"I'm going to set you down so I can get the door open. I'll put you in the back. There's a blanket, okay?"

When he leaned forward to set her down, his shirt slipped away. Her breast was bruised and swollen; a large bluish mark was forming around her side. Blood marked her abdomen and down her legs. Bruises and bite marks were interspersed with blood. She hung her head.

"It's okay. I'll get him," he promised.

Her once beautiful face was swollen into a misshapen orb, her brown cat eyes purple and swollen into slits. Dried blood was smeared across her cheeks and matted her hair. She wouldn't look him in the eye. His heart sank at her broken spirit.

Dorian got her settled, gave her a little water, and dialed 9-1-1. He gave the coordinates and called John.

His voice cracked when he spoke. Not wanting her to hear him, he walked away from the vehicle. "John. I found Jasmine. She was in the mine. The son of a bitch beat the shit out of her. I think he raped her. I've called 9-1-1. We're going to need Jenn on this; she knows what to do."

"Morgan?"

"Nothing. She's not here."

"We're almost to the cabin; Jenn wanted to check something. I'll call Bask. He can get her there faster. Let me know where they're taking her."

"Dory…"

He barely heard the hoarse whisper of his name. He ran back to the car.

"Rob…he's gone…after…Morgan." Tears trailed down her cheeks.

She jumped when his palm slammed the side of the truck. "Sorry, Jas. I think he must have her. She's gone."

"Noooo…" It came out as a long, low moan.

"I'll find him. I promise I'll find him."

He heard the sirens in the distance. He turned on his flashers and waited. The ambulance pulled up beside him. When two women got out, he was relieved. He didn't know how she would react to men in her fragile state. He explained what he suspected had happened as one went with him to the truck and one pulled out the gurney. He stepped back and let them tend her.

"I had to put her shoulder back in," he added, but left out any explanation of the slight burn on her wrist. They would figure it was from Jasmine trying to free herself.

"Where are you taking her?"

"She'll go to Greensboro. She's stable enough and it's a better facility."

As they moved the gurney toward the ambulance, he took her hand. "Morgan has a friend, Jenn. She's going to come see you. I think she can help you." He kissed her knuckles.

"Mor...gan," she moaned again.

"I'll find her." He backed away as they loaded her into the ambulance. They moved into the clearing in front of the mine, turned around, and sped past him.

Chapter Fifteen

Morgan swam toward consciousness, battling her way through a miasma of pitch black sludge. She was careful this time. She knew if she so much as let a muscle twitch, a needle would jab her vein and the blackness would overtake her once more. She lay on a cot of some sort, the mustiness bringing bile up her throat. She swallowed trying not to let the muscle in her throat move too much. She cracked one eyelid. Her lashes brushed against material. Something was over her head. Not tight, but there. She forced her eyes open ever so slightly. The weave wasn't so tight that she couldn't make out light in the room. And movement. She shut her eyes and prayed whoever it was wouldn't see the glow of her eyes.

Morgan strained to listen. Feet shuffling back and forth, back and forth. Someone typing on a keyboard. A hand slammed down on a table. She jumped. He grabbed her arm again and jabbed a needle into a vein. *Dorian,* she screamed in her head as everything went black.

****

Dorian slouched in the waiting room chair, legs stretched in front of him, demanding his body to rest. There was nothing he could do but wait. Everything depended on someone else. He hated depending on anyone but himself. He waited on the doctor to finish his exam and treatment of Jasmine. His heart cringed every time he thought about her.

He waited on the arrival of John and Jenn. He'd waited on the team from Abbott House to retrieve the rug and stones from him. He'd found the rug and most of the crystals in the mine when he went back in, looking for clues as to where Rob might have taken Morgan. He'd used the gloves he'd gotten from the EMTs and "bagged and tagged" the items as carefully as possible. He'd finished just before the local sheriff's department arrived, followed by the FBI. Bask would turn over any information he had once he'd had his team study the evidence. He didn't feel bad about that either, since Abbott House was a financial gorilla when it came to state of the art equipment. Now, he waited on their findings.

Several times he thought he felt Morgan. It was brief, just a whisper. Then it was gone. Cut off. He wasn't sure he could get a fix on her, even if they had full contact. He shifted in the chair, frustration making him restless.

Voices in the corridor drew his attention. He looked up under hooded lids. Jenn's bouncing blonde curls led the way as she rushed toward him, an ever-vigilant John behind her.

Dorian pushed himself out of the chair and found himself enfolded in a warm hug.

"Wow, you look like hell," Jenn leaned back and looked at him.

He tried to smile. Failed. "Thanks," his voice was hoarse. "Where is she?"

Dorian nodded toward the closed doors marked "Authorized Personnel Only" and shook hands with John. John's expression told him there was no news from anywhere else.

Jenn sat down, drawing Dorian down into the chair next to hers. "Have you called the Briscoes?"

He hadn't had the heart. He'd only talked to them, what, a day before. They were so upbeat, so loving, so supportive of their daughter. He didn't know how to tell them she'd been taken and he couldn't begin to find her. He simply shook his head.

"Do you want me to call them?"

"No. I'll do it."

"Have you been able to talk to Jasmine?"

"No. She's not talking right now and they're running a CT and a MRI to make sure there's no internal damage."

"Oh, God," Jenn said. "I am so sorry. Family?"

"I called Teresa, her cousin. She doesn't have anyone else."

"When she can be released, I'd like to bring her back with me. We have a great staff that can help her. Get her on the right track."

He let his head fall onto his hands. "She didn't deserve this."

"Nobody does," she rubbed her hand up and down his arm.

The doctor walked through the doors. All three rose. "She's sleeping right now. We have turned the physical evidence over to the police. She doesn't have any internal hemorrhaging. Her physical wounds will heal…" he voice softened to a mere whisper, his features showed strain.

Jenn approached him and handed him her card and ID. "Can I have a word with her?"

The doctor looked at her credentials and handed back her ID. "I'd like to keep your card. I've heard of Safe Harbor. I will ask her to let you talk with her. Thanks for coming."

He then looked at the two men. "I do have a message for Dorian." Dorian stepped forward.

"She said Rob's gone after Morgan. That she did her best to stop him. And that he's crazy."

Pain flickered across Dorian's brow. The doctor took his arm. "I'm sorry. That was all she said."

The doctor turned to Jenn. "Why don't you come with me?" He led Jenn through the closed doors. She looked back once before she went through. Dorian saw the fear and sadness in her features an instant before she transformed her expression into professional calm. He nodded his assurance that he would do whatever it took to find Morgan. She turned and was gone.

John waited for him over by the windows. Several people had come in and sat in the chairs, speaking softly, their own concerns utmost on their minds.

"There's an APB out on Rob. The university was extremely helpful and gave the police access to his personnel file. Bask said it was interesting reading. How Bask got access, I have no idea. The man continues to amaze me." John was a private investigator that Bask used regularly, since John knew more about the history of Ruthorford than even Bask knew. John's ancestors were the tribes that surrounded the area, protecting it. "He didn't have good news," John continued. "It seems the bastard has vanished off the face of the earth."

****

Morgan lay perfectly still. She couldn't have moved her arms and legs had she tried. Their heaviness was unfamiliar to her. It was as though she were lying among a tangle of miscellaneous arms and legs—cold, heavy, lifeless forms. She wanted to move away from the corpse-like appendages but forced herself to remain motionless. Her head throbbed. Her tongue seemed stuck in her parched mouth. She could still see light through the hood. She listened. It seemed like she'd been listening for eons. It wasn't completely silent, just lifeless. There was a faint distant hum. When she reached out with her senses, something sparked back at her. Stinging. *Don't move. Don't even breathe,* she silently commanded herself. Her breath eased shallowly into her lungs. She had been breathing this way for so long, she'd become lightheaded. Disjointed thoughts ran through her mind. She wanted to call for Dorian. Every time she tried, someone shot her full of drugs. The drugs were disconnecting her thoughts and separating her mind from her body. *Dorian.* His name was like the air she fought to keep in her lungs. Screw it. She focused all the energy she had and cried loud and long, hoping her mind would carry it along whatever pathway it needed to reach him. Bee stings of electricity rushed over her body. But, no injection. She risked inhaling deeply, focusing Dorian in her mind's eye, every detail of his handsome face, pulling to his eyes. His deep blue, compelling eyes. She let her thoughts thrust from her in a rush, straight to his mind. As she watched, the aura surrounding her conjured image spiked. A sliver of a smile crossed her lips as she passed out.

****

"No, no... *No!*" he yelled. "Hang on," Dorian screamed as John dragged him through the emergency room doors. Nurses and doctors watched. Several stepped forward. John held up his hand. They turned away, figuring grief was overtaking the poor man.

In the parking lot, Dorian spun around. He grabbed John by the arms, his grip fierce. "I had her. Or, she had me. A real connection." He broke away, spun around, and marched back and forth, head up, searching the sky.

John watch Dorian's demeanor shift, his shoulders lower, his head come back down. He ran his hands through his hair, as though he could clear his mind. "She's killing me, man," he said to no one in particular.

He spun on John. "If he touches one hair on her head..." he let his voice lower, "he'll pray for death, and it won't come soon enough."

They were both thinking of Jasmine. There were no reassurances John could give Dorian.

"She's strong. She might not know it yet." Dorian was rambling. "I didn't get to tell her about the change."

John put his hand on Dorian's shoulder, directed his gaze into Dorian's now blue black eyes. "She's smart, too. She'll figure it out. She's starting to communicate with you, isn't she?"

"Yeah. But if anything happens to her, it's my fault."

"That's bullshit. You had no idea. Our lives aren't filled with intrigue for the most part. At least not until recently," he amended.

They saw Jenn come through the doors. They met her at the bench and sat down. Deep lines etched her forehead. "I got to talk with her a little. She's upset. More about the danger to Morgan, than what happened to her." She shook her head. "She was trying to keep him away from Morgan."

"What do you mean?" Dorian asked.

"Well, when she met him in Ruthorford, he was 'Morgan this, Morgan that.' Jealousy reared its head and she led him to believe that she has the same powers that Morgan has. He's convinced that Morgan can illuminate veins of rare gems. Thinking Jasmine could do the same, he waited and followed Jasmine when she went on vacation. He wined and dined her. However, when she wouldn't have anything to do with his plans, he drugged her. When she came to, she was shackled in the mine. He demanded she use her…" Jenn raised her fingers and made air quotes, "…powers." Of course, nothing happened. She convinced him she needed the rug, hoping he'd get caught. Unfortunately, he returned with the rug and the stones. When she couldn't perform, he beat the shit out of her. He threatened to go after Morgan. She…" Jenn lowered her head and took a breath, "she convinced him it had to be a sexual connection, hoping to distract him and also hoping that he would let her loose. She didn't know how crazy he was. He never unshackled her. He raped her repeatedly. Every time it didn't work, he'd beat her. Then, he would start all over again. The last thing she remembers was him telling her to 'die bitch. I'm bringing back Morgan.' That's when he dislocated her shoulder."

"How did he get the notion Morgan could find gems?"

"Apparently, he had been sneaking around for a while and saw something in the cottage. Stones glowing or something," she said and looked at Dorian for insight.

He and John exchanged a glance, unsure what Jenn knew or what to tell her. Jenn interrupted their non-verbal communication, "I get the bit about the gargoyle creatures, but I didn't know about the rocks." When they both stared at her, she shrugged, "She's my BFF, guys. We share—with a capital S."

John wanted to hug her. This spry blonde had given Dorian a moment of mirth. Anything to lessen the hell that Dorian seemed determined to carry with him right now. John's phone rang.

"Yeah." He listened intently. "Thanks. We're on our way."

"That was Bask. He got a call. They've found Rob. Alone. His truck was in a ditch not far from the cabin. Looks like he's had some sort of seizure. He's pretty messed up. Bask has a plane waiting for us at a field just north of here."

They started toward the truck, remembered Jenn, and turned back.

"Go on. I'm traveling with Jasmine. Call me when you know something." She turned and disappeared into the hospital.

"Quite a woman," Dorian said, as they sped out of the parking lot.

"My thoughts exactly," John admitted.

Chapter Sixteen

The pastoral setting surrounding the small private hospital near Williamsburg where Bask had Rob transported did a good job of hiding its function and security. As a major financial contributor with a lot of influence on its board of directors, Abbott House made sure their patients were provided with the utmost deference to privacy and security.

The helicopter that Bask had arranged to carry John and Dorian from North Carolina set down on the pad with a minimum of disruption. Dorian and John hopped out and moved toward the back entrance.

"I had no idea," Dorian commented, having viewed the building and grounds from the air.

John didn't comment; being an employee of Abbott House, he was privy to many things Dorian had never been exposed to.

It was beginning to dawn on Dorian that his upbringing had been more sheltered than he realized. He found his irritation growing. He wished someone had given him an inkling as to the extent of Abbott House's activities. Dorian wondered now just what his and Morgan's part was in everything. When this ended—and that meant with a positive conclusion for Morgan—he intended to have a heart to heart with Bask. Regardless of his and Morgan's relationship, he wasn't going to allow either one of them to become puppets of the Abbott House.

A man in a sports jacket, with an ever so slight bulge at his side, stopped them as they entered the building and asked them for identification. He passed the cards over to woman behind a desk, who scanned the ID's and handed them back.

"Rob Milineaux?" John tucked his ID back in his wallet.

The woman searched the database. "Room 228. Restricted visitors."

"Yeah. We're part of that restriction," Dorian commented as they walked to the stairwell.

A doctor stepped into the hallway from Room 228 as Dorian and John approached. He turned to them. "May I help you?"

"We're here to see Rob Milineaux," John said.

Dorian stepped around the doctor.

"I'm afraid you can't go in there."

John showed his PI license and pulled the doctor away, firing question after question, while Dorian slipped quietly into the room.

If Dorian hadn't met the man in Ruthorford, he'd never have recognized him. A frail, gaunt man lay under the sheet. Tubes ran from his arms, his mouth, and his nose. A grey pallor blended with dingy scrags of hair. Dark circles around his eyes gave a cavernous appearance. It was like looking at a corpse. Dorian would have sworn the man was dead except for the shallow rise and fall of the chest.

As Dorian approached the bed, his skin prickled. The closer he got the more intense the sensations became.

"Rob," he said and watched the EEG monitor. No shift in the barely perceptible brain activity. He reached out and pinched the man's arm. Nothing. His own discomfort from being so close was extreme. He backed away, still watching. Turning, he stepped back into the hall.

The doctor looked at him. "He's been in a coma since they brought him in. They say he was having seizures, but I haven't detected any." His pager went off. He pulled it out. "If you'll excuse me." He walked down the hall.

Dorian kept his voice low. "I would swear there were Gulatega in there. If Morgan and I were together, we could confirm it." An obvious sadness hooded his eyes. He took a breath and continued. "I've only dealt with two, maybe three, at the most. From what I'm sensing, there's a lot more in that room."

John nodded, pulled out his phone, and called Bask. "We have a situation," he began. "Dorian thinks the Gulatega are surrounding Rob." He paused. "Sure. I'll let him know." He slipped the phone back into his pocket.

"He'll bring in the Virginia couple to do a sweep and clean. Until they corral them, there's no way to know how much permanent damage Rob's sustained."

"Jesus." Dorian started down the hall. He stopped. "I'll meet you outside. You go talk to security. Keep people away from that room. I need to think." Without waiting for a reply, he pushed open the door to the stairwell and left.

Once outside, Dorian looked around. Now what? Rob was his chance to find Morgan. He had to think. He walked out toward the now vacant helipad. *If the Gulatega got to him in Ruthorford, then he's been going downhill ever since. He had to be pretty far gone when he came to get Morgan.* He tried to visualize the cabin. The outside. *Morgan's strong. She would have put up a fight. Maybe she got away.* No, he'd be able to feel her. He couldn't feel her except for short bursts. *She's drugged.*

His phone rang. It was Jenn. "Hey," he said.

"We're on our way to Safe Harbor. Jasmine's doing well," she said.

"Give her my love, okay?"

"Of course. Anything from Rob?"

"He's in a coma." He didn't elaborate.

"Listen…" she paused. It was obvious what she was going to say was difficult. "I got a call from the Briscoes. I didn't tell them anything. They know something's wrong. You need to tell them."

"I know." This was something he'd hoped to avoid. "We'll swing by there in a little while."

"Thanks. Please call me when you find out something." She sounded so sad, not the bubbly woman he'd met a short time ago.

John came toward him. "Everything here is taken care of." He tossed Dorian a set of keys. "Bask had transportation waiting for us. I'm going to head over to look in on Kayla and Meadow." He looked at his friend. "Give me a call when you've talked to the Briscoes."

It didn't look like he could put off that conversation any longer.

They walked toward the parking lot. Two SUVs sat side by side. Dorian wanted to have that heart to heart with Bask. A couple of *thank yous* would be added, he decided as he climbed into a black Explorer, after he read him the riot act for keeping him in the dark. One thing was certain: Bask was good with details. The SUV was fully loaded.

John handed him a piece of paper. "It's the Briscoes' address."

"Thanks for everything," Dorian said.

"Keep me in the loop. I mean it."

Dorian nodded and punched the Briscoes' address into the GPS. Thank God for technology.

****

The sudden motion of the hood being ripped off her head brought Morgan to consciousness. She squinted against the glare. Lights shined on her, making her hot. Someone moved to stand in the shadows.

"Rob?" Her voice cracked.

A deep laugh roared at her. "That pipsqueak, not bloody likely. For a physicist, he wasn't the brightest bulb in the box."

She didn't recognize the voice. It was a deeply accented baritone, the brogue thick. With so much static noise in the room, she found herself straining to make out the words. She had to concentrate to think. "The noise," she tried her voice again. "Please."

"Sorry. Serves my purpose to keep it on."

"What do you want with me?"

"All in time, Lass... All in time." She heard a door close.

Morgan looked around. She lay on a cot in a room not any bigger than twenty by twenty. The lights made it hard to tell. She tried to concentrate on Dorian, but the noise made that almost impossible. Painful. Cloth restraints bound her wrists. She couldn't rise up, only twist around to get circulation moving in her limbs. Her head pounded. Waves of nausea came and went. Her mouth was dry. The drugs still coursed through her system. She tried, but couldn't get a handle on her thoughts. *Dorian.* It felt distant, dilute. She gathered her thoughts and tried to concentrate. Just one single thought. *Dorian!*

****

With a strong arm holding his wife close to his side, Talbot let her cry against his chest while he kept an eye on Dorian. His anger boiled just below the surface. He knew releasing it on the man sitting across from him would not get his daughter back. He restrained himself and tried to speak calmly.

"You seem to care about her," he stated.

"Yes, sir, I do. Very much." More, he realized, than he'd thought possible. He knew he desired her. He'd expected that, with their compatibility, and everything Mel and Thom had told him. He didn't want to, but it had happened as naturally as breathing. She was a part of him. Care wasn't the right word. No, it was more than that. Love? Was he falling in love with Morgan? Or…had he already fallen in love?

The sound of her voice coursed through his body. He jumped up.

"Morgan," he called.

Talbot and Becky both looked up at him. His face reddened. He rubbed the back of his neck in frustration. He sat back down and tried to figure out how best to explain his link to Morgan. "I seem to have a connection to Morgan. I think I'm hearing her call me. But I'm not sure."

Becky tilted her head, studying him. She looked at Talbot then back at him. "Like when I put my hands in water and concentrate on her calling me and she does."

"Yeah. Something like that." *Times a thousand.* "But it's brief. Like she can't keep the contact. And her voice sounds fuzzy." He said the latter more to himself than them.

"Maybe you need a conduit," she suggested, "like the water."

He leaned forward, resting his arms on his legs. His shoulders slumped.

"You look exhausted." She stood and walked over to him. "I'd like to make a suggestion, Dorian. Why don't you get some rest?"

"I can't…I have to find her."

"And you will," she took his arm and gently urged him up. "Believe me when I tell you I want you to find my daughter more than I've wanted anything in my life. But, you are exhausted and no good to anyone. I'm going to take you upstairs and let you lie down in her room. I'll wake you in, say, half an hour."

He resisted.

"You're no good to her the way you are and she might need you to be in top form before this is over. Do it for her," she said softly, encouraging him with her words. "Think of her as you drift off. Picture her in your mind. Now, get some rest."

Dorian let her lead him upstairs. He was beyond exhausted. He couldn't think anymore. Maybe if he closed his eyes for a few moments he would be better at grabbing the connection. At least here he would be close to her in some sense.

Becky took him into Morgan's old bedroom and watched as he sat on the side of the bed. He looked at her.

She smiled. "A half hour. I'll wake you." She closed the door.

Talbot waited at the bottom of the stairs. "That went well." He kissed her on the cheek. "Think it will work?"

"I don't know." She shook her head. "If it doesn't, he'll have gotten some much needed rest. If it does, we might be closer to finding our baby girl."

"You're ability to mesmerize is truly a gift."

"Let's pray it works." She patted his arm as she passed and went into the kitchen. He nodded as he followed her.

****

Dorian began to drift. His consciousness fought and lost. He went deeper into the fog. It was too thick to make out any definitive shapes. He knew she was here, somewhere. The fog swirled and thinned as he moved forward. He looked down. On a cot lay Morgan, her wrists bound. Her red tresses flowed out across the cot and cascaded over the edge. Auburn lashes feathered across dark shadows beneath her closed eyes. He reached out to touch her. His hand rammed into an invisible barrier. He knelt and tried to wake her but no sound came from his mouth. Her lids fluttered. Iridescent green orbs stared back at him. A faint smile formed on her lips. She studied his face. Her brow furrowed. He tried to talk again. Nothing. Instead, he thought the words. *I'll find you.*

Her head moved minutely.

He wanted to look around but was afraid to take his eyes off her. Afraid she would disappear. *Can you help me?"*

She looked around her and squinted. She slowly shook her head.

Are you okay?

A small nod.

The fog thickened. Panicking, he tried to reach for her. Again, some sort of barrier impeded his movement. *I love you.* The words game out in a rush.

As the fog closed around her, he saw her smile.

He snapped awake and blinked. He was in her room. He concentrated. He couldn't feel her. Damn. Had it been a dream?

He walked down the stairs as Becky came out of the kitchen. "Anything?" she asked.

"Yes, I…" he studied her for a moment. "You knew."

She smiled. "Come into the kitchen; I made you a sandwich."

She led him to the kitchen table, already set with a sandwich and iced tea.

"Thank you," he said, remembering his manners. "You have been so kind. I appreciate the hospitality."

"You're welcome." She patted his hand. "Hopefully, you'll be back to enjoy it—maybe during the holidays."

She sat down across from him. Talbot remained standing, leaning against the kitchen counter. Dorian studied the older man's posture. It was one he knew well. He'd adopted that same stance on many occasions—one of guarded observation.

"Tell me what happened," Becky encouraged, waiting until he'd had taken several bites of the club sandwich and downed half the iced tea.

Dorian could feel the cold liquid fall into his gut. He took another drink. "How did you know?"

"First, I'm Morgan's mother." She got up, refilled his glass and set it in front of him. "Morgan mentioned she'd had dreams of you." She laughed when he blushed. "Don't worry, I didn't ask for details. Sometimes, dreams can be used to communicate. I just gave you a subtle suggestion and hoped for the best."

Dorian looked at the woman with renewed respect. Had he really thought Morgan lived devoid of her talents? Maybe she hadn't known she'd even used them. He found it sad that Morgan's family had had to help Morgan with her burgeoning abilities without any of the assistance that could have been available to them. Of course, he didn't know that assistance hadn't been offered and rejected. He doubted it. Having met her parents, he knew they would do anything to help her.

"Unfortunately, all I can tell you is she seems to be okay, for the most part." He left out the bound wrists, not knowing how accurate the vision was.

"You couldn't tell anything about her surroundings?"

He shook his head. "It was foggy. I couldn't see anything but her."

"You need a stronger conduit. Something you have in common." She smiled sheepishly, then asked, "Want to try water?"

He thought about electricity running through water, but something didn't feel right. "I don't think that will work." He returned her smile, admiring her for the calm she conveyed.

A conduit. A common link. Meadow came to mind. "I may have something." His voice held an edge of excitement.

"What?"

"A young girl, who has abilities similar to Morgan's. First, I need to see if she's up to it. She had surgery recently."

"Meadow," Talbot nodded his head, speaking for the first time. "Morgan told us about her. I hope she's doing well."

"The surgery went well. She's still recovering."

Dorian's phone rang. "Hi, Jenn, I'm with the Briscoes now."

"Dorian," Jenn said, excitement in her voice, "I thought you could use some good news. Meadow's talking."

"That's great."

"Yeah, she's doing very well. I think we have a lead. It has to do with her father."

Dorian tried to remember what Kayla had said about the native Scotsman. Other than the fact that he'd attempted to have Meadow kidnapped, the information eluded him. "Why don't I head that way? I want to talk to you and Kayla about Meadow anyway."

"I think that's a great idea," Jenn said, adding, "And Dorian...hurry."

Dorian stood. "Meadow's talking," he told the Briscoes. I need to get over there."

Becky stepped toward him. "Give Jenn our love. And Morgan." She smiled up at him, her eyes glistening with tears.

He leaned forward and kissed her on the cheek. It was warm and smelled faintly of vanilla. He took her shoulders in his hands, let a small warm current pass between them. "I will bring her home. I promise."

Becky nodded, afraid her emotions would overflow. She patted his arm.

Talbot extended his hand. They said nothing as Dorian accepted the firm handshake.

Becky stood at the door long after Dorian's vehicle disappeared.

****

When Morgan's eyes opened, it wasn't to the glare of spotlights. The soft light of a table lamp illuminated her cot. She sat up before she realized she was able to sit up. Unfettered. Her head swam. She grabbed the cot.

"Easy does it," a strong male voice cautioned gently.

She blinked. The man stepped closer. She looked up. The light from the lamp shined on his form. He was shorter than Dorian. Stockier. Not in muscle. Not toned. His hair was deep red and streaks of gray. His beard was more whitish than red.

"I'm Ian MacIntosh. I need your help." His brogue was thick, his tone melodious.

This was the man that had married Kayla. She was surprised. The man in front of her looked to be in his fifties.

She tried her voice. "Why did you drug me?"

"An unfortunate mistake." He looked into her eyes. "I apologize. I've reconsidered and decided to implore you to hear me out before calling out to your mate."

She fought not to betray the surprise she felt at his knowledge.

He smiled a knowing smile. "Let me get you some refreshments," he said instead, as though she'd come for tea.

Her wariness heightened, but she remained silent. She wondered if there was any way she could reach out without him knowing. He walked to a sideboard near a door. As he walked out of the lamplight his outline took on a faint glow—a faint lavender glow. As he turned back, holding the tray in his hands, he looked up at her and smiled. His eyes had the same faint color as the light outlining his body. She remembered her dream. In her dream it was a human size Gulatega staring back at her. She swallowed. Her hands tightened into fists but she didn't move. Her gaze shifted to the floor. Several violet outlines moved around his legs. Her intake of breath was audible.

"So you *are* like my daughter. Meadow can see them as well." He walked forward and set the tray on the cot next to her, pulled a chair forward, and proceeded to fix her a cup of tea. After placing a scone on a small plate, he handed it to her.

She contemplated tossing the hot liquid in his face. His next words stopped her.

"I'm dying."

He had her attention.

"Please hear me out. I'm desperate. If you can't or won't help me, I will let you go. I promise."

Morgan looked at the cup but didn't drink.

"Go ahead, it isn't drugged. I use more direct means."

Remembering the injections, Morgan took a sip of strong, sweet tea. It helped clear her head immediately.

"Eat some of the scone. It should help. I'm afraid some of the drug may take time to exit your body. I used an anti-seizure medication. It dampened your abilities." He added softly, " I'm sorry, but I needed time."

She wasn't buying the remorse. She thought of the small young girl who'd been attacked. "Do you really expect me to feel sorry for you, after what you let happen to your daughter?"

The cup stopped midway to his mouth. He blinked. She watched his eyes redden. A tear rolled down his cheek, unchecked. "I had no idea. The man was in my employ, therefore I take the blame." He looked at her, his eyes hardened. "He won't harm anyone again."

"Don't you want to know about your daughter?" her voice dripped with accusation.

"I know she had surgery for a tumor and is recovering nicely." He saw her surprise. "I'm a very resourceful man. I know how she is and I know where she is. I promise you, I will do nothing to hurt her."

He tilted his head and studied her. "You're much stronger. Your help is preferable."

Was that a veiled threat? If she didn't help him, would he go after Meadow? "What do you want?"

"I would like to tell you a story. Maybe, after you know the facts, you will help me."

"I'm listening."

"First, finish your tea and scone. Then let me show you the facilities. Afterward, we'll talk. I want your word that, until I'm finished, you won't try to contact anyone." He looked at her for a second before adding, "Please." That single word seemed to come with great difficulty.

She looked down at her tea. She could feel the energy moving in her body. She let it swirl but didn't thrust it outward. Instead, she closed her eyes, lifted her head and focused her sight on her captor. The man in front of her sat very still. She knew that he knew she was scanning him and he let her. The lavender glow was close to his body. From that, his aura spiked outward. It was jagged and imperfect. There were definite breaks in the energy field surrounding him. She closed her eyes and looked down.

"Do we have an agreement?" he asked quietly.

Morgan nodded.

He stood and motioned for her to follow him. He opened the door and they passed into an ornate hallway, wide and full of heavy dark furnishings. He led her to a bathroom off the hall. She closed the door behind her and saw herself in the mirror. Darkness encircled her eyes. Her hair was a tangled mess. She finger-combed her tresses and took some time washing her face.

It was silent in the room, as was the hallway. The static noise appeared to be limited to the room where she was being held. She reached out and let her fingers move over the wallpaper. It was cold beneath her fingers, as only stone would feel.

Ian waited for her, leaning against the wall across from the bathroom. Silently, he led her further down the hall, away from the room where he'd kept her manacled. Whether he wanted to disaffirm her previous treatment, she wasn't sure. She followed him into an ornately appointed library. In front of heavily draped windows, a glass case enclosed a large tome. She walked over to it, drawn by its heavily embossed leather.

"'Tis the history of my clan, such as it is. I am the last of that clan. It dies with me." There was sadness in his voice.

"Meadow," she corrected softly.

His smile was morose. "I end the male line. When I am gone, I am turning this over to you to give to the Abbott House, in her name. I am trusting that you will do this." His hand settled against the glass—a caress.

He motioned for her to take a seat in a large chair—its carved wood shining, the leather seat and back soft. The furnishings befitted a castle somewhere on the highland moors. He moved toward the chair's mate, his steps slow and measured. As he took his seat, Morgan saw fragility, but only for a second. Then he sat straighter and became the very image of a Highland Chieftain. As he spoke, his brogue thickened and his eyes took on a faraway look that transported him, and her—through his story—back hundreds of years.

Chapter Seventeen

Dorian stepped into the bedroom. Adorned with clouds and unicorns, it was every young girl's fantasy. Meadow was holding court in the canopied bed as regally as any royalty. John leaned against the wall near the foot of the bed, one eye trained on the door. Kayla sat in a chair next to Meadow and Jenn stood at the foot of the bed. Meadow's youthful voice flowed into the hallway, catching his ear long before he entered the room. It was full of happiness and merriment, with little semblance to the frightened girl he'd first met only days before.

"Uncle Dorian," she called, giving him an honorary title that tugged at his heart.

"Your highness," he walked to the bed and bowed from the waist.

She giggled.

He stood and smiled at her. "You look a whole lot better than I remember."

"I feel a whole lot better," she chirped. "I can talk again," she announced.

"I can see." He laughed.

John added, "Nonstop."

"Uncle John," she pouted, the green eyes flashing.

"It's okay, Princess," John turned his own charm on her, "I brought earplugs."

She groaned.

Meadow turned back to Dorian. "I've been talking to Momma and Uncle John. I think Papa has Miss Morgan." She said it matter-of-factly. Dorian's gut tightened. John shifted, put his hand on Dorian's arm and squeezed.

Dorian forced a neutral expression. "What makes you think that, sweetheart?"

"Well, it's like I was trying to tell Momma and Miss Jenn: Morgan's like me and Papa needed my help. I would have tried, too, but the man he sent to get me started acting funny. Then Papa's pets were attacking him—"

"Pets?" Dorian interrupted, thinking dogs.

"*You* know, the little trolls." She tilted her head and studied him, her brow furrowed, her eyes sharp.

John whispered, "Gulatega."

Dorian nodded to John and looked back at her. "They were attacking him?" He had never heard of them doing anything that was actually interactive on this plane. He had assumed their mere presence was enough to cause harm.

"Yes, he was holding me. I was fighting. They started swarming all over him. He let me go and I ran away. I didn't look back. I couldn't tell anyone. I lost my voice. I was so scared."

"It's okay, Meadow." He looked to Kayla, worried about asking the wrong questions. She nodded.

"How did the man get you?"

"He came to school. He said Papa was sick and needed me. I'd seen him before—I knew he worked for Papa." She looked thoughtful for a moment. "He'd never said anything to me before." She started fumbling with the sheet. "On the way, I noticed he was mumbling to himself. He started acting more...more...crazy. He stopped the car and started talking funny. I couldn't understand what he was saying. His eyes looked wild. When I tried to get out of the car, he pulled my hair. I tried to pull it back and hit my head on the door. Then I couldn't talk." She talked faster. Kayla reached out and placed her hand gently on Meadow's forearm.

Meadow looked at her mother and placed her other hand on her mother's. She took a calming breath before continuing. "I fought and finally managed to get out of the car. He ran after me. When I saw Papa's pets, I turned. That's when he caught up with me. When he grabbed me, they jumped on him. I could feel them. They made my skin tingle but it didn't hurt." She frowned. "I don't know why he was screaming. When he let go, I ran."

Dorian watched her eyes change. When she was telling the story, the pupils appeared to dilate and contract. The green facets darkened and sparkled ever so slightly.

She looked from him to her mother and back. "I've been thinking," she said. "If Papa needed me, Miss Morgan would be even better." As she turned back to him, her eyes had returned to normal—or to what was normal for her or Morgan.

"Why do you say that?"

"She's so strong—like you."

Dorian looked at the innocence before him. He thought of Jasmine at the same age. They were so different. Jasmine had been mouthy and self-centered, so sure of herself. Meadow had a fragility about her. She seemed years behind Jasmine at that age.

Sadness gripped his heart when he thought of his lifelong friend. He hoped to see her soon, when Jenn okayed it. He pulled his thoughts back. Right now, he needed to find Morgan and he would do whatever was necessary to get to her.

He'd called John from the Briscoes' to feel him out on using Meadow. John had talked to Kayla and called him back. They didn't have any problem with it as long as Meadow was agreeable. It was up to Dorian to ask Meadow.

"You might be right. Meadow, I have something to ask you." Dorian said.

"Okay." The bandage went around her head like a headband, in bright pink gauze. He smiled at her expectant eyes.

"Remember how Morgan held your hand and I had my hands on her shoulders? Together she could see your tumor."

She fingered the bandage over her ear. "I forgot to say thank you."

"You're welcome. But that's not why I brought it up," he said. "I think... if you and I hold hands and we concentrate on Morgan, maybe we can find her."

"We can try. I know Papa is worried about something. I can feel that."

"You can feel your Papa?"

"Oh yes. I can feel Momma, too. When Momma was so worried about me, I could feel it. Papa's worried about me, too. But, he's also worried about being sick as well. I could tell he was really angry when the man hurt me. He knows I'm okay now." The words tumbled out.

Dorian moved to the side of the bed, took the chair that Kayla vacated, and sat down next to Meadow.

"You will feel a tingle when we touch. If it hurts, I want you to pull your hand back."

"Okay," she said, reaching out toward his hands.

Meadow's small, cool hands slipped into his. He could feel her current; it was vibrant, full of energy.

Meadow closed her large, brilliant green eyes. Dorian did as well. He pictured Morgan in his mind and pushed. His current joined with the younger, slightly more erratic energy flow.

"I can feel Papa," Meadow announced happily.

All Dorian could feel was a heaviness. He didn't want Ian knowing what he was doing. If he had Morgan, he didn't want to risk her getting hurt. He whispered to Meadow, "Try not to contact your Dad, Meadow. We just want to find Morgan."

He watched her scrunch up her eyes and concentrate. It was hard not to smile. She was a joy, her energy so light. He closed his eyes again and sought the essence he knew was Morgan. He felt her. She pushed back, gently, faintly. He could almost see her. Then, he was seeing through her. He could feel her energy against him, like a soft stroke. He tried to push Meadow's presence in so Morgan would know the child was there as well.

"I feel her," Meadow chirped with excitement.

Dorian could see Ian. He was sitting across from her. He looked bloated, grey.

Look around, Morgan. I need to place you.

The image lifted from Ian and he was seeing a huge library, decorated in a dark gothic, renaissance fashion. He could see that Ian was speaking but he couldn't hear. Then he felt another push and the current stopped. He frowned. He let go of Meadow's hands. Morgan had broken the connection. Why?

"I know where they are," Meadow bounced up and down. "I know where they are!"

Kayla put her arm on her daughter. "Meadow, you promised. The doctor doesn't want any sudden movement. You are definitely moving."

"Yes, Momma." She calmed down. "But I do know where they are."

Dorian's heart beat faster. "Where?"

"Papa has a house at the beach. It's a castle. It's not on the beach but you can walk down the road and cross the highway and be on the beach."

"He's at Meadow's Keep?" Kayla questioned her daughter.

"Yes, I could see the library."

Kayla turned to Dorian. "Ian bought this place after I got pregnant with Meadow. It looks like a small castle. He named it Meadow's Keep. He said it reminded him of his homeland. It's a fortress. Nothing like a beach house." She shook her head. "I thought he'd sold it. We haven't been there in years."

"Momma," Meadow interrupted, "Papa's sick. I can feel it."

Dorian looked at Kayla. "How old is Ian?"

"Thirty-eight. Why?"

"I could see him. I would have sworn he was in his late fifties."

Tears formed in Kayla's eyes. She fought them, stroked Meadow's hair, and said nothing.

"Can you tell me how to get there?"

Kayla nodded and went to her purse, wrote down the address, and handed him the paper.

She walked into the hallway and waited for Dorian to follow. Jenn and John followed as well. When they'd gathered around her, she turned to Dorian.

"I thought it was the blatherings of a madman. He was nothing like this until about three years ago." She shook her head and let the tears fall. "If what she said is right, he is very sick. Maybe dying. Please." She grabbed Dorian's arm. "Please try not to hurt him."

It was John who spoke. "If he needs help, we'll see that he gets it. First, we have to get Morgan."

Kayla nodded. She looked back at Dorian. "Be careful; he's like you. Maybe stronger."

"Thank you," he said softly.

Jenn stepped forward. "Did you see her? Is she all right?"

"I couldn't see her; I was seeing through her. I believe she's okay. Tired. Her energy level is pretty low, for her."

He touched her arm, "How's Jasmine?"

"Healing. She's been talking with our staff psychologist. I think she's going to be okay. Give her time."

He nodded. He couldn't help but feel that, somehow, it was his fault she'd gotten hurt.

"Don't do that to yourself," Jenn said softly, reading the expression on his face. "It won't help anyone."

He leaned over and kissed her cheek, "I can see why Morgan has you for a best friend."

Dorian started down the hall; John caught up. "Don't for a minute think you're doing this alone."

Dorian kept walking, but smiled just the same. He'd take all the help he could get.

His thoughts shifted to Morgan. He didn't feel the fear coming from her like he had earlier. One other thing baffled him—it had been Morgan who'd broken the link. He was sure of it. He could see Morgan doing something like that to protect him, keep him away. However, he wasn't reading it that way. He would have to see when they got there.

****

Morgan watched Ian watching her. He looked exhausted but weary. She had listened intently as he told his story—a pretty fantastic story at that. Ian claimed that his ancestors, or the ancestors of his ancestors, had come through the portal and mated with humans. Apparently, they were human-like, very much like him. Ian insisted he was a genetic regression. Whether or not he was a throwback mutation of some original "visitors," she had no way of knowing. Certainly, Dorian hadn't mentioned anything coming through the portal except the Gulatega. Ian was convinced that he, like the ancestors he claimed came here centuries ago, would die on this plane of existence and that he had to find a way to go through the portal himself.

It looked, to Morgan, as though the man was definitely dying. Not immediately, but he wasn't the heartiest of individuals, either. Then there was the lavender glow that surrounded him—just like his little critter friends at his feet. Could they be causing the illness? Humans—an odd thought—seemed adversely affected by them. Well, not she or Dorian, or people with their marks.

"Mr. Macintosh," she interrupted him.

"Please, call me Ian," he grinned a devilish grin and she could see his charm.

"Ian, do you have a crescent moon shaped birthmark on your hip."

"Ah, lassie, want to be seeing me strip now?" He laid on the brogue.

She scowled at him.

He waved away her rebuke. "Actually, I have a crossed crescent." He stood and unfastened his pants.

Embarrassed, Morgan looked down.

"Don't go all girly on me, Morgana." He turned sideways and lowered one side of his trousers. The two crescents, identical to the individual ones on her and Dorian, appeared darker, with their backsides abutted, prongs outward. He pulled his pants back up and fastened them.

"My wife has a single, as does my daughter. This is another indication that I am a throwback to an original—"

"Did it ever occur to you that you might be mutating forward, not backward?" She looked up into his eyes, the blue in his eyes beginning to show a lavender hue.

"Can't say that it did. But aren't mutations meant to further the species, not end it?"

She shook her head. "Mr. MacIn...Ian," she corrected. "I don't know. I'm new to all this myself. Have you talked with Bask or Dr. Yancy?"

"I'm not ready to become someone's specimen." He snarled. "I got my introduction to Bask when I married Kayla. Sign this, agree to that. The man's a legal pervert. As to Yancy," he huffed. "Your Dr. Yancy is more minion to Bask than these creatures are to me," he pushed his foot at one of the creatures. It scurried several feet before returning to its original spot. It could feel him. Could he feel them? Could she? Morgan shivered. She wasn't willing to find out.

"Why kidnap me? Why Meadow?"

"You really don't understand anything, do you?" He was becoming agitated. He realized he was frightening her and went back and sat down, instead of pacing, as he'd been. He ran his hand through his thinning hair.

"The descendants go back much further in Scotland than here. You think Abbott House is rich?" He smirked. "They're nothing. *I'm* rich."

Morgan wondered why this vent but said nothing.

"I knew of Kayla. I did my research before I came here." He looked toward the draped window and said half to himself, "Obviously, not that great a research or I would have known about you."

"Me?"

"Yeah. You see, there aren't that many 'blended' offspring, anymore. Those that aren't paired, anyway."

Morgan shifted uncomfortably.

"You're paired. Dorian got to you first. I was hoping...," he took a deep breath.

Morgan didn't say anything, but felt her face flush.

A slice of a smile crossed his lips but didn't go to his eyes. "Don't be so naive. You couldn't anymore resist a match-mate than breathing. If I'd have known about you, Dorian wouldn't be slobbering after you now. Unfortunately, I lost. Once paired, another can't transgress."

"But you're married to Kayla," Morgan reminded him.

"Not the same. She's only half. Together we created a blend."

Morgan shot up, a horrible possibility of his intention toward Meadow. "You weren't going to—"

"Oh, good God, no. Sit down. I would never hurt my daughter. As long as she's unpaired, I can use my current with hers to open the portal. That's what all this is about. That damned portal."

Morgan sat. "Why didn't you just come to Dorian and me? We would have tried to help you."

He just shook his head. "Lass, you are so naïve. One, do you honestly think Dorian would let another match near you? Risk someone else pairing with you? Two, it's not as simple as it seems. We don't know what will happen. I'm willing to risk it, but are you?"

"You were willing to risk your own daughter," she accused.

"No!" He was emphatic. "By the time I sent Leon after her, I knew it was too dangerous for her. Then everything went to hell. Son of a bitch hurt my bonny lassie." His voice went sing-song, then flared. He looked down at his feet. "They killed the sorry SOB, saving me the trouble."

"So," he became more controlled, "I knew I had to ask you. But I knew Dorian wouldn't let you come." He shrugged. "Here you are."

"There are others," she said. "What about Mel and Thom?"

"I went to Melissa and Thomas Kilraven a couple of years ago. They turned me down flat. Of course, I didn't know they were protecting you."

Ian stopped talking and appeared to be staring into space. He gave a laugh. "Well, I'll be hanged. Looks like Sir Galahad approaches." He jumped up, grabbed her by the wrist and pulled her back toward the room where she'd been held.

When Dorian's presence had come to her earlier, she'd tried hard to keep Ian from knowing. That's why she'd broken contact. Apparently, Ian could sense him before she could. She had no idea he was nearby.

Ian appeared to sniff the air.

"Don't." She pulled against him. He was stronger than he looked. "Please don't. I'll talk to him. Don't fight him."

He turned on her, his eyes purple flames. He pushed her into the room and slammed the door.

Morgan beat on the door. "Ian, please. We can help you. Let us try."

She kicked the door, pulled at the handle. "Dorian!" she screamed. Static noise flooded the room. Morgan slammed her hands over her ears. She couldn't think. Couldn't concentrate. She spun around. At least this time she wasn't tied to that damn cot. She reached out to the side and flipped on the switch. The bare cot where she'd lain was against the wall. Hand restraints dangled from the side. At the end, a silver tray with china cups sat in stark contrast to the dingy mattress on the barren iron cot.

She scanned the room. It was empty except for the cot, a side table and a chair. The lights that had shone in her face were in the ceiling and over the door. Heavy drapery hung along one wall. Morgan ran to the drapes and pulled them back. A small window, high over her head, was covered with some sort of inset barricade. She pulled the chair over and climbed up. Wire mesh was stapled to plywood. Metal hurricane clips held the plywood in place inside the stone window frame. She wasn't strong enough to remove them by hand. Her eyes searched frantically about the room. She jumped down and grabbed a silver spoon from the tray. She stuck it under the edge of the metal, forcing the clamp, using it to pull the edge of the board toward her. She quickly worked on each clip. The spoon bent. Pain swept up her arm as her knuckles scraped against the stone edge of the window. The board edge finally gave, and she pulled it out of the window, letting the low afternoon sunlight cascaded into the room.

She thought about trying to break the window, but the glass was too thick. She took the tray to the window, hoping to catch a ray of light and send a signal. As she placed the tray against the window, she felt a sting. A small jolt went through her arm and was gone. The noise stopped. She must have shorted a circuit of some sort. With her hands pressed against the tray, she cleared her mind of everything but Dorian.

Tremors ran down her arms to the tray. She concentrated on the flow of current. Suddenly, she could see him in her mind, at the gate, against the wall. She pushed harder. She saw him stop, stand dead still, and stare. Current flowed back to her and warmth infused her. She took a deep breath. It was him. Dorian was with her. In her. Part of her. She smiled as energy flowed back and forth between them. She felt as though she was growing stronger. The hair on her arms stood on end. She tingled. She pushed it back.

She understood. She got it. She waited for his signal. Waiting for the energy to build, she paused and concentrated. She felt the tug and gathered everything she could and pushed it to him. She heard a loud pop. The tray zapped her and, and unable to control her movements, she watched as the heavy silver tray clattered to the floor. Morgan jumped down to retrieve it and stopped. She heard movement in the hall. Yanking the drape across the window, she ran to the door and flipped off the light, backing up to the cot. She sat, placing the tray on the floor. She shivered.

"Please, God, let Dorian be through the gate," she prayed.

The ensuing moments were torture. She found herself torn between just wanting to escape and wanting to help Ian. If his story was true, Morgan believed she and Dorian could help him. There was another part of her that doubted him. She knew—somehow—that he wasn't telling her the whole story. One thing was certain. The flare in his eyes was unlike anything she had ever seen. It wasn't human; it wasn't sane.

The door crashed against the wall. She knew Dorian had made it into the house at the same time Ian pulled her off the cot. His grip was fierce. His current was erratic; it sparked chaotically. She could feel Dorian reaching out to her, but it was as if Ian shielded her. He yanked her toward the hall.

"Dorian," he yelled. "I have Morgan. If you don't want me to hurt her, you'll show yourself."

"He's bluffing!" she screamed.

Ian slapped her with his other hand. Dorian stepped into the long corridor.

"Let her go." His voice was deep—deadly.

Ian pulled her against him. At the same time, he released a ball of electrical fire, aimed directly at Dorian's chest. Dorian dove to the floor, rolled and looked at Morgan. She felt the pull. Dorian's nod was so slight she wasn't sure she saw it. As Ian pulled her head back, pain shot through her neck. She pushed as much of her energy toward Dorian as she could. She heard a crackle and a bolt threw her down the hall and against the wall.

Pain shot through her.

Her head felt fuzzy and her vision blurred.

She heard Ian scream across from her. She blinked, focused, and saw him slide down the wall.

Flurries of outlines cluttered around him. She tried to yell to Dorian as he approached the fallen man. The creatures leapt in mass at Dorian. She watched him twitch and brush at his body, a look of confused agony on his face. Too dizzy to stand, she crawled to him and grabbed his leg, pulling herself up. Wrapping her arms around his waist, she put her legs against his and her head against his chest. She breathed deep and felt the current flow between them. The creatures slid down his body and circled around their legs. They appeared confused. Slowly they returned to the unconscious form on the floor. She had to look closely to tell he was breathing.

John poked his head around the corner. "Is it safe?"

"For now," Dorian sounded out of breath. He was holding Morgan against him, not loosening his grip. Ever so often he planted a kiss on her head. He breathed deep.

"I'm not immune to voltage, like some people I know," John said sheepishly. "However, I did disable his rather impressive security system while I waited."

"What do we do with him?" John walked near Ian.

"Careful," Morgan said, "the Gulatega surround him."

John took several steps back.

Morgan thought for a moment. "The room where he had me. There's a small sink in the corner."

"Good girl. We'll ground him. If we handle him gently and together, we should be okay."

The man was no lightweight. Under protest, John was relegated to moving the car to the front while Dorian and Morgan attempted to move the unconscious behemoth down the hall and into the small room. Since Morgan was the only one who could actually see the creatures, she wanted to keep them as far away from the two of them as possible.

At first Dorian suggested they try carrying him, with Dorian carrying most of the torso weight and Morgan grappling with the feet. Watching her dance around Ian's feet became amusing. She would gingerly move in and reach down, then jump back shacking off her hands, like she'd encountered spider webs.

Of course, all this was going on while Dorian held Ian's upper body off the floor. The dead weight of the man increased exponentially. As she danced back for the third time, Dorian set the man down with an oomph.

"Can you actually feel them?" he asked, trying the keep the mirth from spilling out of his mouth.

She turned on him, hands on her hips. "If I hadn't actually seen them attack you, I'd let you take the damn feet. They…they…" she fought for a word, "slither. I don't feel them exactly; I think I just think I do." She shuddered.

"Okay, they seem to want to stay at his feet. Let me just drag him from the shoulders. You get the door."

Dorian shifted his arms under the man's shoulders and arms, twisted around and began dragging him across the floor. "He's limp as a rag," he huffed. Ian's shoulders would slouch together making him damn near impossible to hang onto.

By the time they had him arranged on the floor next to the sink, with his hands handcuffed to the water pipe, Ian started to rouse. Morgan ran out of the room. By the time she was back, Ian was out again.

"What'd you do?"

Dorian shrugged, "I cold cocked him." He rubbed his knuckles.

"John's back. I told him to wait in the library. I have something that will probably work better than shoving your fist in his face every five minutes." She held up a vial and a syringe.

"Where did you get that and what's in it?"

"I saw it in the library when Ian was talking to me. I'm assuming it's what he used on me."

He took the vial from her and looked at the label. "Carbamazepine. I didn't know it came in this form." He looked at the vial. "This ought to work." He took the syringe, turned the vial upside down and withdrew half a syringe.

She handed him the alcohol wipe and went down to the feet. "I'll distract them." She shuddered and knelt down. They swirled around her. "Kinda hurry, please."

Dorian pulled out Ian's arm, swabbed and stabbed. "Okay," he said and backed away.

Morgan stood and took two steps back. At first, they followed her. Her eyes widened as she looked at Dorian. They turned and studied the unconscious man on the floor and crawled back to him, settling near his waist.

"All gone?" Dorian asked.

"Yes." A shudder ran down her body. "But I'll be glad when they really go away."

They closed the door to the room and joined John in the library. Morgan was still shaking off imaginary creatures. John turned to them as they entered.

"Look what I found." He was standing beside a credenza against a side wall. The huge pastoral oil painting hung away from the wall on a hinge. A large wall safe gleamed shiny black behind it. "The security system is off, but without—"

Dorian walked over, put his hand over the keypad, waited a few seconds, grabbed the lever and pulled down. The heavy door swung open.

John whistled. "If you ever want to enter a life of crime..." he slapped his friend on the back.

Dorian looked at Morgan but spoke to John, "You'll be the second to know."

John pulled out documents. He flipped through several. "I've got his will." John pulled out a leather folder, flipped through the pages. He whistled. "Meadow is going to be one wealthy young lady," he commented. "Kayla has guardianship, and is also named as an heir." He studied it some more. "Know anything about a MacIntosh tome?"

Morgan pointed to the glass enclosed case. John walked over and glanced down. "That goes to the Abbott House, through Meadow, as does...hey, hey...listen to this," he turned to his friends, "...all research papers, notes, paraphernalia, equipment, and lab experiments of one Dr.

Robert Milineaux, while under my employ..." He looked at Morgan.

"I'll be damned." Dorian commented and turned to Morgan, who stared down at the leather bound tome, not meeting their gaze.

"You okay?" Dorian put his arm around her shoulder.

She nodded slightly, squelching the embarrassment she felt about her "ex."

Dorian let his energy run from him to her.

She felt warmth gather in her core. She leaned into him for a second, then moved away.

John was back rifling through the safe. "I've got several personal journals here as well. I better call Bask."

"Wait," Morgan said.

John closed his phone.

She looked at them. "He's dying. Something's wrong with him genetically. He's more like the creatures than he is human." She walked over and sat down in one of the large chairs. Her shoulders slumped. "He asked me to help him. I'm assuming he wanted me to help him cross through the portal."

Dorian went to her, knelt in front of her and took her hand. "I don't think that's ever happened." He looked into her eyes. "All the stories I've heard have been of the Gulatega. Period."

"That's not entirely true," John spoke hesitantly from across the room.

Both pairs of eyes turned to him.

"We have tribal stories we haven't shared with anyone outside the tribe about glowing men. You're talking ancient history. Oral history. Some drawings, maybe. I would have to check our records." He walked over to them. "And I have a feeling Abbott House might have information that not everyone is privy to."

Morgan squeezed Dorian's hand. "I think I want to help him."

"Even after…" he didn't finish.

She simply nodded as Dorian looked at her. Their communication was silent.

Finally, Dorian stood and turned to John. "Look, I know you work for Abbott House. But, if we do this, we're going to need your help."

"When have I ever turned my blood brother down?" He smiled at Dorian.

"I need you to stall Bask. Give us some time. I don't care how you do it, just do it. I'll call you when we're done."

"Don't you think you're jumping the gun here?" John asked.

"I'm going with Morgan on this. She's the one that can see them. Him. I trust her gut."

John didn't look convinced. He looked at the papers before he spoke. "I can call him. I'll think of something." He sat down at the desk.

"I want you to leave," Dorian walked to him. "Take the will with you. But I want you out of here."

"I don't know if I want to do that," John stood and faced his friend.

Morgan came forward. "John, give us time. We need to look around here. I don't know if it can be done here or not. Somehow, I think it can. Of the three of us, you are the most vulnerable. I don't want anything happening to you. Think of Kayla and Meadow."

"God, I hate it when you're right," he said to Morgan. "You've got six hours. If I haven't heard from you by then, I'm coming back with a team."

Dorian smiled and shook his hand. "If you haven't heard from me by them, bring lots of reinforcements."

Chapter Eighteen

Morgan turned back toward the long corridor as Dorian closed the front door. She figured they'd better take a look around while they could. She gave the drug two to four hours before Ian woke up, based solely on her own experience. He was much larger and male, so it might be less effective. Ian had mentioned a lab. She wanted to find that lab.

"Where do you want to start?" She called back over her shoulder. She heard him drop the duffel bag John had handed him before he left.

"Right here." Dorian grabbed her and turned her in his arms. His mouth came down hard on hers, insistent.

Morgan tensed at the unexpected assault on her senses. His energy enveloped her. As suddenly as she tensed, she began to relax. As his mouth softened, he teased, coerced her response. She moaned and met his tongue, stroking it with her own. She couldn't get close enough. She pressed her chest into his, wrapping her arms around him and allowing her hands to push up under the back of his shirt, exploring the muscles on his back.

"God, woman," he groaned into her, "You scared the hell out of me."

"Didn't do me too much good, either." Her voice came as a caress, muffled, as her tongue ran across his neck. The lights flickered.

Morgan felt her need for him intensify. With each caress, she grew stronger. Something about them seemed to be genetically altered, so that each one's strength was enhanced by contact with the other.

She backed out of his arms. "Maybe we should explore a little first."

He smiled. At least she wasn't saying no. They were both drained. They needed one another—badly. He took her hand and went forward, opening doors, glancing in, shutting them.

"This isn't a race," she laughed and pulled back.

"That's what you think." He moved to the next door. So far, they'd seen a parlor, dining room, the library—which they were familiar with—several closets, and a bathroom. Toward the back was the room Ian was in and through the door under the arched stairway would be the kitchen. Upstairs were the bedrooms. That's where he wanted to explore. Alone. With Morgan. He stopped.

"What's wrong?" She looked at him.

"Nothing. I'm being a guy. I need to stop being a guy."

She nestled closer. "No, you don't," she purred, "but, you might tone it down a bit." She let her hand brush across the front of his jeans.

"Not if you keep doing that," he groaned and grabbed at her. She jumped away and went toward the kitchen, pushing open the heavy door. She let out a low whistle. They stepped into a massive kitchen fit for any chef's fantasy.

The island had to be a good eight feet by eight feet. Two prep sinks occupied diagonal corners. A huge—big enough to wash a dog comfortably on one side—double sink sat under a large expanse of windows in the back. She turned around and whimpered, "I want."

"Just remember who comes with it," he challenged.

"Oh...yeah...well, never mind." She let her fingers trail over the five-foot wide stove.

Off the kitchen, a door led to steps going down. "Bingo," Dorian said, and flipped on a light.

"And creepy," Morgan added as she begrudgingly followed him down the narrow stairs. They came to a landing and turned, twice. At the bottom, Dorian found another switch and turned on three sets of overhead fluorescent lights, illuminating a large laboratory and workroom. The lab was a mess. At the far end of that was a set of arched, heavily reinforced doors.

Dorian made eerie sounds as he approached. Morgan jumped. "You're not funny."

"Actually, I'm pretty scared, myself." He turned to her and smiled at her expression.

"Would you stop that?"

"Just trying to lighten the mood."

"Well, just remember, I'm the person who can warn you if creepy critters are about to attack."

He frowned. "Yeah, I want to remember that."

He held his palm up in front of the arched doors for a few seconds and pulled them open. He stepped into what looked like a cave. Dorian found a switch by the door. When the light came on, it sparkled off bits of rock and gems embedded in the wall. The floor was natural—dirt, sand, and rock. It looked similar to the grotto, except it was manmade. It had to have been since there was no natural rock this close to the beach. Still, he could guess its use, or potential use.

Morgan stepped inside and chills went down her arms. "I know this place," she whispered.

Dorian looked at her. "Did he bring you down here?" His voice was taut.

"No." She concentrated. "I dreamt of it. Recently. I thought there was a giant Gulatega. It was Ian." Her voice trailed off and she rubbed her arms.

"Come here." He pulled Morgan to him.

She seemed distracted. She looked at him. "Now?" she tried to back away.

"Not that. Five points, remember?"

"Oh. Okay." She moved into his arms.

He lowered his head to hers. The energy began to pulsate, then hum. The room took on iridescent glow. The gems and stones sparkled as the harmonics changed. Not two feet away, Morgan saw what looked like a fissure in the floor. A lavender light shot up. She broke contact.

He looked at her but dropped his hands.

"Unless you want a portal opening up, we need to back off."

He nodded. The room went back to the way it had been when they entered. They went back into the lab and closed the door.

Morgan looked around, trying to make order out of the mess. Walls were lined with papers taped on top of other papers. Formulas filled chalkboards and dry-erase boards. It was chaos. She picked up a paper and looked at Dorian. "This is Rob's handwriting. It looks like he's been losing it for some time." She looked at the date. "It also looks like he was working here when he met me." Then added under her breath, "The jerk."

"I'm sorry." Dorian put his hand on her shoulder.

She shrugged and walked to the stairs. "Well, it looks like we found the avenue. And, we have the means. Shall we try to wake him?"

He looked at his watch. "I don't think he's going to be any good to anyone for some time. Let's look around some more." He walked past her and headed up the stairs. If he noticed, he chose to ignore the smile she gave him.

Morgan cracked open the door where Ian rested, curled up on the floor. The Gulatega, there appeared to be four or five—it was hard to tell, since their outlines seemed to meld into one another—lay curled up next to him with their eyes closed. She watched Ian's chest rise and fall in a steady, even pattern and quietly closed the door.

"Apparently, our experiment downstairs didn't faze them," she told Dorian as she backed out of the room. "They haven't moved."

"Shall we?" He motioned toward the steps.

She noticed he carried the duffel bag.

"Something your mother put in the truck when I left."

"The clean underwear syndrome," she said, walked around him, and preceded him up the stairs.

Dorian watched the gentle sway of her derriere as the moved up the stairs. He felt a tightening in his loins and cursed under his breath. He heard her chuckle.

The stairs wound around to the opposite side. At the top of the landing was a large hallway with doors on either side. A high arched window overlooked the front from on end.

She started at the left. The first room was decorated befitting a faery princess. It had to be Meadow's room. It was bright and airy, done with love. She closed the door. The room next to Meadow's was simple, feminine and had a door leading to a huge bath, which led into another room. She figured the first of the two adjoining rooms was Kayla's. The large bath was a shared Master Bath and led to Ian's suite. His suite looked as though it had been plucked out of a medieval castle, all heavy furniture and dark wall coverings.

Dorian was opening and closing doors on the other side.

"Morgan, come here," he called. She walked out of Ian's room and crossed the hall, stepping into a circular turret room. It, too, looked as though it had been plucked straight out of a medieval romance. Tiny windows, starting at floor level, spiraled around the room ending at the ceiling, which was an inverted cone shape. A large stone fireplace hugged the inside wall. Tapestries hung around the room on the stone walls and the bed was covered in more embroidered fare.

As Morgan stepped into the middle of the room, the door swung closed behind her. A heavy metal latch fell in place. Dorian turned and grinned, walking slowly, purposefully, toward her. She swallowed, her throat tight. She felt his warmth around her neck, then the sizzle of energy as it moved down her spine.

Electricity filled the air, emanating from the man walking toward her. His eyes were hot with desire; they had changed from ice blue to blue black. He stepped in front of her, holding her gaze captive. His hands moved slowly up her arms, across her chest and down, until he cupped her breasts. Dorian moved his hands to her sides and pulled her close to him. As his mouth took hers, he let her breath mingle with his and their currents meld. Any hesitation she felt disappeared as she responded to his body's silent call.

He backed her to the bed, stripping off her clothes, piece by piece, until she stood naked before him. His lips followed his hands as he trailed molten kisses down her sensitive skin.

The fire spread from the core of her being through her limbs and settled in the vee at the top of her legs. She was ravenous for him and began tearing at his clothing. He pushed her back on the bed and stood between her legs, devouring her with his eyes as he ripped off his clothes. His body was hard and hot as he moved over hers. She spread wider, inviting him into her center.

As he entered her, the currents of their bodies surged, pulsing between them. He fought to retain control, to feel her velvet muscles hold him. He heard her sudden intake of breath, felt a ripple across her abdomen and, in a tight spasm, she gripped him. His control slipped and he took them both over the edge in quick, conjoined movements.

Their bodies slick, their breathing hard, they didn't move. He put his forehead against hers. "I adore you," he breathed. "I just want you to know."

"Yeah...me, too," was all she could manage.

He kissed the tip of her nose.

"You know," she tried again, "we probably shouldn't have done this."

He rolled off her, looked down, and trailed his fingers from her neck to the mound of red curls. "Look at it this way—we're recharged and we didn't mess up his library."

She shifted up on her elbows, scanned the hard muscles of the man next to her. "There's still time." She smiled at him impishly.

"You're a hard task master. I guess I must be strong for the both of us." He sat up and got off the bed. "I do believe there's a bathroom through that door. We can avail ourselves of the facilities and change into fresh clothing." Naked, he grabbed the duffel bag and walked through the doorway. By the time she reached the bathroom, the shower was running and he held a beckoning hand to her. She took it and stepped under the spray.

He lathered her body from top to bottom, slowly exploring all of her curves and crevices until she could barely stand. Then he sat on the stone bench in the back and let her straddle him, allowing her to move at her own pace. The spray beat against her back, over her shoulders and ran down her breast. He took her hardened nipple into his mouth and suckled. Her movements increased in intensity. He moved to the other breast and let his hands close over her buttocks, supporting her. She bucked against him, straining. He thrust deep inside her and their climaxes peaked. She leaned her head against his.

"If we're going to have any energy left, we better stop this," she panted.

"You first," he looked up and took her mouth.

She crawled off him. "Yes, I am woman. I am strong."

As she stepped out of the shower, he let his hand brush down her back and buttocks.

"Stop that!"

He laughed and stuck his head under the hard spray.

****

Morgan rummaged through the duffel bag, finding clothes for both her and Dorian. By the time she donned the underwear—God love her mother—jeans, and long-sleeve knit tee, Dorian stepped into the room, a towel slung low on his hips. She completely stopped the finger combing of her tangled hair and stood staring in appreciation of the incredible male form striding across the room. She felt her pulse quicken and the blood pool in her groin. Oh, God, she was becoming a sex fiend. She swung around and tried to get her clumsy hands to pull her hair back into a ponytail.

Warm lips on her neck stayed her hands, her pulse, and her breath. She closed her eyes and moaned.

"I like it when you do that," he said against her neck.

She leaned her head back, turning it to the side, giving him better access. "Dorian…I…can't…think…" she groaned and forced herself away from the fire following his hands as he moved them up her sides to her breasts.

"Geesh!" The word came out in a whoosh. "Please get dressed. Please," she begged.

He was already pulling a black tee over his head. She watched as he pulled it down over rippling muscles.

"You're not helping, either, you know." He smiled at her. "Those emerald orbs have fire in them," he leaned over and kissed, first one lid, then the other. "It makes my blood boil."

"Dorian?"

"Hmmm?"

"Do they glow in the dark?" she asked him.

He looked at her, his brows coming together in a frown.

"My eyes? Like the Gulatega?" She had always worried about it. Since Dr. Yancy had said that she saw beyond the normal spectrum, she wondered—no, hoped—that she was the only one who saw them glow in the dark.

Dorian studied her, looking into her eyes. "Your eyes glitter, like cut emeralds, and sometimes I see a sparkle in the dark. But glow, no." He laughed a small laugh. "Melissa used to read an old comic called "Brenda Starr" about an adventurous reporter. Melissa loved the fact that they would print a star in her green eyes. That's what I think of when I see your eyes. They are nothing like you describe the Gulatega."

Morgan felt better. No, she felt good. As close to normal as she ever had.

"You know, by the way," Dorian said, thoughtfully, "I can see Ian's eyes glow and his outline. Is that how the Gulatega appear?"

"Yes and no. Ian has substance. The Gulatega don't have that substance. It's the glow that actually defines them."

"I've been thinking," Dorian said as he went and sat down in one of the chairs beside the fireplace. "Ian wants to go through the portal. We don't know that he'll live once he gets there."

"He definitely won't live much longer here," she walked over to the narrow window and looked out. She could see the ocean in the distance. It was calm, the waves breaking small. Very different from what she was feeling inside. She felt like she had the ocean's store of energy and it sought land upon which to crash. She turned to Dorian. He was tossing a ball of energy from hand to hand. He shot it up in the air and it popped. She felt the tingle as her hair reacted to the static.

She pulled her attention back to the problems ahead of them. "I'm worried about Kayla and Meadow as well. I know he left the will, leaving them everything. If we help him go through the portal, he disappears. No body, no death. I don't know much about this sort of thing, but I think they'll have to wait seven years for him to be declared dead."

"As much as I hate it, I think we need to bring Bask in on this. And I have a feeling he's not going to like it at all."

"I want to help Ian, in spite of what he's done." She moved back to the chair opposite him. "I don't know why, but I seem almost compelled to help him."

"Do you think it's him? Is he making you feel this way?" Dorian looked concerned.

"No. He could have done that earlier. He didn't." She shrugged. "Maybe we should talk with him first. Then call Bask."

"Just be careful, Morgan. I don't—"

She moved to stand between his legs, looking down into his upturned face. "I've got you," she interrupted, brushing back an errant lock of black hair. "Besides, he needs both of us to open the portal."

A horrifying thought entered his mind. Ian had taken Morgan, but it took two to open the portal. Who did Ian expect to help Morgan? Ian. God, had he planned to drag her through with him? As the thoughts played through his mind, his arms went around her and he buried his face into her midriff, inhaling the sweet scent that was Morgan. He could have lost her.

Without telling her the direction of his thoughts, he stood, took her mouth with his and poured himself into the kiss. When he pulled back, they were both breathless.

"Let's go talk to Ian," he whispered. "But keep your distance. I don't trust him."

"Me either," she laid her head against his chest for a moment. "Me either."

Ian was awake when they entered the room. He was sitting up, his back against the wall. The creatures were moving about his feet, a little further away from his body. Morgan pulled Dorian further away, across the room toward the cot where she'd been tied. They sat, side by side on the cot.

Ian lifted one side of his lip in a half smile, half sneer. "I see you've availed yourselves of my hospitality."

Morgan blushed. Dorian smiled back. "And nice accommodations they are, too," he challenged.

Ian laughed. "No fool you. Keep yourself and your mate strong, by all means."

"By all means," Dorian hissed through clenched teeth.

Morgan took a breath, ignoring Ian's slight. "We've come to discuss helping you. You might want to choose your words more carefully." Her tone was even and clipped, her eyes blazed.

Ian looked at her, tilted his head and studied her. "Why?"

"You're dying and, unlike you," she added the dig, "we have a sense of humanity."

"So the witch and her wizard are going to send the wicked sorcerer back from whence he came."

"Ian," she straightened, fighting not to let his ugliness alter her intent, "you didn't come from there any more than we did. However, something has you convinced that you will survive on the other side, better than here. If you can convince us of that fact, maybe—just maybe—we will consent to help you get there." His sneer propelled her. "Or to hell, for that matter—it makes no difference to me."

Ian looked at Dorian. "She has spunk, that's for sure. Shame I didn't get to her first."

Dorian started off the cot. Morgan's hand grabbed his wrist. She felt his energy pulse and rise.

"You didn't," she chided. "And…" she paused for effect, "I seriously doubt you would have been successful. I still have free will."

Ian harrumphed.

Morgan found him appalling. For two cents, she'd shove him and his little creatures right through the portal, ready or not. Dorian sensed her anger and took her hand in his. They looked at one another. It was one of those moments when they knew exactly what the other was thinking and it didn't need to be spelled out. They smiled at one another.

Dorian spoke, "Say we decide to help you 'cross over.' You disappear. What happens to Kayla and Meadow?"

"Besides becoming very wealthy women?"

"There won't be any body," Morgan stated.

Ian smiled. This time it seemed genuine. "I've taken care of that. I will need to talk to that asshole of an attorney you have—Bask—first. I would prefer to do that in private. The less you know about my business the happier I'll be."

"As long as Bask okays it, we're good to go. Oh, one thing. I want John here during our little experiment. As a safety. Well…actually…his *safety* will be off." Dorian stated matter-of-factly.

Ian shrugged. He was growing weaker. His bravado was slipping.

Dorian dialed Bask. They spoke for a few minutes and he handed Ian the phone. The man, even slumping next to the sink, held quite a presence. Dorian took Morgan's hand and led her out of the room.

Someone knocked on the front door. Dorian opened it to John.

"You want me?"

"How does Bask do that?" Morgan asked.

Dorian just shrugged and led them back down the corridor, explaining the make shift plan that they had so far. John's response was to check his weapon.

"I'm ready. I would like nothing better than to have to shoot that son of a bitch."

Morgan placed her hand gently on his arm. He looked at her and shook his head. "I suppose I have some anger issues where Ian's concerned."

"I don't blame you. He's not a very nice man."

"Ironically, he was. When he was dating Kayla, we all liked him. He was funny and fun loving, and seemed to adore her. Things started changing about three years ago."

"He's sick, John. In fact, if he stays here, he's going to die."

"Couldn't happen to a…" John let the words trail off.

"How are Kayla and Meadow?" Morgan reached for a better topic.

John immediately brightened. "Great. Meadow's healing very rapidly. I guess I can be grateful to Ian for that one fact. Kayla's talking about getting an apartment in the area. She likes it up here."

Morgan brightened. "I might have a great idea. I have an apartment. It has two bedrooms and allows pets." She was thinking of Mrs. T. "You might mention it."

Dorian watched her. This was the first mention she had given that she might be going back with him. Her eyes caught his and held.

John saw the exchange. "I think I'll go call Kayla right now." He pulled out his phone and walked toward the front of the house.

"You're coming home with me?" Dorian asked.

"I…I've been thinking about it," Morgan whispered, her voice failing her.

"Please, come home with me," he said and stepped in front of her, framing her face in his hands.

"Hey out there!" Ian yelled through the door. "Come get this infernal phone. He wants to talk to his minion."

Morgan and Dorian broke apart. Dorian stepped toward the door and turned back to her. "This discussion is only tabled."

She nodded and followed him into the room.

Morgan was astounded. For all of his bravado, Ian looked like he'd aged five more years. There was a sheen of sweat across his brow and his skin had a grey pallor and was now etched with deep lines. She took Dorian's hand and closed her eyes. When she reopened them, she looked at his aura. There were pits in it. Even the glow that surrounded him had taken on a mottled look. The creatures were swirling closer to his middle again, almost as if they were trying to give him strength. However, she couldn't be sure of that. When Dorian stepped forward to retrieve the phone, they turned to him in unison, their eyes widening, their glow deepening. Where they warning him off, or finding an attraction to his energy? They made no move toward him. When he stepped back out of range, they settled back around Ian's middle.

She blinked, returning his image to normal, or what was normal for him. The violet glow, even broken, encircled him, whether she looked at him with enhanced vision or not. She glanced down at the small creatures nestled close to him. They were the same color. The closer they got, the more even his aura became. Morgan believed he might just be a throwback of the humanoid individuals he claimed once crossed into this plane.

"I've a fax machine in the library. Bask will be sending some legal crap for me to sign. When you go get that, bring the white envelope on the desk back with you. You will give that to Bask. He knows about it. Let's get this show on the road." He dismissed them and settled back against the wall.

Dorian talked with Bask as they walked into the library where the fax machine was already spitting out papers. Morgan pulled out the documents, took them to the desk and stapled the sets together, grabbed a clipboard from the desktop and a pen from the drawer.

Dorian picked up the envelope from the desk. "Do you trust this to be what he says?" he asked into the cell phone.

"Given our discussion, yes," Bask said. "Have him sign all copies and fax them to me. Then, you two will do your thing and pray it goes as planned. Give John the envelope, as well as the signed forms. You'll take John's car and head back to Morgan's parents' house. John will wait there for the Abbott crew."

"What do we say to Kayla and Meadow?" Morgan asked Dorian, who relayed it to Bask.

"John will take care of it. I want you two as far away from this as soon as possible, understand?"

"Yes." Dorian said and hung up.

Morgan didn't want to think about the implications of what they were doing. She knew she was an accessory to something. She didn't want to go any further than that. She kept Meadow in her mind and tried to think how much better she would be without Ian in her life. Kayla, too. His death was imminent. Putting him through the portal could save him, if his theories were right. If not... She didn't want to think about that.

John's beaming face pulled her away from the morose thoughts that were setting her nerves on edge. "Jenn says she's going to take them over to see the apartment this afternoon. She thinks it's a great solution. Says she wants to talk with you later—no if's, and's, or but's."

"I'll call her tonight." Her voice broke.

She felt Dorian's arm slip around her. "It's okay," he whispered in her ear. "It's going to be okay."

Morgan looked at him. He was the picture of calm. She didn't feel it. The unknown was scaring her to death. Maybe she didn't have what it took to do this. Or…to be part of the Abbott group…or Ruthorford.

He kissed her temple and leaned his head in against hers. She felt the current build and converge on her spine, where his hand rested. She took a deep breath.

"Thank you," she whispered. She felt better. Stronger. She wasn't used to needing help from anyone. All her life, she'd been strong, physically and emotionally. She'd never had an illness. Her exuberance with living seemed to encompass others. People tended to be happy when she was around. There seemed to be no carry over from the nightmares. Now that she knew she'd been dreaming of the Gulatega, her concerns about them had vanished. The idea that she might need strength from someone else was a new concept, but one, at least for the moment, that she was willing to embrace.

"Shall we go in?" Dorian gently guided her toward the small room across the hall.

Ian was lying on the floor, his arm pulled back. Morgan rushed to him. He looked to be sleeping, except his breathing was shallow and wispy. "Mr. Macintosh?" she touched his arm, ignoring the creatures swarming around her. She felt feather-like sensations along her legs and arms where they came in contact with her.

Ian opened his eyes and blinked. "I guess I fell asleep," he said as he struggled to right himself. Dorian moved toward them, but she waved him back. Morgan helped Ian sit up. "I have the paperwork you asked for," she said softly.

He smiled at her, "You really are a bonny lass," he said and took the clipboard. He looked for the signature lines and signed his name, over and over, never once stopping to read the documents.

"Do you want me to read it to you?" she offered.

"No, lass," he smiled at her. "Bask and I have come to an agreement." He handed her back the clipboard, then grabbed her wrist.

A second of panic went through her until she saw the furrow in his brow. "One thing you can do for me. When this is over," his voice broke, "check in on my Meadow, now and again. And tell Kayla I'm sorry."

"I promise." Morgan covered his hand with her own. She felt energy go down her arm and into his hand. She heard his intake of breath. She hadn't intended it. She remembered thinking how weak he was and trying to give him sympathy. She jerked back her hand.

"It's okay, lass," he chuckled. "I appreciate the effort. I see you don't quite have a handle on it yet."

Her face reddened and she tried to smile.

Dorian reached down, his voice not as accommodating as Morgan's had been. "Let's get these cuffs off you. John and I will get you up while Morgan faxes back the paperwork." He looked at Morgan. It wasn't a suggestion.

She took the clipboard and left the room.

By the time Morgan was finished faxing the documents, re-stapling them and putting everything in a manila envelope for John, she had calmed. This was the best way. For everyone involved. If he stayed here, if she helped him heal—and she had no doubt from what she'd done in that room that she could—he could still be a threat to Meadow and Kayla, and possibly herself. But, she felt she still had to offer.

He was sitting on the cot, looking like a tired old man, when she walked back into the room. She swallowed and looked around the room where he had held her prisoner. And drugged her. It didn't change things.

"Mr. Macintosh," she began.

"Ian, child. Call me Ian." His voice came out a bare whisper.

"Ian. I can help you. I felt it when I put my hand over yours. You felt it, too. You don't have to do this. You can stay here."

Dorian grabbed her arm. "What are you doing?"

She pulled away from him, went and knelt down in front of this weary man and stared into his faintly glowing eyes. She ignored the creatures gathering at her feet. "Ian, let me help you. You don't know what will happen when you go through that portal. You could die."

"I've planned this for years, Morgan." He gently patted her hand, but removed it before her energy moved through him. "I'm ready to do this. But I truly appreciate your offer."

She nodded and stood, tears forming in her eyes.

Chapter Nineteen

It took the effort of both John and Dorian to get the increasingly weaker man down the steps into the lab. As Morgan watched from behind them, she was amazed that they didn't trip over the Gulatega swarming and swirling around and between their legs. They seemed to have no interest in Dorian. John seemed to be unaffected as well. Still, she watched the creatures for any change in movement and John for any sign of confusion. She still couldn't tell if they had substance in this dimension. Neither Dorian nor John seemed to take much notice of them. Every now and then, she would see one or the other shiver, as though they'd walked through a spider's web, but their footing remained even and strong.

In the lab, Ian had them help him sit on one of the stools so he could explain some things he thought were pertinent to what they were going to do. Apparently, it wasn't going to be as simple as Dorian and Morgan touching and opening the portal. The embedded gems and crystals were placed in specific locations for a reason. There were more stones that had to be strategically placed. He had them searching through the milieu of papers strewn across counters to find a diagram. He swore he had it memorized but he wanted to be damned sure to get it right this time—since this would probably be his only chance.

In a safe, Morgan found several bags of gemstones, none of which looked familiar but all of which she was sure were worth a fortune. Following Ian's direction, she took the stones with them into the cave room and placed each stone exactly as Ian indicated. On the wall, he had her feeling for a ledge here and there and placing one just so. Twice, he had her exchange stones. When she was done, he had John and Dorian help him move about the room to make sure of every stone's placement. By the time they were done, Ian was gasping for breath and sweating profusely.

"Are you sure you want to do this while you are so weak?" she asked.

"I don't think it's going to get any better, lass. We best be getting on with it."

Ian took a yardstick and walked to the center of the room, looked around, and turned slightly. He drew a line in the dirt. "This is where the portal should start to open."

Morgan looked around. It definitely looked like the location from earlier. "Does it come from the floor?"

"Very astute." Ian pointed to the line. "I've embedded stones beneath the floor. They correspond to the earth's energy grid that crosses this location. There are also stones to the side and in the ceiling. I need the portal to be large enough for me to cross. Generally, they are small and the Gulatega barely squeeze through." He reached in his pocket, withdrew a beautifully carved stone, set it in the middle of the line.

"Two things…" he turned to them, "When I am gone, I want you to take the stones in the walls with you. I am turning the house and everything over to Bask. For now, I don't want just anyone following me willy-nilly. Please. I beg of you."

Morgan looked at John and Dorian. They nodded. She turned and nodded as well.

"And the second thing?" Dorian asked.

"I want you two to stand over there, by that ledge. When this opens and widens, I don't want you two being sucked through."

Morgan immediately stepped back.

"John, your safest place would be in the lab, but knowing you won't do that, please at least stay at the entrance, as far back as you can. I don't want your natural rhythms to screw this up."

When Dorian nodded agreement, John walked back to the entrance and pulled his gun holding it at his side. Ian smiled.

"I'm game when you are," he said. "Oh, I have an envelope for Meadow in the safe. It's for her birthday."

"I'll see that she gets it," Morgan promised.

"Whatever you do, don't break contact. This could take a bit longer and require more effort. Please, see this through."

Dorian took Morgan's hand and led her to the area by the ledge. They turned sideways, so they could both see Ian. Dorian leaned forward and lightly kissed Morgan's mouth. She felt the tingle. Then she felt his arms embrace her, his legs move to either side of hers and he placed his forehead to hers.

Surges of energy raced between them. Erratic at first, then pulsing, Morgan felt her heart rate change to match the pulse. She could feel the energy, hotter than before, move between them. She tightened her palms against his sides. The current deepened, widened.

About the room, stones began to glow. At a certain point, the light from the stones began to pulse. The pulses quickened. As Morgan watched, the line on the floor emitted a spark. Beams of lavender light shot up from the floor, through the stone in the center, and fanned out toward the ceiling. The creatures circling Ian's legs moved back and forth, more and more erratic. Ian was beginning to slump.

Morgan started to pull away, to go to him. He saw her and yelled, "No!"

She held on to Dorian, tears stinging her eyes. The current was moving up and down her spine, then down to the floor and back again. She couldn't tell if she was energized or drained. She and Dorian stood as one.

Suddenly, she could see the portal. She stared. Lights of lavender and a rainbow of other colors pulsed in the area where the portal should be. She knew it was open when one of the creatures went through. Then another. Ian, having slumped to the floor, began dragging himself toward the brilliant, flashing pulses of light. The last creature disappeared into the glow. The portal seemed to blink.

"Please," Ian begged, staring at the portal opening as though he could see through it to the other side. "Please help me."

Morgan tried to break free. Dorian held on tight, clasping her in his arms.

Ian stretched out one hand and she saw it disappear into the glow. The glow changed color and encircled his wrist. He pulled back, looked at his hand. Thrust it through again. Pushing with his feet, he inched toward the portal. His breathing became labored, he could barely move, yet he refused to remove his hand from the portal.

Suddenly, one of the creatures appeared back through the portal. Then another. As more came through, Morgan sucked in her breath. What had they done? They watched as a mass of Gulatega encircled Ian, and, by sheer will, inched his form slowly toward the portal.

Morgan didn't realize she was holding her breath until the last creature began to move through the portal. The creature reached down and pushed the stone that Ian had placed in the middle through the portal and followed it through. The portal collapsed upon itself. Ian was gone.

She began to shiver. Dorian tightened his arms around her and held her. Tears poured from her eyes. She took great gulps of air into her lungs. Morgan knew that, had Dorian not been holding her up, she would have collapsed.

The stones no longer glowed. The only signs of what had transpired were scratches in the dirt. No one would know what had occurred. No one would believe her.

"You all right?" Dorian leaned back and looked at her. His expression was strained, his brow furrowed.

She nodded. She could do nothing else.

John walked into the room and handed Dorian the velvet bag. Silently, they walked around the room collecting the rare stones and placed them in the bag as Morgan leaned weakly against the ledge. John brought the diagram over, folded it and slipped it into the bag. With one last look around, the three of them walked silently out of the cave, the lab, and up the stairs to the main level.

Dorian sat Morgan in a chair in the hallway and disappeared into the library with John.

"You okay with us leaving?" Dorian asked.

"Bask will have the clean-up team here anytime. I'm pretty sure nothing's going to come through that portal—at least not while I have these." He held up the bag of stones.

Dorian clapped him on the back. "Thanks, I owe you one."

John smiled. "It all works out. I'll catch up with you later."

Dorian walked back into the hallway and helped her to her feet. As they got to the door, John called. Dorian stopped, took the duffel bag John handed him, smiled at his friend, and led Morgan to the SUV.

Morgan glanced at the side view mirror as they wound their way down the drive. Looking back, one would never guess that this estate sat so close to the Atlantic Ocean. They turned onto a narrow road. Sand scattered in windblown wave-like patterns across its gravel and asphalt surface. She could see the divided highway ahead with beach cottages and dunes separating it from the ocean. Most of the cottages were boarded up for the winter now, with a few permanent residents the only holdouts.

Dorian turned onto the divided highway and drove in silence. Morgan let her head fall back against the seat and closed her eyes. She opened them again. She kept seeing Ian disappearing through the portal and she wasn't sure she was ready to handle that imagery yet.

Dorian swung into a fast food drive-thru, placed a double order, and retrieved it while she watched in silence.

"I bet you don't have any idea of when you ate last." He handed the bag to her and set the drinks in the cup holders in the console.

The smell of hot fries escaped the bag and she sniffed longingly.

"Go ahead," he encouraged.

Morgan slipped her hand into the bag and pulled out a container of fries. Her favorite kind—fresh and piping hot. The tang of salt and heat touched her tongue and she reached for another. She held out the carton in offering. Dorian grabbed a few, cursed when they burned his fingers and sucked in air around the hot grease he'd just popped in his mouth. She smiled and nibbled on another, closing her eyes in appreciation of the distraction.

He turned down a short road and parked the vehicle at the end, overlooking the ocean, now cloaked in night. Morgan could make out the white of the waves' crests as they raced toward shore. Even with the windows up, she could hear the sound of the ocean.

Dorian doused the lights and reached for the bag of food. He pulled out his burger and set another carton of fries on the dash. They ate listening to the sound of the waves.

"Want to take a walk?" he asked as he shoved wrappers back into the bag and tossed it behind the seat.

"Sure." She was feeling better. The food helped. Maybe a walk along the sand would help her regain perspective. The ocean always seemed to give her strength.

Dorian took her hand as they stepped down onto the sand. The waves sounded louder although they weren't breaking very high. The blackness of the ocean pulled at her, its unknown beckoning. They walked down to where the water had dampened the sand, giving them a firmer path. They turned and headed toward the distant lights of a pier. Morgan crossed her arms over her midriff as a chill breeze ruffled her hair. Dorian threw his arm around her and pulled her close, slowing to adjust his gait to hers.

"Are you all right?" he asked.

She nodded, watching the twinkle of the sand in the dark and wondered if he could see its sparkle. She turned and looked up at his strong profile, the unshaven line of his jaw, the unruly curl of his hair. He turned and looked down at her, his eyes clear in the night.

They stopped. He turned her toward him and pulled her gently against his body, dipping his head down to kiss her lightly on the lips. The heat of his mouth warmed hers and she parted her lips, welcoming his exploration. Her arms moved to his chest and up around his neck. He pulled her tighter and deepened the kiss. She felt the comfort of the current moving between them, giving and taking, advancing and retreating, as the water kissed the shore.

As he lifted his head, he kissed her temple. Morgan looked down. They were encircled by the perimeter of sparkling sand, glittering in the night.

"Can you see that?"

He looked down. "Yes."

"I'm glad. I never know what things only I can see."

"If it's within a spectrum I can perceive, I can see it. Probably not as vividly as you, but I see it. "Which means," he lightly kissed her and turned to walk back in the direction they had come, "others can see it as well."

"Oh, I hadn't thought of that." She laughed softly.

She felt much better. Energized. As she always did when they connected. Even a kiss set up a connection between them.

"Do you want to go back to your parents tonight?"

"It'll be late. I don't want to bother them. I should call them, however."

"Bask already did that. I'm sorry; I forgot to tell you. I knew you'd want them to know you were okay."

"Then let's go to my apartment," she said, then added, "If you don't mind?"

"Sounds like a plan."

Chapter Twenty

It felt like years since Morgan had put her key into the lock of her apartment. Suddenly, self-conscious about what Dorian would think, her hand trembled as she pushed open the door. A soft mewl greeted her. Everything fell away as she stepped in and watched Mrs. T stretch out a paw and roll over on her side on top of the hutch.

"Hey there, gorgeous," she called softly and took the paw in her fingers. Mrs. T splayed out her paw for a mini massage. They must have brought Mrs. T over in the afternoon as a surprise. When the cat saw Dorian she flipped back over, withdrew her paw and tucked them, ladylike, under her ruff, while tilting her head to inspect the newcomer.

Dorian reached up, let her sniff his fingers and, laughed when she rubbed the side of her mouth across his fingers, lightly scrapping a tooth against his skin.

"She's giving you a subtle hint who's boss," Morgan informed him and walked into the room. She looked around. She'd forgotten how small it was.

"It's you," Dorian said. He inhaled the basil and citrus scents he remembered from his first meeting with Morgan. She had become so infused with the lavender that pervaded the shop and cottage, that he'd almost forgotten that fresh scent that was her.

Morgan walked over to the table in the kitchen alcove. A basket with fruit, bread, cheese and a bottle of wine sat in the middle, with a note leaning against it.

We thought you might be hungry. There's some ham and turkey in the fridge. Call us tomorrow. We love you, Mom and Dad (p.s. Dorian's quite charming—Mom)

When she turned to Dorian, she was smiling. "It's from my folks. I didn't know you met them."

"Wow. I forgot to tell you that, too. Yes, I went to see them. I like them a lot. Your Mom fed me and put me to bed. Your Dad pretty much inspected me."

"My mother put you to bed?"

"Yes. After giving me some sort of suggestion or psychic push or something. That's when I first saw you. Oh, and they sent the clothes."

Morgan hadn't thought about the fact that Dorian had brought her clothes or where they had come from. She'd just accepted that they were there. It showed what a jumbled mess her mind had been in earlier. She shook he head. It would take a while to sort out her thoughts.

"Well, now they've sent food."

Dorian walked over to the patio doors, flipped on the light and looked out. Someone had put covers over the herb plants to protect them from the chill. Probably her parents. Further evidence of the little things they did for her. Their caring reminded him a great deal of the way Mel and Thom went about their lives, caring for him and others. God, he missed them.

He turned back to the room. Morgan stood near the table, watching him, a frown on her face. He moved toward her. She took a step back. He stopped. He studied her expression and saw she was puzzling over something. He took another step and stopped.

A smile broke across her lips and Morgan moved forward until she was in front of him. She lifted her hand, slipped it around the back of his neck and pulled him down, fitting her slightly parted lips to his. She eased her arms around his neck and deepened the kiss. His hands moved to her waist and moved upward until his thumbs rested on the side of her breast, making small circles. She could feel her nipples harden, anticipating his touch. She backed away, took his hand in hers, and led him to the bedroom.

Morgan had never been very aggressive sexually. She had never wanted any man quite like she wanted this one. Even without the current flowing between them, her body hummed with need when she was around him.

She closed the bedroom door and touched the lamp on the bedside table. A small glow emanated from the bottom of the lamp. She saw his eyes focus on the lamp. "A gift from a friend of my mom's. It's a touch lamp. I've had it since I was a girl. I'm sure she didn't have this in mind when she gave it to me." As she spoke, she began slowly pushing up his tee shirt. She leaned forward and pressed her mouth to the muscles of his midriff, using her tongue until she encircled his hardening nipple. Her fingers splayed and moved around his side to his back, gently massaging his muscles.

In one swift motion, he pulled the shirt over his head. In another motion, he pulled hers up and off her, letting her hair fall down her back and across her breasts. He ran his fingers along the scalloped edges of her bra, feeling her breasts swell in anticipation. He slipped his hand around and, in an instant, the bra lay at her feet. He put his hands under her breast, gently cupping them, while his thumbs circled her nipples. She moaned and his mouth took hers.

It seemed to be a race to free themselves of all traces of clothing until they were lying facing one another on the bed. He pushed her on her back and starting at her ear, used mouth and tongue to explore her body. His mouth trailed fiery kisses, his hands explored and gently kneaded muscle and skin. He inched his way down her body until he pushed her legs apart, and let his fingers slowly trail heat through her moistened curls. Where his fingers explored, his tongue followed, until she writhed with pent-up passion. Sensing her reach toward satisfaction, he eased back, slowing the pace.

In one quick move, she pushed him back until he fell across the bed. Quickly, she shifted positions and used her tongue to lick his jaw and down his neck, while her hands followed the inside of his arms to his sides. She laved his nipples and followed the dusting of hair down his abdomen. When her mouth took him, he grabbed the sheets in sweet agony. His whole body went rigid.

She looked up and watched his eyes darken. Suddenly, his hands were on her sides and he was lifting her, pulling her up. Her legs straddled his hips and she came down slowly on his shaft, letting her heat engulf him. He pulled her head down and took her mouth, their tastes mingling. As he deepened the kiss, he started a rocking rhythm that she quickly picked up. His hands cupped her breasts and teased her nipples. She leaned back and rode him. The air around them sizzled and sparked. Energy coursed back and forth between them, sensitizing their flesh. Tension built and when their climax came, their moans were as entwined as their bodies. Morgan collapsed on top of him.

A moment later, Morgan stirred to heated kisses on her neck. She stretched. Without saying a word, he pulled her up and led her to her bathroom. Fitting both of them into her small shower proved to be a challenge, which they accomplished, even if it meant mopping up the floor when they finally stepped out, sated and clean.

They munched on bread, cheese, wine and each other, making love one more time before falling asleep. By the time

Morgan's eyes closed for the last time, she was wrapped in the warmth of his arms, safe and content.

She woke with his hardness pressing into the soft flesh of her rear, tempting her to wiggle ever so slightly. He responded by shifting and sliding into her warm wetness from behind, giving him full access to her breasts and the tender flesh between her legs. Fully sated once more, she snuggled into his arms.

Dorian moved slightly. She rolled onto her back. He raised up on this arm and looked into her eyes. "You are so beautiful." He lifted a lock of red curl and laid it gently across her breast. "I love you."

Her breath caught.

He smiled, creases forming at the corner of his eyes. "What? You didn't know?"

She smiled back at him. "I do now."

She was quiet for a moment, then spoke, her voice soft, "I don't know how it happened so fast, but I love you too."

"Destiny," he said, a smile lifting the side of his mouth.

His look turned serious. "We are paired. You are my mate, as I am yours. That's fate. Do me the honor of becoming my wife. That's your choice." He spoke softly, his voice deep.

She tried but couldn't seem to swallow. It took a moment for what he'd said to sink in.

He brushed the hair away from her face, studying the emerald eyes he loved. He waited.

She studied his face, trying to read his thoughts.

Finally, he spoke, "I know it's quick. I understand if—"

"Yes," she interrupted him.

He stopped, a smile spread across his face. His eyes looked as though they twinkled. "You sure?"

"Are you?"

"I've never been more sure."

She answered him with a kiss. A kiss in which she put all the feelings she felt in her heart and soul. He was her mate. There was no other.

"I would like to ask your parents, if I might. I understand it's a formality because I'd marry you if the entire world were against it. But, they have been through a lot and they love you so much."

Morgan threw her arms around him. "Thank you. That would mean the world to me."

The door rattled and they looked at the door. A scratching sound started slowly and increased in urgency. "I think Mrs. T would like some breakfast. Or lunch," she amended when she glanced at the clock.

"That cat has no sense of romance." Dorian swung his legs over the side of the bed.

"Don't say that. She behaved all night. It could have been very different." Morgan slipped on her robe and tied the sash as she opened the door. Mrs. T looked up at her, crooked her tail and marched down the hallway toward the kitchen.

"I see," he mused.

Dorian entered the living room, dressed, to find Morgan on the phone, laughing. "Yes, Mom, a late lunch sounds wonderful. I love you, too. We'll be there about two. Oh, thank you for the basket."

He lifted a brow.

"Don't expect a sandwich. Mom's idea of a late lunch is actually an early dinner."

****

As the Briscoes gathered in the living room of their home, Dorian found he was actually nervous. He wanted them to like him and to believe that he would make a good husband for Morgan. His palms dampened. He sat on the sofa next to Morgan. Her mother and father sat on the loveseat across from them. He wasn't sure he was going to have a voice when he needed one.

Morgan slipped her hand into his and smiled at him. Her green eyes sparkled and a slight tingle ran up his arm. The surprise showed in his eyes. It had generated from her. She grinned and squeezed his hand.

Dorian cleared his throat. "I know we haven't known each other for very long, but Morgan and I have found what we want for the rest of our lives. I would like, very much, to have your blessing in taking Morgan as my wife."

Becky sniffled. Tears welled in her eyes. She looked at her husband. Talbot put his arm around his wife. "After all you've been through. Your willingness to face an unknown future together demonstrates your commitment. You have our blessing and our love." He stood, extended his hand. "Welcome to the family."

Dorian was surprised to feel moisture in his eyes as he took the man's hand. Then Becky bounded around the coffee table to hug, first Morgan, then Dorian, then Morgan again. "This calls for a celebration," Becky announced. "I guess it's a good thing we're having red snapper for lunch. It goes well with champagne. And I guess that cake I made won't go to waste."

Dorian leaned toward Morgan, "Are you sure she doesn't have Georgia ancestry?"

Morgan merely shrugged and followed her chattering mother into the kitchen. From the looks of the buffet her mother had set up, Dorian was convinced she knew his intentions before he did. Lunch was sumptuous and joyful. They toasted with champagne and feasted on coconut almond cake. Dorian promised himself to get the recipe for Teresa, who, he realized would never forgive them if they didn't call her next. Bill answered the phone, telling Dorian that Teresa was in Virginia with Jasmine. He looked at Morgan and her family and thanked him. He knew the next place they would visit might not be as joyful.

Morgan couldn't remember when she'd seen her mother so excited. Of course, most mothers' dream about their daughter's wedding. She was already asking when, where, and how big in a steady stream of exuberant questions. Morgan looked at Dorian, who only shrugged, giving her no help. They promised to make some decisions before they left to go back to Ruthorford. When her mom began quizzing them about that, they both burst into laughter. Morgan took her mother in her arms and held her tight.

"I love you, Mom."

Becky hugged her back, finally calming down. "I love you, too, Pumpkin. Just be happy."

"I am. I promise."

****

Morgan and Dorian spent the trip to Safe Harbor's main house discussing her parents' enthusiasm over the upcoming nuptials. They knew that, no matter where they chose to be married, someone would feel slighted. Morgan understood that people who stayed in Ruthorford generally married in Ruthorford, so Ruthorford could be in attendance. The bed and breakfast could accommodate quite a few people and, if Morgan could keep her mother in line and limit the guest list, it would be easy to fit everyone there. With Morgan's inheritance, she could easily afford to help people who wanted to come, make the trip.

Morgan's family consisted of Becky and Talbot. Becky's family was long gone and Talbot's father was in a home with Alzheimer's, no longer cognizant of anything but the most distant memories. Morgan hadn't visited her grandfather in almost six months. He no longer knew who she was and found her eyes disturbing. With what Morgan had learned about the Gulatega, she had had momentary hopes that maybe, just maybe, her grandfather was affected by the creatures. She knew better. She would have sensed it. She was sure of that. But, just to be certain, she might drag Dorian by the nursing home on the way home. Home. She had just referred to Ruthorford as home. She looked at Dorian and smiled.

It was time to bring up one other thing. "When we get to Safe Harbor, I want a few moments to talk with Jenn."

"I understand. You want to tell her in person." He was smiling at her.

That too. But, that would come after Jenn answered her questions. There was something she needed Jenn to explain to her. Not wanting to worry Dorian unnecessarily, Morgan took his hand and smiled. "I knew you'd understand."

Jenn knew they were coming. You didn't arrive at Safe Harbor unannounced. If you got past the layers of security to get to the front door, you could, at the very least, expect a firm tongue-lashing. At worst, you would be arrested and toted downtown to spend a few uncomfortable hours in the poky.

They turned into the gated drive. There was no call box. Safe Harbor had a functional gatehouse, staffed 24/7 by an armed guard. There were several surveillance devices scanning the entrance. If you weren't on the list, you didn't get in. The whole compound—and that's what it was—had state of the art surveillance and security.

Dorian and Morgan each handed their driver's licenses to the guard who shined a flashlight in their faces and studied them against the pictures on their identification. Handing back they ID's, he pressed a code into the panel and the gate pulled aside. They followed the winding drive—done intentionally—around, up and over a raise and down into a valley, before they came upon the main house. As they approached, security lights flashed on. Morgan saw Jenn standing at the foot of the steps. Dorian pulled across and parked in a space directly across from the entrance.

Jenn was at Morgan's door before the engine died. She pulled open the door and flung her arms around Morgan, almost throwing them both back into the car. Dorian just shook his head and headed up the steps where John was waiting. They stepped aside and spoke quietly while Jenn and Morgan squealed and hugged like pubescent teenagers. Jenn wiped the tears from her eyes and stepped away.

"I was so scared. I didn't want to lose my best friend."

"I was pretty scared myself." Morgan looked over at the men and watched Dorian glance back at her. He purposefully led John inside giving her the privacy she had asked for.

Morgan turned serious. "Jenn, I have something I have to ask you." She leaned back against the car, not moving forward to follow Jenn toward the building.

Jenn walked back to her. "What?"

"When we were driving to the cabin, I heard you call someone and tell them you had me. Who was it?"

Jenn looked confused. "What are you talking about?"

Morgan didn't like the way this was going. She steeled herself. "You thought I was asleep. You pulled out your phone and called someone. If you value our friendship, you will tell me who you called."

Jenn scratched her head. She honestly seemed confused and looked like she was trying to remember. Morgan watched her, her irritation rising. She didn't want to think her friend could be influenced by someone like Rob or Ian. She found it almost impossible to believe, given her determination to protect endangered women and children.

Jenn dropped her hand as she became aware of the importance of Morgan's question. "Morgan, I would never put you in danger. I couldn't do anything so contemptible."

She walked around trying to remember. She pulled out her phone and tried to go back through her log. She searched and searched. Her eyes widened.

"It was Uncle Mike!" she yelped. "I remember now. He wanted me to get you away from all the brouhaha that was going on and I was so thrilled that I called him. I didn't want to wake you so I assumed he would know what I meant."

There were tears in Morgan's eyes. She let the tears fall. It had been so hard to think Jenn wasn't the friend she'd always accepted her to be. Jenn, in turn, started crying and put her arms around her friend.

Morgan hiccupped, "I am so glad. I couldn't think of asking anyone else to be my maid of honor."

"I know that," Jenn cried, "Anytime one of us gets married—"

"How does December sound?" Morgan asked.

Jenn stepped back and wiped her eyes. "December?"

Morgan nodded.

"Oh my God!" Jenn screamed. "Dorian proposed! Oh my God!"

Dorian and John watched the women jumping up and down and Dorian turned to John. "I guess it's okay to tell you Morgan and I are getting married."

"You think?" John said stoically.

"What? No jumping and screaming?"

John smiled and held out his hand. "This will have to do."

"You will be my best man, right?"

"I've always been the best man," John joked.

They turned and waited for the women to join them.

****

Jenn led them into a large conference room. Morgan had been to visit Jenn many times at this facility, which Jenn also called home, but she had never been into the administrative wing of the facility. They settled around a large table, Jenn taking the chair at the end. Jenn's air of confidence and professionalism displaced the shrieking, jumping friend in the parking lot.

"First," Jenn said and smiled. "I have an announcement to make." Jenn opened a folder in front of her. "Safe Harbor has been the recipient of a sizeable endowment."

Morgan could see the excitement in the way the corners of Jenn's blue eyes crinkled. Her heart beat a little faster for her friend.

"With this money, we can provide secure facilities in this and several more states. And, apparently, it's just the beginning." She took a moment to breathe and lightly bit her lower lip. "The reason I am telling you this," Jenn looked at Morgan and Dorian and let her eyes pass over John, briefly, "is that the endowment is from the Abbott House."

Morgan listened to Jenn's voice hitch. She watched her eyes glisten with tears. She reached out and covered Jenn's hand, squeezing gently. Jenn looked at her. "I had no idea. I mean...you..." she stopped as tears fell. She took a tissue and dabbed at her eyes.

"Congratulations, Jenn," Morgan said. "You deserve it. You probably know more about the Abbott House than I do at this point. I am so happy for you. I know how long you have worked and dreamed for this."

Jenn nodded, tears brimming. She sniffled and straightened. "Damn it. I knew I would do that. I told myself I wouldn't, but damn—there I went."

That was the friend Morgan knew. She grinned at her. Jenn grinned back and reached to gain control of her emotions once more.

"I did want to go over a few things before you go see Meadow. Bask called me. John has told Kayla and Meadow that Ian has gone back to Scotland. You went to visit him, when he called you for help. You couldn't help him, so he's returned to Scotland."

Morgan looked at Dorian. He took her hand in his. Warmth spread through her, pushing back the weight of the sadness that threatened. She didn't know how much Jenn knew. She looked at John, whose handsome stoicism wasn't betraying anything. He gave her an almost imperceptible nod. She remained quiet. With the other hand, she reached into her pocket and touched the envelope that was for Meadow from her father. The sadness was almost more than she could bear. She squeezed Dorian's hand.

"Shall we go see her highness?" Jenn stood. "She's become quite popular here. There aren't many children right now so she's getting a ton of attention. A ton of spoiling, too, I might add."

They followed Jenn out of the business wing and up the stairs. Off to the right was a large open area with couches, tables and chairs for games, and a huge flat-screen television on one wall. Morgan looked at Jenn.

"Yes, it's new. I figured they deserved it."

Meadow jumped up as soon as they entered the room. She'd been sitting at a table working on a large puzzle. She was wearing flannel pajamas with unicorns on them. All that remained of her bandage was a small gauze pad behind her ear.

"Uncle Dorian!" she squealed and launched herself at him. Morgan was amazed at the youthfulness of the just turned thirteen year old. "Aunt...Miss Morgan," Meadow corrected and turned to her rather shyly.

"It will be Aunt soon, so I guess we ought to practice," she hugged the young girl.

Another squeal. "Really? Can I be in the wedding?"

"Meadow," Kayla admonished.

"Of course you can."

Meadow grabbed Morgan's hand and drew her over to the table. A picture of a castle, with unicorns in front of it, was slowly taking shape. Morgan reached in her pocket and drew out the envelope.

"Your father asked me to give this to you. He's sorry he missed your birthday."

She handed it to Meadow, who took it gingerly, like it was the most precious thing in the world. Meadow moved to the chair at the table and, after looking at her mother, tore open the envelope. She reached inside and pulled out a beautiful card and a small bundle, wrapped in lavender tissue paper and tied with delicate ribbon. For something so simple, it was very beautiful. Meadow read the card, tears gathering in her eyes, set it aside and slowly opened the bundle. As she unfolded the paper, a locket fell into her lap. She lifted it. On the front was an inlay of a white unicorn, rearing. The sparkle in its eye came from a dark lavender gem. It was encircled by a silver Celtic braid. She gently opened the locket. Inside, on one side, was a picture of Ian holding Meadow in his arm. On the other was tiny portrait of a gorgeous woman, sitting regally, yet with wild flowing hair. Hair the color of Morgan's.

Meadow looked at her mother. "It's Daddy's Nanna. And me and Daddy." Tears brimmed and fell.

John stepped forward. "Here, princess, let me." He took the delicate locket in his large hand and with easy movements, unlatched the chain and hung it around Meadow's neck.

Meadow smiled up and him and reached for the locket, holding it in her small hand. "It's so warm." She smiled at her mother. "Daddy says it's been in his family forever and it was time for me to have it."

"Well, I think it's time for this princess to say goodnight, go to bed, and dream of unicorns."

Meadow turned to Morgan. "Thank you so much." She hugged her, picked up the envelope and card, and hugged Dorian, John, and Jenn in turn. She started down the hall. She turned back, "it's okay if you want to work on the puzzle." She turned around and walked down the hall with her mother.

"Did you see the stone?" Morgan whispered to Dorian.

He nodded and changed the subject. "Do you think Jasmine is up to receiving visitors?" he asked Jenn.

"Have you ever known me *not* to be up to receiving visitors, you lunkhead?" Jasmine's sexy voice trilled behind them.

Morgan spun around as Jasmine joined them. She walked straight into Dorian's arms and hugged him tightly, reached up and kissed him on the cheek. She looked into his eyes for a moment before turning to Morgan.

"I hear congratulations are in order," she walked over and put her arms around Morgan. It was not a cursory hug. She wrapped her arms about her and held her. Morgan slipped her arms around the other woman and hugged her back. A small burst of energy passed between them.

Jasmine stepped back, looked at Morgan with twinkling eyes. "Welcome to the family," she said with warmth.

"Thank you, Jasmine. I mean that." Morgan didn't have a clue how Jasmine knew they were getting married.

Jasmine looked wonderful. A small yellowing bruise on her cheek and a tiny purplish scar beside her lip were the only evidence of the brutal attack. That healing trait must have been passed on to her.

Morgan took her arm. "I am so sorry—"

"Don't!" Jasmine said firmly. "I mean it. You had nothing to do with what happened. The fact that you knew him doesn't put you at fault." She led them over to the couches.

"I am getting some excellent counseling sessions, from a counselor here and from Dr. Yancy."

Morgan looked at Jenn. Jenn smiled.

Jasmine went on. "There are things I need to understand about myself and what happened to me." She looked at Morgan. "I was a bitch when I first met you. I was jealous." When Morgan glanced at Dorian, Jasmine laughed. "Well, that too," she shook her head, her spiky dark hair framing her beautiful face. "I was jealous of you," she leaned forward. "I don't have the..." she searched for the right word, "...traits that you have. My mother was like Melissa, my father like Thomas. I should have been like you. However, I'm not. I guess that jealousy has been in me for a long time."

Morgan started to speak, "But—"

Jasmine interrupted her. "I'm not." Her statement was final. Morgan wondered about the small transfer of energy she'd felt when they hugged. She kept quiet. For now.

"Are you planning to come home with us?" Dorian asked.

Jasmine looked at Jenn. "I've asked Jenn if I can stay here for a while. I've been impressed with what she's doing here. I'd like to stay and learn more, if she'll let me."

"You know I'd love that. I can use all the help I can get."

"What about your shop?"

"Bonnie has offered to run it for me for a while. Sales are up. I can't argue with that."

Before Morgan or Dorian could interject, she raised her hand. "Yes, I do know about the slight punk look that's taking place." She shrugged. "Maybe an infusion of younger blood is a good thing. Besides, I have Teresa and you guys to keep an eye out for me."

"Speaking of which, where is she?"

"Oh, she had to head back. Bill managed to book a small convention of romance writers, and then decided he couldn't handle it on his own."

Kayla walked in and joined Morgan and Dorian on the couch. She slipped her arm through Morgan's and gave a squeeze. Morgan reached over and patted her hand.

Jasmine got to her feet. "I still tire a bit quickly, so I will say goodnight."

Morgan and Dorian both rose. John, who had said nothing, remained seated but smiled at her. Jasmine gave them both a hug, stopping at Morgan. "You take care of him or I'll come kick your butt."

Morgan laughed but saw a challenge in Jasmine's eyes. "I promise."

They watched her walk down the hall, her step a little slower, her shoulder's slightly drooped. Morgan realized the bravado had been just that, bravado. She tuned to Jenn.

"She'll be a great help to me," she spoke to Morgan's unasked questions, "and she'll be able to heal. It takes time."

"What's the latest on Rob?" Dorian asked.

John spoke up. "He came out of the coma yesterday. He appears to have amnesia. He's confused about who he is but has retained his education memories. He remembers nothing about Ian, what happened, or what he did. Whether it's selective or dissociative, they don't know. He does seem to have an altered personality. He's too weak to work with yet." He relayed the discussion he'd had with Dr. Yancy earlier.

"Does Jasmine know?" Morgan asked.

"No. We don't see any reason to bring it up. Unless she asks, we aren't volunteering information about him. Her counselor prefers she approach the event in her own way."

Morgan walked over to the chair and dropped into it. "God," she said, remembering the man she'd known. "It's hard for me to fathom what he did."

Jenn sat near her. "What upsets me is it could have been you. Not that I wanted Jasmine hurt, or anyone else for that matter, but he was working for Ian before he started dating you."

Sadness etched Morgan's features. "Do you think we'll ever know the whole story?"

"I doubt it," Dorian spat. He felt the anger rush to the surface. He still held murderous thoughts about Rob. He kept seeing Jasmine chained in that mine.

If Bask has anything to do with it, he'll know every detail about everything before the year is out. That man is a pit bull when it comes to Abbott business," John added.

Kayla's voice interrupted. She spoke quietly, softly. "I don't mean to change the subject, but I want to ask Morgan about the apartment."

"Sure," Morgan said. "Did you like it? It's not very large. You can keep the furniture. And Mrs. T," she finished. She was going to miss that cat but didn't see uprooting her at this time in her life.

"Meadow adores Mrs. T. And, Mrs. T has a real fondness for Meadow. And I have a real fondness for the things my daughter likes."

"Mrs. T will grow on you."

"I have been offered a job with Jenn. Your apartment would be perfect."

"It's a great school district, too." Morgan was getting excited for them. "Have Jenn introduce you to my parents. They will love Meadow."

Tears welled and fell down Kayla's cheek. "Thank you," she choked out, "for everything."

Morgan reached out. "That's what families do. Right?"

Kayla nodded and sniffed.

John broke up the sob fest. "I'm starving. I say we raid Jenn's larder."

Jenn punched him in the arm. "Don't let me stop you, you oversized lunch pail."

Five adults raced each other down the stairs.

Chapter Twenty-One

Morgan stood before the cheval mirror in the master bedroom above the shop. Her fingers brushed the ivory velvet that ran down the sides and the back of her gown. Ivory brocade covered the front and fell in flowing pleats from the deep vee in the front waistband of the medieval-style wedding gown. The gown had belonged to Melissa, Melissa's mother, and her mother's mother. A few tucks and it fit Morgan's figure to perfection. How the gown remained in such exquisite condition was surely attributed to the Abbott House, where it would be returned after the wedding. Her fingers gently touched the owl necklace that had also been her mother's. A kirtle belt of hammered gold and silver draped around her hips and hung down the front of her gown, gems twinkling in the light.

She glanced past her reflection in the mirror to watch her mother gently lifting the veil that was attached to a silver and gold band, encrusted with the same stones as the belt, which would encircle her head. Her mother raised her eyes as she came toward Morgan, caught her look in the mirror and smiled at her.

Ruthorford had been literally cordoned off for the wedding, which had only been put into production a little over a month ago. Morgan had had her doubts as to whether such an event could be arranged in such sort time. However, as soon as Becky and Teresa got their heads together, Morgan stepped back and let them take over. It would have been dangerous to do otherwise. The women had taken to each other immediately and Becky and Talbot had become frequent visitors to the bed and breakfast.

Her parents fell in love with Ruthorford and Ruthorford responded in kind. Morgan couldn't believe it, but her parents were actually considering selling the house she'd grown up in and transplanting themselves to the small town in Georgia. They decided to put off the decision until after the wedding, which had been set for December 22nd, the winter solstice.

The month and a half had flown by. Dorian and Morgan arrived back in town to find that Teresa had orchestrated the cutting and hanging of the herbs from the garden. The cottage beams were the customary location for this and the cottage was perfumed with the scents of drying flowers and herbs. When she and Dorian stepped into the cottage upon their return, she was astonished to find, not only had all the stones been put back in their original locations, but the rug was lying in its spot as well, looking none the worse for wear.

Not one Gulatega had been seen since their experience at the castle in Virginia Beach. They came together upon the rug, touching in more than five points, but raising the current nevertheless. The portal shifted but no creatures appeared near them. The portal quietly collapsed. She and Dorian spent more than a few evenings contemplating possibilities. Although they hadn't mentioned it to anyone else, they had discussed the stone the creature had pushed across the portal and the fact that the eye of the unicorn in Meadow's locket looked to be a tiny version of the same stone.

They had no way of knowing whether or not Ian had survived being pulled, however willingly, through the portal. Nothing was said about the incident except between themselves. A few days after their arrival in Ruthorford, it was announced on the evening news that financial tycoon, Ian Macintosh, had disappeared when his plane went down in the Atlantic Ocean. He apparently was on a solo flight to Scotland when the accident occurred. Minimal wreckage had been found and no black box. She had called Kayla and talked with her, extending their sympathies. Morgan still didn't know if Kayla knew what had happened. She hadn't had a chance to ask John, who was spending more and more time in Virginia.

Kayla and Meadow were, in fact, staying in the cottage for the wedding. Meesha loved the idea of having Meadow around, even if it did mean putting up with Mrs. T, who took a swat at her whenever the chance arose. Meadow wouldn't go anywhere without Mrs. T. Morgan figured it was a good thing the Gulatega were not to be found, since poor Mrs. T would have resumed her enraged porcupine status immediately.

The only other accommodation that had been made in their absence had been the gentle packing and storing of Melissa and Thom's clothing from the master bedroom. Morgan wasn't sure how she felt about that, but Dorian didn't seem to mind. His clothes had been moved in with hers and his old room was converted into a guest suite, where Becky and Talbot were staying. They planned to move into the bed and breakfast for the night to give Morgan and Dorian more privacy. Meesha had been invited to spend the night at the cottage with Meadow, so they would have the shop all to themselves. Even Miss Grace and Miss Alice had promised to refrain from calling until the second day, at which time the two sisters were promised their pastries would be greatly appreciated.

Morgan stepped out of the limousine in front of the chapel next to the bed and breakfast. The sun glinted off the silica in the dirt next to the stone path. A chill breeze ruffled her veil. She took her father's hand and they walked up the steps to the chapel and into the front hall.

Meadow stood holding a basket of deep red rose petals, their fragrance permeating the air. She looked up as Morgan stepped into the room.

"Oh, Miss… Aunt Morgan, you look like a Scottish Faery Princess." She came over to hug her. Morgan heard her mother's intake of breath and smiled at her. She knelt down in all of her finery and looked into Meadow's glowing green eyes.

"*You* look like the princess," she said. "Thank you for attending me as my lady in waiting."

Meadow beamed.

The music began.

Suddenly, Morgan's nerves bunched. She saw her mother slip through the door. Then Jenn and John. Oh, God. Her stomach did a somersault.

"You ready, beautiful daughter of mine—at least for the moment?"

She heard her father's voice falter and blinked back a tear.

"I love you, Pumpkin," he said. The doors opened and they stepped through.

The chapel was full. Everyone she knew, and many she didn't, crowded into the chapel to see her marry Dorian, their beloved son. All eyes were on her.

She looked up. The only eyes she saw were Dorian's. He stood in the front, waiting for her, wearing a short tuxedo jacket. Pinned to his shoulder and hanging down the side was a tartan plaid, its purple, green and black colors dark and dramatic. He was tall, rugged and handsome. Her breath caught. His lips parted in a smile. His eyes twinkled. He waited for her.

Morgan didn't remember the trip down the aisle or much of the ceremony. She vaguely remembered placing a Celtic braided ring on his finger after receiving a matching one from him. Until they kissed, everything seemed a blur.

As they were announced man and wife, he lifted her veil. His eyes looked deep into hers and they stood there, the energy flowing between them. The stones in the windows and around the altar vibrated and began to glow. A hush moved through the chapel.

"My mate, my partner, my wife," he said as he lowered his head and the warmth of his mouth took hers.

Down the street, the sign above The Shoppe of Spells shimmered, its outline an iridescent violet.

THE BEGINNING

~*~

ABOUT THE AUTHOR

Shanon Grey weaves romance and suspense with threads of the paranormal. THE SHOPPE OF SPELLS, published by Crossroads Publishing House, is the first in her series, THE GATEKEEPERS.

Shanon spent her life on coasts, both the beautiful Atlantic and the balmy Gulf. Hurricane Katrina taught her the fragility of life and the strength of friendship, family and starting over. She currently lives in northern Georgia, trading the familiarity of the coast for the lush beauty and wonder of the mountains, where her husband fulfilled her lifelong dream—to live in a cottage in the woods. There, she garners inspiration from horses grazing on rolling pastures and deer that wander by to tease her beloved dog.

Stay up to date on other Shanon Grey books and events by visiting her website at www.ShanonGrey.com. You can also visit Shanon on facebook and twitter @ShanonGrey.

Coming in 2012
from Shanon Grey

Meadow's Keep
The Gatekeepers, Book Two

Jasmine Monroe once felt like damaged goods. But, not anymore. Her latent abilities, although appearing too late to save her from a brutal attack, will keep her safe from anyone ever hurting her again. She's made sure of that. Secure in that fact, she's moved on. Until she meets her first love's doppelganger.

Eryk Vreeland, a misfit and embarrassment to his upper-class/upper-crust family, is a magician. His shows are renowned, his contributions to charity astronomical, his illusions precise. Except, not everything is an illusion. Sometimes there is real magic.

Jasmine stumbles upon a secret that will change Eryk's life forever, and in doing so, she must face her own destiny as well. When Jasmine and Eryk are forced together to rescue and protect a young woman, each must overcome the barrier that protects, yet hinders any personal attachments. The safeguards must come down to combine their abilities and, when that happens, their attraction strengthens—beyond their control—until they can barely tell where one person stops and the other begins.

Can their hearts take the toll? Will they surrender to one another or risk a disaster to stay apart?

Crossroads Publishing House thanks you for spending your time with The Shoppe of Spells.

We invite you to visit our website to learn more about our quality Trade Paperback and Digital Book selections at www.crossroadspublishinghouse.com

<u>Adams Grove Novels by Nancy Naigle</u>
Sweet Tea and Secrets
Out of Focus

<u>Johnson Naigle</u>
inkBLOT

<u>Rick Cunningham Suspense Novels by Sam Phillips</u>
Deadly Voyage
Deadly Friendship

Made in the USA
Columbia, SC
04 August 2017